MW00776072

An Evening with Birdy O'Day

An Evening with

Birdy O'Day

A Novel

GREG KEARNEY

ARSENAL PULP PRESS
VANCOUVER

AN EVENING WITH BIRDY O'DAY
Copyright © 2024 by Greg Kearney

All rights reserved. No part of this book may be reproduced in any part by any means—graphic, electronic, or mechanical—without the prior written permission of the publisher, except by a reviewer, who may use brief excerpts in a review, or in the case of photocopying in Canada, a licence from Access Copyright.

ARSENAL PULP PRESS
Suite 202 – 211 East Georgia St.
Vancouver, BC V6A 1Z6
Canada
arsenalpulp.com

The publisher gratefully acknowledges the support of the Canada Council for the Arts and the British Columbia Arts Council for its publishing program and the Government of Canada and the Government of British Columbia (through the Book Publishing Tax Credit Program) for its publishing activities.

Arsenal Pulp Press acknowledges the xʷməθkʷəy̓əm (Musqueam), Sḵwx̱wú7mesh (Squamish), and səlilwətaɬ (Tsleil-Waututh) Nations, custodians of the traditional, ancestral, and unceded territories where our office is located. We pay respect to their histories, traditions, and continuous living cultures and commit to accountability, respectful relations, and friendship.

This is a work of fiction. Any resemblance of characters to persons either living or deceased is purely coincidental.

Cover art and design by Jazmin Welch
Interior art and text design by Jazmin Welch
Edited by Catharine Chen
Proofread by Alison Strobel

Printed and bound in Canada

Library and Archives Canada Cataloguing in Publication:
Title: An evening with Birdy O'Day / Greg Kearney.
Names: Kearney, Greg, author.
Identifiers: Canadiana (print) 20230549845 | Canadiana (ebook) 20230549853 |
  ISBN 9781551529417 (softcover) | ISBN 9781551529424 (EPUB)
Subjects: LCGFT: Novels.
Classification: LCC PS8621.E23 E94 2024 | DDC C813/.6—dc23

In memory of Robert Matte

Some boys are very tough. They're afraid of nothing.
They are the ones who climb a wall and take a bow
at the top. Not only are they brave on the roof,
but they make a lot of noise in the darkest part of the
cellar where even the super hates to go.

—GRACE PALEY, "SAMUEL"

News

THERE ARE TIMES in the day—typically midmorning and midafternoon—when my vision dims and flickers, and I feel like I could collapse and die, or at least collapse. I am tired. It's hard to be an old-fashioned hairdresser, both chatterbox and confidant, when you have literally nothing to say and want only to lie down somewhere cool and silent. But then I think of my Birdy, touring the world, loath to cancel a concert, no matter the malady, and I can push past my exhaustion and get on with the task at hand.

I have one more client today, a new client named Rita. I haven't stopped all day, not even for a cigarette out back. My colour correction for Brenda took a good two hours, and by the end of it she was crying in pain from the sting of the bleach. And there was Mrs. Miner's perm, which came out frizzy despite several attempts to tame the frizz with various smoothing treatments. She was happy with it, which of course is the important thing. But she's eighty-eight and only has the one eye.

I am sixty-nine. I've been a hairstylist for forty-three years. It's always been slightly less than a passion, but equally, more than a chore. The work has taken its toll. My lungs are scorched from inhaling bleach and dye fumes for four decades. My head sits forward on my neck from years of leaning in to better inspect weight lines and wonky bangs. I have carpal tunnel in my right wrist. My back and feet pain me from constant standing. I am beyond burn-out, which isn't as horrible as it sounds; there are long stretches where I simply get down to the task at hand with a Zen neutrality. It's an okay living, better than I'd hoped for when I dropped out of grade eleven to be a barfly: my boyfriend's disability income plus my tips from the salon. Our apartment has a dishwasher and in-suite laundry, and we can usually afford to go to the casino once a month. Could be worse.

Rita arrives. She is tiny and middle aged with a pleasant, open face and huge dark eyes like Liza Minnelli's. Her hair is slightly wavy and thin.

"This is what I was hoping for," she says, pulling a picture of Beyoncé from her purse.

I nod. One must be tactful during a consult; you never tell a new client that her hair goal is impossible.

"Okay. Well. So, you're looking for a lot of body, a lot of move-ment, and a very warm blond. That can absolutely work. Your hair is very straight and fine, so I can't guarantee that I'll be able to exactly reproduce the picture. Have you considered extensions?"

"Extensions. You mean, like, bits of fake hair?"

"Yes. Although it's real human hair."

"No. My daughter tried those, and they always looked so ratty and cheap, even when they were first put in. I'm very much a wash-and-go person, you know?"

"Absolutely. I do need to tell you that the style you want would involve a fair bit of maintenance. Blow-drying is essential. The right sequence of products is essential also."

She sighs, annoyed. "Okay. Just do the best you can. Do what-ever you need to do. My daughter's getting married this weekend."

I sit her in my chair. We are alone in the salon; the other stylists are young and haven't yet built the client base that I have. I've moved from salon to salon over the years, and my regulars follow me, even now that I'm way in the north end of Winnipeg. Women hug me, invite me to dinner, weep over their incarcerated children, ask me to look at the rash underneath one of their breasts. Against the odds, I've made a name. My name is Roland. I've always hated my name.

I fit the cape around her neck.

"Let's give you a wash first."

"No, that's all right. I don't like the sensation of someone washing my hair."

"Okay. No problem." Who doesn't like a nice head massage? I am struck by this woman's strange bearing, which is hunched and defensive, as though she doesn't trust gravity to keep her upright.

I wet her hair and go to the back to mix bleach. It's ten after four. Tony will be on the couch, smoking a joint and watching *General Hospital.* He said he was going to try to go to Canadian Tire for new torches for the balcony, but his fibro has been so bad this week, he likely didn't make it out the door.

"What's that smell?" asks Rita when I return to my station.

"What smell, honey? My smeller's wrecked from all the bleach."

"There's a smell coming from somewhere. A smell like someone has ... had a bowel movement."

"Really? Huh. I'm sorry. I'm not sure where that could be coming from. I'll spray some Lysol."

"No, don't! I'm allergic to air freshener. I'll just have to put up with the bathroom smell."

"I'm really sorry." I section her hair with clips and start to paint it with the bleach. It's always a challenge starting a rapport with a new client. I have my affable salon persona, calling people "honey" in a benign, chummy way, but I'm really very shy. And tired. I think I mentioned that already.

"Do you live in the area?" I ask.

"Sort of."

"That's interesting. I like this neighbourhood. I know everyone says it's a bit dangerous in the north end, but I haven't found that at all. Well, there was that family reunion last year where everyone shot everyone, but otherwise ..."

"I was at that reunion. That was my family."

"No! Oh, I'm so sorry. I'm so glad you're okay."

"Thank you. I'm not okay, truth be told. But I've coped better than my sisters. They're both on Ativan. Gertie has an emotional support dog. And not a very good one. It bites her and pulls her into traffic."

Where do you go from there? I work in silence, mortified. When I'm done with the bleach I mull over putting her under the rotating heat-circle thing, this newfangled appliance that the owner just acquired but that I have my doubts about. I decide against it. Thin hair like hers will almost certainly break if heat is applied. I tell her I'm going to let the bleach develop and nip out the back for a cigarette.

There is a yellow cat on the stoop. It hisses and bolts when it sees me.

Could you imagine being at a nice family reunion only for it to end in gunfire? Awful. No wonder her sisters are on drugs. I would be too. And I'm already deep into the booze as is. Birdy O'Day has been very public about his struggles with prescription medication and has been to rehab three times, most recently in 2014. He went to Betty Ford. Or Promises. It's one of those—I can't remember, which is strange for me. I know everything there is to know about Birdy O'Day.

Date of birth? May 5, 1955. Star sign? Taurus. Biggest hit in America? "Yes," number two in 1978. Biggest flop in America? Everything he released after 1991; his last song to chart on the *Billboard* Hot 100 was "Fun and Then Some" at number eighty-three in February 1991.

"Stop it," I say aloud. If I'm not careful I could get irretrievably lost in Birdy trivia.

I step on my cigarette butt. *Things could absolutely be worse*, I constantly remind myself. I'm prone to wildly uncomfortable bouts of jealousy: I'm jealous of other, more successful stylists, and I'm jealous whenever I'm out socially with Tony and people cruise him but not me, and naturally, I'm jealous of my best friend from childhood, who left me in the dust to become Birdy O'Day, rich and famous pop music legend. I snap the rubber band I keep on my wrist and say, *No!* I'm alive, after thirty-eight years with HIV, and I have Tony, even though we bicker constantly and sometimes look at each other with such resentment and exhaustion that it's a wonder we're still together. But Winnipeg is small. There's no playing the field, because there is no field.

I go back to my client.

"Ooh, yes," I say, studying her head. "You're lifting nicely."

"Did you just have a cigarette?"

"I did. I'm sorry. I know it's a revolting habit."

"Cigarette smoke is another one of the smells I have a hard time with. Would it be okay if you don't smoke?"

"For sure, yes. I can go for hours without one. I guess we all cope in different ways."

Rita is silent. I finish with the bleach. I tone her to a pretty honey colour. I set about trying to animate her lifeless hair. I snip and tease and backcomb it for nearly an hour, smiling widely to allay her obvious concern. When I finally concede defeat and put down my comb and scissors, she looks like she's wearing a fun-fur toilet lid cover on her head.

"Wait," she says. "That *cannot* be the finished product."

"I really did struggle to create the shape you wanted."

She puts a hand over her mouth.

"I look crazy. I look like I live in a ravine."

"This is for sure fixable. I'd suggest that we go back to your natural colour."

"But this is my wedding hair. I wanted it like the picture."

"I understand. I did warn you that it might be difficult to achieve that look, given your hair type."

"No. No, no, no. You've destroyed my hair. I'm not paying for this!"

"You will need to pay for services rendered. Like I said, I'm more than happy to return your hair to its original state."

She stands, grabs her purse off the counter. "No. I refuse."

"Ma'am, you still need to pay."

"Why? I asked for a service that I did not receive."

"And I offered you colour correction. I did tell you to temper your expectations. Truthfully, Beyoncé is probably wearing a wig in the picture you showed me. Maybe you could consider a wig."

"A wig? I've spent two hours in your chair and now you're telling me to buy a wig? Wow. I'm mother of the bride and you want me to buy some shitty wig that comes in a bag at a costume store?"

I want to spray the place with gasoline and light a match. "There is a wonderful high-end wig store on Corydon. You'd be surprised. The wig industry has come a long way. The Raquel Welch line of wigs is—"

"I don't want to talk about the fucking wig industry. I'm not going to my daughter's wedding looking like a cancer patient. I'm not paying for this."

"I understand. But please know that you will be barred for life, unfortunately."

"Good!" She stomps out. The door chimes go chiming.

I exhale hard. A run-in like this happens maybe once every other year. There was a time when I'd have been able to shake it off, but my nerves are shot now. I lock the door. I ponder retirement, as I do almost every day. But a pauper doesn't get to retire. I'll die here at the salon, scissors in hand.

I TAKE THE BUS to Club 200, the only gay bar left in the city. There used to be a thriving scene: Gio's, Happenings, Club Desire. But the young queers don't need bars anymore; they have their phones, and they're spooked by old-school social interaction. I still need a bar. A beer among old acquaintances still nourishes me.

When I arrive, there's only Jean, eating a Reuben and drinking a 50. Jean is my age; she's battled various cancers for twenty-five years. Everyone loves Jean. She's grizzled but thoughtful.

"Roland. Was thinking of you the other day. How's Tony?"

"Oh, you know. He has bad days. We're gonna go to the casino this weekend. That always perks him up."

"So, I seen Marvin on the street the other day. That young boy-friend of his run off with all of Marvin's fur coats."

"No way. Shit. Marvin loves his fur coats. I never liked that kid. He made AIDS jokes. Idiot. Hopefully they'll catch him."

Jean nods, distracted by her sandwich. I stare absently at the movie on the big screen by the VLT machine. Bette Midler is running down a hallway in a black wig.

I get another beer. Jean leaves. Some guy in dirty overalls comes in to use the washroom.

I have another beer. The day's chaos recedes, and my sore shoulders return to their normal position. I love beer. It has magical properties, as long as you know when to say when. I have one more. The cute ginger who works at Sephora comes in. I smile and wave. The cute guy smiles and moves to the other end of the bar. The downside of beer is that it sometimes makes me forget I'm no longer young, and I embarrass myself by flirting with young men who clearly aren't interested.

I walk home. It's a warm, breezy evening. I think of Marvin and his stolen furs. Some of them were kind of ratty looking, but others were very nice. Marvin even has a walk-in fridge that he stores his fur coats in. His obsession has sometimes bordered on the absurd; it's not uncommon to see him in full-length fox in the middle of a heat wave. I try to think whether I have a comparable obsession, but all I can come up with is my obsession for the past: my mother's honeyed smell and fun times with my best friend Birdy, our avowals of love and devotion, our defiance in the face of so much hatred, until Birdy ran off to become who he needed to be, and I faltered and became for a time—yes, I can admit it now—trash.

The elevator is still broken when I get home. I slowly make my way up the six flights, gasping, pausing often. When I get to my floor I can hear our television blaring at the other end of the hall. Tony always blasts the television, despite having perfect hearing. Drives me crazy.

I open the door to a fog of marijuana. Tony is splayed out on the sectional. He offers a half nod as greeting.

"Hey. Could you turn the TV down a bit, Tony?"

"Yer drunk."

"I am not. I had three beer at the club. It was really stressful at work today."

"There's beer in the fridge. Would've been nice if you'd come home and spent time with me."

"I know. I'm sorry. I just needed to sit by myself for a bit. Work was hell."

"Queen, please." Tony is hopelessly masculine, his speaking voice croaky and his diction staccato, and when he attempts to talk in gay patois he sounds like Sylvester Stallone doing a cold read of *The Boys in the Band*. I still find it endearing.

"What does that mean? Are you saying my job can't be stressful?"

Tony pets Linda, our elderly cat. "I'm saying that if you spent a day in my shoes—not that I can wear shoes anymore—*then* you'd know stressful. It took me five minutes to lower myself onto the crapper today, and I was still crying out in pain."

"Have you taken your pills?"

"Yes, I've taken my fuckin' pills. Don't I always? They barely touch the pain. I'm gonna have to go back to Dr. Eadie. I need a higher dose."

Tony's already on a shockingly high dose of hydromorphone. Whenever he ups his dose he's stuporous and prone to falls, and I have to pay the woman next door to sit with him while I'm at work.

"What about you?" he asks. "Have you taken your pills?"

"Always. Come on. You know that. Have you eaten?"

"I got McDonald's from Skip."

"Oh, Tony. That's not a real dinner. I'll make you some spaghetti."

"No, I'm full."

I sigh and plop down next to him. "I can't eat either. My guts are still in knots."

"What happened? Was it too busy?"

"Some woman wanted to look like Beyoncé even though she only had three strands of hair. And it came out horribly, like I knew it would. I told her to maybe consider a wig, and she flipped out and left without paying."

"But wigs have come so far in the last few years, I thought."

"That's what I said. She wouldn't hear of it."

"What a bitch. You're too good for that salon. You should have your own place again."

I chuckle. I had my own salon once. Keener and Company, right on Portage. We did really well, but I found it so stressful that I started drinking at work. It got ugly. There was a staff walkout. At the end it was just me and Florence, a junior stylist so uncertain of her skills ("I can do this, I'm sure I can do this," she'd say to herself during a simple wash and set) that she also started drinking at work, and walk-ins would find us lying on the floor or dirty dancing. Tony was still working construction then; he came by one afternoon to take me to lunch, and I was already hammered.

"You're Tony, and my name is Ida," I remember saying before I blacked out. I closed the place for good two days later.

"I can't ever retire, Tony. Never. We have no savings, shit credit. What are we going to do?"

"We'll figure it out. When my dad goes, I'll get some money. We'll figure it out. Did you see the paper today?"

"The paper? Like, the newspaper? We don't get the newspaper."

"Yeah, there was a *Free Press* in the hallway, so I took it. Anyways, there was a big write-up about Birdy. He's doing some shows at the concert hall."

"Birdy? Really?" My heart leaps. "But he's never played Winnipeg. He swore he wouldn't when he left. And he doesn't have a record out. What could he be promoting?"

"Fuck if I know. I didn't read it all. Go look. It's on the kitchen table."

I rise and walk to the newspaper on the table. My heart leaps again; even though I keep a scrapbook of every press clipping, every advertisement, I do so with a mixture of pride and despair. Birdy O'Day, my best friend from grade school, so blazingly gifted in so many ways, now a pop music legend who hasn't spoken to me for fifty-odd years despite my letters and emails and flowers when he won his Grammy in 1979, has been my neurotic hobby since forever. When I'm washing my brushes at work, I think of Birdy cavorting in his infinity pool in Malibu. When I'm struggling to make love with Tony, who is also giving his all despite the pain of my body atop his, I think of Birdy, cooing astride his current lover. I still measure my life against his, which is silly and pointless, but there you go.

Tony fires up another joint. "How come he hasn't come out? Is he ashamed of it?"

I roll my eyes as I flip through the entertainment section of the paper. "How many times do we have to have this conversation? He's not ashamed of it. He's just living his life. People aren't obligated to come out if they don't want to. It's not like he's *getting away* with something, Tony. He's busy being a brilliant recording artist. Gosh, be an ally!"

"I am an ally! I'm an ally up the arse and out again, so don't hand me that. I'm just saying, he's so famous. And so mainstream—my grandma had his records. We all watched his Christmas special on CBC. He'd be such an inspiration if he came out."

"He already is an inspiration. I'm sorry, I can't have a conversation until I've seen the article and put it in my scrapbook."

I find the article. "Legendary Songbird Flies Home." There's a big glamour photo of him, one I haven't seen before. He's leaning on an elbow, with his platinum hair windblown. There's not a line on his face. His nose has been whittled down through the years so that now it resembles a discrete peak of meringue. And he's had a couple facelifts, but he doesn't look pulled at all. He is as beautiful as he's ever been, at least in this picture.

"I'll be right back," I say.

"Hurry and put it in your scrapbook," says Tony with affection. "You're so goofy."

"I'VE NEVER BEEN more excited about a performance as I am about this one," he says, with his trademark breathiness, from his home in California. "I only hope that my Winnipeg fans can forgive me for being away so long."

If only because his homecoming concert seems to signal a reckoning with his past, I have to ask him the question: will he finally acknowledge the open secret of his homosexuality?

He laughs his breathy laugh. "Oh, you! I'm sure there will be a surprise or two during the concerts. I'm so excited. It's really just so exciting. The rehearsals have been dreamy—all we do is laugh! It's hard to get any work done, because we're all laughing so hard! I don't know why, but I love it. Oh! There's someone at the door. Thank you for talking with me. I'll remember it forever."

He's so full of shit. I miss his bullshit. He wasn't always quite the bullshit artist he is now, certainly not when we were kids. But there was definitely some bullshit back then too. We came up hard, in a hard city. Birdy's bullshit was protective, protective and provoca-tive at once. I maybe would've fared better if I'd also possessed a bit of Birdy's bullshit when we were growing up.

I Meet Birdy

MY MOTHER AND I were on the bus home from downtown. We'd been shopping for back-to-school clothes. I was seven. My mother, Margaret, in her granny glasses, taupe house dress, and comfortable, ugly Hush Puppies, was twenty-three and already girded by the austerity and stern logic with which she would live the rest of her life.

"Mom, what does *husky* mean?" The man at the clothing store had looked me up and down with frustration and said, "He's really gotten quite husky, hasn't he?"

"It means that you're fat, despite my best efforts. The rapist was overweight too, so it's to be expected. Don't obsess over it. We'll get it under control eventually."

From the time that I could first comprehend speech, I have known that I am the product of rape, that a man in a parkade pulled my mother into a truck and raped her. She was sixteen, in love with Jesus, planning to enter the convent the day after graduation. But she was raped, fell pregnant, was thrown out of the house when she refused to go into hiding and then surrender the baby. She got a job as a night janitor in office building, finished high school, and enrolled in college to become a pharmacist.

Margaret was the most dogged, unflappable person I will ever know. Betrayed by Christ and her own family, she didn't believe in innocence, or sentiment, or Christmas.

We rode past a burning house, several blank billboards, and people asleep on the sidewalk. On the bus, there was the sound of the bus and nothing else.

"How come we have to take the bus?" I asked. "Why don't we have a car?"

"Don't be cloying, Roland. You know that a car isn't in the budget. Be grateful that I sleep on the couch so you can have your own room."

I leaned my head against my mother's arm. She stiffened.

"Sit up. It's far too warm for contact. You're very sticky. Dan is bringing us dinner tonight, so there'll be no snacking when we get home."

Dan was Margaret's boyfriend; they were both in their last year of pharmacy school. He was tall and skinny. He was nice but boring.

"Dan is nice, but he's so boring."

"I know, but he's very stable, and he's brought out the woman in me, which I thought was lost forever."

I didn't know what she meant by this. I pictured a strange miniature lady popping out of my mother's mouth, like a cuckoo from a clock. But I was used to listening blankly as Margaret mused on the subtleties of her existence.

ONCE HOME MARGARET ordered me to put away my new clothes in their proper dresser drawers. As I folded them and put them away I was reminded of how much I hated my new clothes, all of them muddy browns and greys and rough to the touch. I thought how nice it would be to wear pants made of slippery satin, like the fabric at the edges of the blanket on my bed.

I looked at the only picture in my bedroom: Dumbo, smiling delightedly in a cocked yellow cap. Dumbo's easy joy was out of place in the apartment, which was dark, all thick black drapes and crammed bookcases. There was no television, no record player, nothing quaint or cozy. The salt and pepper shakers were shaped like salt and pepper shakers, not anything fun like corncobs or smiling fish. The wallpaper was as plain as blank newsprint. For a time there were placemats covered in daisies on the kitchen table, but my mother threw them away.

I returned to the living room. Margaret was sitting on the couch, reading. I was still energized from the trip downtown, and I stood beside my mother, bouncing in place.

"Could you please stop bouncing. And could you also not breathe through your mouth like that."

"Do you want to play Go Fish?"

"I'm reading. Why don't you settle in with a book."

"Don't feel like it. Tell me about when I was a baby."

"Roland, I am not a jukebox. I've told you that story a hundred times."

"Okay. Sorry."

She sighed, softening, and put down the book.

"You were an uncommonly beautiful baby. Eyes big as dinner plates, lashes so lush they could've been made of mink. Perfectly formed everything. You were a perfect pod of a baby. The nurses couldn't stop gushing. One of them came up close to me and whispered that she'd pay to adopt you."

"You never said about that part before!"

She folded her upper lip over her teeth, her version of laughter. "I was tempted. Well, not really, although god knows I needed the money. But in the end, I didn't have the heart to part with you."

I knelt on the floor beside her. "Because you loved me so much. Because you loved me so much, right?"

"Well, of course. Don't be maudlin. Anyway, that's all I can recall."

"What about the part where you were giving me a bath and you had a picture of how I was going to be when I grow up?"

"I don't remember that. Oh, wait. Yes, it flashed through my mind that you were destined for a life of public service."

"What does that mean again?"

"Public service? As in helping the poor, possibly even going into some form of health care."

"Oh!" I burst into laughter. I was mostly a placid kid, but I was also thrilled to exist—typical for a tyke but also probably because my mother repeatedly mentioned that, had I been born to any other teenage girl, I would've been aborted. I ran my cheek along the bald upholstery of the couch cushion. I was deeply in love with all sensory input. The sound of a car engine struggling to start. The musty smell from the closet in the hallway. I also liked the sound of my own voice, and while Margaret could mostly manage to just let me prattle, sometimes she'd snap: "If you don't stop talking right now I am going to die!"

"What else went through your mind?"

"Nothing. Nothing else went through my—"

A knock at the door.

"That's Dan. Now, don't be a pest, and if he's brought something yummy for dinner, just know that I will be watching your intake. Each and every bite. We have to counteract the genes of the rapist."

There was Dan, with a pizza and something in a covered dish. He gave Margaret the awkward peck on the cheek he always gave her in greeting, and he patted me on the head.

"I'm sorry I'm late. Am I late? I had a protracted phone call with my father. He's buying a vacant building on Smith and wanted my advice."

"Are you versed in real estate?" asked Margaret.

"Not at all. I think he just likes the sound of my voice when he's worked up about something."

"Your voice is very calming."

They embraced, two nerds trying to be sensuous. I pretended that I was a tree until they finished.

"ARE YOU EXCITED about grade one?" Dan asked me as we ate. My mouth was full, so I waited to reply. Talking with your mouth full was the most disgusting thing in the world, according to Margaret.

"Grade *two*," I said at last, slightly snooty. "I'm at a new school this year."

"Ah. That can be nerve-racking. I'm sure you'll fit right in. You're a charming young man."

Even then, I knew empty flattery when I heard it. I was not a charming young man. In grade one, at the old school, I'd had only one friend, a girl named Tanya who threw up several times a day for no reason. Kids said that I was spooky as a ghost because of my pallor and vacant face and that I used big words because I was from Russia, which I puzzled over endlessly until finally telling Margaret what they'd said. She always enjoyed a good non sequitur and did her lip-over-the-teeth laugh. "Russia! Why on earth would they—see, this is what enjoy about having a child. The strangeness." I remember searching her face for reassurance that I wasn't some mutant from a faraway place. But she was still savouring the non sequitur.

When we'd finished with the pizza and the metallic-tasting apple crumble in the dish, we adjourned to the living room. Dan and Margaret talked about school things, their impending pharmacy placements for their last year of training. I sat on the floor, seeing how long I could go without blinking.

"I was always very nervous before every new school year," said Dan. I didn't realize that Dan was speaking to me.

"Dan is speaking to you, Roland."

"Oh. What did you say?"

"I was just saying that I always got nervous before the start of a new school year. So don't, you know, feel somehow less than."

"Less than what?"

"Like you're not good enough."

"I don't feel like I'm not good enough."

"Oh. Well, that's good!"

Margaret fixed me with a dark corrective look. "I don't like your tone, Roland. Dan is trying to have a conversation with you. He would like to get to know you better."

"If you ever feel like you need someone—another male—to talk to, I want you to feel like you can come to me."

"Okay. Thanks."

Now Margaret fixed Dan with the corrective look. "I prefer to think that I offer Roland sound advice unhindered by any kind of man/woman sorting."

"Oh, no doubt. No doubt," said Dan, cracking the knuckles of the toes of his right foot. Margaret did not look mollified. She liked Dan, but as she would later confide to me, she struggled sometimes with his passivity, his almost limitless ability to squelch his instincts in the name of getting along.

Whenever Dan came over there would come a point when they rose as one, and Margaret would announce that they were repairing to the bedroom for intimate adult time. She announced this without any inappropriate inflection. She raised me to be without shame, or at least without confusion, about all topics, all manner of human exchange. At seven, I knew that Dan found pleasure in putting his penis in Margaret's vagina, and in the years to come, when schoolyard banter dissolved into giggles over words like *boobies* and *dinkies*, I'd just shrug and wait for the topic to change.

Today, though, this didn't happen. Margaret fiddled with the tiny chopsticks that held her bun in place and then told Dan that she was feeling introspective and needed to be alone. Dan nodded and bowed abruptly, as though he'd just been stabbed: this was how he conveyed empathy. He gathered his apple crumble dish. They hugged, then Margaret did this almost imperceptible sweeping motion with her hands to shoo Dan out the door.

"I try not to have expectations of you," she said to me when Dan was gone. "But I do hope that you will live by your own policies and not get hung up on 'being nice,' like Dan. So many lives are squandered in the name of niceness. Do you understand what I'm saying?"

"I think so."

She ran her hands down her dress, lost in thought. "No one is going to supply you with the solution to your worries in life, Roland. It's essential that you understand that. Companionship is very nice, but it's incidental. Dan is disappointing in so many ways, but he's reliable. That's more than enough, for now. Suddenly I feel less than charitable. Do you think I'm a terrible mother?"

She never asked me questions like this. I wanted to cry but knew that wasn't the proper response. I then dithered over whether or not she was, indeed, a terrible mother, as she would've done when asked her opinion on a weighty matter. She was a demanding parent, and quite often her constant instruction left me so exhausted that I wanted lie down wherever we were—in the mall, on the sidewalk—and fall into a deep, dreamless sleep.

"You're the best mom ever," I said finally, touching the hem of her dress. She smiled, but it was obvious her mind was elsewhere. It often occurred to me that she had to be at least a little fretful over the fragility of our life in that dingy apartment. We were poor. The lock on the front door was so flimsy anyone could've kicked it open and killed us in our beds.

Monday morning I wiggled into my husky-boy pants and shirt. I was too nervous to eat the boiled egg and toast that my mother made for me.

"If you don't eat, your blood sugar will crash, and you won't be able to concentrate."

"I feel like I'm going to throw up and poo at the same time."

"Well, do it now if you must."

"I think I'll be okay."

"Good. Then eat your boiled egg."

GLENVALE ELEMENTARY WAS much bigger than my old school. There were kids milling about everywhere, screaming and pushing each other, brandishing forefingers as pistols. My old school was sleepy enough that I could slip about mostly unnoticed, but here it was as though everyone was looking at everyone else, always. As I walked toward the front steps, two boys, who in my memory were spinning as a unit, like tumbleweed, barrelled into me and sent my brown bag lunch flying.

Our teacher, Miss Monk, was very tall and very close to retirement age. She was cheerful, sometimes to the point of mania ("Welcome, class! Welcome! Welcome! Welcome! Welcome!" she beamed that first day), and while some kids made fun of her, I adored her. For seven hours, five days a week, she was a firewall of optimism, and I felt like nothing bad, or at least nothing criminal, could happen as long she kept smiling, and laughing until she doubled over, and clapping the chalkboard erasers together to gaze in wonder at the pastel dust they issued.

My mother was right about skipping breakfast; by lunchtime I was glassy eyed with hunger. When the bell went I tore into my squashed lunch and devoured the bologna from between two pieces of toast ("Bread is fattening, but toast has all the calories burnt out of it," Margaret always said) and the badly bruised apricot, and I guzzled my little carton of skim milk.

The kids were all screaming again. Much satisfaction was found in antic gaping mouths full of food. Until that first day I'd considered myself easygoing, or at least not easily rattled, but here in grade two I was already shaking with anxiety and longing for the mandatory nap of kindergarten.

There was commotion in the back of the room. Boys had gathered around someone's desk.

"You can dress like a boy, but you're really a girl! You're such a sissy! Sissies get murdered at recess!"

This was 1962, so there was still some innocence to the bully-ing. It would be at least two more grades before we learned *faggot* and *queer* and wondered at the almost hallucinatory improbability of someone actually enjoying getting a dick up the ass.

When the crowd thinned I saw the object of the boys' teasing. This boy was fine boned, blond, and stone faced; if the harassment affected him, you couldn't tell. I understood the boys' confusion over the kid's sex, but his androgyny didn't anger me. I was cap-tivated. He was incredibly pretty, and he sat with a poise that would've been prissy if it weren't for the immensity of the folded hands, the huge, all-seeing eyes.

"What are you looking at?" he demanded. I spun around in my seat. I was panting. I'd just seen the most riveting, confound-ing person I'd ever meet. I don't care if I sound like some corny *Reader's Digest* anecdote in saying that. My life hasn't been very eventful. There have been some pleasant moments, some swaths of sadness, but generally I'm a very average, even tedious person, and I don't come across charismatic people in my wan little journey from home to work to gay bar and home again. Is it any wonder I've stayed obsessed for six decades? Tony is forever saying I need to let go, that it's unseemly for someone my age to be keeping a scrapbook of some old pop star. He's not wrong. But how else would I mark the passage of time? I have no milestones of my own; Tony and I can't even remember our anniversary. So I revel in stolen milestones: Birdy's Grammy win is my Grammy win, his Junos are my Junos, his guest spot on *The A-Team* is—well, that last one was unfortunate, with that stuffed panther and that duet with Mr. T. Serious Birdy O'Day fans gloss over that one.

By two o'clock I could no longer hold in my nervous poo. I went off in search of the boys' bathroom, afraid of the empty, echoing hallway.

The bathroom was next to the janitor's supply closet. The jani-tor was in the closet, and he looked at me warily.

"Where you going, boy?" he said. Instantly I felt like a pickpocket.

"I just have to go to the bathroom."

He returned to cleaning his wrench. I wasn't used to being spoken to so sternly by an adult. In grade one everyone had spoken to us with a soothing lilt, as though we were deer.

I went into the bathroom and sat in a stall. I've always been shy about using public bathrooms and making telltale bathroom noises, so I tried to excrete silently.

Someone started singing in another stall. "It's My Party," by Lesley Gore. The voice was high and faultless, like a choirboy, but with some tooth, like an orphaned choirboy. I knew it was the beautiful kid from the back of the class. No one else could have made such a haunting sound.

"You sound really good," I said, shocked at my own forwardness.

"Thanks. I like to sing. You're in my class."

"Am I?" I winced. The choirboy was too canny not to know that I knew who he was.

"You're new."

"We just moved to this neighbourhood. Do you like it here? In this school?"

"Everyone's really dumb. But I don't care. I'm going to be on *Jammy's Talent Hut*."

"What's that?"

"It's that TV show."

"Oh. We don't have a television set. My mom doesn't believe in it."

"That's crazy. Everyone has a TV set. My mom took me to audition, and Jammy said he's never heard anyone my age who's so good."

"I wish I could sing like you."

"Everyone has their own talent. My mom says that sometimes someone's special talent doesn't show up until you're really old."

I didn't understand what that meant. How could talent not manifest until a person was really old? Obvious talent bubbles up immediately. I maintain that belief. I'm sixty-nine, and I know there is no latent gift for chess or tennis waiting for me to stumble upon.

There was a flush from his stall. "Your name's Roland, right?"

"Yes. How did you know that?"

"Duh. Miss Monk said 'Let's welcome our new student, Roland.'"

I had no memory of that. My first-day nerves had occluded my hearing. "What's your name?"

"Gerald. But I'm going to change it. It's not catchy enough. I'm going to change it to Birdy. Okay, bye."

I sat there, baffled. It made no sense. Kids didn't change their names, and they certainly didn't change it to something wacky like "Birdy." The nerve of it made me slightly dizzy. Margaret was all about the empirical world—this is an apple, this is a roll of dimes—and that left me unprepared for brilliant, assured little boys named Birdy. I know I've bored countless people with my stories of Birdy O'Day and how he transformed me from a sheltered dolt into a rabid fan who wanted only to merge with him, leaving no trace of myself. "Sounds like you're in love," people say, but that's too pedestrian to me. Had I been some aerial soul wafting around, looking for a mortal form to steal into, I would've stolen into Birdy.

At the end of the school day I looked at the packed school bus and decided to walk home instead. I noticed a boaty Cadillac in the parking lot, cherry red. It shimmered like it was brand new.

I was just walking past Kresgie's Loaf and Jug when the Cadillac slowed beside me. The window rolled down: Birdy.

"Do you want a ride?"

I started to shake like a lost dog. I couldn't believe that Birdy would want to give me a ride. "I'm on Dufresne Street, is that too far?"

"Just yeah, come on. It's okay."

I slipped into the back seat behind Birdy. He introduced me to his mother behind the wheel, who turned and smiled. She looked very sick, gaunt and yellow and sad-eyed, but she was still very friendly.

"Gerry says you're new to the school. How did it go?"

"It was okay. Lots of people. I'm not used to so many people."

"Gerry didn't like how busy it was at first. But how's he gonna cope in front of a big concert audience? He's gotta get used to it if he wants to be a famous celebrity."

"It's Birdy, mother. Birdy."

"Oh, Gerry, don't start in with that bullshit again, I can't hack it. Maybe Roland would like to be your friend. Birdy can't have friends, because he's not an actual person."

"I don't mind. I can call him whatever he wants."

"You're very obliging, Roland, but I get so nervous when he starts up with the Birdy business. He's had so many run-ins with kids at school. Last year he almost lost an eye."

"Please can we stop talking about it. Ughhhhh." Birdy sounded like a vacuum cleaner turning off. I would come to know that sound as a sign of ultimate frustration. I'd hear Birdy make that sound several times a day.

"I'm Judy Perner, by the way. Everyone calls me Judy, so ya might as well get a head start!"

I smiled. I liked Birdy's mother already. In years to come I'd encounter a lot of women like Judy at the salon: sweet, a little brassy, endlessly magnanimous, but also braced for future disappointments after a past filled with them.

"I'm just here on the right, by the firehouse," I said.

"That's a nice firehouse," said Judy, coming to a stop. "It's nice and old-fashioned. Okay now, great to meet ya, Roland."

I said goodbye and walked the path to our building, beaming, shaking again. I'd made friends so easily with an interesting, slightly dangerous person. As I turned the key in the lobby door it hit me that I'd been deeply lonely in the company of mostly only my mother.

She was doing homework at the kitchen table when I came in.

"Well, hello, young scholar. How did it go?"

"It was okay. My teacher is nice. I made a new friend."

She put down her pen. "A new friend? Progress. Great progress. What is this new friend's name?"

"Birdy. Birdy Perner."

"Perner ... doesn't ring a bell. What's she like?"

"She's a boy."

I watched her think. "Oh. A boy named Birdy. Okay. Yes, why not. I don't know why that name strikes me as feminine."

"What's that?"

"Feminine? Pertaining to all things female."

"Oh. Well, yeah. He is kind of like a girl, but he's not."

"Interesting. Variation is only ever a good thing. Does Birdy have supportive parents?"

"I—I don't know. I think so. His mother gave me a ride home, she's really nice. I don't know that much about his dad."

Margaret nodded. "Huh. That's no surprise. Men are unknowable. Unless they're having an orgasm. Or a stroke."

"I think Birdy's mother worries that someone is going to beat him up."

"That's a valid concern. This isn't a very sophisticated city. I worry that you could get attacked. Did you feel that you were in any danger today? Did anyone pick on you?"

"No. I didn't really talk to anyone though. I'm just going to be quiet and try not to talk to anyone."

"Sit." She smacked the chair beside hers. I sat. "I know that you're a sensible, intelligent person. It's good that you're cautious in new situations. But I don't want you to cower, Roland. We don't cower, ever. I'm a reasonable person, but I can also be a viper. A viper. I've had many occasions to cower in my life, and I've always done the opposite. I'm not saying that you should provoke people, but if a situation comes up, you need to stand firm. Maybe ... should I get Dan to show you how to box? No, he probably doesn't know how either. After the rape my grandfather showed me how punch somebody in the throat. I'll show you that after dinner."

THE DAYS PASSED at school. I sat with Birdy at lunch and recess. I listened as he detailed his future, down to the purple suit he planned to wear for his first appearance on *The Tonight Show*. He'd also rhapsodize over female classmates he found charming and boys he found cute. (We were in grade two! I couldn't breathe when he told me of his crushes; I'd felt a dark swirl in my stomach whenever the dad from *Flipper* took off his shirt, but I'd no idea someone could fall in love with someone of their own sex! Birdy was vastly more precocious, seasoned even, than I was, so much so that I often wondered if I had some kind of mental deficit.) Occasionally he'd let slip some tidbit from his family life: his father was incredibly old, sixty-something, and liked to gamble, and Birdy's mother was his best friend and liked to drink, elegantly but constantly. Birdy mentioned a brother, Terry, who was stupid and wasn't home much.

Here and there he'd ask me about myself, and I'd seize with fear; no matter how florid my own life might've been, I knew I'd never be able to offer it up with his level of élan.

> *Birdy:* What does your dad do?
> *Me:* I don't know. I've never met him.
> *Birdy:* Why? Is he dead?
> *Me:* I don't know. He might be.
> *Birdy:* Have you seen a picture of him?
> *Me:* No.

Birdy: That's so sad. What do you think he looks like?

Me: I don't know.

Birdy: My dad is very handsome. Well, he was, but he's sixty-seven now. My mom is his second wife. He's so mean. He was in the war. He saw his best friend get shot in the face. He talks about it when he drinks with my mom. Then he calls her a greasy whore and kind of beats her up. But then he goes to bed. And she keeps drinking.

Looking back, I was already in love with him. I'd wake up each day excited to see him, to hear his voice, to see him thwart bullies with a perfect put-down or, when pressed, a punch in the face (I asked him who taught him to fight, and he said that his uncle once came to visit and taught him to tie an assortment of knots and to throw a punch). If there was even the shortest lull in conversation, I'd ask some vague question about what he thought heaven would be like, and hell, and wouldn't it be great to have your driver's licence. I'd start every morning feeling vacuous, dim as a pigeon, but by day's end Birdy's presence would have filled me with so much nervous energy that I'd come home giddy and motor-mouthed. One time my mother asked me, with real concern, if someone had been feeding me coffee beans.

ONE AFTERNOON IN the spring, Judy gave me another ride home.

"I think Gerry has something he wants to ask you. Go on, g'wan, Gerry."

Birdy rolled his eyes, embarrassed but—possibly?—hopeful. "It's my birthday in two weeks and I wanted to know if you want to come over for my thing."

"Come on now, it's not your thing, sweetie, it's your birthday party."

"That nobody's coming to."

"I'll come!" I cringed at my obvious enthusiasm.

"See, sweetie! Now you've got two kids coming to your party."

"Cheryl doesn't count. She's a garbage picker. She rides in the garbage truck with her dad."

"Get off your high horse, fancy man! You and Cheryl were babies together. Her mum and I used to walk our baby buggies to Pigeau Park together. We'll see you real soon, Roland."

"**BIRDY INVITED ME** to his birthday party," I said to Margaret that night. "Do you think we can afford to buy him a present?"

She didn't respond right away. Her eyes were casting left and right, like she was looking for something. I guess she was figuring the logistics of her fey son being friends with a fey boy, how to encourage the friendship without getting us killed.

"You can't go to a birthday party without a gift. What are Birdy's interests?"

"I don't know. I've only known him a few months. Oh, wait, he wants to be a singer. He was singing when we were in the washroom at school. He has a really nice singing voice. It's better than nice. It's like he could be on the radio."

"I always wanted to have musical talent. Does he play an instrument?"

"I'm not sure."

"He must be able to accompany himself. He needs to be self-sufficient. All right, let me work on it."

The day before Birdy's party, my mother produced a small stringed instrument from the hall closet.

"What's that?"

"It's your birthday gift for Birdy. It's a baritone ukulele. I got it at the pawnshop on Hargrave."

"What if he doesn't know how to play it?"

"He'll learn. If he truly has a passion for music, he'll learn how to play it. The man at the shop said it's quite easily mastered."

I looked at it. It looked used.

"But it doesn't have the box it came in. And there's a scratch on it." I instantly regretted saying that.

"I went all over town on my only day off to find a suitable gift for a child I've never met, Roland. I spent money I do not have. We are poor, Roland. We cannot afford to pretend to be middle class. Hopefully, when we *are* middle class, we can pretend to be upper middle class, if that's something that is important to you."

I fought to keep from crying. I wanted to throw myself at her and beg for forgiveness. When Margaret was mad at me I felt as though I'd committed some grave moral trespass that would stain the rest of my life.

"Sorry," I said softly. "It is really nice. I'd like to learn to play guitar."

"We aren't musical. My parents had no artistic ability. My father was so literal minded. I remember him looking up from the newspaper once and asking me what *fairweather* meant. 'Says here that Conservative voters in Manitoba tend to be fairweather. What is that? Does that mean they bring fair weather?' Your grandparents are morons, I'm sorry to say. Or they were morons. They could be dead, for all I know."

MY MOTHER WALKED ME to Birdy's house the next day. It was nice out, warm but not stifling. Margaret wore a thin white-cotton skirt that in direct sunlight revealed her dark panties. Sometimes my mother could be inadvertently licentious. It embarrassed me, but if I'd mentioned it, she'd just have shrugged and said that all her other underwear was in the laundry hamper.

Birdy's house was a sprawling bungalow in pink and white. The front lawn was long and the shrubbery misshapen and spiky.

There was an old washing machine on the front porch. Margaret, who ordinarily never noticed those sorts of things, paused briefly at the bottom of the driveway.

"Have you met your friend's whole family?" she asked, eyeing the washing machine.

"Just Judy, Birdy's mom."

"All right. Well, if anything should happen, or if you're feeling like you want to leave, you'll call?"

"Why would anything happen? What's going to happen?"

"Probably nothing. I'm just having a pang, a maternal pang. I don't often have them. You go on now. Have fun. Actually, no. I'm just going to introduce myself. It would be rude not to."

She tried to take my hand, but I wouldn't let her. It was bad enough that my mother had to see me to the door. I wanted to seem independent and footloose, like Birdy.

Judy answered the door. She grinned and put her hands to the sides of her face, like she was imitating a fish's gills.

"It's Roland!" she wheezed, smelling of alcohol. "Is this your mother? Hi, I'm Judy! You're so young and pretty! My goodness."

"Hi there. I'm Margaret Keener. Thanks for having Roland over. He's really been looking forward to Birdy's birthday."

Judy's grin dissolved. "Oh, now Gerry's got you talking his nonsense. We don't call Gerry by his made-up name. Please don't indulge him. His dad gets so upset. Won't you come in for a drink? It's just me and little Cheryl and Gerry. I'd love some grown-up conversation. Have you read *Peyton Place*? I'm on the last chapter. It's just this side of a blue movie!"

"I really have to go, I have a previous commitment. But definitely another time." My mother grabbed a tuft of my T-shirt and gave me her sternest, most cautionary look, the one she saved for Jehovah's Witnesses at the door or Dan when he was pestering her to let him stay over and she wasn't into it. "Be good, and remember what I said to you in the driveway. Do you remember? Say that you remember."

"I remember. I'm fine."

"Okay, then. Well, have fun." She backed down the front steps.

Birdy's mother put her hand on my back and nudged me inside. "It's birthday party time! Gerry, look who it is!"

THE PERNERS' HOUSE was uncomfortably bright, with fluorescent panels of light in the ceiling, like you'd find in a doctor's office.

Birdy drew close until I could see the dark of his nostrils. "I'm soooo glad you're here. Cheryl's so—I mean, I like her, but I can't talk about interesting things with her. All she wants to talk about is stuff she found in the garbage. My mother's pretty drunk. I don't know where my dad is."

"Happy birthday." I handed him the ukulele, nestled in the sewing box Mom had sacrificed so that it wouldn't look like a wrapped ukulele.

He gasped. "I have no idea what you got me but I know I'm going to really like it."

I followed him into the living room, which was brightly lit by more office lighting, as well as several floor lamps, some beautiful, others vulgar. There was a jade serpent lamp that I wanted to steal; the snake's exuberant forked tongue had a hole in the middle for the chain to pull the lamp on and off. There was also a tacky lamp in the shape of a delighted fat baker, replete with baker's hat, baker's apron, and rolling pin held high and somewhat menacingly, like Death's scythe. Birdy's friend Cheryl sat under the light of that lamp, her mouth held neat and tight, like a zipper.

Judy teetered in, her coffee mug clinking with ice cubes.

"This is so nice," she said. "Gerry, did you introduce Roland to Cheryl?"

"This is my friend Roland. This is my friend Cheryl."

Cheryl offered a wide, oddly maternal smile; with her comfortably splayed legs and lacy gingham top, she looked like a contented country grandma, except she was seven. I smiled and sat on the other end of the couch.

"Now, we have all kinds of board games, and lots of records for dancing," Judy said. "This is your special day, sweetheart," she said to Birdy. "You can do whatever you want. And I'll make myself scarce—I know you don't want your silly old mother hanging around!" Then she sat down between Cheryl and me. "I'm so proud of Gerry. I was thirty-nine when I had him. Almost died. The blood and afterbirth just whooshed out of me like a garden hose. I felt myself leaving my body, and I heard the doctor say, 'Uh-oh, she's a goner! Oh well.' But he denied saying that when I asked him about it after I came back to life. Gerry! I'm telling your friends about when you were born!"

She yelled this at Birdy, even though he was two feet away, by the record player.

"I'm right here, Mother. You don't have to scream."

"Oh! Gerry's so quick witted, so clever. I love both my boys equally, but Gerry is for sure the more—what's the word—not brainy, but along those lines. Terry is very gifted with his hands. He wants to be in the RCMP. He's really been struggling with grade twelve. How's your mum and dad, Cheryl?"

"They're good. My mom fell in the bathtub, but she's okay. My dad found a Queen Elizabeth plate in the garbage yesterday."

"Oh, yeah? Now what's a Queen Elizabeth plate, exactly?"

"It's like a plate that has Queen Elizabeth on it. It's nice. It's not chipped or anything."

"That's just great. It's nice to have nice things. I like the Royal Doulton products. I had a little collection going, but most of it got broken."

"Mother."

"I wish you all good things, you kids. You never expect that you're going to end up living in hell, but—"

"Okay, Mother. You can go now."

"He has spoken. Well, say no more. I'm just going to toddle off to the kitchen. Help yourself to the chips and pop! It's not a birthday party if you don't go home with a tummy ache!"

She rocked back and forth to get the momentum to stand. I'd never heard an adult ramble on about personal problems like that. My mother was matter-of-fact, but only if the topic at hand demanded it. She wouldn't just let rip with the particulars of her sorrow, like Birdy's mom.

Once Judy was gone, Birdy sat where his mother had been. "She is so embarrassing. She said she was just going to flit in and out." He turned to me. "Sorry. Do you still like me?"

"Yes. Definitely." I looked guiltily at Cheryl; I assumed she didn't need an apology because she'd long since been exposed to Birdy's mom's tipsy melancholy.

"My mother has mental problems. I try to make her laugh, but sometimes she just won't. I like her more than my dad though. I hope he doesn't come home until late."

"Does he yell at you?"

"He … gets mad easy. Something makes him mad and his eyes go bulgy and—let's play a record. My mother got me the new Dionne Warwick record. Do you like her?"

"I think so. I might not have heard her before."

"My dad says that he found your dad passed out at the garbage dump," Cheryl said, unaware the subject had changed. Now she resembled an ancient sea turtle, slowly craning her neck, taking us in really, really slowly with her tiny sea turtle eyes.

"Shut up, Cheryl. Your dad is full of shit." Cheryl gasped at Birdy's casual use of the S-word. Birdy got up and put on the Dionne Warwick record. The first song was "A House Is Not a Home." I'd never heard such a beautiful voice. She sounded like a pained angel. Then Birdy started to sing along, faultlessly, in his own ashy soprano, not unlike Dionne Warwick's. I started to cry and turned away. Birdy brought out strange and emphatic feelings in me that made me worry I was turning into the man who sat all day at the bus stop by our apartment building, talking and laughing and crying with unseen friends.

Judy came in with pink coconut-flecked balls on a tray. "Who's ready for my famous hoo-hoo balls? They're Gerry's favourite."

"I don't really like hoo-hoo balls anymore, Mother. You can tell they came from a cake mix."

"Oh, Gerry, you're so hard on me. I can't do everything from scratch. I'm sure your guests will enjoy my balls."

I made a big show of taking a hoo-hoo ball in both hands and biting off half of it. It did taste like it came from a cake mix, but it was still delicious. Margaret never let me eat sweets. I crammed the rest of it in my mouth and took another.

"See, sweetie? Roland can't get enough of 'em. Cheryl, you look like a girl who likes her food, have a ball. Have two!"

Cheryl shyly took a ball. I instantly recognized her as another kid whose mom hassled her about her diet.

"You kids look like you've just lost a pet, for God's sake. It's that sad music you're listening to. Gerry, who is this sad person you're listening to?"

"It's the record you gave me this morning. 'Member?"

"Well, of course I remember, sweetie. I'm no dumb Dora. But she sounds like she's been rode hard and put away wet. You need peppy music for a birthday party. Put on the record with that song I like so much! *Well you've got the sixteen pounds and what do you get? Another ten pounds and you wanna bet! Oh* ... so and so, however the rest of it goes ..."

"Okay, can you please go away again?"

"Party-poopers. All right, I'll leave you be."

I turned away again to finish my second hoo-hoo ball; I didn't want Birdy to see my gluttonous appetite.

"I'm going to open your presents," said Birdy. He opened Cheryl's first: a miniature chalkboard with a box of coloured chalk.

"It's a little chalkboard," Birdy sighed, already so adept at subtle shade. "For when I ... need a little chalkboard. Thanks."

"I know it's stupid," said Cheryl. "I didn't know what to get you."

"Did you buy it from a store or did you find it at the garbage dump?"

"I bought it. I wouldn't give you a present from the dump. Unless it was something really special."

Birdy smiled and nodded. He unwrapped my ukulele. "It's a little guitar?"

"It's a baritone ukulele. So you'll have something to play when you're singing."

He held it to his chest. His face registered both dread of having to learn an instrument and delight at having an instrument other than his voice.

"Is it hard to learn?"

"My mom said the man at the store said it wasn't that hard."

"This is the best present I ever got." He looked at Cheryl. "When you give someone a present, you should think about what the person likes to do and what their interests are."

Cheryl started to cry. "You're so mean, Gerry. You used to be nice. I don't want to be friends with you anymore."

"Good. Neither do I, and my name is Birdy now."

She tore out with a jerky walk that suggested one leg was shorter than the other. Birdy's mom returned.

"What happened with Cheryl?"

"Nothing. I don't know."

"I was just going to bring the cake out. She was crying, she ran right out the door. What did you say to her?"

"Nothing. I don't know."

"Don't hoodwink me, Gerald. You can be so short with people. You're going to have it hard enough in the world without your backtalk. You have to get along with people."

Birdy smacked his thighs and shook in his seat on the couch. "I can act how I want to act. You act nice all the time and you still ..."

"I still what? You can go ahead, Mumma doesn't mind. I act nice and still I get into scraps with your dad, that's what you want to say. And there's nothing I can say in my defence. You're really getting an earful now, Roland. I'm sorry. Your nice mother is going to think we're all a bunch of pea pods over here."

"No, she won't. I won't say anything."

Birdy glared at me. "You won't say anything? There's nothing to say. Do you think you're better than me? You're not."

"I know."

"You stop right now," Judy said to Birdy, stern like I'd never heard her. "Roland is probably your one and only friend at this point, and you're going to send him running too, if you're not careful. Is that what you want, Gerald? Eh?"

In my memory of the moment, I heard a gathering, hissing wind before Birdy spoke.

"My name is not GERALD! My name is BIRDY! This is my BIRTHDAY and I am NOT HAVING FUN!"

He stood and stuck out his hands like they were bear's claws. He shook his head back and forth as if concussed. He twirled around furiously. He was moving like someone lost in rapture, but he was utterly disconsolate.

His mother approached him slowly. "All right, now. Come here with me now on the couch. Mumma's sorry, sweetie. I know things are a wee bit scratchy right now, and I feel just awful about it. You shouldn't have to ... well, I'm just sorry about all of it. I know Roland understands."

I nodded, understanding nothing. They were speaking English, but their back and forth was like a movie I'd missed most of.

Birdy hid his face in his mother's chest. He cried and cried. At that age we were still prone to these implosions. I tried to think of something useful to say.

"Do you want me to go get the cake?" I asked feebly.

"Oh, could you? Oh no, wait. I don't want you lighting candles by yourself."

"It's okay, my mom showed me how to make a fire when we went camping." This was a lie—my mother had no use for nature—but Judy bought it.

She looked down at Birdy. "Would you like your birthday cake, sweetie? A nice slice of your birthday cake?"

The sobbing slowed. "What—what colour is—is the icing?"

"It's pink icing. Like you asked for. I was at the Safeway bakery, dithering. I knew your dad would have a fit. Then I thought, you know what, to hell with him—excuse my language, Roland. Anyway, I got you nice pink icing, with a little plastic ballerina in the middle of it."

Birdy pulled away, wide eyed. "Really? Does she have the ballerina skirt that sticks out?"

"She does, my love. She's all decked out."

"Oh! Thank you, Mum. Cheryl always has a ballerina on her cake. One year I stole it when nobody was looking."

"You're awful!" They laughed and hugged. It was nice. Then we heard the front door open. We heard something metal drop onto the kitchen counter.

"Oh, Christ," said Judy. "Wouldn't you know it. Okay. All right. You just stay put. I'll go and see what's what."

She got up, drunk and anxious, sighing before she greeted her husband with a canned, thin "Hey!"

"If my dad sees the cake he's gonna be so mad. Don't leave. Are you gonna leave?"

"No. I want to have birthday cake with you."

Judy came back with a tall, stooped, worn man in stained clothes. Birdy's dad was probably very handsome in his youth, as Birdy had said. But now his face was covered with deep wrinkles, probably caused by sorrow, and tens of thousands of unfiltered cigarettes.

He looked around his own living room as though it were a crime scene; he inspected the coffee table, the record player, and his own young son before he landed on me.

"Stop the presses, the kid has a friend," he said, and for all the world it felt like he was scanning me for feminine infractions: a fringe, a heel of any dimension. I guess I passed the test; he stuck out his big hand for me to shake. I shook it as firmly as I could.

"Ken, this is Roland. Roland, this is my—Gerry's father, Ken. Roland's in the same class as Gerry."

"Well, I figured as much, Judy. Christ. I'm gonna lie down for a bit."

"No, you are not," said Judy. "This is your son's birthday party. You're going to sit and be part of things."

Ken started wagging his finger but then collapsed on the dingy fabric recliner. "I've said before, I don't think he's mine. I'd gone off you in the sack at least a year before he come along, and he don't look or act a thing like me."

"What a nice thing to say on Gerald's birthday. There is not one bad thought or feeling you don't have, is there? I could bring up just looking at you. You know, I wish I had been an adultery— adulteress. Both my boys have to contend with your shitty genes. I wouldn't wish that on a dog I liked."

"You keep it up, Judy. I'll give you something to cry about. What a life. Did you get him a present? It better not have cost anything or I'll belt ya."

"Don't worry about it, Ken. It didn't cost you a goddamn nickel, okay? I've got my own money, thank Christ."

"Whores always do."

"Stop! Please," said Birdy. He sounded so broken that both his mom and dad drew back and looked at their drinks.

"Where is Terry?" Judy asked after a lull. I could tell she was trying hard not to slur her words.

"I dropped him at his girlfriend's. They're having steaks. Go get me a rum and Coke."

"What about my cake?" asked Birdy.

Judy did this long, slow blink, so slow I thought she was falling asleep on her feet. "We'll save the cake for later."

"But you said we could have it now." There was an edge to Birdy's voice. He knew his pink cake would upset his father, and that prospect thrilled him, despite the bruising aftermath.

"Gerry, please. We'll have the cake later. There's no rush." She went to fix her husband a drink.

"Where's that fat girl you used to chum with? The garbage man's girl. Myrtle."

"Cheryl. She had to leave. Her present was dumb."

"Yeah? That's no surprise. That whole family—well, you know they're brother and sister, the mom and dad."

"That is not true," Birdy said. "That's a mean made-up story. I asked Cheryl, and she said her mom and dad definitely aren't brother and sister. They're barely related."

"Oh, well then, pardon me." Ken spotted the Dionne Warwick album sleeve on the ottoman. "What's this? This isn't one of ours."

"It's Dionne Warwick. Mum got it for my birthday."

He flipped the cover over. "She's as black as night. Nice looking, but still." He shook his head. The tension in the room made me tuck my chin under the neck of my T-shirt.

"I got a present for ya," Ken continued. "I'm gonna show you how to use a gun. We'll go in the bush, and I'll have you do some target practice with my pistol. Would ya like that?"

"No! That's violence. I'm not going to try and blow some deer's head off."

"You're soft, Gerald. If you don't watch out, you'll end up drawn and quartered. I sure don't see a whole lot of good fortune for you."

Judy returned with her horrible husband's rum and Coke. She handed it to him with strenuous deference.

"What all are we talking about?" she asked. The look that passed between her and Ken—I recognize that look now as coming from the back end of a lifetime of intractable mutual contempt. I kept my eyes on Birdy. Birdy's face kept me from running out of the house like Cheryl.

"What all are we talking about? Oh, I can fill you in, Judy. We're talking about the record you got for his birthday without consulting me. Looks like the kind of record whores dance to in dirty bars. You throw that record out, Gerald."

"No way. I like it."

Judy—skinny, jaundiced, drunk—let out an awful sound like someone sick being yanked from sleep. "Enough, Ken. It's just a record. Why are you so hard? Did you lift a finger to get a present for Gerry? No. But still you come home and cause a ruckus. It's not fair to Gerry."

"Not fair to Gerry. You know what's not fair to Gerry? Letting him grow up in this house with you, drunk as a skunk, while he turns into a full-on deviant. I don't have a chance to set him straight and give him a shot at life with you hovering over him all the time. He's gonna learn how to use my pistol. That's the best gift he could ever get."

"Like hell. He's a small child. I'll never let my child go into the bush with you and a gun. Sick. You're sick."

Birdy started crying again. This was how his mom and dad conversed. I suddenly understood the ferocity of Birdy's imagination: it was his only armour.

"Gerry, you and Roland go to your room for a bit while I talk to your dad."

Birdy didn't move. I gently took his arm and pulled him away.

His bedroom looked a bit like a prison cell. There was a bed, a dresser, and a little desk with a little chair. The walls were bare. I was shocked—I'd been sure his room would be colourful, the walls covered in posters of his goddesses: Marilyn Monroe, the Supremes, Julie Andrews. Afterward I realized that his father would likely have ripped down these posters, so Birdy didn't bother.

We sat on his hard bed that was identical to my own hard bed at home. We listened to his parents argue through the walls. Birdy wept, and I put my hand on his knee.

Ken, you can go to town on me, I don't even feel it anymore. But you're not gonna torture our son on his birthday. No way.

If you could see yourself, you would jump off a bridge, Judy. Ugly and dead drunk. People come up to me and ask me why I'm with such an ugly drunk.

Keep it coming, Ken. But what did give your son on his birthday apart from more reasons to hate you? That's how you'll be judged right before Jesus throws your ass in hell forever.

Get bent, ya whore. I'd be happy to go to hell as long as I didn't have to look at your ugly puss.

"Do you still like me?" Birdy asked.

"Yes. You're my—yes. A lot."

One smack and I could send you ass over teakettle.

You don't scare me at all, Ken. There is not one thing you can do to scare me anymore.

We heard Birdy's mother fall against furniture. Birdy covered his face.

"If I go out there it gets worse. It always gets worse. Sometimes I have to call the police. I should go check on her."

"Don't go out there. Please don't."

I put my arms around him. I wanted him to be smaller so I could hold him like a baby.

"What about now? Do you still like me now? I know this is so bad. Your mom won't let you come over again."

"I won't tell her. Promise."

"No, I want you to. Maybe she can write a letter to the police or the ... rescue people, I don't know what they're called."

I couldn't tell if it was untoward, a boy in another boy's arms, but I didn't care. The poky propriety of my short life no longer mattered. We heard Judy trying to pull herself to her feet and Ken telling her to *Stay down, stay down, stay there on the floor and don't move.* I remember sending my mother mental messages to come and rescue us, and later I would lie in my small, hard bed and tearfully tell her every detail as she worried a dent on my headboard with her thumb and incanted, "This is not good, this is unacceptable," but all I could do at the time was hold my friend and tell him that I loved Dionne Warwick, that she had such a nice voice, that she was super pretty.

AND NOW I think of Birdy O'Day's autobiography, which is only 120 pages and sanitized to the point of inadvertent satire.

> *Lucky Boy: My Story*
> by Birdy O'Day
> Page 17
> My childhood was filled with so much love and easy affec-
> tion. Just thinking back on it makes me well up. My mother
> was strong and vivacious but never vulgar, quick to laugh,
> quicker to scoop me up in her arms. And my father was
> my hero. He was strict but fair, a man's man in the best
> sense. I'll never forget when Daddy got me a wiener dog
> with a big bow tied to her collar for my seventh birthday. I
> called her Dionne after my favourite singer at the time, the
> immortal Dionne Warwick. Daddy loved Dionne Warwick

almost as much as I did. As he handed me my brand-new doggy, he said, very sombrely, "I have faith that you're ready for this responsibility, son."

I guess that's why I do so much charity work with children's agencies: I had the so-called "perfect childhood," and if I can spread just a smidge of that childhood happiness to children less fortunate than I was, I'm there in a heartbeat.

I don't want to sound like some messiah—heaven knows I'm not perfect—but sometimes these children, be they battered or starving or dying, reach out to me and touch my hand or even my shirt sleeve, and I try to bathe them psychically with healing light. Parents have written me to tell them that I cured their child's cancer. I don't necessarily believe that I was the direct cause of the recovery, but I'm pretty sure I didn't do any damage either!

We are all vessels of love, imbued with healing light. Maybe my healing light is—for whatever reason—more potent than other people's. I do know that I was sent to Earth to spread things. Good things, I mean—not herpes or anything like that! And if I can help even one person by speaking my truth, I feel so fulfilled. I love you! I thank you!

THE WHOLE BOOK is punctuated by these declarations of love and thanks, as if the reader is a live audience. I've read Birdy's memoir start-to-finish maybe three times. It's pure fiction—and shitty fiction at that. But I understand its purpose. If I'd seen what Birdy saw growing up, I'd want to concoct an alternate, comforting backstory too. Hell, I only heard his parents fight the once, and the memory still makes me gasp. Birdy's done what he's had to do, and I confess to feeling proud of his resourcefulness.

Birdy Is My Friend, My Only Friend

WE WERE SLOUCHED on my bed when Birdy played me the first song he'd written. He'd mastered the ukulele within a few weeks of receiving it three years ago. He'd since dashed off several wordless melodies, but this was the first time he'd married words to music. I could see his fingers tremble on the strings, so I sat up and leaned in avidly.

> Here is a lake, a lonely lake
> The lake misses swimmers, or even a nice clambake
> But the lake is empty, nobody's around
> There are no sunbathers, not even a sound
> I am the lonely lake, I am the lonely lake, ooh, I am the
> lonely lake
> Swim in me, I am not fake

It was a beautiful tune, but the lyrics were kind of stilted. I mean, we were only ten years old, and I didn't know the first thing about poetry, but even then I was confused by the gulf between the beautiful music and the weird words.

"That was so good, Birdy."

"Really? I know the words are dumb."

"I like the words. You should play it for Margaret when she gets home."

We went into the living room. Our new living room was spacious and airy, so unlike our old living room. Margaret and I lived in a pretty yellow house now, just down the street from our old apartment. My mother had been a pharmacist for two years and was already beloved at her pharmacy; her three assistants, all older women, approached her with total deference, wowed by her unwavering competence. Whenever I dropped by they'd all be doubled over with laughter over some small aside Margaret had offered up as she portioned pills. They all had sweet, benign crushes on her. This made me proud.

Birdy was at our house almost every day. These days his mother was weaker, bedbound more often than not. We'd spend all day together at school, then walk home, reflecting on the science teacher's new, stringy bangs, or what Birdy would wear on his first album cover, or who he thought was cute. Occasionally he'd ask me who I thought was cute. And I would throw up my hands, still terrified of the topic, wanting only to tell Birdy that he was my love object, my cute one, the person I most wanted to kiss gently on the lips.

My mother liked Birdy. She liked him with an enthusiasm she'd never displayed for me. I understood. Birdy was a cut above with his talent, vivacity, and perfect porcelain face, and I was happy that Margaret liked him and welcomed him into our home, but sometimes I felt a bit like an also-ran. This preference of hers was never blatant, so it would've been churlish to bring it up.

Case in point: that March afternoon in 1966 my mother returned from work looking tired, complaining of a would-be shoplifter she'd had to run around the counter and grab by the sleeve to intercept. Thieves were getting so brazen, she huffed. In her day, thieves at least had the decency to slip the item under their shirt.

"Birdy wrote a song with words," I said.

"It's dumb, but yeah," said Birdy.

"That's remarkable. I can't wait to hear it. Just let me change out of my work clothes. I feel so gamey."

Mom went off to change.

"I love your mother. She's so tough. My mother is scared of her. I mean, in a good way. Back in grade two, when your mom talked to my mom about my dad being mean, when my mom got off the phone, she said—I forget what she said—oh, wait, she said 'every home should have one,' like every home should have your mother in it."

"Your mom is nice too."

"That's what I said to her. I said, 'Mother, this home already has a nice mom.' But then she got all sad and said she wasn't a good mother, because she has her drinking problem and should've left my dad a long time ago."

"Why didn't she ever leave your dad?" Just thinking of Birdy's dad took me back to that horrible birthday party and made my heart pound.

Birdy shrugged. "At first it was because if she left him, she would've been the only divorcee she'd ever known, except for this one lady who had a tattoo and ended up falling off a cliff. And then it was because she didn't have any job skills, and then it was because she's always drunk."

I sighed. There was a lot that was bad about Birdy's life, but Birdy himself was, as far as I could tell, already fully formed, already tethered to the glittering life that awaited him. Whenever he spoke of the bad things at home it was like he was describing a stage play to a blind person. Meanwhile, I already knew that I was not destined for greatness, that I would be lucky if I ended up collecting errant shopping carts in a grocery store parking lot. Every now and then I would bristle a little at the thought of Birdy's awesome potential. This day was one of those times.

My mother returned in jeans and a pale-blue top, with no bra. "Okay!" she exclaimed, clapping her hands together. "Let's hear that new song! Finally, something pleasant after such a draining day. Whenever you're ready, Birdy."

She sat in our new leather loveseat and folded her legs under her in an expectant half lotus. She never sat like that when I had a book report or a poem I wanted her to hear.

Birdy picked up his ukulele. "Okay, so this is dumb, like I said. I'm not as good at words as I am with music."

"Nonsense. Whenever you're ready."

Birdy sang his song that was filled with clunky couplets. He held the last note a really long time, and my mother whooped. *Whooped*.

"That was exceptional, Birdy. Exceptional. I saw such vivid pictures in my head. The lonely lake—how many of us have felt exactly that but lacked the insight to describe it? Well done. Wasn't it well done, Roland?"

"He already played it for me."

"Aren't you the lucky one, then. Don't be territorial, Roland. We support each other's creative efforts in this household. Is there something creative that you'd like to share?"

I pretended to think about it. "No."

"Well, when you do, we are all ears. Aren't we, Birdy?"

"Yeah, oh yeah. I always tell him that he should learn an instrument. I've never heard him sing, but he probably has a nice voice too."

My mother nodded a desultory nod. I wanted to cry. I'd grown accustomed to her austerity, but now that she was so effusive about all things Birdy, I wanted her to at least tousle my hair or toss a casual arm across my shoulders.

The doorbell went, and I ran to answer. It was a slightly sooty man with wild hair. I didn't recognize him.

"Hello there, Roland. It's your old friend Dan. How are you?"

"Fine." I hadn't seen Dan since Margaret broke up with him the previous year. They'd fallen into a rut, my mother told me. She'd heard all his stories, and he no longer brought out the woman in her. I remember listening to him sob and watching as she gently but decisively led him toward the front door.

"*Mom!*" I waited for her to come to the door, not wanting to leave him alone in our nice new house.

She looked at him from several angles, as confused as I'd been.

"It's Dan," said Dan finally.

"Dan? Dan! Oh, Dan. What happened to you?"

"Maggie. Hello. I've been living rough the last little while. How are you?"

She pushed me behind her protectively. That felt nice. "How did you get our new address?"

"It's in the phone book."

"It is?" My mother had a nimble mind for all manner of minutiae but sometimes tripped up on the most obvious stuff. I chalk that up to her being thrust into adulthood too young, not having learned all there is for a growing girl to learn. "Well. Dan. I'm really sorry that you're in a bad way. Have you tried to access supportive services?"

"Do I look that far gone? I guess I do."

I saw her mouth open and close. She knew she was inept at this sort of situation, one that called for both empathy and remove.

"I'm so sorry you've been through so much hardship. But at the same time, we really did make a clean break. I was very clear. Very clear. It's not appropriate for you to just drop by unannounced, even with ... all you've been through." She plucked a short twig from his beard.

He pressed his forehead against the door jamb. The last time I saw him he was wearing red suspenders and a bow tie. He'd fallen so far. I didn't necessarily want him in our living room, but I was curious to hear what had turned him into a hobo.

"I'm sorry, Maggie."

"It's Margaret, Dan. Margaret. Margaret. Even when we were together I told you not to call me Maggie. Maggie is what someone would call their dachshund."

"Sorry. I'm sorry, Margaret. I'm not myself. I was in the hospital a few weeks ago. I've also been ... in prison."

"Prison! Oh, Dan. You're a pharmacist. What were you doing in prison?"

"I stole a ready-made sandwich from a deli. I know. I'm ashamed. But I was so hungry."

My mother's hand quivered on my arm. She sighed. "Do you— are you hungry right now? Do you want another sandwich?"

"I don't want a sandwich, Margaret. I miss you. You're all I think about. It's true. I know you think I'm just some—some push- over pantywaist, and maybe I was back when we were courting, but now ... I'm like an animal. I am. I sleep on the forest floor. Last week I ate a chipmunk for sustenance. A chipmunk. I'm an animal now, Margaret. My mind is gone and I'm—I'm all viscera now."

"Oh, Dan. I'm sorry. But if your mind were truly gone and you were truly only viscera now, you probably wouldn't have the capacity to announce it like you just did."

"That gives me hope, it does. Thank you. All I want to do is take you in my arms and—and, yes, I don't care—I want to be with you. I want my body to be—"

"Dan! My child is in the room." She said the right motherly thing, but I could tell that Dan's desperate soliloquy was bringing out the woman in her.

"Are you bothering her?" Birdy's fluty voice came from the hallway. I turned around: his face was all contorted.

"You're Roland's friend. Nice to see you again."

"Get lost!"

"Birdy! Go back in the living room. This doesn't concern you." Margaret had never admonished Birdy before. I'll admit to a burst of satisfaction just then.

"I know all about guys like you. You think you're so important, but you're not. So you can just go. We're having a nice time. These are my friends."

"Birdy, you're rude," I said. "Dan is a pharmacist. He looks crazy right now, but he's not."

"I'll only be a minute, Birdy," my mother said. "Go back in the living room."

Chastened by Margaret, Birdy folded in on himself and tiptoed out of sight.

Margaret folded her arms across her chest. "Dan, I know you think that's what you want, or possibly it's what you think I might want to hear, but neither is the case. We had our nice moment, and now it's over. You're looking for a wife, and I've no doubt you'll have lots to choose from. I mean, once you emerge from the forest. I am nobody's wife, which maybe makes me deficient somehow, but that's my concern. As for all this"—she gestured at his matted hair and torn shirt—"I don't necessarily buy it. For all I know you could've dressed up like this just to come over and shock me. And if you are sleeping on the forest floor, so did the Group of Seven. Maybe take up the paintbrush."

"Take up the paintbrush," he parroted, slumping halfway down the wall to our nice new yellow linoleum. "If you're being glib, I don't ... I don't know."

"Dan. You're not some lovelorn beatnik. And you have every advantage in the world. You're a young white man with rich parents. You have no excuse! Imagine if I'd fallen to pieces after the rape—Roland here would be in the foster care system. Or worse, he could be floating in formaldehyde in a jar on a shelf at the teaching hospital. So. And now you've made me angry." Indeed, my mother's cheeks were warming to a deep pink.

"You're so cold, Margaret. I knew you were cold but—not this cold."

"Then I've done you a solid, haven't I? You might've ended up shackled to a cold woman. Now, it's time for me to shut the door. Goodbye."

Dan swayed in place. My mother nudged him onto the porch and closed and locked the door.

"He looked bad, Mom."

"We all look bad sometimes. He just needs a bath. I know men, Roland. They'll stop at nothing. Avarice. It's all about avarice. Men are ... avaricious."

Birdy was standing in the living room, his face filmy with an anxious dew. "I'm so sorry, Margaret. I thought something bad was going to happen. Please don't be mad at me."

"Sit. Let's all sit."

We all sat.

"Birdy, you are a fine young person. You're smart and tough as nails. But you don't have to look out for me. In this house, the grown-up looks after the kids. And that will always be so. Roland knows this. Roland, has there ever been a time when you've felt unsafe with me?"

"No. Maybe sometimes in the car, because you like to go fast."

This annoyed her. "Am I not a skilful driver? Have we ever had an accident?"

"No. Well, we went over that pit that time, and it was scary."

"It's called a pothole. We hit a pothole. I'm not asking you to sift through every last occasion where you've felt jostled, Roland. I'm asking you, when we are at home together, do you feel like something horrible is going to happen?"

"Umm. No."

"Good. Thank you." She turned to Birdy. She briefly cupped his chin. "You poor soul. What you must've seen in your short life. And your mother ... I know she's her own worst enemy in many ways, but I can't help wanting to scoop her up too."

"We're all gonna die soon, I really think that," said Birdy. "Something bad is gonna happen. On *Dark Shadows* on TV this lady's house burned down, and her and her niece got burnt to death."

"You are not going to burn to death. You are not going to die, get that straight. I won't let that happen. And neither will Roland." She pulled me closer on the couch. "I know I'm not as demonstrative as other mothers, but I'm not—I have the full range of emotions. We have a nice familylike situation going here, don't you think, Roland?"

I am not a particularly selfless person. I was not a particularly selfless kid. I loved my mother with a doggedness that never wavered, and I loved Birdy with a proprietary viciousness that continually surprised me. So when my mother offered Birdy her protection and a tacit invitation into our family, I couldn't help but wish I'd kept my two loves separate somehow. At the time I smiled and leaned into the awkward group hug that Margaret and Birdy soaked up like it was salvation itself, but when Birdy went back to his possibly-burning house after a dinner of pork chops and scalloped potatoes, I was relieved.

"We're so fortunate," my mother said to me softly, as I brushed my teeth before bed. "Are we not a couple of fortunate souls?"

My mouth was full of minty foam, so I nodded in agreement. We were fortunate, the two of us. My mother was young and tireless. I was ruddy average in every way. But I had this nasty case of intuition, which has always been a source of pain. I could always sense when I was in the presence of someone formidable, and I could sense, more or less, all the ways in which the person was more formidable than I was and the middling outcome of any attempt I might make to mould myself in the shape of the formidable person. What saved me, then and now, is my bottomless capacity for hero worship. I'd watched my mother and Birdy in their protracted hug, and it bothered me, but I also wanted to take pictures of them as they were, and from various flattering angles.

I WAS NOMINALLY better in science than Birdy—his eyes would glaze over at the mere mention of photosynthesis—so when science fair came along, he made a beeline for me. Normally our partnership would be a no-brainer, but I was hesitant about science fair; I couldn't see how Birdy might contribute and worried that I'd end up doing all the work, and then, at the fair, he'd turn on the charm for the judges and intentionally or not take all the credit. But Birdy solved this dilemma right off the bat: our science project, he proposed, would be all about women's hairdos.

"But that's not science," I said.

"It's very science! It's all about angles of people's faces and—when my mother mixes up her hair dye, that's chemical—chemistry. And the hair—like, the hair itself—you could put a ponytail or something under a microscope and look at it. And we could call it 'All About Hair.'"

"Maybe. But what if Mr. Binns doesn't approve it as a subject?"

"Mr. Binns loves me. He gives me dirty looks in class, but other times I catch him looking at me like I'm a dream come true."

I was dubious. Mr. Binns was at least sixty and not at all lecherous. It was hard for me to believe that he would cast a longing glance at Birdy Perner, his ten-year-old student. But there was Birdy, beaming with his impenetrable certainty. So I gave in. He went up to Mr. Binns and told him that our project was all about the science of human hair. He didn't mention hairdos, or how bangs might make someone pretty look ugly, or someone ugly look pretty. And Mr. Binns nodded avidly and appeared to speak at length on our chosen topic, while Birdy's expression went from spunky salesgirl to bored salesgirl.

My mother got us some red bristol board for our display.

"I'm sorry," she said, as we worked at the kitchen table, "but I have a hard time believing that you two are really going to write about the structure of human hair. I do have a microscope from school somewhere in the basement, if that's really the direction you want to go, but I know you two. You really want to write about women's hairstyles, like that redhead's from *Gilligan's Island*. Am I wrong? Roland?"

"I think we can put scientific things in and also have hairdo things."

"It's going to look so good when we're done," said Birdy. "That's what's important. When the judges look at it, they won't notice the science part, because it'll all look really great."

I had a sinking feeling. Birdy was going to cut out pictures of Elizabeth Taylor from movie magazines and plaster them all over the bristol board, and I'd be left with one skinny column for my scientific essay.

> *Me:* Human hair is made from keratin, which is a protein. Protein is made up of amino acids. Amino acids are made up of many elements, such as carbon, oxygen, hydrogen, nitrogen, and sulphur. Hairs are attached to the skin by follicles. The base of the hair follicle is called the bulb.
>
> *Birdy:* Look at how pretty Shirley Bassey is with her big permed hair! It goes around her face so nicely. It might be a wig, but even so. And here is Julie Andrews with super nice bangs. Everyone says she's stuck-up and a goody-goody, but even so. Some people look fat or simple minded with bangs, but not Julie!

OUR SCIENCE PROJECT turned out exactly as I'd feared: My write-up about the structure and composition of human hair was shoved over to one side, and the rest of it was pictures of female movie stars with short adoring captions by Birdy, and across the top of the board, in glittery marshmallow letters: "ALL ABOUT HAIR!!!!!!" Six exclamation points.

"It's very vivid," my mother said warily, as we stood back from the finished project. We exchanged a glance. As much as Margaret adored Birdy, she didn't want him to sabotage my grades, which were erratic to begin with.

Grades five and six were lumped together for the science fair, and we all set up our projects on long, wobbly tables around the perimeter of the gymnasium. Birdy bolted over to the table closest to the entrance. "It's the best spot, it's the most noticeable," he said, as though we were fruit vendors vying for space in a street market.

The judges were vice-principal Abbott and another woman, I can't recall her name, from Esther Scanlon Elementary (I guess they imported an outside teacher for impartiality's sake). They did a preliminary walk-through together, two blocklike women in belted dresses, lumpy nylons, and black Mary Janes, nodding at students and occasionally whispering things to each other. When they came to us Birdy broke out into a gigantic paparazzi smile and waved at them. Mrs. Abbott nodded. The other woman did not.

"That lady didn't look like she liked our thing," I said, pulling at Birdy's shirt sleeve.

"She's just keeping a lid on how much she's into it. They have to pretend they have no favourites. Look at Carol and Martha's project. It's so sad. Looks like their bristol board is drooping too. 'Why Dogs Don't Live as Long as People.' Who cares? I like Carol, and Martha sort of, but look at their awful drawing of a beagle. It looks like a pizza folded in half."

I was distracted; I really was curious to know why pets die so much quicker than humans.

There was some sort of delay, and Mrs. Abbott and the other woman slipped away somewhere. Most of the kids got restless, hopping in place and whipping wadded-up paper at each other. Birdy fell to singing the chorus of "Stop! In the Name of Love" over and over. The room was about to tip into bedlam, when Mrs. Abbott and the other woman returned from wherever they'd been. They smelled of fresh cigarette smoke.

We were closest to the door, and they started with us.

"Roland, Gerald," said Mrs. Abbott.

"Hi! I'm so excited about this! I can't believe it!"

"Good to hear, Gerald. This is Mrs. Hays (yes, that was her name—Hays!), and she's going to be evaluating your work with me. So. 'All About Hair.' What led you to choose this topic?"

I tried to speak, but Birdy beat me to it. "Well, you know, we were thinking and thinking about everything in science, cuz there's just so many interesting things you could choose, and then I just suddenly thought, *hair*. What's going on with it? You know? And Roland thought that was really interesting."

"Is that true, Roland?" Mrs. Abbott sounded suspicious. Birdy glared at me.

"Once I started looking into it, there was a lot of interesting information. And Birdy—Gerald was really excited about it, so he got me excited about it."

Mrs. Hays snorted. "You sound like an old married couple!"

Mrs. Abbott said "Oh!" and threw up her hands, trying for levity. Birdy did his celebrity smile. I coughed and looked at the ceiling. My heart began to hammer.

"So yeah, I wrote—we wrote—about human hair and its—like, what makes up a human hair. And that's all in this column over here on the left."

Mrs. Abbott read my write-up, nodding with tepid approval. Mrs. Hays gave dirty looks to Shirley and Julie and Barbra and Tina Louise.

"I don't understand what these women have to do with the structure of the human hair," Mrs. Abbott said.

"Well, it's not just about the structure of the human hair," said Birdy, who was now leaning against the wall. "We also wanted to take a look at how hair can make someone look pretty and also how it can make someone look ugly—or less pretty, I should say."

Mrs. Abbott continued to look at my write-up even though she'd clearly finished reading it.

"Pictures of movie actresses are not part of a serious science project," said Mrs. Hays. Her face was closed and hard. I swallowed a bit of nervous barf.

"I think it really adds to it," I said weakly.

"It really doesn't, young man. It cheapens the whole enterprise. I'm not sure what you might think you're getting away with, but this sort of thing is a real slap in the face to other students, who have made an effort at serious study."

"Bernice," Mrs. Abbott said softly, "I know this isn't a typical science project, but it is a valiant attempt. It also reflects the particular academic talents of both Roland and Gerald. And if you read the text over on the left, it's quite thoughtful."

"I'd like to read it, but I'm so distracted by the rest of it."

"So don't read it." Birdy's face had gone dark, and he was baring his incisors, like a cat mid-hiss.

"It's my duty to read it. And please don't roll your eyes at me. You're not a sixteen-year-old high school girl."

"It's okay, it's okay," I whispered to Birdy, because he was ready to blow, and when Birdy blew, there was nothing to be done.

"I can tell you hate it," he said. "So go and look at somebody else's project. Go and look at the dead dog thing."

"Gerald, please," said Mrs. Abbott. "Let's move on, Bernice. I've read the write-up, and I'll give you an oral précis."

Bernice shrugged and began to walk away, then returned to us.

"It's probably not my place, but you two are clearly operating in a state of conspiracy, and it's wrong and … not right. The two of you should really be separated. That is just my opinion."

Mrs. Abbott grabbed Mrs. Hays's arm fairly roughly. I wanted to cry, and I could tell that Birdy also wanted to cry, but he'd clamped his jaw hard and stuck his head in the air, so I began to cry for the both of us.

"She's not our teacher," I said through my snot. "She can't say mean things like that."

Birdy touched his short blond hair and pulled at the long phantom locks he'd have for real in a few years.

"I've had way worse. You'd better start getting used to it."

There are scenes emblazoned in every baby gay's memory that confirmed for us our social strangeness, or that marked the moment when we were recognized by gruff grown-ups unmistakably as a problem. At least that's how it was for my generation; kids now probably have more respite from that bald-faced cruelty. I hope.

Birdy had faced this form of abuse pretty much from infancy. I'd gone unnoticed because of my silence and willingness to bundle myself into the smallest, most toothless version of myself always, even at home with my mother, who surely would've accepted me if I'd been at all demonstrative. So this science fair, when I was newly eleven years old, was the first time I was clocked as a burgeoning queer, or at the very least, as a worrisome accomplice. I wanted to call my mom and watch as she stormed into the school and informed Mrs. Hays of the ways in which she'd failed as a judge, educator, and human being.

WE PLACED SECOND TO LAST, ahead of the Allen twins, whose project was a set of those novelty wind-up chattering teeth, which they kept winding up to chatter. I don't know how they got past the classroom pre-screen. The one Allen twin, so the rumour goes, dropped out of grade eight and promptly impregnated his mother, then later died from a heart attack at twenty-six. The other Allen twin is a collection agent.

Birdy tore up our bristol board and tossed it in the parking lot. We walked home slowly, dragging our feet through the pearly gravel on the road's shoulder.

"I hate Winnipeg," he said. "When I'm famous I'm going to say mean things on TV about everybody here. Except for you and your mother and my mother. I'm never coming back here. I don't care if they want to name a park after me or whatever they do for famous people who come from here."

"Yeah." I wanted to say that I too would leave Winnipeg and never look back. But where would I go? I didn't possess the restless engine that propelled my best friend. I knew I'd stay here for the rest of my life. Unless Birdy took me with him. But he'd have no use for me as he scrambled toward celebrity.

I couldn't wait to tell my mother about our dismal day, but when we got home she was furiously pacing the house, absently patting her chest with both hands, murmuring broken sentences. "I really didn't know ... This can't be happening ... I did due diligence ... but I didn't ... it's not like I'm ... am I a murderer?"

"What's wrong, Mom?"

"Is she having a stroke? Are you having a stroke, Margaret?"

She put her hand up as if to buy time while chewing a mouthful of food. "There's been—something has happened—there's been something—"

Birdy, clearly versed in calming a person in distress, approached her softly, took her hand, and told her to sit and take a deep breath.

"Dan—you're children and I shouldn't be telling you this, but you've caught me in a moment—Dan has been found in the Red River. Dead. He took his own life. He killed himself."

I thought of Dan as I'd first known him—smelling of shaving cream, decked out in his suspenders and bow tie—jumping off the

Disraeli Bridge into the squalid waters of the Red River. It was hard to believe.

"How do you know that? Are you sure he killed himself? Maybe he fell. Or maybe he was pushed."

"Roland, you know I don't announce such things willy-nilly. It was in the newspaper. And I got this today." She took a piece of paper from the end table. "He wrote me a note."

"Read it," Birdy said.

"I'm not going to read it to you. But he made it clear that he was going to take his own life. And that he blamed me. So now. Maybe I did cause him to commit suicide."

"No way," said Birdy. "That's so dumb that he did that. You're so nice. And pretty."

"Thank you, Birdy, but you don't need to be sycophantic. I'm very upset, but this is something I'll have to navigate on my own. I'll be fine. So, distract me. How did the science fair go?"

"Good," I said.

"Yeah," Birdy said. "We came really close."

As much as we wanted to vent, we couldn't add more despair to my mother's horrible day. This was probably the first time that Birdy and I used discretion in unison. I basked in the feeling this produced, that Birdy and I were, as Mrs. Hays had feared, very much like an old married couple.

Birdy called home to see if he could sleep over. When he got off the phone, he said his mother sounded funny, and not in the usual way. Birdy had asked his mother if he could sleep over, and it had taken at least a minute for Judy to respond, after making a long groaning sound. Birdy felt bad that he wasn't at home for his mother, but he couldn't face it, not after our dismal day.

Margaret warmed up a shepherd's pie from the freezer. We talked about death: the various ways a person could die, what it might feel like, what might happen after we die. We all spoke in small, thoughtful voices. It seemed as though the meal and our gentle exchange were helping to soothe my mother. But then, as we spooned our way through bowls of peppermint ice cream, she started to go off again.

"I can't think of a time in all my life when I've ever consciously done the wrong thing," she said, addressing, for no reason, the fridge. "I've taken great care. At every turn. Haven't I?"

"You're the most—I don't know the word—"

"Decent?" she offered. "Moral? Good?"

"Good, yeah," I said, although *good* still didn't quite fit.

"But what if that still isn't enough? It's so callow of me to ever have thought that there was such a thing as absolute right and wrong. Why did I ever think that? Doing the right thing—you're still making a judgment call, which could be wildly off the mark. It could've been the rape that made me so arrogant in my morality. But no. I was like that as a little girl. I remember once, when I was in the grocery store with my mother, she kept ripping open bags of apples and picking through the bruised ones so she could make one bag of perfect apples, and I went and told the cashier. I was such a brat. I don't know. What do I know? I don't know."

We were barely following what she was saying. We were both wincing from the effort.

"Sometimes I don't know what the right thing to do is," said Birdy haltingly, unaccustomed to scrutinizing his own behaviour. "So I just do *something*, just so I can say that I've done something. Like I found a dirty magazine under my brother's mattress, so I ripped out all the pages and flushed them down the toilet. That was maybe wrong, but I hate my brother. I sound dumb."

"Not at all," said Margaret, still looking at the fridge. "Not at all." Then she took her ice cream spoon and started tapping it against the table, two taps to the right of the bowl, two taps to the left. She repeated this sequence three times. I started to think of what I might do if my mother went crazy.

"**DO YOU THINK** Margaret is turning into a wacko?" I asked this into Birdy's neck as we spooned in my narrow bed. This was something that we'd fallen into after countless nights of awkward, uncomfortable half sleep on the edges of the mattress. He was wearing a pair of my pyjamas. At such times we were guileless, indivisible as conjoined twins, slack with ease at last after long school days of strenuous self-defence.

"Your mom could never turn into a wacko. She's too—my mother told me that your mother is the kind of person she would've liked to be if she hadn't met my dad."

"She said that? That's so nice. Your mom is really nice."

"Sort of, yeah. She stays in bed a lot now. When I think about her I feel like I'm going to throw up, I get so upset. When we were talking about dying and being dead with your mom, and you said you thought dying would feel like walking into nice, warm, dark water—that's what I think too. I feel like that's what's happening to my mom. It's like she's walking into dark water, like you said. It's like she's shutting down."

Birdy started crying silently. I could only tell by the shudders of his chest under my arm. I kissed him on the back of his neck, at the top of his spine that was as delicate and explicit as a seahorse's.

"What?" he asked, like I'd said something too softly. "We shouldn't kiss each other."

"Why? We love each other. It's nice. I didn't mean it in a perverted way."

He was quiet, and then: "I guess it's nice. But you're not going to be my husband, okay? My husband is going to have a moustache. He's going to have really big hands. Okay?"

"Okay." There was mild disappointment in this partial rebuff, but I also knew that Birdy's dream date was years away, that he could be my special one in some gauzy, undefined way until at least high school.

I slept a bit, until Birdy shook me awake.

"Let's go read Dan's letter," he said.

"But my mom would be really mad."

"It's okay to be curious about stuff like that. If you don't take a look at bad stuff, you'll never—you have to take a hard look at things. Otherwise, you know—why are we here, on Earth? We have to take a hard look at things."

WE WENT DOWNSTAIRS to where my mother kept items she wanted hidden but not discarded: the bottom drawer of her rolltop desk in the living room. That's where she kept police reports from the rape, and the letter from my kindergarten teacher, who'd worried that I slept too quickly at nap time and was too difficult to rouse at nap time's end. And there were love letters from an assortment of men, all of them stupid with ardour. Dan's letter was on top, neatly tucked back into its envelope. I picked it up and carefully tugged the letter out. I looked at the calamitous handwriting, only just legible as language. Birdy and I knelt, and he read it in a whisper while I followed along.

> Margaret,
>
> I want to apologize for coming to your house unan-nounced. It was thoughtless of me—but do let me say how picturesque your new home is. It's such a nice colour. I'm happy for you.
>
> But I also curse the day I met you. You were so plain-spoken at the start, I was disarmed straight away. I fell in love in the span of an afternoon. You were very clear in stating that I shouldn't expect much. I adjusted my expectations accordingly. We had fun. Then you showed yourself as the chimera that you truly are.
>
> It was YOU who started in with the romantic banter. You can't deny that. I brought out the woman in you, you

said. You said if you weren't careful, you'd fall in love with me. Lying in my arms you said your defences were giving way and you felt, for the first time, that you could pair-bond with someone. I was so afraid of spooking you I couldn't respond, I could only hold you closer. You said you'd been daydreaming about having my child.

"Wow," I whispered. "That doesn't sound like her. Mom's always said that she doesn't want another child. She said if she ever got pregnant again she'd run screaming to the abortionist."

"People can be super two-faced," Birdy whispered back. "Even friends and family."

If I act like an animal now, dear Margaret, it's because you've turned me into an animal. Your seduction was, in retrospect, pathological; it was as though you thought you could say all those sweet, promissory things in the afterglow of our lovemaking and I'd somehow forget it all come morning, as you pulled your hair into a bun and resumed your stony persona, demanding I dress and leave as quickly as possible so you could prepare for a frantic day of work, and study, and the flattened, non-stop instruction you call mothering. I forgot nothing.

I don't care if I'm craven when I say that you drove me to these next steps. Perhaps it's that you didn't evaluate me correctly before we began. You thought you'd procured a placid man, low in testosterone and adept at the domestic arts. You were wrong. I'm a man crazed with love, probably always destined to fall, alone and howling, to an early, ugly death.

Yours always,

Dan

Birdy and I looked at each other, both of us woozy from this onslaught of masculine despair. I felt like my innards had been carved out and replaced with nothing but air.

IN THE MORNING the three of us ate sugared bowls of Cheerios; my mother alternated with big gulps of coffee.

"What's on the itinerary for you two today?" she asked cheerfully.

"Oh, the usual," said Birdy. I couldn't respond. I couldn't look at my mother, who was probably a treacherous romantic bandit who drove men to their death.

"Roland? What about you?" I lifted my eyes to hers. "What?" Her tone was brittle.

"What? I'm—the usual."

"I see. Well. As you were."

WE WENT TO SCHOOL. We sat through the school day. We parted at the parking lot and went to our respective unhappy homes. I barely spoke to my mother. This went on for several days.

Finally, over seven-layer dinner, my mother cut the tension.

"I may be losing my mind, but why are you not speaking to me?"

"No reason."

Her eyes bored into me.

"I read Dan's suicide note. I mean, the one he sent you." I braced for backlash. But there was none.

"Ah. Okay. I suppose I should be angry, but I probably deserve to be ... exposed."

"Did you really say all those things to Dan? That you loved him and wanted to have his baby?"

"I did. Oh. You're a child, but at this moment, I feel like you hold the moral high ground. Yes, my pillow talk could sometimes be capricious. I did get carried away, here and there. Go ahead, ask your questions. Nothing you can say will make my self-loathing any worse."

I shrugged and puffed out my cheeks, rattled. I didn't like holding the moral high ground over my mother. "I guess ... did you really want to have a baby with him?"

"No! Well, maybe in the moment I did, but the impulse passed quickly. Sometimes, during sexual intimacy, a person can get carried away. Your brain clouds over from the hormones. And I failed to clarify my true, considered feelings with him afterward. So, I guess you could say that, yes, I was a factor in his death." Her eyes went up into her head, and she started in with her spoon tapping. "I guess you could say that I killed him. You could say that, and you wouldn't be wrong."

I went around the table and touched her arm. "You didn't kill him. You didn't. It's not like you pushed him off that bridge or anything."

"I've taken a turn, Roland. I've taken a turn, and I don't know what to do."

My wariness went away, and I cleared and washed the dishes, enumerating my mother's many virtues until she told me to dial it down. I ran upstairs and grabbed pillows and blankets, and we settled onto the couch, swaddled and facing each other. We watched the local news on the television I'd finally pestered Margaret into buying. The news that night was filled with shootings and Third World plagues, but I pretended it was all just pleasant noise, anything to keep Margaret from her dark train of thought. Then there was a rerun of *I Love Lucy*, and its black-and-white hilarity had a sedating effect on us both. We went to bed.

It was midnight when the phone rang. My mother yelled, "I've got it! I've got it!" so urgently it was like she had polio and was warding off visitors. I ran downstairs to listen on the extension, as I liked to do.

It was Birdy. "My mom passed out and now she's in the hospital."

"Are you at the hospital right now, Birdy?"

"No, the ambulance came and took her there."

"Is your dad there?"

"No. We don't know where he is. It's just me and Terry."

"All right. Sit tight. I'll be right over."

"Really? Thanks. Can Roland come?"

I heard my mother draw breath. "Yes!" I chimed in. "I'll be there too!"

"I'VE BEEN DREADING this day," Margaret said as we sped over. "She's probably in liver failure."

"Can she die from that?"

"Yes. Mrs. Perner is a lovely person, but she's been drinking herself to death for some time."

"Really? On purpose?"

"No! And I could be wrong. It could be a drop in blood sugar, or even anxiety. I could be wrong, Roland."

THEY WERE WAITING on the stoop. Despite the emergency I couldn't help but notice Birdy's adult brother's denim cut-offs, his hairy, meaty thighs spread open.

"I wasn't sure what to do," Terry said, sounding more like a child than his younger brother.

"That's all right. You must be so upset. We'll all go in my car."

AT THE HOSPITAL we made our way past various tableaux of illness and injury and the sounds and smells they issued until we came to Judy, tiny but bloated under a paper-thin blanket.

Judy saw us and said "Hi!" all lit up like we weren't in the hospital but at some bustling house party.

"Judy, I hope it's okay that we're here," my mother said. "Birdy called us."

Birdy ran to his mother's side and folded himself in beside her. He was weeping soundlessly.

"I'm so glad you're here," Judy said. "I'm sorry for all this. I think I'm fine. I just—well, you know. When the pigeons come to roost, what can you do? It's my own fault. I'm a bad example. I'm sorry."

My mother told Judy to stop apologizing. The air was heavy, as though it had just rained in the room. I didn't know where to look.

"What has the doctor said?" my mother asked.

"He said I'm for sure jaundiced, and I have upper—upper—"

"Upper quadrant?"

"Yes! Upper quadrant tenderness. They're gonna put me through some machines, but dollars to doughnuts, it's the liver failure. And not just from the booze. Both my parents died from it."

"No!" Birdy looked petrified.

"We don't know that for sure, sweetheart, but we should prepare for the possibility."

"Are you going to die at any moment?"

"Oh no. I don't think so."

We listened to Birdy crying into his mother's pillow.

"Has your husband been notified?" my mother asked.

"Not that I know of. I was woozy there for a bit. He may have swung by."

"I can't get a hold of him," Terry said. "I even tried him at that woman's house, but there was no answer."

"That bitch. They probably have the phone off the hook. Christ, I hate that man. I'm sorry, kids. Normally I can keep a lid on it, but I'm on my last goddamn legs here and he's stuck in the muff of his sidepiece. You couldn't write a sadder story."

We all went quiet. I watched my mother realize that she really had no relationship with Judy Perner, that they'd met maybe three times. Birdy murmured affectionate, worried things in his mother's ear, which was still pinched by a blue-plastic clip-on. I could see that Terry, hirsute and blockish in the chair in the corner, wanted only to slip to his mother's other side and rest his big hand on her head.

"Can I sleep over at Roland's?" Birdy asked his mother.

"If that's okay with Miss Keener."

"Of course. Of *course*. And Terry, if you'd like to stay over too, you're more than welcome."

I could tell Terry wanted to stay with us, but he said he'd be okay on his own.

We sat there a long time. I fought to keep from dozing.

"We should probably slip away," my mother said at two a.m. "We'll all be back tomorrow, as soon as I can get away."

"I want to stay with my mum," Birdy said.

"Oh no, Gerry, sweetie. This bed is much too hard. You won't sleep a wink. You go on now with Miss Keener and Roland and your brother. We'll see you tomorrow."

BIRDY DIDN'T WANT to talk when we were finally in bed. When we woke up it was afternoon. My mother had let us sleep in.

When she got home from work she fed us TV dinners and then we went to the hospital.

"It's very possible that she's bounced back a little today," my mother said in the car.

"No, it's not," Birdy said. "It's bad. Thank you for saying that, though."

JUDY LOOKED HORRIBLE; one side of her face was droopy, and she only just recognized her son.

"Well, hey there!" she said, ever the hostess, despite a thick tongue and crooked mouth. "I had a little bit of a stroke. Not a big one, a little one."

Birdy started in with fresh tears. "A stroke is really bad. I don't know what's going on. Where's Dad?"

"He was here for a few minutes. Just before I had the little stroke. He said he was sorry I wasn't feeling good but that I had only myself to blame and that he was nobody's nursemaid. I told him I had a dream where somebody cut his balls off. And then he said some other things I can't remember and then the nurse came in and he stared at her tits. I'm not even fifty years old and I feel like I've lived through every chapter of the Bible. Know what I'm saying, Miss Keener?"

"Maybe you kids should go to the pop machine and get yourselves some Pepsis," my mother said, rifling through her change purse. Birdy was hesitant, but I pulled him away. I was thirsty.

I got an Orange Crush and he got a Pepsi. We sat on plastic chairs across from the pop machine.

"Everything is going to be fine," I said.

"Her face is all lopsided," he said. "Why is this happening?"

We went back to Judy's room. My mother had pulled her chair close to Judy's bed, and they were talking with antsy conspiracy.

Birdy returned to his spot next to his mother. He held the can of Pepsi between them like a keepsake they both treasured.

"If you die," he said, just loud enough for us to hear, "if you die, I won't have anyone who loves me."

"Oh, my girl," Judy said to her son, probably confused but also spot-on. Birdy's gorgeous inner girl was clear to us all, and we leaned toward her, wanting to hold her, brush her hair gently. "If there's any way I can, I'll come to you in your dreams, and we can chat."

My mother snapped her fingers three times, suddenly angry seeming. "You stop that right now, both of you. You have me, Birdy, and you have Roland. There's no need for you to return to Earth, Judy. As long as we're around, Birdy will have people. Who ... love you. Isn't that right, Roland?"

"Yes. I love you, Birdy."

Birdy put his hand over his face. "But my dad. He won't read Nancy Drew with me. He only knows how to make hot dogs. If I do something wrong, he'll hit me with the phone book."

My mother drew back slightly, tapping her chin with a forefinger in the same focused way she'd recently been opening and closing cupboards, locking and unlocking the front door.

"Your mother and I have been talking about that very thing. With her encouragement, I am proposing that you come and live with Roland and me, if that's something that appeals."

My Birdy blinked and scanned the room, like someone on a TV show who has been surprised with a clump of long-lost relatives.

"Is that—really?" His voice was a sigh. I wanted to smother his face in countless quick kisses.

"Would that be all right with you, Gerry? I haven't known Miss Keener very long, but I know in my bones that she's a real solid person who really cares, like. The last thing in the world I'd want is for you to be stuck with that—with your father, who I'm royally sorry to say really is your father. Never marry a person just because they have nice hair and a sports car. I've been a dim bulb most of the time."

I was overcome by the candour. "Let's all hug each other!"

"That would probably be physically painful for Mrs. Perner, Roland. The three of us will have a little hug in the parking lot."

"I can't believe I get to live with you guys," Birdy said, not distraught for the first time in recent memory. "My best friend and my second favourite lady in the world. I'm so lucky. You're so lucky, Roland."

I didn't know what to say. My mother was my number one favourite lady, and occasionally I'd catch her in some bit of domestic business—signing a cheque with a flourish, dismissing a door-to-door salesman with unassailable finality—that made me sigh with pride, but I'd never considered myself lucky. It often seemed that we were inches away from vagrancy or home invasion. But Margaret didn't hit me or berate me for being myself. Before Birdy, we'd mostly sat in silence, reading. There were times when that silence had made me panic; surely so much quiet could drive someone crazy, or could become a solid mass that would crush and kill you. But mostly, it was peaceful.

We gradually fell to talk of current events and the quality of care at St. Boniface, palate-cleansing niceties after so much intensity. When it was time for us to leave, we lined up to kiss Judy Perner on the forehead, like she was a sacred chalice.

Birdy had to poo before we left the hospital. Margaret and I slumped against the nurse's desk, waiting for him.

"I really regret not asking you first," my mother said.

"About what? Birdy? I can't wait for him to move in."

My mother nudged me hard, like we were drunkards at a bar. "Birdy is going to live with us. Permanently. I'm going to get him his own little bed. That sort of thing. This will be a big adjustment. It's not like he's sleeping over and going home again."

"I know. It's like a dream come true. He'll be my friend and almost like my brother."

"All right. Good to know." She jangled her car keys like it was the percussion in a bumpy Christmas song. This was annoying, and I wanted to slap the keys out of her hand. "This is a lot. This is really a lot. I can do this. I am not insane, and I can for sure tend to two boys. Yes."

"I love Birdy. I want to marry him when I grow up."

"Oh god, don't say that. Please don't say that. Am I knitting you two together in quasi-incest? Oh no. Stop it, Margaret. Okay. Okay."

"Does Birdy's dad know about this?"

"Yes. I didn't want to say anything. When Judy told him our plan he said—oh god, it's atrocious—he said 'good riddance.' Good riddance! Giving away your child like he's an old rug. It's like some old movie with Joanne Crawford."

"Joan," I corrected, never having seen one of her movies, startled by this almost mystic knowledge, preordained and passed down, like an old, private prayer, from gay to gay to gay.

"Maybe it's my new nervous condition, Roland, but I can't help but feel we're being overcome by dark forces."

I had no response.

JUDY DIED AT the end of May—either the 26th or the 27th, I can't recall off hand, but I have it written down somewhere—and Birdy did come to live with us in what was pretty much a seamless transfer. But my mother was right: we were being swarmed by dark forces, and when I look back on that time, I see screaming crimson birds swooping in on black-crayon vapour trails and ruining our sleep, and our meals, and every bit of optimism we may have been keeping for sustenance. It wouldn't always be this way, of course. We righted ourselves—Mom and Birdy for sure, and me for the most part.

Ken Perner drove up to the house one afternoon and pounded on the door. Margaret screamed at the sudden sound; she'd only gotten more anxious and strange that spring, and by mid-June she'd stopped sleeping, plagued constantly by her repetitive tics, which we now know were obsessive-compulsive disorder but at the time just made her look like a possessed Tinkertoy. Her work at the pharmacy had grown sloppy, and she once caught herself about to give a dying man's morphine to a six-year-old with a rash.

"What should I do?" she asked us, amid the banging.

"Don't let him in!" I said. Birdy went running to the basement. "He probably has his gun."

"Oh my god. Okay. This is something I can absolutely handle." She stood up from where she was crouched. "He is not going to kill us. He is *not*." She went to the door. She stepped out of her slippers and into the plastic clogs she wore for work. She practised her greeting. "Hello, Ken. Ken, hello. How can I help you? Can I help you? What brings you here? Hello, Ken."

She opened the door but kept the screen door locked. Ken walked gingerly up the steps. He had a box under his arm.

"Ken. How can I help you?"

He stopped in the middle of the porch. He didn't look at my mother.

"I don't want no trouble. I just come with Gerry's books. I've got the Nancy Drews and some other ones. I know he likes his books, 'specially the Nancy Drews."

"Thank you. That's very thoughtful. You can just leave them on the porch there. Thank you."

He put the box on one of the lawn chairs.

"I know you think I'm a right arsehole, to give him away like that. All's I can say is that he'll be better off. We just never got along, him and me. Even when he was a baby. It's not just because I know he's probably a pansy. Although that's sure not ideal either."

"I happen to like your son very much. He's vibrant, and he's strong."

"I guess so. I don't even know what to call it, when a dad and his boy never hit it off."

"There are words I can think of."

"Yeah. Yup."

Birdy's dad turned around and got back in his truck. He died three years later in his sleep, seventy-four years old. Birdy didn't go to the funeral and thereafter mentioned his father only a handful of times, and then only when pressed.

Birdy and Me and the Handsome Man

ON THE LAST DAY of grade five we ate gigantic, slightly stale cookies from the Vietnamese bakery (it only just closed in 2015). We found the gigantic cookies shocking and delicious, as we chewed in unison. Then Mrs. Mitchell gave out a whole bunch of merit awards. Best math student, best English student, best athlete, most courteous, most tidy. Birdy and I were passed over again and again. Our heads began to roll laconically. Birdy's sighs from the back row grew increasingly shrill.

"And now, our final award," Mrs. Mitchell announced, but was suddenly interrupted by Jeannie Cotton and Elaine Luby calling each other prostitutes.

"Hey!" our teacher snapped. "Stop that! Do you two even know the meaning of the word *prostitute*?"

The girls were quiet and then Elaine Luby spoke. "A prostitute is a lady who calls your house and asks for your dad and then your dad pretends he didn't know who it was that called."

Mrs. Mitchell was about to correct her, then gave up. "Moving on. Our final award is the Courage Award. We give the courage award to a student who has shown great bravery despite difficult circumstances."

"There was no courage award last year," said Elaine, on her third go at grade five.

"I know there wasn't, Elaine, but there is this year. Is that okay with you?"

"What?"

"As I was about to say, this year's courage award is presented to Gerald Perner."

I smiled and turned to look at Birdy. I applauded. I was the only one to applaud, until Mrs. Mitchell also began to applaud. Birdy put his hand to his mouth and looked around in hammy disbelief. He stood and walked up the aisle, past hissing and snickering. He took the certificate that Mrs. Mitchell handed him and then pulled Mrs. Mitchell into a hug that was reciprocated with a pat on the back.

Instead of going back to his desk like the other winners, Birdy stood facing us, fanning his face as if staving off tears. He was going to give an acceptance speech. I winced. I supported him in all his endeavours, but sometimes he could lose himself so utterly in fantasy that he'd forget where he was.

"Thank you so much. I promised myself I wasn't going to cry, and I'm not going to. There are so many people I need to thank, I'm sure I'm going to miss a few. I'd like to thank Mrs. Mitchell for this award—I can't tell you how much it means to me. I don't think of myself as a courageous person, but if you think I am, well, who am I to argue. Thanks so much to all my friends and—"

"Faggot!"

"Duncan Zurkan, I will not tolerate that kind of language. Thank you, Gerald. You can go back to your seat now."

"But I haven't finished my acceptance speech."

"You don't need to give an acceptance speech."

"But I want to. I'll be really quick."

Mrs. Mitchell tilted her head in a weird way, like her head was being yanked by a big unseen fish hook.

"Quickly, then."

"I just wanted to thank all my friends, especially my special friend Roland."

I clamped my eyes closed. I hated being singled out, even when Birdy did it.

"Ooh, special friend," hissed Carl Nyberg from his desk behind mine. "Ya faggots."

"And I just want to say that I'm going to be famous, and you're all losers. Everyone knows Elaine sucks cocks for half a sandwich. And everyone knows that Duncan's mom gave birth to him out of her mouth. And—"

"Be seated, Gerald. I am deeply, deeply disappointed in all of you! This is not a barnyard! You are representatives of this school, remember that. I feel like revoking all of the awards now. There are games and races planned for the rest of the afternoon, but none of you deserve to participate."

Everyone was silent. We didn't know what was going to happen next. What if she kept us after school, all afternoon, and all evening, possibly all night even? Several moments passed. I stole a glance at Elaine—her head was bowed, and her bottom lip trembled.

"All right, out! Out with all of you. What an ugly end to the school year. I've been teaching for sixteen years, and I've never been so ashamed of a group of students. Go! Go!"

We all filed out noiselessly, like we were barefoot and bubble wrapped. The other kids tore off for the playground. Birdy and I walked slowly to our spot at the far end of the parking lot, behind the big garbage bin.

We sat on the boulder we always sat on.

"Why did you have to make an acceptance speech? It was embarrassing for me."

"When you win an award, you give an acceptance speech, *Roland*. I'm sorry I embarrassed you. I didn't know you cared so much about what stupid people think of you. Sorr-eeeee."

"It's not about that. I don't like it when people pay attention to me. And then when you said all those mean things about Elaine and Duncan ..."

"I'm not really a mean person. When they say mean things I say mean things back, but I never start off mean. I don't just take it though. You can't just take it. Roland, what happens when you grow up and someone is mean to you, if someone tries to steal your wallet?"

"I would say something."

"You would say something? That's not enough."

"I think I know how to stand up for myself."

"No, you don't."

"I think I do."

"No. Sorry."

I was just about to keep this monotony going when a tall figure, backlit by the sun so that his face was in shadow, poked his head around the garbage bin.

"Hello, there," he said. His voice was deep and soft. "I heard you chatting and thought I'd say hello."

Our backs straightened. We couldn't see his face, but we instantly knew that a handsome man was in our midst. His voice was measured, so unlike the brutal horns of all the men we knew. Birdy couldn't speak.

"I'm Caesar Stock. I'll be leading a new choir at the school come fall. I was supposed to visit all the classrooms to introduce myself, but it seems like you've let out early for schoolyard fun."

"I'm—we—our teacher got mad at us," Birdy managed to say, all throaty.

"I'm sorry to hear that. I'm sure it was a miscommunication. In any case ..." The man came around the bin and sat on the boulder beside our boulder: blond hair slicked back artfully, and big green eyes that seemed to throb with wisdom, and a chin square as Superman's, and enormous hands with long fingers like a concert pianist's. We'd never seen anything like him. I flashed on what Birdy might say once the coast was clear, and for once I knew I could match his rhapsody, sigh for sigh.

"I like to sing," said Birdy. "I'm a really good singer."

"I am too. I am also."

He glared at me. "No, you're not. You never sing."

"You don't know that. I sing sometimes. When you're not around."

"No, you don't. Don't be fake."

"Boys, there's no need for this. You're both welcome. I've also started a youth choir at St. Alban's, if you're interested."

"I'm very interested," Birdy said. I rolled my eyes. I couldn't name my distaste at the time, but looking back, we were children, precocious but still naive, vying for the attention of a grown man who—what? Would scoop us up into his arms and lead us into an enchanted gingerbread house? Where we would—what? Play Yahtzee?

"Excellent. Well, I look forward to seeing you both. Just get your mothers' permission, and soon we'll all be lifting our voices in song."

I looked at Birdy to see if he was upset about the mother reference, but he was still transfixed by Caesar Stock, who was now reaching into his leather tote and feeling around for permission slips.

"I LOVE HIM," Birdy said, once Caesar Stock had loped off. How free he was with this kind of talk! If it weren't for Birdy's certainty in all things, I might still be floundering for the words to describe my desire for men.

"He's really nice," I said. "His eyes are so … nice."

"He must be new. New in the city, I mean. I bet he's from New York. Or Hollywood."

I didn't say so, but I thought Birdy had misread Mr. Stock completely. Neither of us had been anywhere, but I hadn't gotten New York or Hollywood or even Toronto from Mr. Stock as I listened to his gentle, august voice. I heard a verdant countryside, festooned with the occasional castle, and placid horses nodding in a vast field. England, somewhere storybook. He didn't have an English accent, but he easily could have at some point; accents can fade away after a long time in a new place.

"I hope Margaret lets us join the choir," I said.

"You don't really want to sing in a choir, Roland. You're just copying me."

I pushed off our boulder. "It could be fun. I don't know. We can both like him, Birdy. He's a nice person."

We started for the road home. "Okay, fine. But just remember that I'm the one who's gonna marry him."

"He's not going to get married to an eleven-year-old boy. He's probably married already. But … we were talking so quiet, I don't know how he could've heard us. It was weird."

"He's a musician like me. Our hearing is more powerful."

I WAS SHOCKED to find my mother already home. She was sitting at the kitchen table, and her hair was in her face, all scraggly. It looked like she was asleep, but when I said hi her head snapped back.

"Oh. Hi, Roland. Hi, Birdy. I had to leave work. I'm so groggy."

My mother's doctor had recently put her on a sedative to calm her obsessiveness and insomnia. She'd warned us that she might not be herself for a bit. Given that she was already not herself, I had looked forward to the new medicated Margaret. But it was bad. She spoke so slowly, with faraway eyes, like an old person remembering the Depression.

"We're going to be in a choir," said Birdy, beaming.

"Last day of school, eh," my mother replied, not noticing that Birdy had spoken. "Did you have fun? Were there, you know—fun things?"

"Birdy won the courage award."

Nothing.

"Mom. Mom?" I touched her shoulder. "I said Birdy won the courage award."

"Oh. Okay. That's great. What's the courage award?"

"It's not a big thing," Birdy said, not wanting to further drain my drained mother. "The teacher just gave it to me because my mum died and my dad didn't want me."

"Oh. I'm sure that's not true, Birdy. You're very brave in many ways. I really admire your—you know—your dignity. I'm going to cry."

Birdy put his head atop my mother's head. "Don't cry, Margaret. Please please. Everything is going good, for everybody, everywhere. Please don't cry."

Margaret ran a hand under her streaming nose. "I think I'm going to lie down for a bit. I don't like these pills at all. Make me so dopey."

"Okay. But can Birdy and me be in the choir? You have to sign a permission slip." I pulled it from my pocket.

"I'm sure that's fine. Just leave it on the table and I'll sign it in the morning. Okay. You're great kids. You both should've gotten the courage thing. You both have—yeah. Dignity."

We bookended her as she wove her way to the bedroom and fell upon her bed silently, like a dress tossed from the closet.

"WHAT ARE WE going to do all summer?" I said to Birdy, as he strummed his ukulele. We were watching *The Carol Burnett Show*. We were ambivalent about *The Carol Burnett Show*, which had only been on the air a few months. Its hammy skits struck us uncool. We much preferred *Laugh-In*; Goldie Hawn was so groovy and pretty in her psychedelic minidresses.

"We're going to be in the choir. And then we'll just—I don't know—hang around. What did we do last summer?"

"Nothing. Well. You wrote songs on your banjo—ukulele, and I ... I forget."

IN BED THAT NIGHT we talked breathlessly about Caesar Stock.

"I want to know all about him. I wonder what his house is like. He's so ... I don't know. I wish I was eighteen. I just want to skip seven years and be eighteen right away."

"I think I'm for sure gay."

"Oh, come off it, Roland. You are for sure gay. We hug and kiss all the time."

"Yeah, but I've never seen someone handsome and felt like passing out before. I felt like passing out today."

"I sort of did too. What are you gonna do when I'm famous? I sometimes get sad when I think about what you're gonna do."

I was too shy to speak my own sadness about this. "I'll come with you, and I'll iron your costumes and make sure everything in your dressing room is the way it should be."

"Would you really do that? You'd be my ... assistant?"

"Yeah, sure. It would be fun."

"That's exciting. Okay. Yeah."

I pulled him closer. We dozed. I felt lucky, stunningly lucky. I would spend my adulthood looking after Birdy, and we'd travel the world, staying first in cheap motels, then in fancy hotels, chatting and cuddling like we'd always done. The daunting riddle of my future had been solved in fifteen seconds.

IN THE MORNING we found Margaret sitting on the kitchen counter, kicking her legs and smoking a long, thin cigarette.

"You two are not joining a church choir. Especially not a Catholic church choir."

"It's not a *church choir* church choir," I said.

"You're going to be singing hymns in a church. That's a church choir. No way, sorry. You know how I feel about organized religion, Roland."

Birdy looked at me, then at Margaret. "How do you feel about organized religion?"

"It's a poison, Birdy. It leads to nothing but heartache. I won't have you exposed to it."

"My mother went to church sometimes."

"Faith kills. I know that sounds harsh, but it's true. We'll never know the root of your mother's drinking problem, but ten bucks says it was at least partly due to religious indoctrination."

I could not let my mother's phobia keep us from spending time with Caesar Stock. "It's not like that, Mom. We met Mr. Stock at school yesterday, and he's really cool and nice. He's going to have a choir at school next year too."

"Huh. And where did you meet this Mr. Stock?"

"At school. Outside of school. In the parking lot."

My mother made this harsh, sardonic gasping sound and looked up at the ceiling. "Ah. A grown man skulking around outside a primary school. No, that's not suspicious at all. One thing I learned in church was how to spot the diddlers. Not that it did me any good in the end. Well, that settles it. Sorry. No. No."

"Maybe you should take your pills, Mom."

She leapt off the counter. "Ah yes. You don't like it when your mother is lucid. You thought I'd just scribble on your permission slip if I were all doped up. Guess again."

Birdy went up close to my mother. "Margaret, you don't understand. I *have* to be in the church choir, and in the school one. It's part of my destiny. It's part of my destiny as a musical entertainer. I have to be in the choir. If I have to, I'll fake your signature."

"I am your guardian now, Birdy. I'm not some dotty bystander. I encourage your gifts, but I'm not going to let you be preyed upon. You might think you're very sophisticated, but you're not. You're a sitting duck. Do you want to be bent over a baptismal and given the rough once-over? No. I may have some issues with my nerves, but I'm determined to care for you as your mother would've."

Birdy started screaming, furious vowel sounds that made my eyes go bulbous.

"I AM GOING TO BE IN THE CHOIR! I HAVE A DESTINY AND YOU ARE A BITCH!"

He ran to our room and slammed the door. I had several emotions in rapid succession: I was worried for Birdy, angry at him for insulting my mother, and worried for my mother in the wake of this dust-up. I knew my mother had valid points, but also the thought of Caesar Stock bending me over whatever a baptismal was and giving me "the rough once-over," whatever that entailed, was not without its scary appeal.

"Mom." I spoke as softly as I could. "Mr. Stock is not a bad man. He's going to be teaching choir at the school. He has qualifications, I'm definitely sure. Maybe—how about—what if you came with us to the church to meet him and talk to him? Then you'll know for sure that he's not awful."

"I will not step foot in a Catholic church, Roland. I will not."

"Please? Please, Mom? I never ask for things. I really want to be in the choir. And Birdy really, really, really wants to be in the choir. Mr. Stock is so nice. Please?"

She rolled her eyes, over and over. She jutted her jaw like some prehistoric dog.

"I am going to be very thorough in my questioning, Roland. And if I get even a whiff of something untoward, it's game over. Understand?"

"Sure, yes, okay."

"When you're grown up and I'm long dead I want you to remember this concession and think of me with love and respect."

"I do think of you with love and respect."

"Sycophant! I'm sorry, I hate myself. Maybe I should take a pill. You go away now and tell Birdy my decision, which is contingent on him apologizing sincerely to me for calling me a bitch."

I bounded to the bedroom; it was always such a thrill to present Birdy with good news. I told him Margaret's verdict, and Birdy instantly stopped crying, flipped over onto his back on the bed, and started doing these weird water ballet wiggles with his legs. We waited a while so Birdy could conjure the optimal apology and then he went to my mother, knelt, and apologized profusely until she told him to stop and did he want a boiled egg.

THE FOLLOWING SATURDAY we drove to St. Alban's. Margaret held off taking her sedative again so she'd be sharp for her interrogation. Her hands trembled on the steering wheel, and she swatted at non-existent mosquitoes.

We were early. There was a sign taped Scotch-taped to the wall inside the front door: "Singers! Please come to the basement rehearsal room," in spiky cardiogram cursive.

"Of course he chose the basement. That's very crafty of him," my mother said. "That way your screams can't be heard."

"Mom. Please. That doesn't sound open minded like you said you would be."

"Yes, okay, you're right. To the basement."

CAESAR STOCK WAS in a dark suit, possibly the same suit we met him in, or possibly a different suit in the same shade; gentlemen have several subtly different suits. He was pulling a music stand to its full height.

"Hi, Mr. Stock!" said Birdy too loudly.

Mr. Stock smiled and walked toward us. I noticed how willowy he was, his long arms and legs moving with liquid grace.

"You made it. I'm thrilled." He made to shake our hands, but my mother deftly stepped in front of us.

"I'm Margaret Keener. Roland's mother, and Birdy's guardian."

"Great to meet you." Mr. Stock stuck out his hand; Margaret shook it hard. "Welcome to our very first choir practice. I'm so glad you dropped in to say hello. Roland and—Birdy, is it?"

"Yes," said my mother, stony, ready to seize on the smallest infraction. "They told me they met you in the parking lot at school. That sounded somewhat, well—in any case, I felt it was important that I meet you before consenting to their involvement in the ... singing group. The choir."

Caesar Stock smiled knowingly. It struck me that he already had several impeccable responses ready to go for any impasse.

"Of course. I applaud your diligence. I'm hoping to meet all the parents in short order. It's funny, I was talking with Ingrid—Mrs. Mitchell, the grade five teacher—"

"I'm aware of my children's teacher's name, thank you."

"I'm sure. I didn't mean to imply otherwise. But we were talking about parental engagement in the education of children, and we were both dismayed at the level of apathy on that front. I understand that our lives are incredibly busy, but as an educator I do sometimes wonder what more I could be doing to involve the whole family in the process."

"Mm-hmm." Margaret looked him up and down continuously, as though he were some confounding vertical hieroglyph. "I think you'll find that I'm very much immersed in my children's education. Very, very immersed. So, you're a teacher?"

"I'm a psychiatrist by trade, but I have also trained as an educator. My primary work can be so draining—endlessly rewarding, but draining—and the pure passion that children have for music is very restorative."

"Hmm. So you find children's passion restorative."

"I find their enthusiasm for music restorative." He was clearly hip to her line of questioning, like he'd weathered similar interrogations before.

"Where is your practice? I'm assuming you have an office."

"I do. I have an office in my home. On Heather Crescent."

"Your office is in your home. Interesting. That must be very convenient."

This was turning into a standoff, and I couldn't bear it. "Mom, why don't you just tell him what you're all worried about?"

"I'm having an adult conversation with Mr.—or should I say Dr. Stock."

Birdy ran to the risers that had been assembled for choir practice.

"Mrs. Keener."

"Miss. I'm an unmarried woman. Proudly so."

"Well done. Miss Keener, I am not a pederast. If that is your concern, let me assure you. I'm a respected clinician with long-standing ties to the community. I'm happy to furnish you with whatever credentials and references you require. I'm here to inspire your children as they study the practice of choral singing. Beyond that, I'm not sure what to say."

This seemed to thaw my mother. She sighed. She swallowed. "I'm sorry if I'm being too—I don't know. I have problems with the setting. The Catholic church setting. Maybe I'm projecting past trauma onto you."

Dr. Stock offered a considered smile, likely one that he used frequently when listening to psychiatric patients. "Please, let me reassure you that the religious aspect of our choral project is really an afterthought. I'm a hopeless agnostic, but I can't deny the beauty of some of the pieces we'll be rehearsing. The Catholic aspect begins and ends with the music."

Other children started streaming in. Dr. Stock pulled a folding chair out of a closet and set it up for my mother. "Please, Miss Keener, I'd love it if you sat in and watched us work."

"I'd like that. As long as I'm not intruding."

My mother suddenly had this stuporous look on her face, a look I hadn't seen since her early days with Dan, when she'd emerge from the bedroom with him after he'd brought out the woman in her. She was falling prey to Dr. Stock's powerful allure, the dark bell of his speaking voice, the way he moved through the room with equine elegance. I was relieved. Margaret wasn't easily impressed, and even when she was, it barely discernible: one briefly raised brow, a swallow that could also be nothing more than mild heartburn. She would let us join Dr. Stock's choir.

I joined Birdy on the riser. "Margaret likes Dr. Stock."

"Of course she does. It's destiny. I know it sounds snooty, but I really feel like my destiny is more, you know, powerful than everyone else's, at least when it comes to singing and the choir and all that."

I nodded. That sounded reasonable. If one person in a group of people had a particular investment in a given situation, it only followed that their force of will would propel the course of things. I hadn't cared much about anything to that point, except for Birdy, and I liked to think my love for him propelled him into my house, and into my bed.

"Afternoon, everyone," said Dr. Stock, once all fifteen kids were more or less lined up. He surveyed us, stopping for a beat at Birdy and me. My face pulsed. He liked us. He liked us both. "Welcome, and thank you for participating in my little experiment, here at"— he shot a glance at my mother—"your local church, which will not be named."

I swivelled around. My mother had covered her mouth with her hand and was, I'm almost certain, tittering. Tittering like a school-girl. This was not part of her expressive repertoire. It was one thing that she approved of our choir leader, another thing altogether that he might be turning her into a fawning tart. I've always been unforgiving when people step outside of the role I've allotted them.

"The first song we'll tackle is 'Wander Through the Palms.' You'll find the lyrics on the stands. Two singers per stand, please."

Birdy and I pressed together in front of a stand. Dr. Stock sang the first line, fast and then slow, and told us to copy him. Although I sometimes sang softly at home, I'd never sung publicly. My face pulsed. Most of the kids were equally intimidated by the strange man and the new song, and after several dismal, muddy run-throughs, Dr. Stock turned to us from the piano bench and shook his head.

"Too many mouthers," he said, stern but still encouraging. "I know you can do this. You're a lovely bunch of people. We'll go line by line. Don't let me down, friends."

He'd called us all his friends. The tiny pep talk was effective; as we slowly worked our way through the song, there was a palpable banding together, and even though by afternoon's end we still sounded like a drunken head falling on piano keys, we were all excited for the next practice.

Birdy's musical gift truly burst forth around this time. He'd collected pop bottles to save up for a guitar, which he'd conquered as quickly as he had the baritone ukulele. I'd watch him practice, lost to the world, and pretend that I had some equivalent minute obsession, studying the three strands of colour that made up the fibres of the living room carpet. It was so hard to keep from distracting Birdy when he fell into these trances; he'd look up periodically with faraway eyes, picturing, I'm sure, his future on the concert stage, in the recording studio, in the back of a limousine after a night of revelry with fellow stars and pretty hangers-on. I had already begun to brace for total desertion. It's gruelling, loving someone talented who's ready to bolt for some other, vastly more interesting place. I'd study the blue-grey-green tendrils of the carpet, hit with a sudden sadness at the thought of treading that carpet years after Birdy was long gone. He swore he'd take me with him, and I believed him, but I also knew his quicksilver disposition; no matter how neatly I might lay out his dressing room brushes and combs or how expertly I teased his hair before he wafted onstage, there would come a time when he'd need someone new to do it, solely for the sake of newness. And I would return to Winnipeg, and my mother's house, and my mother, who might be irretrievably insane or restored to full mental health, and we'd tread that carpet until we deemed it too tatty to remain and bought a new one.

MARGARET DROVE US to the next rehearsal, again unmedicated so she could drive, her fingers a blur as they tapped the keys of an invisible typewriter until she remembered to retake the wheel.

"I wonder what he has up his sleeve for you this time," she said, glancing at us in the rear-view mirror. "Hey? What do you think? Hello? Earth to Roland and Birdy!"

"Yeah, I wonder," Birdy said, in the world-weary voice he affected when he wanted to come across as prodigiously hip. We were grateful for the ride but miffed that Margaret might infringe on our time with Dr. Stock.

"I'm sure she won't stay like she did last time," Birdy whispered.

"Hmm." I'd seen my mother's ruddy face the week before. I'd seen her take the stairs two at a time with the zeal of a new army recruit.

And she did stay. Dr. Stock greeted her like she was a dignitary, with continental kisses on both cheeks.

"I'm sure I must be an annoyance, sitting in again," she said, patting her purse as though it contained something precious but incriminating. "There's just something about the process I find so interesting."

He was about to speak but then ran to the supply closet to retrieve her folding chair. He propped it open in front of her, and she slowly lowered herself onto it in an almost unseemly way. This was my mother being flirty. I hated it.

The kids came in all at once. This time there was another mother, a beautiful, somewhat blowsy woman with enormous black hair dense as moss. Her breasts were huge and sprawling. Dr. Stock set up a chair for her next to my mother. My mother almost smiled, but defaulted to the robot face she gave to canvassing Jehovah's Witnesses.

"My girl said Dr. Stock is kind of a miracle worker when it comes to singing," the other mother said to Margaret. "I had to see for myself."

"I don't know if I'd go that far. He's a bracing presence, for sure."

The other mother had no response to that.

WE WENT THROUGH "Wander Through the Palms" until it sounded almost not awful. I stayed in tune. I'm pretty sure Birdy shot me a dirty look, which filled me with pride. I had no talent, but clearly I had encroached on his terrain.

At one point, close to the end of rehearsal, Dr. Stock covered his face with his hands. We thought he was crying. We didn't want him to cry. He could do almost anything—he could do rage, sending pages of sheet music fluttering through the room like lazy birds, or he could do contemplation, which was how we knew him up to that point—but sorrow would destabilize us. Dr. Stock crying would remind us of messy domestic scenarios—the drunken, guilt-laden blue-collar father, the wan mother astonished by the barrenness of her daily routine—and our team spirit would dissolve. We needed—I needed—Dr. Stock to be convivial, deft, always. I held my breath as his hands fell away.

He was grinning. "That was remarkable. Remarkable! The progress you've made in two rehearsals—I've never seen anything like it. Well done, everyone. You're becoming musicians. How's that for transformation?"

The girls on the front riser whipped their heads around, giggling. Their coarse hair and huge teeth, their blatant lack of personality— like Margaret, they were infringing on our private enjoyment of Dr. Stock. Birdy and I shared a smirk; we didn't crash their bake sales and sock hops, we weren't about to poke our heads in the window when it came time for them to neck with boys in cars, so why should they get to gum up the fun of two gay embryos?

Dr. Stock approached us at rehearsal's end. He was wearing a heady woody cologne.

"If your mother's not in a rush, I'd like to chat with her for a moment or two, if that's okay with you."

We nodded like manic hand puppets. We went to where Margaret and the other mother were. Dr. Stock said hello to the other mother, who threw her head back and made a throaty barking sound, a chain-smoker's laugh.

"That was great, oh, that was so good," she said. "Holy shit."

Dr. Stock's face fell at her profanity. Margaret pursed her lips. She didn't have a problem with profanity but obviously welcomed the other mother's sudden fall from grace.

"Thank you so much for your kind words," said Dr. Stock. "I need to speak with Miss Keener for a moment, if you'll excuse us."

"Oh, sure thing," said the woman, shooting up from her seat. Her nylons bagged at the knees. "I'm Anita Brasseur, Kiki's mum. We'd love to have you for supper sometime. I love to—when you put the food in the oven—umm, cook. Oh, what is wrong with me! I had to take a pain pill for my back—I'm so chesty it hurts."

She looked down at her burdensome bosom, then looked up with moist, parted lips.

"I understand," said Dr. Stock.

"So! When are you free? Eh?"

"My schedule is full to overflowing these next few weeks, Mrs. Brasseur, but I'm grateful for the invitation."

"Oh, no problem. For sure, no problem. My husband is a truck driver, so yeah, he's gone all the time. Oh, my back! This darn bust! Whenever's good for you. Just let Kiki know when you'd like to come over and it's a done deal."

"Again, thanks."

"Oh, no problem." I cringed as she backed away, rebuked but still trying to look affable. Flirtation can go so horribly wrong so quickly.

"I'm sorry, Dr. Stock," my mother said once the woman was out of earshot. "I feel like I pre-empted her in some way. I've developed this nervous condition."

Dr. Stock folded his hands solemnly, looking like an old photo of a Quaker in his Sunday best.

"Miss Keener, it's downright spooky that you mentioned your nervous condition, because I was just about to ask—perhaps we should speak privately."

Margaret looked at Birdy and me. I was dumbfounded by the whole exchange. Birdy seemed delighted by this adult intrigue.

"Oh, no need," my mother said. "I'm an open book when it comes to my recent mental issues. I've always felt that it's important to let children observe the reality of a given situation. Within reason, of course. I would never, for example, invite a strange man over for *dinner*, with obvious desperation in my voice, in front of my kids. Again, I've spoken out of turn. I am sorry."

Birdy, bored now, announced that he had to go to the bathroom and ran off.

"May I sit?"

Margaret motioned at the empty seat beside her. Dr. Stock sat. He leaned forward, smiling with studied bedside concern.

"Are you satisfied with the care you're receiving from your care team, Miss Keener?"

"Margaret. I feel like something out of Dickens when you call me Miss Keener. Frankly? No, I am not satisfied with the care I'm receiving from my care team. I don't even have a care team, just my old GP. He put me on Valium and told me to get a hamster."

"No!"

"Yes. I'm not a neurotic, Dr. Stock. I'm a very determined person. Until recently, I haven't had even a moment of anxiety. Well, anxiety that I can't account for, I mean. It's hard to sleep. And even when I do sleep, I sometimes wake up screaming, with these awful visions of—actually, on second thought, Roland, would you mind excusing us for a few minutes?"

"It's okay, Mom. Like you said, I can handle it."

"Yes, well, I've changed my mind. Just go stand over by the Ping-Pong table and wait for Birdy. I'll be five minutes, tops."

I sighed, embarrassed to be chastened in front of Dr. Stock. I walked halfway to the Ping-Pong table.

"I can still hear you guys."

"So keep walking, Roland!"

I walked all the way to the Ping-Pong table.

"I can't hear you guys anymore."

"Good. Shush now!"

I leaned against the Ping-Pong table, pretending that Dr. Stock was still looking at me. I did things I thought he would be impressed by: shadow boxing, swatting forehands and backhands in a game of air Ping-Pong. I glanced over at them. Dr. Stock had pulled his chair to face Margaret, and they were bent forward, lost in what looked like a wrenching exchange.

Birdy returned. "Oh my god, are they still talking?"

"She's telling him why she's going crazy."

"But I thought she didn't know why she's going crazy."

"Well, she's telling him all the ways she's acting crazy, and he's telling her ... what to do about it."

Birdy and I both leaned against the Ping-Pong table, bored to death. The grown-ups' conversation went way past five minutes. Birdy started making donkey sounds. I bumped his shoulder with mine.

"It would probably be so easy to tip this table over," he said. "Let's lean on it until it tips over."

It sounded fun. "Margaret will get really mad."

"We really didn't sound bad today," he said. This was the first time he'd spoken positively about our group undertaking. He so rarely softened on such topics that it always startled me. "Remember that show we saw on TV that had Dionne Warwick with a gospel choir? I'd like to do something like that. But that sort of thing you can't really do until you're an established superstar, otherwise you just look full of yourself."

A feverish impatience swirled in me. I was not a bratty kid, far from it, but as the minutes passed I grew more and more huffy, more and more twitchy. What could they going on about? My mother had bad nerves, and she typed on an invisible typewriter, and she'd often come home from work pale and shiny and full of work anecdotes about making co-workers cry, making customers wait upward of an hour for prescriptions she'd long ago filled and hidden in a drawer just to be spiteful. How long could it take for her to tell him that and for him to tell her to get more fresh air, or a perm?

"I'm going to say something," I said at last.

"No, don't," said Birdy, suddenly circumspect. "She never gets the chance to talk with people her own age. Maybe she is really going crazy. I don't want her to give me back to my dad."

This mollified me, until it didn't. I walked over to them.

My mother looked up at me, her tearful face like a wet tomato. "We're almost finished, Roland. Go back. We're almost finished."

"You said you'd be five minutes. It's been, like, twenty minutes."

Dr. Stock encircled my right wrist with his thumb and forefinger. I shuddered. His hand was hot but gentle.

"You two must be going stir crazy," he said huskily, like he'd just been woken from sleep. "I'm sorry. We're—well, we're devising a treatment plan, aren't we, Margaret?"

"What? Oh. Yes."

"Five more minutes, Roland. You're doing us a real solid, and I won't forget it."

"Okay, sure. No problem." Suddenly I was Anita Brasseur, flummoxed, grinning, incapable of saving face. I went back to Birdy.

"Are they almost done?"

"I think so. They're making a treatment plan."

"What is that?"

"I don't know. He was—he put his fingers around my wrist. And he sort of squeezed it, but gentle."

"Oh! I want him to squeeze my wrist. Did you notice that he smells like a Christmas tree?"

I hadn't been able to pinpoint the main note in his cologne, but Birdy nailed it: the doctor smelled like Christmas.

WE'D BEEN WAITING half an hour. Birdy pulled a thin hardcover book from his backpack.

"What's that?"

"It's my diary. Margaret gave it to me. She said it might be helpful to write down my feelings, cuz I've been through things."

"Oh." I tried to keep my voice light and neutral, but I felt betrayed. I'd been through things. I hadn't lost my mother or been abandoned by my father, but I *was* the product of rape, and Margaret was in the midst of a breakdown, and I was chubby and socially inept. She could've given us both diaries. My mother was clearly favouring Birdy, months after he'd stopped crying in the night and reaching out in the dark for his missing mother and didn't need doting on anymore. I like to think that I was mostly magnanimous when it truly counted, but I was not without need. I was not a cactus, nourished by the occasional spurt of water. I was only eleven; I needed my mother to comfort me as I brushed against the horror of adolescence. And here was Birdy writing with a yellow pencil crayon in his spiffy diary, while Margaret wept and fluttered in the bright light of Dr. Stock's undivided attention.

Finally, finally they adjourned, and my wobbly mother made her way over to us. Dr. Stock stacked the chairs and came over too. My mother's blouse was dark with sweat across her breasts and beneath her armpits. Dr. Stock looked unruffled, as fresh and immaculate as he had when he arrived.

"I'm so sorry to have kept your mother so long," he said. "I can be quite the chatterbox when I encounter another supple mind."

"Thank you so much, Caesar. For the first time I feel like I have a path out of the darkness."

I let out a small derisive sigh. A path out of the darkness! She made it sound like she was Helen Keller.

"Roland, don't you dare judge me right now. People who mock other people when they're at their most vulnerable—well, the penitentiaries are full of people like you."

I flinched as though I'd been smacked.

"No, no," said Dr. Stock. "Please, it's entirely my fault, Margaret. Roland is tired and probably hungry at this point."

"You're right. I'm sorry, Roland. I'm so drained. I'll—we'll have a nice, quiet evening. We'll order a pizza."

"Don't act for him." I was not myself. I was speaking in an alien voice, guttural and snide. My mother took a step back. My mother didn't act for anyone, ever. But still that unknown voice came out of me.

Birdy grabbed my arm. "We should go. What time is it? Oh, look, it's almost five o'clock. Can we go?"

Margaret nodded. Dr. Stock started to say one of his soft, sage sayings but stopped and clapped his hands as if to dispel the stand-off. He said he'd see us next week, then bolted from the room to address some non-existent emergency elsewhere in the church.

The three of us filed out. Nobody spoke until we were halfway home.

"I know you're fans of Dr. Stock. He has more than allayed my concerns. It's important to have role models who ... aren't on tele-vision. And I'm not going to impose myself on your choir practice anymore. But he offered me a lot of good advice today. He's an insider, he knows the wheat from the chaff on psychiatric matters. I'm sorry that you've both seen me at sixes and sevens. I like to think that I'm turning the corner though."

"That's exciting," said Birdy. I didn't say anything.

"How does that sit with you, Roland? Am I forgiven?"

"Say something," said Birdy.

"So ... where did he tell you to go? Did he put you on new pills?"

"He's not my prescribing physician. In fact he's not a fan of medication at all."

"So, what did he say?"

"He's referring me to this woman who, he says, is the best in the world."

"For what?"

"For groceries. For what. She's a therapist, silly. She'll be offer-ing me therapy. He said she offers real-world solutions that can carry a person through the rest of their life."

"Did he ask you on a date?"

Margaret burst into raucous laughter. "He most certainly did not! Did he ask me on a date!"

"You keep repeating what I'm saying and then saying your answer."

"Don't make fun of how she talks," said Birdy. "We all talk different sometimes."

"I think I know that. And I wasn't talking to you. *Birdy*." I laid into his name with some venom.

"Stop now, both of you. Today was a good day, that's the important thing. And I can confidently say that I didn't feel one bit of desire for him. It was strange, actually. He's definitely an attractive man, charming, attentive. But ... he has this sort of priestly bearing. Not that he's unknowable exactly, it's more like— it sounds stupid, but—it's almost like he's ... an apparition. Or a hologram. Or a fallen angel. No, that makes him sound like Satan. It's more like he's—"

"Oh god, which one is he, Mom? Pick one."

"Stop being so mean!" said Birdy.

"Stop telling me what to do."

My mother shrieked and pulled the car over on the road's shoulder.

"I am going to drive us into the lake if you both don't shut up right now. I know I've been off my game of late. But that is going to change. There will be order and there will be thoughtful exchanges, and we are all going to pull together and share household chores. I will treat you with kindness and consideration as long as you stop this ... banshee back and forth. All right? All right? Say it. Say it!"

"All right," we said.

I WAS QUIET during supper. Birdy and Mom talked about choir practice.

"I didn't think I'd like singing with other people, but I kind of do. When everyone was singing together and we were almost all in tune, it was—I almost started to cry."

"Oh, me too, Birdy. It was very moving at times. Especially the choruses. You've all got the chorus down pat."

"And could you hear me? Could you pick out my voice from everybody else?"

"Definitely. Your voice—well, I've prattled on about your beautiful voice so often."

"Aw. Thank you!"

"You know what? No. Thank *you*."

I found that I hated them both, right then. They both had such optimism. Margaret's optimism beat lightly against Birdy's optimism, and together Margaret and Birdy were like waltzing suns. I excused myself and lay down on my unmade bed.

I got bored. I looked around our shared room. My side was bare, save for the new poster above my bed. Ringo Starr in a Speedo. Birdy got it for me at the mall. He'd insisted I put it up; it was easily my boldest declaration of budding gayness, but my mother had yet to mention it. Birdy's side was a mess. Dirty clothes in multiple piles, movie magazines, knock-off Barbies with matted hair, and his knapsack with his diary.

I couldn't resist. I unzipped the bag. I felt entitled; Margaret and Birdy were happy, dancing suns, and I had the right to invade my friend's privacy. At the time it seemed fair.

The first few pages were a bore. "I feel okay. I thought I felt bad, but I don't," followed by doodles of saucer-eyed women with enormous, gaping mouths and hair piled high in coils like Dairy Queen sundaes.

JUNE 30, 1965

I'm really tired today. Roland and me talked way into the night about Dr. Stock and what his house probably looks like. I love Roland. He's trusty. Sometimes he's boring but he's always there, kind of like if I had a dog. But I love him so much. In some ways I'm lucky. Margaret is so nice to me. Sometimes after Roland falls asleep I get out of bed and sit with her and watch TV, and we talk about what's good and bad about everything and she tells me about going around in her everyday life as a woman who is strong. She tells me that men can be really nice but also they can be dumb, like sometimes you'll be talking for a long time about something with a man, and then at the end the man will say "oh, I thought you were talking about something else this whole time," and you'll want to hit him with a brick. I am so lucky to have a woman friend who is smart and calls me Birdy and not Gerry. I have to go now. Will try to write tomorrow?

Birdy and my mother had late-night heart-to-hearts while I was asleep. Given my agitation, I should've been incensed to learn of these illicit conversations, but Margaret and I also had heart-to-hearts, just not at night. And I liked sleeping. And we were all Birdy had for family, apart from his brother, who'd called a few times early on but then fucked off altogether.

What turned my hands into claws on the pillow was that Birdy perceived me as a dog. Not a best friend nor a future boyfriend. To Birdy, I was as predictable as a pet.

JULY 7, 1965

Tomorrow is our first choir practice. I'm so excited. I hope Margaret doesn't think Mr. Stock is a criminal when they meet. Mr. Stock is so handsome I can't even stand it. It's like he fell out of the sky. It was fun talking about him with Roland. I am so lucky to have Margaret and Roland as well. I miss my mother but I couldn't really talk to her because she was always upset or drunk and I didn't want to bother her. I am so glad that Roland and me found each other. We can say anything. Now I feel bad for saying that he was like a dog in the last thing I wrote. I'm no good at all with writing in sentences.

I looked behind me, spooked. He'd written that he was sorry for the thing he said that I was just angry about. Had he caught me in the act? But he couldn't have, because I was reading his diary, and his diary wasn't him, of course. Logic sometimes failed me when I was young. I sometimes miss those young lapses in logic. They made for a spaciousness in my mind. That spaciousness is long, long gone.

> I wonder what Mr. Stock is going to wear at choir practice. Maybe he'll have his shirt open a little bit, and he'll have that little bit of hair that some men have sticking out of their collar. Roland likes him a lot also but I can't help feeling like I like Mr. Stock in a way that is I don't know, more interesting. I hate it when I have snooty feelings like that but I can't help it. We are both gays, me and Roland, but I'm cuter. That's not stuck-up, it's a fact.

When we hugged and talked at night we were equals; I'd say my small thought and he'd say his, and we were peers. By day, though, there was the asterisk of his beauty, and that gave him primacy, which was fair enough, if sometimes frustrating. I wanted him to feel important. He'd need to feel important all through his life, if he wanted to be a pop star. I didn't need to feel important.

IN THE MORNING my mother darted about silently in her work clothes, preoccupied. She was always preoccupied in her nervous condition, but that day her distraction had focus. As she tossed the breakfast dishes in the sink and rinsed them negligently, I could see words forming on her lips, some enunciated so crisply that I could make them out. *Decision. Weeks. Foolish. Trust. Please.*

Birdy and I played lawn darts on the sad greyish grass of our tiny backyard. Our hearts weren't in it.

"Don't just whip it as hard as you can, Birdy! What if a cat runs past? You'd kill it."

"This is dumb. I hate activities. It's almost time for *Days of Our Lives*."

"We can't lie on the couch all summer. My mom will make us get paper routes. Let's finish this game, at least."

I threw my dart. It went wayward and pierced a petunia.

"Come on, Roland. We're both awful at this. What's the point?"

"It's not healthy to watch soap operas all day."

"So? Since when did you care about healthy things? You're acting all different."

"No, I'm not. I like lawn darts. We have to try to be more, I don't know. Active. Normal."

Birdy pretended to barf. "Normal. Healthy. What are you going on about? It's like you woke up as a different person."

He was right. I found myself using those ugly words—*normal, healthy, active*—and meaning what I said. It was as though I'd stumbled upon a new arsenal of bland aspirations to counteract Birdy's magnetism and make myself heard again in a tiny house that now rattled with conspiracy and favouritism. This startled me as much as it did Birdy, my yucky new lexicon, my need to stick my neck out, but I kept going.

"We have to start trying to be more normal. We'll be in junior high in a year. We should try to have more friends. I don't want to be … all feminine and everything."

"I feel like you're breaking up with me." He was almost crying.

"No. Come on. I'd never break up with you. I—need to be more of a people person. I need to find out what my interests are. You have that all figured out. I want to do chess club this year, or the bird-watching thing with Mrs. Ostapenko."

Birdy looked stricken. He cast his eyes around like he'd just realized he was stuck in some sooty, penal snow globe.

I gathered up the lawn darts stuff and threw it in the shed. Birdy went back inside to watch his soap operas. As I locked the shed I was hit with a wave of guilt; I'd shown him my innate mediocrity, and there was no going back to our secret world. I was too boring. I started to panic. I would go back in the house and tell Birdy I was only kidding about health and normalcy and ask him what I'd missed on *Days of Our Lives*.

He was sitting on the floor, knees pulled tight to his chest.

"What did I miss?"

"You're going to start hating me."

"No, I'm not. I was—sometimes I get scared that nothing interesting is going to happen to me. When you're playing your guitar and making up songs, I just sit there. What do you think I should do, in the future, like?"

"I don't know. We can just watch TV until we graduate, and then you'll come with me when I do things to get famous."

I sat beside him on the floor. I tried to copy his pose, but I wasn't bendy enough, so I leaned back on my elbows. "But what will I do while you're doing your famous things? I can't just sit around. Well, I mean, I *can*, but that isn't normal. Sorry, I said that word again. I need to have my own thing that I do."

He shrugged. We never did spend much time on what I might do with my life beyond lining up his hairbrushes and ironing his costumes.

The preteen version of desire washed over me. The preteen version of desire is eccentric; I wanted to bite the fleshy part of Birdy's upper arm or gnaw on his hair.

"I could still be your husband when we're old enough," I offered.

"Oh my god, how many times have we talked about that?"

"I know. You can talk about something more than once. Maybe we've changed our minds."

Birdy looked at me with affection. "I haven't changed my mind, Roland. When it's for me to settle down, I'm gonna need a man. A big man."

"I'm going to be a big man. My mom says I look like the rapist, and he was big."

"You know what I mean. I need a strong man who will, you know, go hunting and hang great big moose heads on the wall but then treat me like a china doll when we're in, you know, in bed."

At the time I had no answer to this, but were he to say this to me now, with fifty-odd years of men under my belt, I'd roll my eyes and quote Quentin Crisp the way he admonished starry-eyed gays with dreams of perfect love: "There is no Great Dark Man." That grim truth learned early could've saved us both a lot of heartache. There simply are not enough suave Egyptian shipping magnates to go around, no matter how badly you pine, how famous you are.

"But we'll always, always be best friends," he continued. You'll live with us. We'll talk about current events, even though current events are dumb."

"Okay." And with that, my anger at him receded. I was getting worked up over nothing. Birdy would always be my friend, and we'd share his compound, and he'd have mellowed nicely by then, so we wouldn't need to talk constantly about his career, and we could indeed talk, airily but earnestly, about current events. I never thought about current events except for when it was my turn to do current events in class and I had to cut an article out of the *Tribune* about something in town that had burned down. But I'd be mature by then too, so surely I'd also care about topics outside myself. I smiled as I pictured this happy future tableau.

MY MOTHER GOT HOME, shaky and pale. The skin beneath her eyes was all pinched and silvery.

"Roland, Birdy. I have something I need to talk to you about."
She sat at the kitchen table, so we joined her. "I've been given an
opportunity, a therapeutic opportunity, that I would be foolish not
to accept."

"Like a … job opportunity?" I asked.

"No, Roland. Did I say it was a job opportunity? I'm sorry. That
was abrupt. I'm sorry. I have been given the chance to undergo
intensive one-on-one and group therapy with a very esteemed—I
would even say legendary—psychotherapist in Minnesota."

"What's that?" I asked.

"What's what? Minnesota? It's a state in the American north."

"I knew that," said Birdy. "We both knew that, Roland. We
wrote down all the states for geography last year."

"So, this is a two-week thing, and of course I dread leaving the
two of you alone for so long. But—ugh. After all my suspicion
about your choir teacher—"

"Dr. Stock," I said, annoyed that she didn't just say his name.

"Dr. Stock, yes, I know. Don't you think I know his name,
Roland? Please, I'm feeling mobilized, just let me get through this,
okay? Dr. Stock has very generously offered to fund this opportunity. Ordinarily I'd find such generosity problematic and possibly
even sinister, but I'm borderline desperate at this point, and also it
would be pigheaded of me to not give him the benefit of the doubt
after all his counsel and—given all his credentials, so—"

"So you're going on vacation and Dr. Stock is paying for it?" I
was tetchy again all of a sudden, after Birdy had just disarmed me.

"It is *not* a vacation, Roland. Have you been listening to me?
This is an incredible opportunity to address my emotional problems with a brilliant doctor. Dr. Stock himself studied under her. I
don't mean *under her*, as in under her body! Oh! A ha ha ha ha!"

We watched her buck and jiggle with crazed laughter. But she
quickly regained her composure.

"The process—it'll be very intense, but I'm ready."

"I think it sounds really good," Birdy said. "Are you going to stay in a motel?"

"No. It's an immersive experience. It's a farm with a big house on it, and we'll all stay there. The patients, I mean, not the three of us. Oh!"

"That sounds so good," Birdy said again, to pre-empt more laughter from Margaret. "Sounds so relaxing. And we'll be fine here. You don't have to worry about us."

Margaret smiled and touched Birdy's cheek. "Nice try, dear Birdy. You won't be on your own. I've made arrangements."

"What kind of arrangements?" I asked. Margaret didn't have friends. Was she going to farm us out to some industrial care complex?

"Well, Dr. Stock has graciously offered to host you while I'm away."

I didn't need to look at Birdy. *Ooh, Dr. Stock's house! His book-shelves and underwear drawer and the mysteries of his medicine cabinet!* Still, it was only weeks ago that my mother'd had the man pegged as a pedophile. That he had effected such an about-face in her so quickly was practically sorcery.

"Don't say it, Roland," she said, her palm a stop sign in my face. "You think I'm flimsy for trusting him after all my misgivings. I can assure you, I've done my research. I've asked around, and all my doctor acquaintances hold him in the highest esteem. He's won some prestigious award several times, I forget what it's called. I have it written down somewhere. I've come to believe that Dr. Stock is truly a community-minded person. It was hasty and well, yes, probably not correct of me to write off another person so quickly. I have—there is—I have regret. Okay? It's been a difficult year, and I am sorry that I—well, I'm sorry. Okay?"

"I feel bad about things like that a lot," Birdy said. "I'm working on trying to be nicer too."

"But if either of you have a problem with staying with Dr. Stock, I can make other arrangements."

"No!" we said as one.

My mother pursed her lips and smiled. "Oh, good. I didn't think you would. I know you enjoy Dr. Stock. We all do. Isn't it nice that we have consensus. You're growing up so fast."

"I DON'T EVEN want to talk about it, it's so exciting." Birdy's breath smelled of vinegar. It was a hot night, and we were face to face on my damp pillow. I was shirtless; Birdy wore a cotton top with pink ribbon straps. I don't know where he got it. Might've been my mom's, culled from one of the boxes in the basement.

"I know. It'll be so fun. But yeah, it's hard to talk about. Anything could happen. That sounds gross. You know what I mean."

"We have to be—not gross. We have to be—not like how we are right now. At least until he gets to really know us. And then we can be—maybe we can all sleep in his—I bet he has one of those beds that has the big poles at the corners."

"A four-poster bed. Probably, yeah. It'll be—I haven't spent a lot of time with a man. I mean, there was my mom's boyfriend, but he was creepy. I shouldn't say mean things about someone who's dead."

He sighed and wriggled. It was such a hot night.

"It's too hot," he said. "I'm gonna go back to my bed."

This hadn't happened before, and I felt spurned. But it was hot. He rolled over my body onto the floor and into his own bed. Within minutes he was breathing his deep sleeping breath. Dr. Stock probably did have a four-poster bed. But not one with a canopy. A canopy would be frivolous, and Dr. Stock was the most consequential person I'd ever met, possibly more so than Margaret, who was equally consequential but prone to nervous breakdowns. There was no way Dr. Stock would ever have a nervous breakdown. A wintry crisis of faith, perhaps, but never would he open and shut cupboards until the sound became dreary percussion, nor would he ever type the air.

WE HAD CHOIR PRACTICE twice before my mother left for Minnesota. She drove us there but didn't sit in. She'd clearly done her due diligence, and now she was preparing herself for her therapeutic odyssey.

We mastered "Wander Through the Palms," more or less, and moved on to a song called "Make Our Garden Grow," which was stately as a hymn but contained no religious references. It was a beautiful piece, much more rousing than "Wander," and as we bumbled through the first run-through I found myself singing louder and louder, until Birdy pinched me on the arm.

"That was a song by Leonard Bernstein," said Dr. Stock cagily. "It's not technically a hymn, but it has a robust sincerity that I find so rousing. If you don't tell anyone, I won't tell anyone."

Birdy and I cackled like fishwives.

"I like this song so much!" Birdy screeched.

"Ah, good. I'm glad."

"I like it so much, I can't even tell you," I said.

"A second vote of confidence! I thank you."

Suddenly everyone else was yapping about their love of "Make Our Garden Grow." We drew back at the sycophantic furor we'd unleashed. Rehearsal was almost over, so we slipped off our riser and out the door. I stuck my chest out and grinned into my hand. We'd been conscripted into an adventure involving, probably, heavy velvet curtains held open with golden rope, and an eerie orchestral doorbell, and a four-poster bed. Intrigue could happen when I was with Birdy, and even as we jockeyed for Dr. Stock's affection, I stared at Birdy with a bewildered, cocked head, like an infant might do at the sight of a dangled diamond earring.

THE NIGHT BEFORE Margaret left for the retreat, she came into our room. We were on our beds, reading Wonder Woman comics. She sat on Birdy's bed, sighing, her arms limp at last after a day of manic flapping.

"It's nice to see you both so snug. You know, I don't have to go. If either of you are feeling at all like you'd rather have me here—"

"No!" said Birdy too quickly. My mother slumped a little. "I mean, we're fine, we're so happy you're going to the therapy farm and you'll be all better when you come back."

"That's the hope, Birdy. I'm quite anxious about it. I know I'm going to have to … delve. And share. That sort of thing has never come easily for me. Roland can tell you—I like to get on with things. That approach has always served me well. Well, until now. I'm sorry, Birdy. You've really gone from one domestic jackpot to another, haven't you."

Birdy slid down the bed and put his arm around my mother. "I like it here so much, Margaret. I still sometimes can't believe that I live with you guys. I wonder what's going to happen to my brother. He's not tough like we all are. If his girlfriend ever breaks up with him … all he has is his girlfriend."

My mother bent her head to Birdy's head. It was a gawky tableau; even with two kids clamouring for her affection, she still couldn't relax into a soft exchange.

"I hope you don't expect me to take him in too! No, but really, I'm sure he's fine. Boys like that, you think there has to be a soft underside, an Achilles heel, but quite often, all there is is more boy. You two are special, which isn't necessarily a good thing. But you'll be fine. And I'm going to be fine, and the three of us are going to be fine. What if the therapist makes all the patients wear pyjamas, or makes us talk like babies? Stop, Margaret. Stop stop stop. Well, goodnight, then. Dr. Stock is picking you up at nine tomorrow morning."

I WAITED UNTIL I heard her bedroom door close.

"What if she doesn't come back?" I asked Birdy. All through my childhood I was prone to these sickening visions of my mother leaving the house to run errands and never coming back. Maybe it was because my biological father was nothing more than a story told haltingly every few years, when Margaret had had more than one cocktail.

"Why wouldn't she come back? Margaret would never do that. She's a Virgo."

"What's that?"

"It's her star sign. She mentioned it a while ago when she washing dishes she'd already washed. She said, 'Don't mind me, I'm a Virgo.'"

"So Virgo people are—they like to wash dishes?"

"I guess so. They're—they like to do things a certain way, or something."

"What's your star sign?"

"I don't know. She told me, but I can't remember."

We went silent. Ordinarily we'd have talked into the night, but that night before we went to stay with Dr. Stock, we both fell asleep with our reading lamps still on. I remember seeing stars behind my eyelids, literal star signs like we'd just talked about, only now they were stuck in the dirt along a strange highway, twinkling their bland warnings as I sped past them in an invisible car. "80 km/h." "Rest Area 1 km." "Stop."

"UP UP UP UP UP!" Margaret was bent over me, wearing more makeup than I'd ever seen her wear: dark slashes of eyeshadow and blush. She looked like she'd been beaten. "Caesar's in the kitchen! I'm all packed and ready. He's going to drop me at the airport and then you'll be free of me. Here we go!"

We frantically danced into T-shirts and jeans. We gathered our duffle bags stuffed with two changes of clothes and all the socks and underwear we possessed, and we padded to the kitchen, where Dr. Stock was sitting at the breakfast table, sipping from a coffee mug held in both patrician hands.

"My two house guests! Good morning!"

"Are we late?" Birdy asked him. "We were so asleep. It's like we were in comas."

"Nothing more restorative than a sound sleep. I did not sleep soundly, I must admit. Not since my nieces were small have I been in charge of youngsters. I'm an old bachelor—you'll have to bear with me while I get my bearings."

There was so much going on at once—my mother in her makeup, making sure the stove was off, the taps shut tight, once again checking the stove; and Dr. Stock, getting up to pour himself another cup of coffee, so tall in our tiny kitchen that I remember him crouching slightly so as to not hit his head on the ceiling, even though the ceilings in that place were quite high; and Birdy flitting about, pretending that he'd forgotten something but really just wanting to be ubiquitous—that I started to hyperventilate. I went to the bathroom and breathed into a bath towel.

WE PILED INTO Dr. Stock's car—not the one he normally drove but a boxy red thing, the sixties version of an SUV—and he told us to buckle up.

"I love that you're a stickler for seat belts," my mother said. "I am too. Aren't I, Roland? What's the first rule when we get in the car?"

"Buckle up," I said robotically. I could tell that she was a breath away from nervous collapse. I'd do or say whatever it took to get her on the airplane.

"I like your new car," Birdy said. "It's like a little fire truck."

"I thank you, but this isn't all that new. I have a few vehicles. I change them up capriciously."

"Me too," Birdy said nonsensically. He could say nonsensical things, and they'd fold neatly into an open-ended conversation, whereas I'd say something stupid and stop things cold. That's a social something I learned from Birdy that I use every day at the salon: if you toss out as many comments as you can conjure, none of them will land as awkwardly as they would if they were issued as periodic edicts.

At the airport my mother hugged us as though she were heading off to war.

"Can we call you?" I asked.

"No, I wish you could. We're not allowed outside contact. But—oh god, I feel like I'm doing the wrong thing."

"You're not, Margaret," said the doctor. "I promise you, you're saving your own life."

Margaret stood and waved at us until we'd driven out of sight. I had another flash of fear: her plane could crash, or she could fall in love with another patient and start a new family from scratch.

"Are we all intact?" Dr. Stock looked at us, heavy-lidded, in the rear-view.

"I'm great!" said Birdy.

"I'm worried that her plane is going to crash," I said.

"No. No, no. We have more chance of being in a car crash than her plane has of going down."

I saw sheared, twisted metal wrapped around a telephone pole, our bodies strewn across the road, broken into the wonky angles of dropped marionettes.

"And *that* is also completely unlikely." Dr. Stock seemed to know my thoughts as I had them. I leaned against Birdy, somewhat reassured.

"I've planned an eventful fortnight for us, jam-packed. Well, with rest breaks. Fun—I've planned instructive fun. But I don't want to overwhelm you."

We headed into the tony part of Winnipeg, all manicured lawns and ancient, coddled trees. The houses got more and more sprawling. As we passed a property with three separate structures, Dr. Stock called it a "gaudy compound" and referred to its owners as "well-meaning vulgarians from Regina."

Dr. Stock's house was very tall and fairly narrow, painted black, with phallic turrets and a widow's walk.

"Home sweet home," he said.

"Ooh!" Birdy bounced in his seat. "It's like a vampire's castle. It's so nice."

"Thank you, Birdy. No need for flattery, mind you, I know my tastes tend to veer from the norm. I've always found the colour black to be—it restores me. You'll find more of the same inside."

He took our bags and led us up the staggered steps. It occurred to me that I'd never slept somewhere other than my mother's house. What if our beds were like prison beds, with wafer-thin mattresses and no pillows? What if I didn't sleep at all for the next two weeks?

Once inside we were hit by the smell of caramel and lilac.

"It smells so good in here," Birdy said. "Do you have a maid?"

The doctor laughed. "No. No servants. I hope I haven't ruined the illusion."

"No. I don't have an illusion. Thanks for having us."

Dr. Stock took us on a mostly wordless tour of the main floor.

"The drawing room." Crimson walls and black velvet furniture: a daybed, an uncomfortable-looking sofa, an overstuffed chair with shards of wood above the headrest whittled to look like antlers. An amorphous sculpture on discrete black pillars. Above the fireplace, a huge portrait of an elderly woman about to fasten the blue ribbons of her bonnet.

"The library." Books on shelves that went from floor to ceiling, with one of those ladders on wheels for access to the top shelves. Another portrait of a nineteenth-century woman, this one young and plump and contented, holding a huge clutch of yellow begonias.

"The kitchen." A long, vast space with an endless island that could've comfortably seated an informal UN meeting. There were brass and steel pots and pans hanging from a metal lattice fixed to the ceiling. It was the kitchen of a raving epicure, with two metal fridges and shelves filled with dried pastas of various shapes and colours.

"Looks like you really like to cook," I said.

"Not really. It's all for show, I'm ashamed to admit. Every now and then I'll whip up something unrecognizable and barely edible just to justify having such a massive kitchen. So if you've come for the food, you'll be very disappointed. I eat very simply. Meat is important to me. I make no bones about my love of meat. Shall I show you your rooms?"

"We each have our own room?" Birdy asked.

"It's a six-bedroom house, and the spare ones are just being wasted. My mother was my last house guest, and she died a year ago. Actually, she died in one of the bedrooms. I won't tell you which one. Does that unnerve you? To possibly sleep in someone's deathbed?"

I did find it unnerving. I found it very unnerving. At eleven, it struck me as grotesque; I thought people burned beds after someone died in them.

"My grandmother died in my mother's bed," Birdy said. "And my mother slept in it that night without even changing the sheets. She said she came from her mother's soil, so it was only right that she slept in her mother's soil. Isn't that gross?"

"I find it quite poignant," said Dr. Stock. "I would've liked to have met your mother. Sounds like she was quite formidable."

"Her liver exploded. She tried hard to be a good person. Roland met her. I hate it when people die."

Dr. Stock straightened to his full height so that he towered over us at the top of the stairs. "It's very important that you come to terms with the major themes, Birdy. Death, disappointment, injury. If you shut your eyes to the major themes, you're squandering your chance at a life fully lived. Do you understand what I'm saying?"

"I think so. I should get used to death. If someone dies in my bed and they go poo, I should be a grown up and lie in it."

Dr. Stock squinted at this. "Well, no. It's not quite that prosaic. We'll have lots of time to discuss this. Roland, this is your room." He pushed open the first door on the right. We went in. There was a four-poster bed.

"Ooh," Birdy oozed. "It has the kind of bed that I thought you would have! And the bedspread is so silky and satiny!"

"It's a very old bed. I got it in Madrid. I know it looks uncomfortable, but it's surprisingly cozy."

He set my bag on the bed, and we went into the hallway.

"I want to show you my favourite room in the house."

He led us to the next room on the right. Its door produced a sepulchral groan as he opened it. Again we were hit by a strange, strong smell, this time of camphor and must. A shaft of light through the window illuminated sparkling particles of floating dust. There was an easel holding a blank canvas. There was a big lump of clay on a crude wooden table. There was taxidermy: a moose head with lurid black glass eyes on one wall, and an eagle caught in petrified flight. It was spooky—in retrospect, spooky and campy. At the time, though, we were frozen with fear.

"This is my studio. I do my painting and sculpting here. I know it's a bit gloomy. Morbid, even. I hope I haven't frightened you."

"No way," Birdy said, full of fake brio. "When I'm writing a song, I like to be in sort of a gloomy, dark room. Makes everything more—like, interesting."

"You write your songs in the living room, Birdy. The living room isn't dark and gloomy."

"I think I know, Roland. Sometimes I write in the dark. You don't know everything about me."

"I think I do."

"Boys, enough. Close friends like you two should encourage and support one another. God knows you'll encounter enough animosity from strangers as you move through life."

I started to cry. Birdy started to cry.

"I'm sorry, Birdy."

"No, I am, Roland."

We hugged, as we tended to do after a spat. Dr. Stock sliced us apart with a gentle karate chop.

"Well, now, we don't need any of that, either. Men don't fall into each other's arms, weeping. Remember your dignity."

We went red with shame. All the men we'd ever known had been ninnies, but Dr. Stock's pedigreed opinion meant the world to us.

"Onward, then. Your room is at the end of the hall, Birdy."

Solemn now, we walked to Birdy's room. His bed was half the size as mine and didn't have posters, only two sad little knobs at either end of the headboard. Birdy's tear-stained face fell. He was really counting on a four-poster bed like mine. And the rest of the room was crowded with stacks of boxes, and dry cleaning still in its wrapper, and an ironing board with a dormant iron atop it.

"I apologize for the disarray. I've mainly used this room for storage. It's messy, but it's not dirty."

"You can have my room," I told Birdy. "I don't care about the four-poster bed."

"Really? Thanks."

"No switching," said Dr. Stock. "I've put a lot of forethought into the room selection."

"But I don't care where I sleep," I said. "And Birdy had like a psychic vision of the exact bed in the other room."

"I've put you in these rooms for a reason."

"What's the reason?" asked Birdy. "Do you like Roland better than me?"

Dr. Stock put Birdy's bag on the crappy bed. "Oh, now. I'm a forty-two-year-old man, I don't play favourites with my students. No, I've thought a lot about our two weeks together and what lessons, if any, I'd like to impart to the two of you. I see how close you are, but it's also apparent that you have very different developmental needs."

"I don't know what that means," Birdy said. "I thought this was going to be a fun adventure. I thought we were going to have nice chats and sing songs and that kind of thing. I didn't know we were here to learn things. Margaret didn't say anything about that."

"There will be lots of leisure time, don't get me wrong. But as an educator and doctor, I can't help but think of these two weeks as prime learning time. I'll be learning as much from you as you will from me. I've always wanted to be a hybrid mentor and parent. It's a pipe dream, but ... how does that sound?"

It sounded dull beyond words. "Sounds good," I said.

"What sort of things will we be learning?" Birdy asked, poking the thin foam pillow on his bed.

"I see so much of myself in the two of you. No, correction: I see myself in you, Roland, and I see you, Birdy, as a particular phenomenon. I'd love to be able to offer some practical and philosophical advice on the proper course of approach for a budding young man. I think that would be quite nourishing for you, Roland. Meanwhile, I don't necessarily have *advice* for you, Birdy, so much as I'd like to introduce the principle of *subtraction* to you, so you'll be able to distill the best of yourself and jettison everything unnecessary."

I watched Birdy think it over.

"Which one of us will have more fun?"

"What is fun, really? Real fun is found in quiet cultivation of a skill, like your music. Leave the amusement park silliness to the masses. No? Yes?"

Birdy cocked his head affably, but I could tell he'd rather be part of the amusement park masses.

"And what would you be learning from us?" I asked politely.

The doctor laughed. "Where to begin? Every generation has its own trajectory, its own motifs. I'm fascinated by generational differences. I want to know what preoccupies you, what your goals are—if you've already arrived at goals—who your favourite artists are, what worries you, what gives you hope. Everything."

"I'm going to be a pop star, and Roland isn't sure yet what he wants to be, but he'll be working for me."

Dr. Stock picked up a porcelain dove from a space on the bookcase and held it in both hands as though it were alive and about to take flight. "I do hope you don't really mean that, Birdy."

"Why? Everybody wants to be a pop star."

"I disagree. You could be a serious artist. I know that you are prodigiously gifted as a vocalist and, from what Margaret has told me, as a multi-instrumentalist. But that's simply not enough. What will feed your gift? Any dullard in rock 'n' roll can whip up a catchy tune filled with heartfelt clichés, but what will sustain you as a serious artist?"

"What? Music comes from a mystery place."

"In part. But you can't depend on the muse alone. A lot of it comes down to craft. Literature, world events, vigilant observation of human nature—your work will die on the vine without those tributaries."

"I don't think so. I think it's going to be really great."

"And *that*, Birdy, is the reason why I've placed you here, in the most modest bedroom. Your self-confidence is an asset, to be sure, but it will also lead to your downfall. You need a bit of a course correction, in my opinion. Eradicate the bad habits, the hubris—"

"What's *hubris*?"

"It's pride, excessive pride. The danger of hubris is ... significant. I'd be remiss as your friend and, dare I say, mentor if I didn't help you recreate yourself as a confident but prudent person. And you"—he pointed at me—"you need a good fluffing up."

This sounded sexual but also mumsy and not sexy. I turned my head away.

"I want to fortify you with a bit of swagger. You're a good-looking, thickset young man with a supple mind. There's no reason for your ... lack of direction. And so, I've placed you in the nicest bedroom to bolster you. Not that a bed is going to transform a person. Please bear with me—I'm clearly not a parent, so all my silly theory may have no real-world value. Let's go down to the kitchen. I don't normally eat lunch, but I know I need feed growing boys. I have a gorgeous beef and kidney casserole from the other night in the fridge."

Birdy clutched my arm as Dr. Stock led the way out of the room.

"Kidney? Like body-part kidney? I can't! I'll have to chew it and then spit it on the floor when he's not looking. I had a nightmare once where my mom made me eat tonsils. Oh my god, Roland. What if he makes us eat tonsils?"

AS DR. STOCK warmed up the kidneys, he battered us with all manner of brainy questions that he must've known we had no way of answering.

"I find myself at such odds with the overwhelming pretense of Susan Sontag. I want to embrace her as a cultural critic, but she's so ... random. What do you think?"

We both shrugged. Birdy silently gagged at the smell of our dinner, ignoring the doctor's question.

"What is honour, as you understand it, in 1968? Does honour still exist, or did it die in some crucial way during the last war?"

I could only shake my head, sweating. He could've been speaking Russian. Why was he doing this? From all the reading my mother had forced upon me, I was maybe somewhat more articulate than the average kid my age, but it's not like I displayed real precociousness—certainly not in the presence of Dr. Stock, who only made me tongue-tied. And Birdy made no bones about his disdain for anything other than showbiz.

Was the doctor just amusing himself? We'd only been in his house an hour and I already felt a dizzying uncertainty, a kind of seasickness.

There were potatoes and peas amid the body parts. I forced myself to swallow everything that wasn't viscera while Birdy pushed around the gore on his plate.

"You two need to develop your conversational skills. It's key. You need only have superficial knowledge of most topics to get by. Major scholarship is not required. After lunch we'll take a drive to the outskirts and go spidering."

"What is that?" Birdy asked.

"One of my passions. Manitoba is surprisingly fertile ground for an assortment of spiders. I like to hunker down, good and close, with my magnifying glass and jot down the spider's taxonomy."

"I don't like spiders," said Birdy. "I hate them. I don't want to get close to them."

"That's understandable. It is the most common phobia. We'll dispel those fears."

"I don't want to. I'll throw up. You guys can go. I'll just stay here. I won't touch anything."

Dr. Stock looked long at Birdy. "No giver-uppers in this household, Birdy. I promise, no harm will come to you."

I was never the enterprising one, but it felt unwise to disappoint Dr. Stock on the first day. His odd hardline approach with us had already snuffed out most of our fantasies, but we were still his students, and Margaret's emissaries.

"Even if you just come for the ride," I said. "You can sit in the car. Please?"

"I—okay."

"Excellent. Go wash your hands, and I'll see you in the car in five minutes."

"THIS IS AWFUL," Birdy said, as we washed our hands in the kitchen sink. "This isn't what I expected at all. He's nerdy and weird. He thinks we're, you know, like boys. I just want to go home."

"He's getting to know us. And we're getting to know him—"

"Yes, and he's gross."

"He's not gross. He's a doctor. He probably thinks this is what Margaret expects of him, to have us doing things and learning things. It'll be okay."

"Yeah, but you don't have the gross bed."

"We can switch after he goes to sleep."

Birdy dried his hands on his pants and then grabbed my arm.

"You promise you won't—what if he locks me in the basement? You promise you'll come and get me?"

"Why would he lock you in the basement?"

"He likes you better. It's obvious."

My heart leapt. He did like me better. "He doesn't. He likes us both."

"Just promise, 'kay?"

I nodded and took his freshly washed hand, and we made our way to the car, careful to separate once the doctor caught sight.

WE WENT SPIDERING. It was very boring. Lots of crawling and poking at foliage. Birdy watched from the car until he gleaned the total absence of danger, then he slouched over and sighed incessantly as we knelt and ogled.

"Ah yes, *Bassaniana utahensis*!"

I jerked back, startled by Dr. Stock's fervour. He handed me the magnifying glass and made me look at it. It was a commonplace black spider, the sort my mother would trap in the bathtub with an upturned glass and release in the backyard.

"The good ole Utah crab spider. No great discovery, but it's a good-looking spider. So imposing, don't you think?"

He searched my face. I smiled.

"Yeah. It's so interesting." I gave him back the magnifying glass.

"Isn't it? We bumble through the days, completely oblivious to this teeming underworld. I find it quite comforting."

"Yeah. Definitely."

"Kill it," said Birdy. "Shouldn't you kill it after you know what kind it is? To be safe?"

Dr. Stock dropped the glass in the grass. "Birdy. What casual brutality. *Bassaniana utahensis* is completely innocuous, and even if it wasn't, do we kill a creature because of its capacity to do harm? If that were the case, would there be a soul left on the planet? What do you think, Roland?"

I looked at the doctor. I looked at Birdy. I looked at *Bassaniana utahensis*, still frozen on its leaf.

"Well, I guess you should probably let something live as long as it's not trying to kill you."

"Nicely said, my boy. Birdy, so much of being a man is about these small negotiations. Nietzsche wrote beautifully on the topic. Will you be a leader, or will you be a follower?"

"I will be a pop star. I'm going to sit in the car."

"If you must. I'm not going to force you."

Birdy went to the car.

"FUCK," SAID THE DOCTOR. I gasped. The awful glitter of a handsome man saying *fuck*—I'd rhapsodize over it after the doctor turned in that night, as I lolled in the four-poster featherbed.

"I'm sorry. I'm sorry. That was inexcusable. I'm imposing all my quirks and obsessions on you, and that was never my intention. I want this to be a free exchange. I guess I'm just so thrilled to have your company. I'm a middle-aged man, and I've always wanted a family of my own, but that's not in the cards."

"You could still have kids," I said. "Men can have kids when they're, like, ninety."

"My predicament is more complicated than that, I'm afraid. I won't bore you with the details. I've considered adoption, but society looks upon a family-minded bachelor with such ... malignant suspicion. I'm grateful to have my students, all of you, even the less promising ones. I want to tell you something, Roland."

He paused. Finally I asked him what it was he wanted to say.

"Birdy is talented," he said, as though no one had ever observed that before. My eyes went to a patch of roadside buttercups. "But what would you say if I told you that you're more talented?"

"Umm. I'd say tell me another one."

"It's true. You're more talented than Birdy, Roland. Take it from me."

"More talented at what?"

"Music. You're the real musician."

I snorted and smacked a knee. Had he not heard me honking and whining in choir? Unless I incurred a brain injury, the kind that makes people suddenly start speaking languages previously unknown to them, there was no way I'd ever make even a mediocre musician.

We walked back to the car. I was stunned speechless by Dr. Stock's opinion. As we headed home, he resumed his genteel commentary.

"Your mother is a force of nature. Once she's well again, I foresee an astonishing future for her. I am sorry that your father isn't part of your life, but with Margaret at the helm, you really don't need anyone else."

Birdy squirmed in his seat. He hated that the doctor seemed to be addressing only me.

"My dad gave me away," Birdy said. "He beat me up when I was little."

"I'm very sorry to hear that, Birdy. What an ordeal. Thank you for sharing that with me. I must say, it does help to explain the contours of your personality."

"Is that good?"

"It's neither good nor bad. Just as it's neither good nor bad that Roland's conception was the result of a brutal attack. I mean that Roland's origin is neither good nor bad. Your mother's assault is horrific, of course."

I bristled. We both had maudlin family stories, Birdy and I. But I wasn't shameless about it like Birdy was. I'd rather have died than tell Dr. Stock that my father was nothing more than unbidden sperm, but it was a given that Margaret would've disclosed that within minutes of meeting Caesar Stock.

Shamelessness: unbecoming but effective. Shamelessness is rewarded almost always. For example, Birdy is famous now, and I sometimes have to pay for groceries with rolls of dimes. And there's a young hairdresser with his own salon on Portage who photoshops his face onto magazine covers and posts them as legit on Instagram. "Jordan Pettigrew Shares His Truth" (fake *Vogue*). "At Home with Jordan Pettigrew and His Cocker Spaniel" (fake *Architectural Digest*). Shamelessness. It's too late for me to learn it.

"I have an idea," said the doctor. "After dinner, let's all go for a jog at the track by my house. After we've digested our meal, that is."

I felt Birdy's fingertips press into my thigh. We'd just been coerced into looking for spiders, and now we were being made to jog. Our fantasy had collapsed. The coming fortnight suddenly felt like hard time.

BIRDY RAN HIS HAND along the lid of the black baby grand in the doctor's living room.

"Can I play your piano?"

"Of course. But I thought you were a guitarist."

"So far I know guitar and baritone ukulele. But I want to learn piano. If you could show me a couple of chords, I can figure it out from there."

"Well! What confidence! Well done, Birdy. You may very well be a prodigy, as Margaret touted you. I'll show you what I know, but I'm not especially adept. I love to play, but my progress plateaued decades ago."

Dr. Stock nudged the piano bench back with a knee. Birdy sat to his right, looking up at him with fawning eyes.

"All right, where to begin ... A Major." The doctor played the chord. "And A Minor."

"Got it. Okay."

"Try those out."

I could tell that Dr. Stock was braced for a bumbling session of pure cacophony. I was excited to see Birdy stun him with his instant dexterity. Birdy played the two chords with confidence. I could already hear the difference between him and the doctor: the doctor struck the keys with too much reverence, resulting in a muddy tone, but Birdy's thin fingers hit the keys squarely, and the chords sliced through the room.

"Very nice. Shall we try C Major and Minor?"

"Yes. Show me everything. I mean, if it's convenient."

The doctor laughed. Not his normal mannered chortle, but an honest laugh. I laughed too; it was a relief to see Birdy's confidence restored after such a bumpy morning. They went through chord after chord, eventually arriving at dark, complicated sounds and strange piano words I'd never heard. *Diminished. Augmented. Adagio.* They were the instructions of the musical pedant, and Birdy heard them, used them, and discarded them. In forty-five minutes he was roaming the keyboard with abandon, immersed in sudden song, meandering but inevitable somehow, like music I'd once known but suppressed. Dr. Stock sat at the edge of the bench, hands useless in his lap, now and then shaking his head at Birdy's virtuosity. I felt proud as his friend but also, in this canny, almost smarmy way, like I was his agent, ready to peddle him for all he was worth.

"As long as you don't fall prey to vice and delusion," the doctor said, "I see great things, great work. I know you've your heart set on—what, rock 'n' roll icon status? But I think it would be a colossal waste if you didn't pursue a career as a concert pianist. That can carry its own celebrity, a much more ... elevated, satisfying celebrity. A famous pianist will draw down only those who know and love his or her work, whereas pop stardom, that draws down rubberneckers and stupid people who only clamour for you because you've been on television."

"That's fine. Any kind of famousness will be great."

"Birdy, Birdy. I worry about you. You present as this juggernaut in waiting, but you're also delicate, fey. I can see you being taken advantage of. You need some good old-fashioned woodshed guidance. And now for Roland."

"Now for Roland what?" Birdy shot me a wounded look, like I'd had a hand in the conspiracy. I shrugged, equally confused.

"Come and try the piano, Roland."

"Try the—what? No. No way. I don't know anything about piano."

"I disagree. Come and ... experiment."

"I don't know how to experiment. I've never played anything ever."

"Come here." The doctor stood in front of the piano as though it were rare game he'd just killed. I had no choice but to sit at the piano and make ugly sounds with it.

Birdy left the bench to make room. I felt like a monster. I grimaced. I poked at a piano key. I looked to Dr. Stock; he made an encouraging blur with his hands. I touched another key. I felt like a tuneless monster.

"Excellent," said the doctor.

"No, it wasn't. I don't even know a chord."

"Yes, and it's that naïveté that will cough up original harmonic movement."

"This doesn't make any sense at all," Birdy said. "He played two notes. I can play any instrument I pick up. Music is my favourite thing in the world. Roland has no interest in it. The only reason he joined the choir was …"

The doctor issued a worldly chuckle and sat in a big black leather wingback chair. "The only reason he joined the choir was what? What prompted you to join the choir, Roland?"

"I guess I thought it would be interesting?"

"That's not why," said Birdy impatiently. "You thought Dr. Stock was nice—and handsome."

"No! That's what you thought."

"You're such a liar, Roland. We both thought the same thing."

"Enough," said the doctor. "There's no need for obfuscation. We're all friends here. It's to be expected that you'd find me appealing. You've both been craving a father's love all your lives."

"I haven't," Birdy said. He crossed his legs and folded his arms. Barricaded.

"That maybe was part of it," I said. It was less mortifying to admit to this than a secret crush.

Dr. Stock leaned forward. "Good, good. Headway. So, Roland, you saw me as something of a father figure. What about you, Birdy? What truly called you to the choir, apart from a love of music?"

"Can we talk about it later? I'm super hungry. Can we have something to eat that isn't a body part?"

"In a moment. What called you to the choir, Birdy? Do you find me attractive? Do you have daydreams of me scooping you up in my arms? Pulling you close for a long waltz?"

"Get out. No. I guess I thought you were good looking. But everybody thinks that."

Now the doctor threw a leg over the side of the leather chair, as casual as we'd ever seen him.

"I do thank you for the compliment, inappropriate as it may be. Various people have paid me similar compliments over the years. I've never traded on my physical appearance though. My own father was quite handsome, and my mother was rather plain. He married her for her money and proceeded to destroy her. She was the homely wife of the handsome Lothario, and he never let her forget it. I learned quickly that beauty is only useful in empty transactions. I can see that you are growing into a beautiful young man, Birdy. I can also see you spending that beauty in sordid, pointless ways. I worry for you, Birdy."

"Don't. I'm going to be fine. I'm not looking to marry some-body ugly and rich. I have a lot of goals."

"And what if those goals come to nothing? What then?"

I could tell that Birdy wanted to storm off, taking the stairs to his room two at a time. But he couldn't shy away from this standoff.

"Why are you being so negative? Why don't you say negative things like that to Roland?"

"Because Roland's trajectory has nothing to do with physical beauty and that sort of ephemera. Not that Roland won't grow into a fine-looking man—he's going to be handsome in a rough, tractor-pull kind of way. But I don't worry about Roland. I worry about you."

"Don't. I don't want to talk about this anymore. Please can we have something to eat?"

"One moment." Dr. Stock got up and went into his office. When he emerged, he seemed more energized. His hands trembled and his head twitched as though he'd been hit with sudden, stabbing dental pain: the trademark tics of a cokehead, I've come to learn. "Where were we?" Now he stood behind the wingback chair, kneading its slick black flesh. "Oh right. Birdy. What will you do if your goals come to nothing? What's your backup plan?"

"I don't have one. Backup plans are for try-hards. I'm really not worried about it."

The rancour in the room made my neck itch.

"Maybe we should eat something," I said.

"One moment. Birdy, I want you to picture in your mind the absolute worst possible scenario for your future. Really picture it, the absolute worst."

"No! Oh my god. Roland?"

"Dr. Stock, I think we both really need to eat something and maybe relax a little bit."

The doctor looked chastened. He was breathing through his mouth. He wanted to continue this interrogation, but he was remembering propriety.

"Oosh. I am sorry. I get so immersed. Yes, let's eat something. Pea soup? Pea soup? Let's all have some pea soup!"

We went into the kitchen and watched Dr. Stock struggle with the can opener, struggle with plucking a pot from the cupboard, struggle with pouring the soup into the pot and turning on the element. We ate the soup with unbuttered slices of white bread. My head was swimming with the events of the day, the doctor's unruly, almost pugilistic demeanour, so unlike the warmth with which he led us through old hymns and hymn-like showtunes.

"I'm not going to go jogging after this," Birdy said.

"I don't really feel like jogging either," I said.

"That was probably too ambitious of me," the doctor said. "Let's have a quiet night in. We could watch television. Please don't tell Margaret that I just parked you in front of the television for the duration of your stay."

"She wouldn't care," Birdy said decisively. "It's okay to relax sometimes, you know. We don't always have to be busy."

"Truer words have never been spoken, Birdy," the doctor said, with a mouth full of bread. We walked to the study. "Is there a particular show you enjoy that would be on right now?"

"*Ed Sullivan*!" Birdy said, instantly renewed at the prospect of variety television. "He's gonna have Diana Ross & the Supremes and also Mary Hopkin."

"I don't know those people, but I'm sure they're very talented. Mary Hopkin ... never heard of her. Roland, do you like this Mary Hopkin?"

"I like her song—what's it called, Birdy?"

"'Those Were the Days.'"

"Yeah. That's a good song."

"I've not heard it. Are you a pop fanatic like Birdy?"

"Not as much as Birdy but yeah."

"I see. Maybe I should *get hip* with the contemporary music scene. Could be curative. I'm adrift, there's no doubt about that. I'll be back, I'm just going to do up the dishes."

Birdy turned the dial on the television until he found the channel with Ed Sullivan. There was a big pillow on the couch that we threw on the floor. We lay on it on our stomachs, side by side, legs kicking idly.

"This is awful, Roland. I don't know if I can stay here. I have a really bad stomach ache. He's being so awful to me."

"I know. Sorry. I have a headache."

"Why is he pretending that you're better than me at music? It's like he's a wacko. Maybe Margaret was right and he's going to kill us or—cut off our fingers or something? He made us eat kidneys. What if they came from a person?"

"No, I'm pretty sure they didn't. He probably doesn't have company over very often. He's probably just rusty when it comes to having company."

Birdy's eyes darted to the TV.

"Ooh, it's Mary Hopkin! She's so pretty. She's like an angel, her hair is so blond."

It was true. Mary Hopkin did look kind of like an angel. Her hair and lashes and brows, on the black-and-white TV, could have been made of icing sugar. Our heads bopped to her oddly jaunty ballad.

"Is this her? The object of your ardour?" The doctor had silently entered.

We nodded, not turning to look at him. He filled the room with the smell of dish soap. We heard his old sofa sigh as he sat down.

"There's a throwback quality to the song. It's almost a madrigal."

Birdy pursed his lips. Dr. Stock was ruining the song with his big words, which had ceased to impress us.

"She's very fair, isn't she? Almost albino. Lovely, though. What's the rest of her work like?"

"She doesn't have other songs," said Birdy tightly. "She's new. This is her first single."

"Ah. What an auspicious debut, in that case. What's that swirl in the background that keeps swirling?"

"How should we know? And now the song's over. We're really trying to watch the show. The Supremes are on next. I really don't want to miss any of their songs. They're doing two songs, back to back. It said so in the TV schedule."

"You sound peevish, Birdy. I hope I haven't ruined the experience for you. Of course, you are a guest in my home, and I'm unaccustomed to being chastised in my own home. But I'll swallow that indignity. You'll find, as you progress in life, that people will generally be less tolerant of your tantrums. For now, though, feel free to let rip."

This is when Birdy got up on his palms in what I'd later recognize as cobra pose, from the time Tony and I tried to follow along to a YouTube yoga video during COVID, until we got bored and watched the rest while chain-smoking.

"I'm not having a tantrum. Don't tell me I'm having a tantrum." On TV it had gone to commercial: a housewife was so impressed by her new laundry detergent that she started jumping up and down, higher and higher, until she burst through the roof of her house.

"Perhaps we should take a step back and have a conversation about self-regulation and not giving in to every impulse. Just because you're in the clutches of an emotion doesn't mean that you're perceiving accurately. In fact, one rarely is perceiving accurately when one is in the clutches of emotion."

Birdy stood. "You've been doing that all day. You've been saying whatever's on your mind."

"With respect, I disagree. There's always strategy behind the things I say."

"Then that's worse than saying whatever comes into your mind. I'm gonna go to bed."

"But it's Diana Ross next," I protested. "You love Diana Ross."

"No. I'm gonna go to bed."

"Please stay," the doctor said. Birdy didn't even look at us. He left the room and ascended the big, squeaky staircase.

We watched Diana Ross & the Supremes in silence. They sang "Love Child," a song about an illegitimate child who won't go all the way with her boyfriend because she's scared she'll have an illegitimate child. It struck a nerve.

"You're going to be fine, Roland. I can see you with a thriving family of your own at some point. You're entering into adolescence, which is so turbulent, but you'll come out the other end as an upstanding citizen, a real pillar. Mark my words."

"I ... thanks."

Ed Sullivan ended; the late news began. I couldn't move. It was as if I'd been stilled by cobra poison. I perspired in random spots, one armpit but not the other, one tiny patch of my back but not the rest.

"Do you ever think about what kind of father you would've wanted, Roland?"

"I guess—it would—I ..." It was hard to move my mouth. "I guess someone nice who would teach me things that are—that would be helpful."

"That's very sensible. Very reasonable. I could be that sort of father. I could be that sort of father for you."

He lowered himself onto the big pillow Birdy'd been lying on. His eyes were all watery, and I was afraid he was going to cry. I never liked it when men cried; Dan had cried in our kitchen right before he jumped off the Disraeli Bridge, and for months after I had nightmares about Dan crying as his limbs popped off, one by one, like a cheap plastic doll's would if you tugged at them. Even now, when Tony's fibro is out of control and he can't help but leak a few tears from the agony, I squirm and tell him to think of playing the slots in Las Vegas.

"What do you feel is missing in your life at home?" It was an uncanny thing to ask just then, and it gave Dr. Stock the air of a clairvoyant.

"Not that much. We are very fortunate. My mother has a good job, and she takes care of everything when she's not—when she doesn't have her emotional problems. But when she's better, there's not really anything I can think of."

He looked at me with friendly suspicion.

"Maybe sometimes, since we took Birdy in, sometimes I feel like she likes him better than me. He can play all those instruments, and his voice is so nice, and they talk way more than I talk with my mom. I know he's special. But sometimes I miss when it was just her and me. But I love Birdy, and I know he's special."

Dr. Stock sat up. "You need to understand something, Roland, and I'm saying this as a fan and advocate of Birdy: talent is not a panacea."

"What is that?"

"Talent is not a cure-all. It does not guarantee happiness. If anything, I see it as a hindrance. Birdy will have to forsake so much in service to his gift and his ego. Simple pleasures will be lost to him. I'm honestly much more optimistic about your prospects. You're bright, handsome, but you're not dogged by obsession."

"Is that why you pretended that I'm better at music than he is?"

"That was ... another one of my strategies. I thought if he was destabilized in his musical confidence, he might be more apt to ..."

"To what?"

The doctor stretched his arms like he was mid-breaststroke.

"I want to be useful here. You are—I'm talking as both a friend and a clinician—you're much more at ease with the basic dictates of your gender. You're a boy, in the fullest sense. You're exquisitely sensitive, which explains your friendship with someone like Birdy, but you sense innately how to perform socially as a male child. You will be a man. Birdy ... has chosen a difficult path. Maybe it will all come together for him, and nothing would please me more. Equally possible is—he could fall into a moribund spiral. There could be—he could be felled by transvestism, or worse. He could be—I've had patients who, in the end, couldn't cope and—I've said too much. Let's just see how it all plays out."

I understood enough of what he was saying to feel nauseous about Birdy's future. I wondered if it was this house, this capacious, daunting house, that was causing turmoil rough enough to make Birdy take to his ugly bed.

"Birdy's not going to have any problems when he grows up. And if he does, he'll do whatever he needs to do to fix them. He maybe looks a bit wimpy or whatever, but you would be surprised."

"And what about you? I've heard so much about your friend, but what are your interests? What goes through your mind before you fall asleep at night?"

I froze, like I always did when someone asked me about myself. How could I phrase my stupid bedtime thoughts so they'd sound less stupid? I defaulted to the hoary sound bite I always offered when asked about myself.

"I'm going to be Birdy's assistant and clean his costumes with a lint brush and maybe even be his manager until he finds a real manager."

"Come on, Roland. I've heard that before. Who are you, really? What gives you pleasure, really? I know you're not the blinkered automaton you pretend to be when you're around Birdy. What makes you happy?"

"Hanging out with Birdy?"

"Apart from that!" The doctor was clearly irritated. "If Birdy didn't exist, how would you fill your days? What career would you pursue?"

"Don't get mad. I'm trying to think of something. I am."

He drew back. "Okay. I'm sorry. Take your time."

I made all sorts of *thinking* faces, tilting my head, looking around the room with fake awe, as though I'd just been freed from a coffin.

"I would—I would like to be around people, and be nice to them, and have them be nice to me, and maybe make them feel really good about everything."

"Okay. Vague, but it's a start." He came close again; I could see the lines around his eyes and the odd silver strand in his hair. "And how would you make people feel good?"

"I'd just be nice to them. Maybe I'd offer to brush their hair. I could even—Birdy and I did a science project on hair a few years ago, and I thought I wouldn't mind it if I was a hairdresser."

He looked disappointed. "And is there anything else you might pursue?"

"I could learn about makeup, so I could do their makeup too."

He was quiet. He turned the TV off. The silence pressed at my ears like I was underwater. I wanted to be with Birdy, safe in the four-poster bed.

"I've travelled the world, Roland. I've consorted with minor royalty, and with deviants and barflies. I've been witness to the arc of so many lives, and it has given me great insight as to what makes for a good life and what makes for a life that ends in the gutter. I like you, Roland. Please, listen to me when I say that you will regret a career in hair and makeup. This isn't opinion, this is straight reportage. I had a friend in Toronto who was a hairdresser, Alistair. There was real innocence about him—he had an auto-graphed picture of Arlene Francis taped to the mirror of his work station, and he'd touch her face every morning for good luck."

"That doesn't sound so bad."

"Alistair fell in with an older person, a man—a man with gold teeth and fourteen children. Alistair gave all his money to this man, and the man bought a Porsche Speedster and drove off, never to be heard from again. Alistair began huffing shoe polish. He started talking to an imaginary friend named Panties. Ultimately he threw himself down a well. Do you understand what I'm trying to tell you with this cautionary tale?"

I was so upset by Alistair's story that I could only shake my head. Actually it was more of a shiver than a shake.

Dr. Stock took several deep breaths. "Much has been written on the topic of the homosexual. I've read widely. The official psychiat-ric literature, of course, as well as the works of James Baldwin, Gore Vidal, and—oh, what is his name, the little one from the American south. In any case, I'm not ignorant on the subject. Capote! That's his name. Truman Capote. I've known many, many homosexuals over the years and have found them to be mostly very pleasant, sanitary, deferential. A homosexual gave me the dieffenbachia in the window there. Lars. Here and there, I have even been mistaken for a homosexual because of the fact that I never married. I am not a homosexual, however. Not at all. I am without carnality. I can't tell you how liberating it is to be without sexual desire. One gets so much done." He paused. "And what about you, Roland?"

"What about what?" This was terrifying, this exchange, but it also set a standard for me, a grinding need in me to always bypass chat and get to the pit of someone, regardless of how revolting or sad. It's not necessarily a good thing. I've lost clients over the years, and friends, and sometimes even Tony will take me to task for not broaching things with enough tact. I've told him the reason for my probing approach: once Dr. Stock lit into me with the force of his backstory and blunt questions, how could I possibly return to pleasantries?

"Do you think you're a homosexual?"

I started laughing uncontrollably. Then I settled myself and tried to speak, and the laughter started again.

"Perhaps you'd rather not discuss it."

This passive challenge sobered me suddenly. "It's not that. I haven't really thought about it," I lied.

"I need to say this, Roland. It may be that you truly haven't given it much thought. We all develop at different rates. But if you *have* been thinking about it, it's important you know that that inclination is not set in stone. You are not fated to any one lifestyle. In fact, you can change your fate in a heartbeat."

"Okay. That's—yeah. Good to know."

"I've treated many, many homosexuals, both as a psychiatrist and informally, as a friend. I consider this particular mode of treatment to be the unspoken focal point of my work. Is this something that might be of interest to you?"

"What?"

"Would you like to know a life of family and happiness?"

"Sure, yeah."

"Excellent. That's all I need to know for now. But, I wonder, what about Birdy?"

"Birdy? Birdy wants to be happy."

The doctor looked unconvinced. "Tragically, there are some inverts—homosexuals, who are so lost to the delusion that they cannot be rescued. My friend Alistair was one of those. And Birdy is headstrong, so caught up in his dream of fame that—well, that can wait for another time. So! I'll leave you to amuse yourself. Watch all the TV you want, but do be aware that we'll be up early to go blueberry picking. I'll be in my office, working on odds and ends, if you need anything."

"Okay. Thanks."

I turned the TV on. It was a Canadian game show where people stood behind a curtain making squeaky noises, and the panel had to guess who it was. We only had three channels back then—CBC, the French station, and another one out of Ottawa. I turned off the TV and went up to Birdy's room.

He was lying on his side, facing away from me, shirtless. I saw the frail column of his spine curved into a subtle S.

"Hey," I said. No response. "Hey, hey, hey."

"I'm asleep," he said finally.

I climbed onto his bed, which was rife with tiny surprise ridges.

"Are you all right?"

"He doesn't like me at all. I heard everything he just said. He thinks I'm going to throw myself down a well. I don't want to do that."

"You are not going to throw yourself down a well. I promise. I won't let you."

"We have to call Margaret and have her come get us."

"But they don't have a phone at the mental farm."

"Maybe there's a main office number or something like that. Could you go ask him for it, please? I can't be here much longer."

I put my hand on his cheek. When he was sad, he spoke his sadness so simply, and I loved him the most then. I was taller and denser than he was, and when I held him I had to beat back the feeling that I was monstrous somehow, that my affection was a form of theft.

He took my hand from his face and pulled it to his chest.

"I love you, Roland."

I almost hated it whenever he said this. I knew that he was sincere, but he was also practising for a future in which he'd profess his love to thousands of people at once, and have fanatics haunting his front door, and collect beautiful men who'd go shopping with his credit card. My love for him was threadbare, contingent on nothing at all, constant as the Winnipeg prairie we both despised.

I waited a bit before going downstairs to ask the doctor for the mental farm's main number. I wanted it to seem like this was my own request, that I wasn't running interference for Birdy.

AS I PASSED BY Dr. Stock's office I heard him on the phone, talking in an animated, almost girlish way. I pressed my ear to the door.

"Oh, I'll just bet you were visiting your grandmother last weekend! This is me you're talking to. You were drunkenly hunting for men at the Rooster and the Paper Rose. So, do tell—were you anointed up the back passage? Uh-huh. Uh-huh. Length and girth? Ooh, really? Well, kudos, Brian. You've always liked it the Turkish way. A ha ha ha ha! Please don't call me Mavis. You know I don't go in for gay patois. I am not! I am not nelly as mistletoe!"

The doctor was quiet for a bit. I realized my heart was racing. I couldn't believe what I'd just heard: Dr. Stock sounded like a different person, so unlike the measured man who had just terrified me with stories of hairdressers huffing shoe polish and my own grisly destiny if I didn't turn heterosexual.

He sighed a long sigh. "Yes, I've had them since yesterday. What? I said I've had them since yesterday. No. No! That's diabolical! I told you, I'm trying to lead them out of the lifestyle before it's too late for them. I feel very strongly about it, I'm not sure why. I see so much of myself in them—well, in the one, anyway. The other one is a prodigy of sorts, no doubt, but so, so effeminate. He reminds me of Donna Reed, but obnoxious. Roland, though, is tabula rasa. He can be moulded into—well, anything, really. It's quite exhilarating. I know it's selfish, but I do feel like Henry Higgins. It's the kind of absolute governance that I can't achieve with patients. Am I horrible? No, I'm not—I donated to the Daughters of Bilitis last year. No. No. What? Oh. Please stop harping on that. I am not a pedophile. I know, but this *isn't* ancient Greece. Well, perhaps if he were ten years older and I'd never encountered him as a child, but. Oh, look at the time! My phone bill will be astronomical. All right, darling. Ah, I see, you didn't tell me you had someone coming over. You're so prolific. No! Stop stop stop, I don't want to know. Think of your bedding! Think of your carpets! All right. Kisses."

I heard his footsteps. I ran into the hallway and up the stairs. My head felt like it was packed with cotton. I'd never heard a man talk to another man that way. My conversations with Birdy sometimes verged on a naive version of camp, but it was interspersed with innocent speculation about space aliens or what it would feel like to be a ghost. I couldn't picture the two of us ever trading barbs like Dr. Stock and his friend. It was so brittle, their rapport. Then, as I got back into bed with Birdy, I grew angry. I didn't know who or what I was, but I would not be manipulated into Dr. Stock's idea of the appropriate me. I would not be duplicitous, scaring kids with portraits of gay suicide and then, behind closed doors, letting rip with the florid talk that I'd just warned against. If I'd been debating my identity after the doctor's lecture, I was immovable now: I'd grow into whatever I was meant to be—hammy fag or dutiful dad and husband—and I would not contort myself or forsake my best friend simply because he'd already sorted this stuff out.

"Did you get the number?"

"No. I think he went to bed. I'll ask him for it in the morning."

"Oh, thank you. Oh god. Thanks, Roland."

"UP AND AT 'EM, bed buddies!" Dr. Stock's voice was rousing but shot through with contempt. He'd caught us cuddling in bed. Birdy only moaned, but I sat up and looked the doctor in the eye. He clucked his tongue and shook his head, but I was resolute now, next to Birdy. I would not chuckle and shrug. I could weather this fraud's judgment. I was suddenly so sure of myself. This surety would wane later, of course, but that morning I was militant.

I got out of bed.

"Birdy," Dr. Stock pressed. "Time to get up."

"He doesn't feel well."

"I don't believe that. There's no getting out of blueberry picking, Birdy. Time to get up."

"I told you, he doesn't feel well. I'm not lying."

"That's disappointing."

I said nothing.

"Okay. Get dressed. I'll see you downstairs."

Dr. Stock left the room. Although it was several sizes too small, I stuffed myself into Birdy's flamingo-print T-shirt.

"I DON'T HAVE to tell you how inappropriate it is for you two to be sharing a bed." He poured me a bowl of Corn Flakes.

"Why?"

"Why? Did you retain nothing from our conversation last night? I'm on your side, Roland. I want good things for you."

"I have good things." I'd never been so mouthy with an adult—Margaret would've levelled me in seconds—but I couldn't stop myself. I looked the man over: all his beauty, the wavy hair and chiselled face, all of it seemed like a put-on now. His hair could've been a toupée, his face a feat of expert makeup.

"You baffle me. So ornery all of a sudden. What happened to the thoughtful young man I've come to know and like?"

I cocked my head like a movie delinquent and shovelled cereal into my mouth.

"We're driving to Beausejour today. The berry bushes there are especially fecund."

"I don't really feel like it."

He pushed his hands across the table, stopping just short of my bowl. "Your mother encouraged me to keep you occupied as I see fit. I could just as easily have the two of you doing yardwork. How would you like that?"

"You're not my mother. I don't have to do what you say."

"Uh—no, you do. You really do. Again, I'm simply astonished by this new, surly Roland. I've been so accommodating. What have I done wrong?"

"Fine. Let's go."

He went upstairs. He returned with two metal pails.

WE DROVE THROUGH the city's core, past the vast, ugly warehouses that lined the perimeter road and onto the narrow highway to Beausejour. The doctor's berry buckets clattered on the back seat. Neither of us spoke until we reached the treeline, the sight of which disarmed us somewhat.

"I heard you on the phone last night." I had no chops for confrontation, but I had nothing to lose. I was speaking for Birdy and me.

"You were talking to someone gay, and you were talking like … a fag."

I'm sure I saw panic crawl across his face before he covered it with a steely smile and a snooty little chuckle. "First of all, that was an incredible breach of trust, Roland. Respectable people don't eavesdrop. And you've completely misread the conversation. I was talking with a patient, and we were engaging in focused role play. Don't insert yourself into foreign terrain."

"You told me I was going to kill myself if I became a gay whatever, and then it turns out that you act like a fag when nobody's looking. You said that if I was ten years older you'd go out with me."

He tried the snooty chuckle again but could only swallow with an antic Adam's apple. "This is just—I don't even know where to begin—I'm a doctor. I have my own home, and a vacation property. I'm a community presence."

"And you're a fag."

"*No!*" He splayed his fingers on the steering wheel. I was sure he was going to hit me.

"You're going to kill me and throw my body in the bush."

He covered his mouth. "I'm not sure why this conversation has devolved so completely, but I am not going to kill you."

"Yeah, right."

WE PULLED UP to where Dr. Stock thought was a good blueberry spot. He got out with the pails. He led me to a verdant, mostly shady spot two minutes from the highway. He knelt to scavenge and pluck. I stood there, sulky, sighing often.

"I didn't mean to deceive you, Roland. My intentions from the outset have been honourable. I only wanted to help you. Both of you. I only wanted to save you from the devastation that has been my constant companion since I was—since I was your age."

"We really liked you. We could've just hung out and done relaxing things for two weeks. We didn't need to hear advice and stories about sad people. What for? Me and Birdy didn't feel all that bad about ourselves, like, at all. We didn't need advice."

"I'm trying not to weep," he said, not looking weepy at all. "I got lost in my own selfish fantasia. I wanted to be this indelible father figure who would—oh fuck, I don't know. Who would keep you from harm. I'm not a happy man, Roland. It's all a ruse. A ruse. After the day's work is done, I sit in my underwear in the library and listen to Ma Rainey and drink. Sometimes there is cocaine. I shouldn't be sharing this with you."

Honest at last, he won me back, kind of, enough that I could look at him again. "It's okay. Why aren't you happy?"

"Where to begin? I'm so alone. I've never been loved. That's not true. Patients have—there has been transference, of course. But I've never been loved, in that wonderful, wholesale way, by someone whom I could safely love back. I've tried. I've tried desperately. Some of the pathetic scenarios I've fallen into in the name of love … you wouldn't believe. Do you know what I'm saying? I'm confiding in a child. I'm horrible. Horrible."

I thought about patting his knee or his shoulder, but I held back. My crush had evaporated. He could speak his sorrow to me, but I didn't want to get stuck in some gummy, weird clinch with him.

"My mom has never been in love, and she's happy. Well, before she went crazy."

"Your mother is a remarkable woman. A one-off. I'm not like her. I'm weak. I don't know how to soothe myself. I need to be loved. I look into my future and all I see is—I'm sorry. I'm sorry. I'm sorry. Please don't tell your mother that I had a nervous breakdown in your presence."

"I won't. I'm good at keeping secrets. Hey—but you have friends, at least? You have that guy you were talking to last night."

"Brian? No. He's a satyromaniac and very unreliable. I met him in one of those pathetic scenarios I mentioned. There was—please don't tell your mother—this hole in the wall at a gas station in

Toronto, and I used to sit beside it for hours, waiting for—what? Contact, any kind of contact. I had … contact with Brian, but most of the time the men walked off because of the—please don't tell your mother—the horrible, horrible sucking and smacking and gnawing bunny noises my mouth made because I was so desperate."

Again I was lost. He sat beside a hole in the wall at a gas station? Where in the gas station? By the pumps? And what would he do with the men on the other side of the hole? Would they talk through the hole? Why couldn't they just meet up at a restaurant?

"Everybody here likes you. All the moms like you. I'm sure some of them want to be friends with you."

"No. No. They fetishize me. And that's my fault. I put up this ridiculous facade—it's summer and I'm wearing a three-piece suit to go blueberry picking! And everyone's mother falls at my feet because they think I'm a great gentleman. It's diabolical. What if they knew about the hole in the wall at the gas station? I'd be run out of town. You should be the one giving *me* advice."

I thought about what advice I could give him. I was a child, but I was already an expert in a kind of silent subterfuge: rather than putting up a facade, I found it was pretty easy to move about unhindered as long as you didn't speak or achieve eye contact. With the doctor, though, it was too late for that tactic. He was already the princely choir director; if he suddenly donned corduroy and got a brush cut, *that* would arouse suspicion. Women would be coming to his house with sympathetic casseroles, peering past his filmy curtains if he didn't run to answer the door. I pictured him dancing flamboyantly through the house, making wavy hula arms, only to be caught unawares by a shrieking housewife with her face pressed against the picture window. That would be bad.

"Maybe you should move to California," I suggested finally. "That's where me and Birdy are going to go once he gets a little bit famous."

"California. I've been. It's not my milieu, not at all. I've been everywhere, Roland. Strange as it may seem, this is my home. It's gritty, unpretentious. It's the perfect counterbalance to my own pretentiousness. Do you not like it here?"

"Not really. It's boring. And it's not very pretty at all."

"Suddenly I don't feel like picking blueberries anymore," he said. "Do you?"

"No. I never wanted to."

He ran a hand through his hair, exposing a thinning swath. He looked very tired. We went back to the car.

"I wrote down some of the things I wanted to say to you two. I wrote it a few days ago, but it seems idiotic now. Still—can I read it to you?"

He winnowed a hand through his right pants pocket and pulled out a neatly folded square of yellow paper.

"Okay. I'm just going to read this. Okay." He cleared his throat. "You are promising young men, but I fear that you may also share a proclivity which, if not squelched altogether, can at least be concealed with constant vigilance. Here are some things that you should never do, ever." He turned to me. "Ready?"

"We want to call my mom at the mental farm. We want to go home."

He brought the yellow paper to his face like it was a handkerchief.

"No! Oh please, no. She'll be furious. She'll have me arrested. What are you going to say to her?"

"Nothing. Just that we're not really having fun and want to go home."

"Really? Neutral like that? You won't tell her I've been terrorizing you?"

"No. Never." It occurred to me again that he possibly could still strangle me and throw me in the bush.

"All right. Of course, yes. I'll call the office when we get home. I'm so sorry. I'm not a horrible person."

"I know. It's okay."

"Could I still read you what I've written? I was going to read it to you at the end of your stay with me."

"Yeah. Okay."

"Oh, thank you. Thank you, Roland."

He cleared his throat.

"Dear boys. I care about you. I want to give you some real-world advice, advice I wish I'd been given at the outset, so I didn't have to fashion my own disguise from scratch. And so: Don't touch your hair in public. A firm handshake when greeting a man is a given, but you must also ensure that your hand is warm and dry; a clammy hand has ruined the ruse of many an invert. Don't compliment a woman on her dress unless it's by way of praising her figure. Leave out shoes, accessories, and makeup, no matter how wonderful, altogether—real men don't notice nice shoes. Cross your legs at the ankle. Should a winsome infant pass by with its mother, do not squeal at its cuteness. Never express your emotions unless the topic at hand is something World War II-related. Never ask the other person if it's you or if they find it hot in here too. Don't hum. Don't roll your eyes or look left, right, or down; train your gaze on the other person and look away only in the event of a sudden, loud sound or the like. Also, do not run your hand along any surface or fabric to get a sense of the texture, ever. Do not inquire as to the well-being of a person's female relatives. Do not sigh or do anything eccentric with the sound of one's breath. It goes without saying that you should never call another man 'darling,' 'dearie,' 'Georgette,' 'Mabel,' or 'Cynthia' unless he's a confirmed fellow invert and you're in a secure, soundproof location. It's permissible to call a woman 'sweetheart,' but only if it's said in a lecherously seductive way. And don't blow on hot soup. And don't drive carefully. Do whatever you must so as not to give yourself away and ruin the ruse. Hide. Always hide until it's safe to share yourself as you really are."

It was so sad, all these fearful contortions in the name of safety. I couldn't help touching him on his padded shoulder.

"Will you stay with the choir? I'd hate it if I turned you off choral singing forever."

I hadn't thought about choir since the end of the last choir practice. But now that he mentioned it, there didn't seem any point to pretending to like choir anymore. Our choir leader was, ultimately, a sad neurotic. His once-bewitching chest hair might as well have been a patch of dried seaweed at this point.

"I love the choir," I said. "I can't wait to learn new songs."

He seemed satisfied by my lie. I'd devised my own code of deceit, nothing as ornate as Dr. Stock's cautionary list, but still a baked-in cheat.

WHEN WE GOT back to the doctor's house, there was banging and screaming coming from Birdy's room. I ran up there. I tried to open the door. It was locked.

"You've locked yourself in," I said.

"No! I've been locked in!"

I called for the doctor. The doctor arrived.

"What is it? Can't he get out? Oh, I've had so much trouble with this door. It's so sticky."

He turned his back to me so I couldn't see him fiddle with the lock. He opened the door, and Birdy shot out, screaming.

"You locked me in! You locked me in! I could've had a heart attack in there. I could've gone crazy."

"It's the door," the doctor repeated. "It's sticky."

"I'm not gonna stay here one more second. Did you call the mental farm office, Roland?"

"Not yet. I will."

"The mental farm? Oh, you mean Margaret's retreat?"

"Correct," said Birdy, oddly formal now. "We're going to call Margaret and tell her that you're trying to kill us."

"Kill you? Birdy. Birdy, Birdy. No. In any case, there is no phone at the retreat. But I could send a letter, express post."

"Hardy har har, I don't think so," said Birdy. We'll go to the post office and *I* will write the letter."

WE DROVE TO the post office. Birdy wrote the letter.

> Dear Margaret,
> I'm really sorry but we are having a bad time with Doctor Stock. It is very terrible but we'll tell you about it later. I'm so sorry to get in the way of your mental retreat but could you please come home?
> Love from Birdy

"May I add a footnote?" The doctor asked.

"No, you may not," said Birdy.

WE WENT BACK to Dr. Stock's and hid in my room, emerging only to steal food from the kitchen. He'd occasionally tap on the door and ask if we needed anything, his voice a contrite purr. We'd bark at him to go away, and he'd go away.

The next three days were very near the escapist vacation we'd been hoping for. We slept late, stuffed ourselves with fancy nut-laced ice cream from the doctor's freezer, and cuddled in bed, pretending we were mannequins.

Friday afternoon the doctor called me to the phone. My mother's voice was steady and strong.

"I'm at the airport," she said. "Are you in any immediate danger?"

"No. Not really. I'm sorry we made you leave the retreat."

"Don't be. I'm already transformed. We'll talk about it later. I'll be home tonight around nine. Did he ... has he—"

"No. But it's been weird and not fun at all."

"Sit tight, the both of you. Do not engage him. I'm on my way."

WE PACKED UP. We waited until nine, then we sat on his veranda, ogling passing headlights.

"That's for sure her."

"This is her for sure."

Finally Margaret arrived. She ran up the porch steps. She looked healthier and prettier than I'd ever seen her. She'd gained much-needed weight, and her hair was long and loose, free of the punitive bun she always wore in public. She pushed us together and hugged us hard.

"You look so pretty," Birdy said.

"I'm so sorry. Is he—where is he?"

"Don't know." I said. "It's a really big house, and sometimes he disappears into hidden rooms and things." I'd made him sound like Nosferatu, but it fit the moment.

"We're not going to engage him," she said. "Let's go. Hurry, come on."

IN THE CAR Birdy described the whole ordeal, frequently forgetting to breathe. Margaret let him ramble. When he was finished she shot her hand into the back seat and felt for our fingers.

"Big changes are about to happen. We're closing ranks. There will be no more of these ... bruising encounters with strangers. I'm at the helm now. All you to need to do is be your sweet selves. You've seen too much, too soon. That stops now. I'm not going to hide you from reality, but I'm not going to rub your noses in it either. I'm at the helm. I drank a mystic juice made of rainforest herbs, and I relived my entire life, from birth to present day, addressing and healing every wound along the way. And then I threw up. I am reborn. Do you think Dairy Queen is still open? I could really go for a strawberry sundae."

MY MOTHER DID confront Dr. Stock but, in keeping with her firm new parenting policy, refused to tell us what was said. Birdy and I both dropped out of choir. The school quietly cut ties with Dr. Stock, citing budget constraints. I saw him out and about a few times, in threadbare, poignant settings: the Sally Ann, the sock aisle at Kresge's. We'd nod at each other. I don't know if he ever found love, or a lover, or even friendship apart from those late-night phone calls with men who were just as depleted by long days of frightened, manly burlesque.

He died in '83, if memory serves. He left to mourn a sister in Buffalo, and that was it. The obituary didn't say how he died, but the in-lieu-of-flowers place to donate was the Heart and Stroke Foundation, so.

We Turn Fifteen

BIRDY'S BAND PRACTISED in the basement of our big, new house on Mondays, Wednesdays, and Fridays. The Rubies were composed of Glen Smoley (sixteen) on drums, Steven Ward (seventeen) on lead guitar, Paulie Winters (sixteen) on bass, and Birdy (fourteen) on piano and lead vocals. They did Birdy's songs as well as Led Zeppelin and Rolling Stones covers. Birdy hated these bands, but the other Rubies were all straight and kind of dumb; they refused Carole King and Joni Mitchell and Carpenters covers and could not be swayed. The Rubies were pretty good, or at least they offered solid backup for Birdy's piano and arrangements and his voice, which had emerged from a dodgy, pubescent crackle to become a soaring, supple tenor, replete with stunning falsetto and baritone notes that left the other boys shaking their heads in disbelief. They'd been a band for three months and had already played two weddings and a high school sock hop.

I was briefly a part of the band at the beginning, smacking a tambourine and attempting backing vocals, but even after several lessons from Birdy, I was still grossly incompetent at supporting his singing with anything resembling harmony. After I butchered a run-through of Cat Stevens's "Sad Lisa" that Paulie Winters said sounded like someone in hell screaming to be set free, I graciously resigned to save Birdy the awkwardness of sacking me.

The drums drove us crazy upstairs; from four to six, three days a week, it was all but impossible to focus on homework. My mother's office was on the first floor too, and she tried to ignore the noise initially, but when one of her clients had a panic attack because the drums made him feel like his heartbeat was being broadcast throughout the house, she moved her practice upstairs, to the spare bedroom.

I seldom saw Birdy. We were in the same history class, but apart from that we didn't intersect until suppertime at home, and even then he was full of stories of upcoming gigs and new songs and cheap studios that could best capture his most polished songs for the Rubies' demo. Apart from blanket enthusiasm, I had nothing to offer to these conversations. Margaret tried to ask cogent questions and say supportive things to Birdy after a long day of clients, but even she struggled. What did we know about reverb? Or legato? It seemed as though Birdy had acquired a new musical lexicon by osmosis. We could only continue to cheer on our prodigy.

Margaret, with her new degree in psychotherapy, saw patients from eight in the morning to six in the evening, Saturdays included. Her office didn't have a direct entrance, so if I was home I'd see a steady stream of people dash through the kitchen (sometimes holding something in front of their faces so I couldn't identify them) and up the stairs. Her clientele was about 80 percent women—all white women, aged twenty to sixty, many of them well dressed but some of them slightly shabby, like they'd escaped from intense housework and run all the way to our house—and the rest young men, mostly hippies and geeky guys attempting to be hippies, with their hair barely grazing their Nehru collars. Some of the guys were kind of cute, and occasionally I'd go upstairs and eavesdrop on their session, just to see if it involved anything remotely sexual. I was proud of my mother. She'd set up her practice the previous year, and word of mouth had already completely packed her calendar.

Her sessions were noisy; Margaret's approach was direct and emphatic, and it was typical to hear her all but screaming affirmation and encouragement. "DO IT! LEAVE HIM, IT'S OVER!" "YOU ARE AMONG THE MOST EXTRAORDINARY PEOPLE I'VE EVER MET, AND YOU NEED TO TAKE OUT THAT BUSINESS LOAN, PRONTO!" "HE IS BRAIN-DEAD, PURE VEGETABLE, AND HE'S NEVER GOING TO RECOVER— PULL THE PLUG!"

It was an unorthodox therapeutic model, at least for the era. Dr. Stock wouldn't have approved. But whatever healing bombast she learned at the retreat had spoken to her, bolstered her already forthright way, and people received these bland shouted orders with the force of revelation. Mercifully, she was able to shut down her work persona in her off-hours. Her advice to us was still ceaseless, but she'd offer it gently, on the couch while blowing on a hot cup of tea. She was better, plainly. But different. In beating her demons, something had been lost; she was less pithy now, less judgmental and sarcastic. I guess those are qualities that should be eradicated in a perfect, sane world, but I missed her pulling me aside in a bit of conspiracy over someone's bad job of parking, someone's wanton act of public littering.

Birdy and I had separate rooms now. It just happened, as soon as we moved to the new house. I was still hurt by the ease with which he decided on the new arrangement. That first night, I'd lain in bed, waiting for him to join me, and he hadn't. I padded to his room and found him under the covers, reading *Billboard*.

"Hey," I said.

"Hey. What's up?" He said it without inflection, like we hadn't spent the last few years in each other's arms.

"I was just ..." I struggled to speak. He was so remote just then; I had no entry into our normal patter. But I pressed on.

"I was just waiting for you. I thought maybe something was wrong."

"No. Nope. Just reading. *Tapestry* is still number one."

"Cool. I was just—did you want to—I don't know if I can fall asleep without you."

He kept scanning the albums chart, not looking up. "Yeah. You'll be okay. I don't think we should do that anymore. It's—we're older now."

"So? I don't know why you don't want to. Just because we're older doesn't mean we're not friends or whatever we are."

He looked up from his magazine. "Whatever we are? We are friends. We're not anything else. I told you a long time ago, I'm looking for someone specific, with certain qualities, and that's not you."

He had said that before, but he'd never said it so tersely, so vehemently. I was being dismissed, and I churned with embarrassment.

"Don't flatter yourself, Birdy." I fought to keep the quaver from my voice. "You don't know what I'm looking for. I was being nice. It's called courtesy."

"Okay. Sorry. I misunderstood, then. Yeah, I'm just going to stay in my bed from now on. But thanks though."

I spun around on dusty soles. How could this essential tradition fall away so easily? Part of me wanted to run back and punch him in the face. I loved him, but that counted for nil. Yes, our sleepovers had changed over the past year or so: we'd become shy with our bodies, especially Birdy. He despised the nascent odours that issued from his armpits, crotch, and feet. He cursed his sudden facial down, now dense as cat fur. It wasn't that he questioned his gender, but back then he hated to be clocked as anything other than a sexless sprite, a pretty riddle. He was understood in public as a teenage boy now, and he felt diminished, cornered.

And there were our near-constant erections. They would pop up, unbidden, from the hum of the car on a gravel road, or the hard chairs at school that pressed against our perineums, or someone's loud yawn that sounded approximately like an orgasm, or a sudden rainstorm, or wind, or the paperboy's thwack of the *Free Press* against our front door.

By fourteen I'd given up on trying to conceal hard-ons; they weren't lurid or at all meaningful, so I lost almost all shame. "Puberty is chaotic," my mother said, lying on the couch with cucumber discs on her eyelids. "Your body is not your own for a good stretch. Just please don't walk around when I'm seeing patients. There are a few who could implode at the sight of a strange boy's erection."

When I dared think about sex, my penis would ache and throb; I knew that penises didn't literally explode, but there were times I wondered if there was something medically wrong with me. (Now, at almost seventy, I would kill for one of those worrisome erections). Still, I'd sit in homeroom and fixate on some segment of the boy next to me: his vascular hand tapping a pencil against his desk, or his muscular thighs in tight jeans, or, in summer, his sculptural, hairy ankle and his bare foot resting atop a flip-flop. My distraction was so intense, I'm astonished that I passed my classes and wasn't banished to the general stream, which coaxed dim-witted kids into sturdy trades like carpentry or something secretarial.

I worried that I was growing into someone too ugly to fuck. I gained height but also width. I was broad of pelvis, padded at the hips and thighs. Were it not for my sizable shoulders, I would've been a classic pear.

Also I was suddenly an outcast. I'd never been popular and would've been friendless were it not for Birdy, but I never cared, because I had Birdy. Now, though, Birdy had this brigade of new friends, pretty, bright, tittering girls in crocheted shawls and straw wedges who were too discerning to go steady with anyone but more than willing to surround Birdy—with his dreamy eyes and wild blond hair and his rock 'n' roll band that was for sure going places!—as they walked down the hallway, like a young pharaoh with his fawning vassals. His effeminate deportment, which had previously only hindered him socially, was now received as a sign of his sophistication, and it also reassured his bright, cautious girls that he wasn't about to cop a feel or ask for a blow job. Even the odd straight guy would wave at him and ask him when his next gig was.

He only smiled at me now, in the hallway. It was a forced smile, and it vanished before I was out of sight. I couldn't figure it out; we hadn't argued or even bickered, and yet he wouldn't be seen with me in public. At home I'd ask him why he was ignoring me at school, and he'd act like he didn't know what I was talking about. How could love be so changeable? It terrified me. I took to asking Margaret if she was angry with me several times a day. If Birdy could tire of me without warning, what was keeping my own mother from tiring of me too?

My grades cratered. I didn't care. I couldn't sleep without Birdy. I'd start to drift off, then startle awake in a panic, again and again until dawn when, depleted, I'd fall into dreamless sleep until my mother shook me to life at seven. I neglected basic hygiene and wore the same clothes for days until my mother insisted I bathe.

"What is going on with you?" she asked me one evening, when Birdie had a wedding gig. "You've always been fastidious about your appearance. And now your hair is so greasy I have to wash your pillowcases twice. Is someone harassing you at school?"

"No. No."

"Have you—have you possibly been molested?"

"What? No. I'm fine."

"It's Birdy. Something to do with Birdy. You two aren't nearly as close as you used to be."

I looked away. Her diagnostic stare could always force the truth from me.

"Birdy's a rock star now. But no. It's not Birdy."

"Birdy is not a rock star. He's got the delicate beauty that teenage girls go crazy for, and he's basking in the attention. It'll pass.

Once they see that they are never, ever going to be anything more than his fan club ... it'll pass. And then he'll come around."

She stopped and sighed.

"Or, possibly, he won't. Ugh. You know that I'm a bone-deep libertine at the end of the day, but this is dodgy territory even for me. I know how you feel about him. It's been lovely, the two of you, being little—being friends. But. This is a new phase. Okay, so. Okay. I'm just going to say this: I am proud of your capacity to love. It's rare. It's great. It's a gift. It's your gift, I'm sure I had nothing to do with it. But one of the most, the most ... savage realities is that you can love someone with everything you've got, and the other person could possibly not care at all."

She went quiet. I took a chance and looked back at her. Her eyes were downcast now.

"I loved God with everything I had ... with a child's heart. And God didn't care. I cried out for him, and he didn't listen. So you have to prepare yourself. Do you understand? I don't want you to freeze over like I did for so long. I won't have it. I don't care if I have to—I don't know—put you in private school. A school for sweet boys, if there is such a thing."

"I'm not going to freeze over, Mom. Please don't put me in private school. That would be so much worse."

"Do you want me to talk to Birdy? Tell him to be more attentive?"

"Oh my god, no. Please. Please don't do that. I'll be okay. I'm just a bit depressed."

She looked placated by that. "I have resources now, Roland. We're not hand-to-mouth anymore. If you need therapy, just say the word. I know all the good people."

I shuddered. *Therapy.* If I never heard the word again—after Dr. Stock, and Margaret's retreat, and now her own practice that drew middle-class basket cases across the kitchen and up the stairs all day, every day—well, that would have been such sweet relief. I patted her shoulder and went upstairs to rub one out before lunch.

I STARTED SMOKING. I was leaning against the baseball backstop at recess, biting my nails, and Freddy Hovi, king of the burnouts and skids, came up to me, holding out a cigarette.

"Hey faggot. You need a smoke." He said *faggot* in a quiet, even courteous way, like it was my given name. I'd always felt some kinship with the skid kids; they were without pretense, some of them without hope even, slumped on the grassy hill that led down to the playground, heads in their hands like a vanquished army.

I took the cigarette. Freddy struck a match and lit the cigarette with the vacant consideration of someone used to lighting the cigarettes of drunken parents. I took a drag. I did not get a head rush. I didn't cough or retch. My eyes popped open. My vision grew crowded with dark sparkles. I suddenly felt smart. I wanted Freddy Hovi to ask me a question so I could answer it, effortlessly and with manic acuity.

"Oh, hey, faggot likes to smoke," he said, again with that odd civility. I wandered over to where the other skid kids were smoking and talking about what kind of cars they wanted and how they would soup them up with custom paint jobs and screaming mufflers. There were two or three girls, all of them skinny, their stick necks ropy with tendons and veins. We were all the same age, but they looked like they'd been living on coffee and nicotine since forever. They were scattered among the boys and shouted to each other husky, almost proud declarations of strange infirmities.

"Gina, holy fuck, last night half my hair fell out on my pillow!"

"That's nothing. Last night I yawned when I was watching TV, and my ear popped, and now I'm half-deaf!"

"I've had diarrhea since I was ten!"

And that's how it went, Birdy with his fan club and me with the burnouts. I don't know why they took to me, the burnouts. Our conversations were absurdly pointless.

"What?"

"What? Nothing. What?"

"What?"

But at least I had people to walk the halls with, and when we passed Birdy and the girls, we'd snicker and spit. My grades rebounded; I'd think of the cigarette I'd later have with Freddy or Gina or with Gina and her boyfriend Skunk, his head shaven after a protracted bout of lice, and be magically able to focus on the task at hand, be it in algebra or metal shop.

"You've started smoking," my mother said, smelling my clothes.

"I have new friends. They all smoke."

"Carry on, then. Tobacco, it seems, is a grounding herb."

OVER THE WINTER, Birdy's band saved up enough to cut a demo. It was all he could talk about at home that spring.

"Okay, so, out of all the songs I've ever played for you, which three do you think are the most like, catchy?"

Margaret and I looked at each other. Birdy had played us at least a hundred songs over the years.

"Okay, let me play you my top five, and then you pick three."

My mother smiled and gave an encouraging fist pump. Birdy took his guitar from its case.

"This is called 'Never Forget.'"

He played the song. It was a gorgeous ballad about lovers who witness a murder. The lyrics were still slightly clunky, but he'd come a long way since his first song, the one that rhymed *lake* with *clambake*.

"I love that one, Birdy," my mother said. "It was like an old Irish folk ballad. Very eerie."

Birdy scrunched up his face. He didn't like that feedback; old Irish folk ballads weren't exactly tearing up the charts.

"Okay, this next one is called 'Going Home.'"

"Going Home" was a boppy ode to a favourite hiding place. Birdy and I didn't have a hiding place, and I got lost in thoughts of where Birdy's hidden hiding place might be, but I quickly concluded that the whole thing was a metaphor for his shattered family.

"I adore that one, Birdy." My mother offered up a giddy bleat, one of many hearty sounds she'd discovered during her therapy retreat and now used when words failed.

Birdy turned to me. "Well? What do you think?"

"Yeah. Nice," I said stingily. To my mind, we'd experienced a horrific rift but were still forced to live together. I couldn't just fall in line again, like the sheep I used to be.

"Don't give yourself a hernia there, Roland. Anyway, I think that one is probably definitely going on the demo. Okay, next!"

He played the other songs, all of them melodically brilliant. With Margaret's gentle guidance, he arrived at his top three. One of them, "Butterfinger," would eventually be Birdy's first single and first hit, in 1971. It had simple, almost nursery-rhyme lyrics (*You know you really put me through the wringer / When your ring slid off that butterfinger*) that were stupid but less weirdly slapdash than previous efforts.

That night we had a dense, heavy chicken salad for dinner. Margaret apologized as we worked our way through the taupe goop. "It looked so good in the display case at Safeway, but I know it tastes like glue."

"I have an announcement to make," Birdy said, all smiley. What next? What new, exciting thing did Birdy have to announce, as I gummed the rubbery chicken shards, my filthy hair falling onto my face?

"I have a girlfriend. Nadine."

If we were in a movie I would've spit my food across the table. "Nadine Jackson? She only has one eyelid."

"Roland! We don't identify people by their infirmity. Congratulations, Birdy. She sounds wonderful."

"But I haven't said anything about her."

"I know, I'm just trying to counteract my son's callousness. What—what is she like?"

"She's really smart."

"Not really." I couldn't help myself. Birdy ignored me.

"She's really pretty."

"Yeah, right."

My mother slammed her fork down. "Roland! Enough! I probably understand why you're so taken aback by this news, but please, show some respect."

"It's okay, Margaret. It's natural to be jealous. I would be. When Roland has a girlfriend, he'll understand."

"Ha! Ha ha ha. What are you even talking about? You're so fake. You'll do anything to fit in."

If my mother weren't there I'm sure Birdy would've slapped me or possibly flipped the table. We'd come to that. I could see it in his eyes. But he didn't say anything.

Margaret cleared her throat. We knew enough not to interject whenever Margaret cleared her throat.

"Birdy. Probably what Roland is upset about—or confused by— is that he's come to understand you as ... someone who wouldn't have a girlfriend, necessarily. Not that your connection to this nice girl isn't—"

"You are a ..." I was filthy and depressed; I didn't care anymore. "A you-know-what. "I'm a you-know-what, and you're an even bigger you-know-what. Oh my god, you were the biggest you-know-what of all time when I met you. And I was borderline, but you made me all-the-way-you-know-what. And my mom knows all this. So don't pretend."

"I'm not pretending."

"I'm saying this as a clinician more than a parent, Birdy—it did seem ... inevitable to me that you and Roland would be poised to lead a more nuanced lifestyle. I'd come to understand that as fact. I think we all—well, at least Roland and I had come to understand that as fact. So it'll be an adjustment for us, but it won't take us very long, I'm sure."

"I'm not so sure," I said. "I'm not so sure at all. Have you gone all the way with her?"

Birdy did this patronizing little smile at my mother, as if to say, *What are we going to do about this one?*

"That's a very personal question. What goes on between Nadine and me is a private matter."

"Quite right," my mother said.

My nostrils flared. I'd been besieged by treachery, and ruthlessness, and bad acting. It made me want to wrap up my belongings in a cloth and tie the knotted cloth to a stick, like a vintage hobo, and walk to the arctic. My mother had her glittering new career, and Birdy had his smart, unsightly *girlfriend*, and what did I have? Cigarettes. Recess with the skids and their dreams of screaming second-hand Firebirds. I excused myself with all the grace I could muster, went up to my room, and locked the door.

I rubbed one out, weeping. I dozed. At dusk there was a knock. I stayed quiet.

"Roland." It was Birdy. He tried the doorknob. "Please let me in. I just want to talk. Please."

I scraped across the carpet and cracked the door open.

"Yes? What?"

"Can I come in? Please? I don't want you to be mad at me."

I opened the door. I stood in the middle of my room, hands on hips.

"Can we sit?"

"No."

"Well, I'm going to sit. Is that okay?"

"Whatever."

Birdy sat on my bed and pulled his legs up and to the side, like a pensive mermaid on a rock. I pretended to be interested in the sunset through my window.

"I know you think I'm full of shit. I do like Nadine, and she asked me to go steady with her, and I thought about it, and it seemed like a good idea."

"Why is it a good idea? Seriously—have you, you know, touched her vagina?"

"Ew, no! She just asked me on the way home today. I thought about it, and I really think it will be good for my image."

"What image? We're fifteen."

He whipped back his long hair imperiously.

"Remember a long time ago, when you said we had to try to fit in more? Remember?"

"That was a long time ago."

"But you were right. The Rubies are really going places. I have to focus on the future. We should both be focusing on the future."

My fists fell away from my hips. I sat at the other end of the bed. "So why do you have to have a fake girlfriend? I don't understand."

"I want to be successful. I have, like, a five-year plan. I can't be gay in public. Publicly, I mean. I have to be strategic. Once I'm famous, then ... and maybe not even then. Liberace—I know he's creepy, but it's just an example—everyone knows he's a fag, but he still pretends he's not."

"You used to be so pure. Uncompromising. You made me be myself because you were so pure."

"Things change. I'm changing. You should be changing too."

My mother passed by and paused. "I just saw a peacock!" she said, and walked on.

"We're not even friends anymore. You always ignore me at school. You're really mean, most of the time."

"I have to be strategic. I have to be practical. You shouldn't be hanging out with the skid kids. People think you're a skid now. It's bad for your image."

"I don't have an image! I wear the same thing every day. I'm ugly."

"You're not ugly. You just need to change."

"Into what? I don't have anything. I don't have a special thing like you do."

"Sure you do."

"Like what?"

"I don't know, Roland." He was all huffy now. "You'll find your special thing. But you need to stop hanging out with Freddy Hovi and the other skids. Please."

I was making him look bad, was what this chat was about.

"I don't want to ruin your *image*, Birdy. I guess I'll have to reject the only friends I have."

"Oh, good. Good." Birdy sighed. He sighed with *relief*. He was so obsessed with his own success that he completely missed my sarcasm. And he used to live for sarcasm.

WHEN I TELL this part of the story to Tony—when Tony still lets me tell my Birdy story—he just shakes his head and says I should've told Birdy to take a flying leap. Tony was a skid in his day and still has skid ways, with his mismatched socks and the little pile of Scratch 'n' Wins that forms on the floor whenever he sits on the couch. I've come to love his skid habits, partly out of fealty to my school friends, probably.

But that evening, after Birdy left the room, I was restless, scrappy. I did something I never did (and never do): I took a walk.

I stomped through the neighbourhood. I turned left at the garden centre, left again at the Mitfords' house. Twenty years later they had to dig Mrs. Mitford out from a lifetime of hoarding as she screamed for her late cat in the freezer, but when I was a kid, we considered it a palace.

I walked past some girls from school. We'd long had an unspoken pact to ignore each other. That night was no different.

Once I was clear of houses I began to talk to myself. "Who do you think you are!" I hissed at Birdy. "You may not make it big, you know. And then what'll you do? What'll you do then? Don't think you'll be welcome at our house. You are still a guest, you know. Guardianship doesn't mean anything. You're wearing out your welcome super fast, you know. I didn't like any of the songs for your demo. Your lyrics are moronic. Just because I kind of loved you *at one point* doesn't mean I still love you. In fact, when I think of you now I just want to barf forever, okay?"

From deep in the west end to downtown, I was all vitriol, then I had to stop talking because there were other people around: straggler shoppers and businessmen teetering to their cars after happy hour. Maybe I wasn't so ugly; Dr. Stock had once said that I was handsome in a tractor-pull kind of way, and he didn't have to say that. So what if I wasn't fine boned, like Birdy? So what if I didn't canter through space, shimmering with virtuosity? I had options, plenty of options. I wasn't stupid. I had lots of time to conjure a future. My mother was nearly thirty when she realized her real calling. Maybe I was also meant to be a therapist, or something in the healing arts. That was unlikely—I didn't know how to give advice or say explosive, corrective things like my mother did with her patients, but I was malleable. If nothing else, I was malleable as hot putty, and not innately horrible. No. No I wasn't. I was capacious, and kind of nice.

I found myself in Prior Park off Osbourne. During the day it was a sad little park; there were a few regal trees, but it was mainly low, poky greenery and a fountain of a nondescript, sexless child who perpetually spewed dirty water downward, as though it were the fallout of a stomach bug. Only homeless people hung out in Prior Park during the day. I didn't know anything about Prior Park at night, but as I walked through it that evening, I could make out the silhouettes of men darting from tree to tree, like slapstick spies in a Peter Sellers movie. And there were motionless clumps of men in the denser swaths of foliage.

I was so young; I thought they were city workers doing night repairs. (Night repairs on trees! I was *so* young.) I went deeper into the park, strangely unafraid of this strange environment. As I passed one of the motionless clumps, I heard faint moans and soft sucking sounds. I pulled up to the clump. I saw a man on his knees, feverishly pumping his hand against another man's crotch.

Someone put their hand on the small of my back. This was my first sex: the man cupped my buttock, and someone else grabbed my groin. I gasped too loud, and someone shushed me. The groin man felt me up at length, then pulled my face close to his. This was going to be my first soul kiss. I closed my eyes, hoping my breath wasn't awful.

"You should not be here," he said sternly. "You're not even chicken—what are you, fourteen? I don't want to get busted for kiddie diddling. Go on now. G'wan!"

I turned and ran. I was at once livid and mortified; what did he mean by "not even chicken"? Did he mean that I was an inferior cut of meat, like minute steak? And how dare he wreck my first sex! Now I'd have to wait until the next night to go all the way with someone.

Back on the street I relaxed again. I'd discovered a stunning netherworld of horny gay men. It was as though I'd been teleported onto a tiny, sexy new planet, dark and rustling with illegible male faces. And this was something Birdy knew nothing about. This was *my* planet.

Margaret was standing on the porch in her nightie when I got home. She reached out to me with strangling hands when she caught sight of me in the dark.

"Where the fuck have you been?" She was trembling. This was the first time I'd ever heard her use the F-word.

"I went for a walk."

"Oh, you went for a walk? Just getting some air? You are fifteen years old. You do not head off into the darkness without telling me. It wasn't even a week ago they found that boy on Ascot Avenue, sawn in half in a suitcase. Is that—do you want to be sawn in half, Roland? Do you?"

"No. I was upset."

"Over what? Birdy's little one-eyed girlfriend?"

"One eyelid. But two eyes."

"He was just showing off. He's an artist. His ego is very fragile. We both know Birdy will never, ever have a real girlfriend. Take him with a grain of salt! You're not normally so reactive."

"Well, and then he came into my room and said that my friends are bad for my image."

Her face contorted, as though she'd just smelled something that had decomposed. "Your image? You're a kid. You don't have an image."

I slid down and sat against the railing, feeling defeated again after my brief sexy respite. My mother gathered the folds of her nightgown and sat beside me. I was not unappreciative of her new sensitivity. I put my head on her shoulder.

"What is it, Roland? I see you in such distress lately. It really does gut me to see you so distressed all the time."

I started to cry.

"I feel dumb. I feel like a loser. Next year is grade ten. I don't know what I'm going to do for a living. What if I ... work at McDonald's for the rest of my life."

"No, no. You're much too self-aware to just slack off forever. You'll find your place. You will. You underestimate yourself."

I felt close to Margaret and thought I caught a glimpse of how our relationship might play out once I left the nest. I pictured cathartic heart-to-hearts, frequent phone calls, an honest friendship. I wanted to tell her about my experience in the park but quickly decided against it. She'd just scolded me for taking a walk.

"I don't think Birdy will take me with him when he moves to Toronto."

"Good. Why do you want to be his handmaiden, anyway?"

"I love him. Even now that he's an asshole."

She played with my hair, stopping at the crown of my head, where I worried my hair might be starting to thin.

"My father had fine hair too. Roland, I don't know anything about romantic love. I've never been in love. It's challenging when patients tell me their relationship problems. I just say something bland and try to steer them to another topic. What I can say—and please take this as pure speculation and don't get all worked up— is that Birdy does not strike me as the kind of person who'd be a reliable partner. He's going to need constant validation by an assortment of men. Gay people—well, gay men—tend to have multiple partners. I have—I shouldn't be telling you this, but I have patient who's had a thousand lovers. On the other hand, I have a lesbian patient who's been in a thirty-year monogamous relationship with a woman who's been in a coma since 1938. So."

I puzzled over that last bit. "Wait—so your patient met the woman *after* she was in a coma? How could the woman in the coma give her permission?"

"They haven't been intimate. I can't get into the weeds of my work with her. It's a journey."

"Well, I'd like to be with one person. But, yeah, they would have to be conscious, obviously."

She sighed. Her head fell upon my head. "Yeah. That's the eternal struggle. But I think you'll find that, in the fullness of time. It might not be with Birdy, mind you, but ... you'll find it."

BIRDY SOMEHOW FOUND the addresses of every record company in the country and mailed the demo to them all. Rejections trickled in throughout the summer, until every record company in the country had passed.

"This can't be happening," Birdy cried in the living room, waving the final rejection letter. "We're so good. How could every company in Canada pass on us? It's like a conspiracy or something."

"You're not even sixteen," my mother said, eating a lumpy iced chocolate object from the corner store. "What record company is going to sign children? Well, I guess there's Michael Jackson and his brothers, and Brenda Lee years ago, but otherwise ..."

"Age shouldn't matter! We're really good. I'm really good, at least. The other guys are okay, but they're—obviously they're dragging me down. I'll have to get rid of them."

"Don't be too hasty, Birdy. They're your friends. And you clearly have a lot of fun playing together. When I saw you at that retirement home last month, your enthusiasm was infectious. Everyone was bopping in their chairs. Fun is important."

"Fuck fun. Fun gets you nowhere. They're dead weight."

BIRDY CALLED HIS bandmates and dumped them, one by one. Their screams and threats carried from the phone receiver into the living room. All that weekend we heard them drive past the house, yelling the epithets they'd suppressed while they were in the Rubies.

Fucking queer user faggot your songs are stupid and faggoty, etc.

"What if they break into the house?" my mother worried. "They don't seem like the type to vandalize, but rejection can really warp a person."

"Don't worry, Margaret. They wouldn't dare. They know I'm packing."

"Packing? Where are you going?"

Birdy reached into his back pocket and pulled out a switchblade.

"That is a knife! Where did you get that knife, Birdy?"

"I bought it. At Pat's Camping Basics."

"I'm almost certain it's illegal for a fifteen-year-old to carry a knife. Give it to me. This isn't some ex-con halfway house." She grimaced. "I know that sounds bourgeois. I'm sorry."

Birdy gave her the knife after she promised to let him know where she'd be storing it, should there ever be a showdown with the fallen Rubies.

ALL THAT EVENING Birdy's basic vim seemed to seep out of him; he slipped around in his seat at the table, eyeing his salmon cutlet with weird fear, as though it might leap off the plate and affix itself to his face. I'd been giving him the silent treatment, but now I was concerned.

"What is it?" I asked him, and my mother nodded at me encouragingly, now that I was speaking again. I found this very annoying and put my left hand against my face like a shutter so I couldn't see her.

"I'm so depressed all of a sudden. Maybe my songs *are* stupid and faggoty. If they were truly good, at least one label would have seen through the bad instrumentation and signed us. Me."

"Who can say what a record label is looking for?" Margaret said. "Popular music trends change constantly."

"No. No. I don't have what it takes. I'm a local musician. I've already peaked. I've had my day."

I was in no mood for Birdy's stagy self-pity; there was a park full of cocks awaiting me. I'd been thinking about returning to Prior Park ever since my walk, and now, with the warmth of summer goading my already-riotous libido, it felt like a good time.

"You know you're good. Even talented people have to pay their dues. Did you think you were going to go straight from grade nine to stardom?"

"No. Well, yes. Everything was pointing that way. But. I'll have to adjust, I guess. Maybe ..." He looked at me like I was a box of old tennis balls. "Maybe you and I can open up a—a fabric store or something."

"Yuck. I don't want to have a fabric store."

"Or maybe a jewellery store."

"Where would we get the jewellery?"

"You're both being ridiculous," my mother said firmly. "Birdy, you are a scrappy, resilient person. You know you're gifted. But you have a lot of hard work ahead of you. Elvis Presley ate bologna for two years before he—wait. Was it bologna or wieners? Or both?"

"I'm not afraid of hard work. I'll eat wieners. I just need a bit of—what's the word?"

"Validation," I said. "You need constant validation."

"Roland ... it doesn't have to be constant, okay? I just need someone to tell me that I'm good."

"I just did," my mother said. "And what about that girl at the birthday party you played last month? She screamed for you until she passed out."

He smiled faintly at the memory of the girl screaming until she passed out, then started to stew again. "I think I'm going to go to bed early. Hopefully I'll feel better in the morning."

Once he was gone I sighed and stretched with studied nonchalance. "I might head out for a stroll."

My mother turned to me, her forefinger poised to wag.

"I know what you're planning, Roland. You're going out to look for men."

"Ew, no! No, I'm not."

"Roland. It's me. I've been hip to ... the culture of the night since I was your age."

A gawky silence took hold, and I felt my face go through a procession of strange arrangements: surprised but relieved, defiant and smiley, contrite and lipless.

"I honestly didn't go out looking for that. I honestly only went for a walk. And then I came across the park. Prior Park."

"Oh, Roland, no. Prior Park? It is so dicey there. It's not safe. And you're only fifteen. I told you about the sawn-in-half boy in the suitcase. I know that wasn't in Prior Park, but you can be sure that equally horrible things have happened there. And—oh god—VD. Did you take anyone in your mouth or rectum?"

"No! I just looked around. I swear."

"I need to put my foot down here. I don't want you wandering through the park anymore. It's one thing if you're making love with someone your own age—"

"Oh my god, Mom, no. Please stop."

"I'm just saying that I have to impose a firm rule about this. No more night walks. Okay? Don't give me your profile, you're not Barbra Streisand. Look at me."

"Okay, yes," I said, looking in her general direction.

She studied me for sincerity. "Okay. I'll trust you. But I'll also be checking regularly to make sure you're in your room."

WE WATCHED A documentary about Emily Carr on CBC. Then I pecked her on the cheek and went to my room. I'd been so excited to go back to the park that I had to take deep breaths and roll my shoulders to come down. I undressed and got in bed with Margaret's copy of Alice Munro's *Dance of the Happy Shades*.

An hour later she knocked.

"I'm here, Mom."

"Good. Okay. Sorry."

I tried to sleep but was still fidgety. I started in again with Alice Munro.

An hour later, another knock.

"Still here."

There was a pause.

"It's Birdy. Can I come in?"

"Why?"

"Please?"

"Okay, yeah."

He came in and leaned against my bureau. He still had his mopey face, but now he was dewy with perspiration.

"How are you? I'm sorry I've been weird."

"Do you mean tonight, or the past year?"

"I don't know. Both?"

I was unmoved. "And now you want something, probably."

"No. I'm not like that. Okay, I am like that, but I can't help it. I don't know how to be a nice person. Nobody showed me how. I'm—Margaret called me feral the other day. I think she meant it as a compliment, but it's not a good thing. My parents didn't show me how to be nice. I love you and Margaret, but I've always known that you're her son and I'm basically a guest. I'm sorry. I'm sorry."

"You've been such an asshole for a really long time. You became another person all of a sudden. I don't want to hang out with the skid kids, but my best friend ditched me."

"Please still like me. Please. When I get to be successful, every- thing will go back to normal."

He looked so helpless and sounded so callow. He truly believed that we'd be close like we were once he was a celebrity. I'd stupidly clung to his vision of us from when we were kids—him rich and famous in a big city, and me answering his mail and screening his calls as his assistant and, quietly, his boyfriend—but that dream had gone to ashes while I spent countless hours smoking with the skid kids, bored out of my mind and slowly disassembling that silly vision we'd devised years ago, back to back in bed.

"Can I sleep in your bed tonight? Just for tonight?"

"Why? Won't Nadine be pissed off?"

"Shut up. You know that's just a thing I'm going along with. She's driving me crazy. She's always looking up at me with that bald eye. She's so clingy. Can I just lie down beside you, and you can kick me out whenever you want?"

I thought about it. I thought about Birdy's perfect body: the hair on his calves gone golden from summer sun, his shoulder blades that jutted like wings when he pulled one of his instruments from its case. I moved against the wall to make room for him.

He rolled into me. Our bodies in concert were different now. We were undeniably men; he wrapped an arm around my waist, and I could feel his bicep working against my skin and the new strength of his guitar-toughened fingers. My breath came in gasps, and he asked me if I was okay.

"Let's just go to sleep," I said.

He turned off the lamp. We were still. And then I could feel him moving his hips slowly. He kissed the top of my spine. He slipped his hand into my boxers and onto my cock, not grabby like the man in the park, but more appreciative and diagnostic as he traced me from head to base.

"It's a lot bigger than I thought it would be. It's nice. I like it."

I ground my butt against him. We were obvious novices, but this tentative touching remains the most hypnotic exchange I've ever had with another person.

He said he wanted to put it in his mouth. I froze. I hadn't bathed for two days, and my mother had always warned me that I'd be more prone to odour, given that I wasn't circumcised. I leapt up and ran to the bathroom, praying that Birdy wouldn't change his mind as I cleaned myself.

"What was that?" he asked when I returned.

"I—nothing. I just had to go to the bathroom." I got back in bed and assumed the exact position I'd vacated. Another pause, and then he put his hand back where it was.

"Maybe we should take our underwear off," he said, already kicking off his briefs. I tried to escape my boxers as expertly but had to shimmy and wiggle like someone electrocuted.

"Sorry."

"Take your time."

Then we were naked together, my lumpy, sprawling body beside his photogenic body. It occurred to me that this would likely be the most beautiful person I'd ever be with, that future lovers would likely be somewhat misshapen and, worse, reluctant, needing to be cajoled, possibly even paid. That was not to be the case: I've had several beautiful lovers, including Tony. That night, though, I took no chances. I ran my left hand up and down his torso rapaciously, like a blind person learning a new room.

"You don't have to do crazy hands, Roland. I'm not going anywhere."

I stopped with the groping and kissed him. I pecked at him with tight lips until I remembered the abortive kiss from the park and opened my mouth. We mashed tongues together. He made a sound: not quite a moan, more like a little sigh of recognition.

"This is great," he said. I didn't believe him, but I could sense that at the very least, he wasn't bored. He wrapped a hand around my cock.

"Are you sure it's not gross?"

"What? This?" He squeezed my penis. "Not at all. This is always fun, even when it's boring. But this isn't boring. It's—yeah."

We kissed some more, and I quickly learned that my tongue was not supposed to flop into his mouth and lie there like a dead squid but should dart about playfully. I grabbed his penis—long and thin like the rest of him, with a tidy circumcised head. I shuddered and pulled his hand away so I wouldn't ejaculate. Here we were. It was Birdy and me, alert and tense, tying our erratic love in a perfect knot.

Then I pulled away.

"You said 'this is always fun.' This isn't your first time?"

"Huh? Having sex? God, no. The Birdies—we sixty-nined all the time. Guys at school at lunchtime. Umm. Guys in Prior Park.

Guys in the parking lot outside of Kickers Bar and Grill. There was this Jehovah's Witness guy who came to the door when you guys were out. And I think that's everyone. No, wait ..."

A horrible little hurricane swirled in my chest. I was dizzy. Our sanctified lovemaking was just another furtive fuck for Birdy. The whole world was having sex constantly, no big deal, as banal as breakfast, and I was a goony virgin, stupidly thinking that what we were doing was tantamount to marriage.

"You've been with so many people. I didn't know that. I haven't been with anybody. I thought—never mind." My penis went rubbery.

"You thought I was a virgin. Well, I still sort of am. Really. Sixty-nining with Paulie Winters doesn't compare to this. This is love. For sure."

"I don't believe you."

"It's true. I love you, and I know you love me. Let me give you a blow job."

I weighed Birdy's infidelity against the blow job.

"Okay."

He slid down—*like a pro*, I couldn't help but think—moved his head around, like a mystic entranced, and sort of sniffed the area—*the way gay sluts likely do, men must like it when you sniff the area*—and then he put me in his mouth. It was an extraordinary sensation, superior to any cored peach or thawed veal or anything else I'd frantically fucked in the past, and I made sounds, all the expected sex sounds; they tumbled out of me like a new language I'd instantly learned, the husky *unh*s and *yeah*s and *oh*s. But my judgment ran parallel to my pleasure—*maybe he has someone lined up after this; our whole friendship has been a lie; does my mother already know that Birdy's a whore; is this how it's going to be the rest of my life, one love object after another, all of them born whores*—and I tossed my head back and forth on the pillow. I was experiencing "cognitive dissonance." My mother taught me that phrase decades later, when we were watching a rerun of *Cheers* and I said that I liked Kirstie Alley as an actress but I also didn't like her because she's a Scientologist. I would have a lot of cognitive dissonance over the years.

Birdy started saying slutty things as he sucked me, his sex babble much more evolved than my oohs and aahs. "Yes, oh my god, yes! Ooh, I shouldn't talk with my mouth full! Wowee!"

I went with it until he started to nag.

"Shoot that load! C'mon, shoot it! Shoot that big creamy load, ooh I love cum so much, shoot it shoot it, c'mon now! Let's go, c'mon!"

"Please stop talking. I can't stand it."

He looked up from his task. "What? It's going really good, don't you think?"

I threw an arm across my eyes and started to cry.

"What? Is that pleasure or are you—are you crying?"

I couldn't speak. I wanted to scrub the whole night from my memory. "I don't like this anymore. You should probably go back to your room."

He moved back up the bed. "Was I not any good? So many guys have told me I suck cock really good."

"I don't want to talk about it anymore. You should just go."

"I don't want to go." He put his head on the pillow and looked at me with big, unblinking eyes. "I don't know what to say, Roland. I can't help it that I'm not a virgin. I'm just—I'm not a virgin. But don't get so freaked out. I mean, if we're going to be friends forever, then you're going to have to get used to me—to sex. All kinds of sex. I like sex. I always will. I like what we're doing, and I like doing it with other guys. I can't—I'm not going to apologize. But I hate it when you cry. You don't cry very often. I hate it."

"I'm so sorry for having emotions. You're two-faced, Birdy. One minute you're telling me we have to pretend we like girls, and then you go off and have oral sex in the parking lot at Golden Griddle."

"Kickers, not Golden Griddle. Although—"

"I don't want to know!"

"I love you."

"Who cares. It's fine."

"I'm not moving from here. I'm going to sleep with you."

"Do what you want. I'm going to sleep."

I rolled over. I was furious and embarrassed, not at all sleepy.

"I'm still awake," he said.

"I'm not," I said, cringing.

We lay there for at least an hour.

"Roland? Hey, Roland?"

I tried to make the classic sounds of someone just wrenched awake.

"What?"

"I was wondering—do you think you could ask Margaret if she might be willing to pay for me to redo my demo?"

Here it was at last. The whole assignation, so thrilling and so sad, was only a prelude to this pitch. If I weren't in love I would've sent the side of my fist down on his face as though I were smashing a mosquito.

"Ask her yourself."

"It would have more, like, impact, if you asked her. Don't you think?"

"No. I'm not going to ask my mother for money for your stupid demo. Not everything revolves around you and your … *fame quest*."

He went all boneless and feline, running a leg across my front. "We're family."

"Ha ha. We just had sex."

"Don't be like that. I'd help you. Why can't you help me? What have I ever done to you that's so bad? I've already said I was sorry for being a bitch to you at school."

"You know, if we are family, then Margaret is as much your mother as she is mine. So you should have no problem asking her for five thousand or whatever it is."

He sighed. He whined. He blew in my ear. I pressed my hand against his face and pushed him off the bed.

"Wow. Okay, Roland. I've got it loud and clear. I see you for who you are, and it's not pretty. Good night. Good night, and goodbye."

I tried to laugh sarcastically, but it came out like retching. I pictured him packing a hasty suitcase and running away in the night. I wanted to die. I wanted to run to his room, but I didn't. I knew he had nowhere to go.

THERE WAS A standoff for two weeks. We didn't acknowledge each other; if we passed in the hallway, we both looked away and pretended to be fascinated by the wallpaper.

A few days into the standoff my mother summoned us into the kitchen.

"What's the problem *now*?" she demanded, vaguely regal in a blue blouse with dark-blue velvet piping and brown linen pedal pushers, her go-to work outfit. "This silent treatment with the two of you is mucking with the emotional gestalt of the house. Patients can sense it. Well? Speak!"

"We're taking a break from each other," I said. "We both have our reasons, I suppose. My reasons are a lot more legitimate, I think."

"Roland assaulted me."

"I did not! You wouldn't leave, so I pushed you out of bed. What was I supposed to do? It's not like I was having sex with a whole bunch of guys at truck stops, like you."

"Fuck off. I've never done it at a truck stop."

"Are you having sex, Birdy?"

"Maybe. Yeah. I'm really—I'm a very erotic person. It fuels my lyrics."

"Which are all awful."

"Sit," Margaret commanded. We scurried to our seats.

"Birdy, I'm going to tell you the same thing I told Roland. I am not going to govern your sex lives, but as long as you remain underage, sex—sex with strange men, or strange women, for that matter—is absolutely verboten. You're not streetwise. You think you are, but you are not. If you persist, I won't hesitate to … have you put away."

"You would never do that."

"Okay, yes, you're right, I wouldn't. But the consequences—I haven't thought of the consequences yet. But I will, and they will be extreme. Do you understand?"

"Yes," Birdy muttered.

"Louder. With fear."

She railed at us a while longer and then made us shake hands, as if we were ten-year-old schoolyard foes. When she was finally pacified, Birdy and I shuffled out the back door together, feigning chumminess.

"I hate you," he said in the driveway.

"That's so interesting, because I hate *you*."

MY ONLY RECOURSE in our war was to become as slutty as Birdy. He wouldn't be wounded—in fact, were we still speaking, he would've been happy for me. My heart wasn't in it anymore, but I had to do something; if I simply receded into my bedroom and shredded Kleenex as Birdy romped about with swarthy men in grubby sedans, I might as well take to my bed forever.

And so I became cheap. Every night I'd wait until my mother started making her signature sleep sounds, so like a nesting pigeon, and then I'd stuff myself into my tightest shorts and T-shirt and tiptoe out the door. I combed the places Birdy told me about, lolling in the parking lots of bars and all-night restaurants, looking aimless and hopeful. After a week I hadn't been propositioned. Somebody's mother stopped her car and asked me if I needed a ride and did my parents know I was out so late.

I walked back and forth past the Stopper, a sleazy bar that wasn't officially gay but was run by an enormous butch dyke whose nickname, I later learned, was Shit. I even went inside once, and Shit screamed, "Beat it, jailbait!" from behind the bar. I didn't go back to the Stopper for a long time.

I resisted going to the park. Anyone could get it sucked at the park, and it felt important to master Birdy's haunts.

I finally scored in the Woolworth parking lot. There was a mud-splattered yellow Volkswagen, the only car in the lot. I peeked through the filmy windshield: a fat, balding man was beckoning me inside, mouth agape. He looked like a guy who had the sort of job that would allow him to nap. I was terrified. This was not sexy. I thought of running, then remembered Birdy proudly telling my mother that he was an erotic creature. I wanted to be an erotic creature too. I got in the car.

"Bit nippy out there tonight, eh? You must find it a bit nippy in just your shorts like that."

"Yeah." There was a pungent, half-eaten salami sandwich on the dash. His zipper was down, and the small, wet head of his flaccid penis poked through the slit in his underwear.

"You like having it in the mouth?"

I nearly said *having what* but caught on.

"Yeah."

He extracted the rest of it. It was as small as a child's.

"Fuck, yeah." He pumped it feverishly. "Mine's a grower. You wanna get yours out?"

"Yeah, maybe later."

"You like it up the arse?"

"Sometimes. Not tonight, though."

"All right. Put it in the mouth now."

I gave him a toothy smile that I'd seen Mary Tyler Moore do on her show. It was not erotic. He ignored it and pushed my head into his lap. I smelled his fetid inseam, his acrid scrotum. I touched his dick with the tip of my tongue.

"Oh, yeah, how 'bout that? Yuh."

I did what Birdy had done to me, moving up and down on the guy's partial hard-on. I wanted to puke, but I had a point to prove.

"Yuh, how 'bout that? Oh yuh. Get it. Right down yer yap. Throat it."

His cock gained some volume but was still too small to deep-throat.

"Get it! Get it! Oh, Tammy!"

I pulled up.

"Tammy? Who's Tammy?"

"Eh? Did I say that? Sorry 'bout that. Don't know where that came from. Put it back in the mouth. Tickle the shithole. Ooh, yeah, that's great. Now eat the shithole."

I went back to work. It was not erotic. It was novel, but horrifying. It felt like I should be earning at least minimum wage. Eventually it was completed, as they say. The man was panting, his head flopped back on the headrest.

He started to say something, but there was knock on the driver's side window. And then a flashlight.

"Shit shit no," the man said, rolling down the window. It was a cop, a guy, young.

"What is going on in there?" he asked briskly.

"Hi, officer. We were just talking—catching up, like. This is … my nephew."

"Why are your genitals exposed?"

"Hey? Oh, well, would you look at that. I didn't even know that the genitals were out. This darn zipper."

"Please step out of the car, sir."

"Should I also get out of the car, officer?" I tried to sound as guileless as possible.

"You stay put for now."

I waited in the car. The man and the cop had a lengthy conversation. Another cop car came. This cop was somewhat older than the first cop. He asked me to step out of the car. He asked me how old I was. I said I was fifteen. He asked me if I was coerced into the car. I said yes, kind of. I said the man tempted me with the salami sandwich. The cop scolded me for being out so late.

He drove me to the police station. He said that any other cop would've thrown me in the slammer, but just this once he would let me call my mother to come get me. "Thank you so much," I said. "Thank you thank you."

The guy whose dick I'd sucked arrived at the station in handcuffs. He was weeping. He said he had a wife and four children to care for.

I called my mother.

"Why are you at the police station, Roland? What's happened? It is one o'clock in the morning."

"Nothing. I just went for a walk."

"Oh no. No. You were having sex in public. After our very lengthy conversation about this very thing. I was unequivocal, Roland. My god. Did they arrest you?"

"The policeman said he'd let me go just this once because I'm underage. But they arrested the other guy."

"The other guy. Oh god. Were you assaulted?"

"No. We were in his car. Just talking."

"Do not lie to me. Listen to me. Do not move. Do not speak to anyone. Do not … sit or touch any surfaces. I will be there in ten minutes."

She hung up. I did as she said: I stood motionless in the middle of a hallway. That part of the station was empty except for the intake person, a policewoman who was intently scribbling something on a yellow pad.

My mother arrived, cartoonishly mumsy in her nightgown underneath a thin cardigan. The only thing missing was curlers in her hair. She spoke to the intake woman; the intake woman summoned me with a forefinger. I slowly walked toward my mother. She looked very angry. My mother was mostly progressive, but I knew the snob in her was appalled by this tableau.

"Do you know how incredibly lucky you are? They're letting you go home. They could've easily put you in some sort of ... group home with no windows. I don't know how to communicate with you anymore. I could not have been more emphatic. And still you went out, and you got *into a car* with a predator. He could've— you could be *in slices* in his fridge right now! Why, Roland? And don't say it's your teen libido, we're sentient beings, we are not dogs. We are not cattle."

Outside, the summer night air was gorgeous and comforting after the stuffy station.

"I guess it was because of Birdy," I finally said. "He told me about all his sex experiences, and I guess I felt jealous."

"Get in the car. Get in the car. Get in the car."

I got in the car. I started to cry.

Margaret struggled to get the key in the ignition. We tore out of the police station parking lot.

"I can't help but feel that Birdy's a bad influence, Roland. But I'm his guardian, and I love him. I'm at a loss. I don't know how to protect you. Birdy is never going to give you whatever it is you have such an ache for. Tell me what I should do."

"Nothing. There's nothing. I just want to feel like we're equal. Me and Birdy, I mean. I don't want to feel like he's better than me in ... everything."

She took one hand off the steering wheel and ran it through her hair. She shook her head a little.

"I was friends with a girl who was somewhat like Birdy, when I was your age. This was just before—"

"The rape." The word was so commonplace by this point that I said it without inflection, like I was referring to a neighbouring township.

"Her name was Tiffany. Tiffany, like the lamp. Need I say more? Anyway, Tiffany was my friend, my best friend, or so she said. Until I met her I'd been pretty much persona non grata all through junior high. I was so devout, weirdly so; I had this faith that came out of nowhere when I was a kid. But there I was, saying grace before lunch in the cafeteria every day. The other kids called me 'psycho nun.' Looking back I would've called myself psycho nun. It was clearly the earliest manifestation of the obsessive-compulsive disorder that resurfaced after Dan killed himself."

"I don't know how this story applies to me."

"Bear with me, I'm painting a picture here. Where was I? Oh. So, yes, by fifteen I'd pretty much made peace with having no friends. I had Christ, and Mother Mary, and all the rest. Then Tiffany Iverson arrived in town with her family, and they were all white-blond, and they all had enormous, perfect teeth. Her dad owned two car dealerships.

"She was in my homeroom. Right in front of me. And every morning she'd smile and say good morning to me. She was really, really nice. I'm a pretty good judge of character, and I felt only goodwill coming from Tiffany. We ate lunch together. She even said grace with me. I'm sure the other kids warned her about me, but it didn't sway her. We had sleepovers. We mooned over Marlon Brando. At last, I thought, at last I had a friend, and Christ also. It was a happy time.

"A few weeks before the end of the school year, she had a little breakdown. She'd sit in class and cry, all day, every day. I don't know what the catalyst was—there was talk of trouble at home, but nobody knew for certain. All I know is that I was sick with worry. I loved her.

"Her parents pulled her from school. It was June, so it wasn't like she'd miss much. I called her constantly, and she'd talk in this faint sort of baby voice and then say she had to lie down. I sent her little get-well cards, little stuffed animals.

"It was August 6th, 1954, that I was raped. No need to revisit that story, obviously. I had my own little breakdown and got on with things. I wasn't close to showing on the first day of grade ten. I was staying in that horrible unwed mother's home. Some of the girls screamed and wept all night. I never got any sleep.

"I saw Tiffany on the front steps at school, and I ran up to her. She looked so old, Roland. She was sixteen but looked forty. And she was so thin. I sat down next to her and tried to hug her. She shivered, like my arm was made of ice. Some other girl—her name escapes me, but she married a Sikh man who was incredibly dreamy, she didn't deserve him—she squeezed between me and Tiffany and told me that I was the problem, not the solution. Tiffany didn't say anything. I was so hurt.

"At lunch she wasn't in the caf. I'd stopped saying grace at that point, so I took off, looking for her. I found her on the front steps again. She was bent over an urn, like she was smelling the petunias.

"I said her name several times. She looked up. I told her how much I'd missed her. She made this sound, like a balloon deflating. I took it as a greeting. I was so lonely.

"'I'm pregnant,' I told her. I'd been dying to tell her. 'I was— accosted.'

"She stood. 'I was pregnant too,' she said, looking at the sky. 'It was taken care of.'

"I told her that my parents wanted me to get an abortion, but I refused.

"'You can't have it,' she said. 'You have to have it taken care of. It'll ruin your life if you don't get it taken care of.'

"I tried to debate the issue with her, but she just kept saying that I needed it taken care of and looking at the sky. She furrowed her brow, still looking forty.

"It was a very tense time. I could only withdraw. And after that day, she was a nightmare. She told everyone I was pregnant, and she started running with all the mean, pretty girls, and she got thinner and thinner.

"My best friend made the next three years hell for me, Roland. Everyone called me 'preg-o' and 'rape-o.' I started to show, and Tiffany threatened to push me down the stairs so I'd have a miscarriage. And then—the treachery, Roland. The conspiracy. I'd never known such casual cruelty. Those three years were the worst of my life, including my breakdown three years ago."

"Why haven't you told me any of this before?"

She shrugged. "It hasn't been relevant. Mothers shouldn't burden their children with their problems. But now. Now, it's relevant. Birdy is your Tiffany, that much seems clear now. He's going to ruin you. He will. You see yourself as his satellite. You think he's your ticket to fulfillment. He's not. His path is not your path. You've seen what happens when you try to emulate him. You wind up in a police station."

"That was just bad luck on my part. He could've just as easily wound up in a police station."

"No. He wouldn't."

"Why? Why wouldn't he?"

"Just listen to me. Listen to me for once. You're a good boy. Please just relax into your own destiny. You're going to be absolutely fine, but you're not meant to—you're not meant to skirt danger."

It sounded to me like she was discouraging me from having a sex life, like she thought I was too wimpy to navigate anything carnal. But I was also struck with gratitude at having a reliable, thoughtful mother, which surprised me; this was the gratitude of an orphan adopted at last, not of someone who'd always had someone looking after them.

It was just after two in the morning when we got home. Birdy was still asleep in his room, which disappointed me. I'd wanted to come home to Birdy awake and wanting to know what happened, so that I could tell him I'd been caught blowing someone really sexy and well endowed and had almost ended up in the slammer. I was going to sit at the kitchen table and wait for him to wake up so I could apprise him, but my mother made me go to bed.

I SLEPT UNTIL NOON. My mother checked on me.

"Do you feel sick? Do you have a fever?"

"I'm fine. Why are you not in your office? It's a workday."

"It is. Come downstairs. Birdy's off somewhere with that Nadine girl. I have something to tell you."

I threw on my Cat Stevens T-shirt and denim cut-offs. I was still woozy from all the stimuli of the night before and hoped Margaret didn't have another rambling ethical sermon planned.

She'd made pancakes, and I was delighted. I hadn't had pancakes in months. I sat before my plate and poured maple syrup until my mother squawked, "Moderation!"

"I've met someone," she said, avoiding my eyes. "A patient— well, a former patient. It's not how I would've planned it, but we can't plan these things. We really can't plan anything, can we? I mean, we *can*, but those plans are almost always thwarted. Well, I shouldn't say *always*, I'm not a nihilist, but a lot of the time ..."

I rolled my eyes. "Skip over all that. You met someone and ... what?"

She sipped black coffee. "I've met someone I quite like, someone I'm somewhat attracted to who is somewhat, very thrilling and also ... calming. Calming and thrilling."

"Cool. Did you just meet him this morning?"

"What? No, I didn't just meet him this morning. I told you, it's a former patient. It's been ... mounting. I'm ... interested."

"Okay. What's his name?"

She opened her mouth as wide as it would go and then closed it. "His name is ... Barbara."

"What? Is he a transvestite?"

"Ugh. It's a woman, Roland! A *woman*. Please try to glean the through line here. This isn't easy for me."

I kept chewing. Once or twice I'd wondered if my mother was a lesbian, or at least flexible. She didn't hold much stock in conventional femininity. She'd recently finished reading *The Well of Loneliness*. I guess I should've been more surprised— this was 1970—but nothing in our life together had followed traditional protocol.

"Please say something. Are you horrified? Of course you're not horrified. I've always supported you in your ... Grecian quest. Oh, what is wrong with me? I'm so clinical. Gay, should say. Gay, gay, gay. Hooray, yes, absolutely. I just didn't think it would happen to me. I'm not going to go into the particulars, but ... she's remarkable. She's a poet. She gave me one of her books, *When Sappho Sat On Me*, and I wept from start to finish. Her work is so beautiful and generous."

"Are we going to meet her?"

"She's coming to dinner tomorrow. But you need to know that she's—she's very, very ... sure of herself. She has a brush cut. She— she wears overalls, exclusively. She's very much a classic—this is not pejorative at all—butch dyke. Proudly so. Do you know what that is?"

"Mom, of course I do." I instantly thought of Shit at the Stopper, and the sound of her corduroy thighs scraping together as she walked.

"Good. I just wanted to prepare you. Naturally I've contemplated lesbian love over the years, but in my fantasies the woman has always resembled—this is mortifying—Jackie Onassis. That's not Barbara."

"Okay. So?"

"You're right! So what? How is it that I can be so broad minded as a clinician and mother and so prissy as a sensuous being?"

"I don't know. Did you tell Birdy?"

"No. I haven't had the chance."

I felt reckless, freewheeling. I'd narrowly avoided prison. I'd sucked disgusting cock and I'd eaten "the shithole." My mother was a lesbo. Erotic rebellion was in my genes.

"Birdy's going to hit you up for money to redo his demo. Just a heads-up."

"That's fine. How much will that be, do you think?"

"A lot. He wants it really slick. Probably like two thousand dollars."

"Oh. I see. That's a lot of money. Hmm. Hmm. Barbara has a Rottweiler named Audrey."

"I ALMOST GOT thrown in jail for blowing some guy." Birdy was barely through the door. He'd just said goodbye to Nadine and closed the door in her still-expectant face.

"When? Last night? I thought I heard Margaret's car pull in."

"Yeah, last night. I was blowing this really sexy guy and he was loving it. He kept saying, 'how 'bout that' and 'get it,' it was weird but really great." I smiled.

"Wait—was the guy in a yellow Volkswagen?"

"Umm. Yeah, I think so."

"Did he have some sort of disgusting sandwich on the dashboard?"

"Salami."

Birdy had been with him. I was one-upped again. I studied his face for any hint of spiteful satisfaction.

"That's Get It Leonard! Nobody goes with him. He has such a small penis. Ah well. Beginner's mistake." He came and put his arm around me. "I'm proud of you."

I twirled away from his grasp. "Don't act all superior, Birdy. It's not some big achievement, knowing which cocks to suck."

"I didn't say it was. I'm just—you've broken the ice sexually, and that's good. God. What can I say that'll make you stop hating me? We've been acting so dumb. We need to stick together."

"I have to go to the bathroom." I went to the bathroom and sat on the toilet lid. I heard Birdy plug in and play his guitar in the basement, so I flushed and went to my mother's room, where she had a little black-and-white TV I sometimes watched when I wanted to be alone.

THAT NIGHT I went out again to look for sex with someone better than Get It Leonard. I needed vindication.

I walked along the waterfront. Eventually I noticed a black truck driving behind me. I didn't know what to do; the waterfront was always fairly busy and not at all a place to park and fuck.

"Roland?"

I startled and stopped. I couldn't place the voice. Dr. Stock? One of my old teachers?

He pulled over and leaned across the front seat, but I still couldn't make out his face.

"It's Terry Perner. Birdy's brother. It's late for you to be out. You want a ride?"

I came closer. It was indeed Birdy's brother, twenty-five now, give or take. His baby face had given way to chiselled features, and his head was all but shaven. I hadn't seen him since Judy was in the hospital. In the street light I could see that the sleepiness had left his eyes. They were stark and knowing now, in the street light.

I was going to decline the ride but found myself opening the passenger door. Terry's truck smelled good, synthetically piney.

"How are you?" I asked.

"I'm fair. I've been back a couple months now."

"Oh? Were you travelling?"

"No. I joined the air force and volunteered for Vietnam."

"Wow." All I knew about the Vietnam War was from TV. I knew that it was horrific, and endless, and pointless, and that a lot of American soldiers became heroin addicts, and that Jane Fonda was super upset about the whole thing. "Why did you volunteer for that?"

"Why not? I had nothing else going on. I was working in a slaughterhouse before I left, and it was the shits." He started driving. "I didn't have a steady girl. I don't know."

It was at this point that it occurred to me Terry had become very handsome. I got hard and thought of how dirty and taboo it would be were I to take Terry as a lover. Birdy would be incensed. Terry seemed abject but wired. I saw myself as newly sexy Terry's clandestine lover, wiping his brow with a washcloth when he awoke in a sweat from a terrible dream of jungle land mines and dying comrades crying out for their mothers. Had he died in the jungle, Terry didn't even have a mother to cry for. But I would be his mother when he woke up screaming in our marriage bed.

Terry gave off zero desire. He kept his eyes on the road. He lit up a smoke and offered me one. I took it. He handed me his Zippo to light it. That act resolved any lingering sexual tension in me; if he were at all interested, he would've lit it for me.

"How's Birdy? I think about him every day."

I didn't want to talk about Birdy. If I'd never had to talk about Birdy ever again, that would've been nice.

"He's good. He had a band and made a demo, but nobody wanted it. So he's redoing it by himself."

Terry smiled. "Fuck, that kid is talented. I thought I was doing okay and then he arrived and blew me out of the water. I'm proud of him. I thought of him when I was over there. He was like a—a light, you know? Not a light, a—like a—"

"A beacon?"

"Yeah! Yeah, a beacon."

I knew what he meant. Birdy was a beacon for a lot of us, a bright hint of boundless possibility. It was a good thing, as long as you didn't measure yourself against him.

"Are you guys still at that place in the north end?"

"No, we moved to a house. It's by the big Eaton's. My mom is a therapist now."

"Yeah? Well. She's a really smart person, I always knew that. Nice looking too. I hope that's not out of line."

"Not at all. But she's a lesbian now."

"Yeah? Well, that's not such a bad thing. Kinda nice to think about, if I'm honest."

I was silent.

"Sorry. I've been alone so long I sometimes forget the right thing to say."

We drove east, not speaking. I looked at his sculpted thighs in his ancient, holey jeans. I did wonder if maybe his war trauma had deranged him, if tonight was the night I'd end up dead in a suitcase, like Margaret feared. But I wasn't afraid of Terry. All I sensed in him was a deep fatigue that could only be resolved through some hard, miraculous change. New love. The sight of a gem-like UFO spiralling through the night sky.

"Where are we going?" I asked.

He gave his head a shake, like he'd forgotten he had a passenger. "Oh. Right. Uh, nowhere. I was just driving. I just drive. Do you want me to take you home?"

"No, it's okay. It's a nice night."

"I've thought a lot about what a bastard my dad was to Birdy. Dad was such a bastard. He should never have had kids. He didn't like kids. There was a reason why he was a bachelor until he was fifty. My poor mum. I saw a lot of fucked-up stuff growing up."

I remembered huddling with Birdy when we were kids, listening to his father beat his mother up. Sixty years later, I still recall that memory more than almost any other.

"I remember. Your dad was pretty brutal with your mom."

"That was nothing. My dad was more brutal with my brother. Not just smacking him around—we both got slapped around. My dad would lock him in the basement all day. He'd make him eat off the floor, I'm not shitting you. Humiliate him all the time. When our dad died, I didn't feel a thing. Except relief. I don't know what Birdy's like these days, but if he's still as—if he's still as—"

"He is. In some ways he's even more so. It's kind of hard to be his friend a lot of the time. He gets so obsessed with his music career and all that, and everything's about what other people think of him and making sure that other people think he's really great."

Terry nodded in the dark car. "I get ya. I don't know what to tell you. If you can, just try to cut him some slack. Well, I know you already do, but I guess try to cut him some more slack. He's never going to be someone who'll talk about his problems in like, a serious way. He's always going to do his, you know, song-and-dance thing. My dad treated him like an animal. So. He's still an animal."

I almost cried, which infuriated me. I was so sick of my sympathy, always having to offer up my concern and devotion, like some penitent nun. But I loved Birdy, so I could only receive these stories of his torture as a reason to forgive him and, when and if I had the chance again, to hold him tight until he complained of shortness of breath.

My libido vanished. I asked Terry to take me home. When we got to my street, he sucked in his breath.

"Hey, fancy here, eh?"

"Not really. Just old. Our house is big, but it needs a lot of work."

"Yeah? Hey, you know, I'm pretty good with my hands. I was actually thinking of getting my certificate in carpentry or something like that. Maybe I could help you fix things up? Don't know if your mum would be interested?"

"I'm not sure. And I'd have to check with Birdy too. I don't know how ..."

"Right, right, of course. I don't want him to feel weird."

I asked him to stop two houses down so my mother wouldn't hear the car. I opened the door. The lights inside the car went on, and I finally got a good look at Terry. He had such hunger in his eyes, literal hunger, like he needed a hot dog or even a plain slice of bread. But I knew I couldn't bring him in the house.

"Okay. Thanks, Terry."

"Okay then, Roland. So could you run that past your mum?"

"For sure, yeah."

"And say hi to Birdy for me? I wouldn't mind seeing him sometime, even for a few minutes."

"I'll definitely ask him. 'Kay. Night."

BIRDY WAS SITTING cross-legged on the couch, strumming his acoustic, head bobbing. He looked like some pretty, self-effacing hippie boy riding a soft grass high. He looked utterly unthreatening.

"Hey, Birdy."

"Hey." He kept strumming.

"I thought you were with Nadine."

"We just went for a walk. She asked me to go with her when she gets her braces off. So I broke up with her. You start doing practical things like that with somebody, they're gonna think you're really into them."

I sat. "I ran into your brother."

"Where?" He stopped strumming.

"I was walking around and he pulled up."

"What? Was he cruising for sex?"

"No! Well, I don't think he was. He gave me a ride. He was nice. He's way nicer now. He was in Vietnam."

I expected Birdy to be startled by that bit of news, but he only nodded and mouthed *Vietnam.*

"What else did you talk about? Did you talk about me?"

"Yeah. He wondered how you're doing."

"And did you tell him I'm doing great? I am doing great."

"I did. He was happy to hear it. He really wants to see you."

"Yeah? Well. I'm pretty busy."

"He said even for a couple of minutes. I think he feels bad for not keeping in touch."

"Right. Since when did he care about that."

"He was in Vietnam. He saw guys get shot in the face and like, little kids exploding."

Something in that sentence, probably the image of exploding children, made him put down his guitar and fold his hands in his lap.

"Can I—he talked a little bit about when you guys were little. He said—is it true that your dad locked you in the basement some-times?" I braced for a drink coaster whipped my way.

"Sometimes. It was—I got used to it. I'd just play my mother's Jo Stafford records and make up dance routines."

"You never told me that. It's still not right. A child shouldn't be locked up, ever. I mean, unless they're going apeshit and might beat themselves up."

"It was a long time ago. I'm a survivor. I believe in ... survival. All the greats had bad childhoods. I think I read that Bob Dylan's mom and dad both had Down's syndrome."

I was pretty sure that Bob Dylan's parents didn't have Down's syndrome, but I said nothing.

"What are you playing? A new song?"

"Just noodling. Trying to find a nice chord progression. I'm not some abused reject, you know."

"I didn't say you were. Did you ask my mom for that money?"

"No. I don't know if ... I'm not just some parasite. I know you think I am."

"I don't think that, Birdy. I don't. Terry said that your dad made you eat off the floor."

He jumped to his feet and threw his hands up, as if beseeching an unseen panel of moderators.

"Fucking hell, Roland. Is that all you talked about with Terry? All the ways my fucking dead father fucked me up? I'm trying to make a life for myself. I don't want to be some loser who can't stop talking about my childhood. Okay?"

"It's just that he feels really bad. And I feel bad."

"And I feel fantastic, so there you go."

"Okay."

He stood there for a bit, no doubt debating some dramatic exit, then he relaxed and fell back onto the couch. He stuck out his bottom lip like a stubborn child.

"Thank you for saying that. Really. I'm not saying it wasn't shitty. I think about it all the time. But then I have to slam it out of my mind, because I have to be tough, super tough, until I make it big, and then I can have a nervous breakdown when I'm famous. You know? And I hope you'll still ..." He started to cry. He cleared his throat. "I hope you'll still be hanging out with me when that happens. Because. Because I know that I can have a breakdown with you around, and you won't get scared. And you won't go to the *National Enquirer* and tell them I've gone crazy."

"I'd never do that."

"I know. You're not going to have a breakdown, because nobody did shit to you when you were little. I sometimes get so jealous of you, because I know you're going to have a nice life. Maybe you'll be a therapist, like your mom. I could see that happening. And you won't have to take sleeping pills or do starvation diets. Because you have a normal mom."

I smiled. I'd once or twice considered what it might be like to be a therapist like Margaret. I knew I'd never have her acumen or her brio. But I did have a blank affect that, with some training, could possibly look like doctorly contemplation. I would abandon that idea pretty fast when things started unravelling for me.

"Did she tell you about Barbara?"

"Barbra? Streisand? Oh my god, did something happen to Barbra Streisand?"

"No. Barbara is Margaret's—" I started laughing and couldn't stop. "Barbara is Margaret's lesbian lover."

"What? No! But Margaret's not—oh wow. When did she tell you this?"

"This morning. She's all fucked up about it. Barbara's a proud butch. Who writes poetry."

We tittered, two know-it-all gay boys still confounded by all things female. Eventually we made our way upstairs and talked through the night, about Margaret and Barbara, and Terry's stint in Vietnam, and the kind of fanciful speculation we'd used to fall into so easily when we were kids. I drifted off softly with Birdy's arms around me. I felt certain that we'd returned to the best of our friendship after a bumpy year.

BARBARA WAS A vegetarian, and Margaret spent the whole day chopping massive quantities of vegetables and broiling tofu, then tossing it all together endlessly until she complained of aching wrists. With annoyingly detailed instruction from my mother, I made my first cheesecake. Birdy set the table, which was significant for him. When he was finished, he kept studying his work like an obsessive maître d', turning plates slightly, lining up utensils, lining them up again.

"Does it look okay?" he asked me.

"It looks fine. It's only dinner."

"Shut up."

I winked at him. We were friends again, cozy, lively.

BARBARA ARRIVED. She was easily six feet tall, easily two hundred pounds. She smelled of sawdust and patchouli. She wore a blazer overtop overalls.

"Barbara Samuels," she said, shaking my hand as if ridding it of gathered rainwater. She was clearly nervous. She did the same with Birdy. We both forgot to introduce ourselves.

"This is where you tell Barbara your names, boys." Margaret was also nervous, and she spoke like she did when she wanted to hide her nervousness, in stiff cadences, like a reporter signing off on location. We introduced ourselves.

Barbara homed in on Birdy. "You must be the singer-songwriter I've heard so much about. I'd love to hear your music. Lyric writing—I can't imagine anything more challenging. I wouldn't know where to start. One must be imagistic and inventive without going opaque. I tip my hat."

"Thanks," said Birdy. "Margaret says that you write poetry."

"Barbara's a very accomplished poet, Birdy. She won the Governor General's Award."

"It was the Stoddard-Klein Fourth-Place Citation for Lesbian Effort, but thank you, Margie."

"No, thank you," said Margie (with a soft *g*), who used to hate it when anyone tried to call her anything other than Margaret. Barbara put her arm around my mother's waist.

"Doubtless you'd love a cocktail," my mother said, scurrying to the booze cupboard. Birdy and I looked at each other; we'd never seen Margaret so deferential. We'd never seen her scurry for anyone or anything.

She mixed Barbara a drink whose recipe she clearly already knew by heart.

"Where should we sit?" asked Barbara. "I want us to engage each other as friends. I don't want anyone sitting on the floor."

"Oh! What about the living room?" my mother said, as though she'd only just realized that we had a living room.

Barbara, Margaret, and I sat on the couch. Birdy sat on the ottoman and shot suspicious looks at Barbara. It seemed like the ions in the house had changed with Barbara's arrival; there was a prickling sense that, wherever Barbara came from or however she conducted her life, she moved with a stately, possibly unnecessary intensity that was foreign to all of us.

"Barbara," Margaret said brightly, "why don't you recite something?"

"Oh, Margie!" Barbara said, tossing back her massive head with studied laughter. "I couldn't! I couldn't possibly!"

"Please, Barbara? The boys will find it so edifying."

Barbara let out a deep, almost yogic breath, closed her eyes, and drew her thumb and forefinger down from chin to groin, like she was pulling at a very long beard. For several seconds she was motionless and silent. The rest of us looked at each other, startled by her sudden intensity.

"*I am Hecate!*" she began.

> Fear me! For I am Hecate! Oh yes, I am!
> Hecate? Who is Hecate?
> Me! I am Hecate!
> Here comes Zeus, with whom I call a truce!
> I will not chop off his scrotum, fry and eat it,
> because I am not that kind of person!
> Hecate!

And now I must check in on my live-in girlfriend Deb,
who has seborrheic dermatitis,
which can be very challenging!
Ha-ugh!

We were speechless. The force of her delivery was so persuasive that it was impossible to tell if her poetry was brilliant or awful.

"Well, what can I say, Barbara," my mother offered, breaking the spell. "Talk about powerful."

"I'm simply a vessel, Margie. I can't take credit for any of it. But thank you."

Barbara turned to me.

"Margie tells me that you're the most spiritually evolved of your clan, Roland. How does that tend to manifest?"

"I have no idea." My mother had never called me spiritual. I began to wonder if she'd manufactured fake, lofty biographies for Birdy and me to impress Barbara, or at least to reassure her that she wasn't going to be saddled with two childish dolts if things progressed between them.

I wanted to be courteous. "Are you working on a new book these days?"

Barbara took a slow, showy sip of her drink. "I am. It's provisionally entitled *Fisting Desdemona*. It's been a particularly difficult birth. But then, they've all been difficult. The poet is a penitent of spirit and must write in her own blood."

"Yes," said my mother. "Always. It's—so important. I should go check on the salad."

"It's a salad," I said. "What's there to check on?"

"Be right back." She scurried. I waited a courteous moment before following her.

"Don't say it," said my mother, tossing and tossing. "I know I'm acting like an idiot. I'm so nervous. I feel like a schoolgirl. I don't know what it is. There's this ... alchemy happening. And I'm helpless."

"But you're acting like—like you're not into women's lib anymore. You're acting like she's your husband."

"No, I'm not. It's difficult to articulate, but oppressive sex roles don't apply to lesbian love. Were Barbara a man, yes, my behaviour would be doormat-ish. But Barbara is a woman, and so my behaviour is deeply, powerfully feminine. I feel like ... a nymph. A sprite."

"Whatever. Are you always going to act this way now?"

"Please be my friend today, Roland. I need your support. Things will level out. No doubt. And I don't even know if she's truly interested. It's all very new."

"Why was she in therapy with you?"

"You know I can't disclose that. Why would you even ask?"

"I'd like to know a little bit about her."

"You already do."

"Please. Mom. Just this once. I guess I'm feeling protective."

My mother pulled at her cheeks.

"She—I cannot believe I'm telling you this—she has automatic thoughts and impulses."

"What does that mean?"

"Kind of like my obsessive tics before I got treatment. Only with her—I can't."

"What? What? I swear I won't say anything, ever."

"She—she—" Her voice fell to a whisper. "She picks her head."

"Like, when people say 'can I pick your brain about something'?"

"No. She picks at her scalp until it forms a scab, and then she picks the scab off and eats it."

"Ew! I've never heard of that. Does it have a name?"

"It's a compulsion. It doesn't have an official name. You are *not* to mention any of this to Birdy. He doesn't have your restraint, and I worry he'll weaponize it. I know Barbara seems strong, but she is very, very vulnerable. If you look closely, you can see the bald spot on her head from the picking. And she's probably a nymphomaniac."

"Like she can't stop having sex?" I thought of my mother, exhausted and gasping beneath Barbara. "Does she—make you—"

"No. We haven't made love yet. That's why I say probably she's a nymphomaniac. She's mentioned her difficulty with previous lovers. It sounds fairly trivial, but it affects her quality of life. Her last lover had to take a leave of absence from work so she could be available to—I should not—well, to provide … *digital succour* when needed. Oh no. I hate that I've told you all this." (Tony still doesn't believe this story but asks me to repeat it frequently. "That's not a real thing, nymphomania," he'll say, laughing. "She was just really sexual. *Digital succour!* Your mum so didn't say that!")

I made Margaret a Tom Collins. She said Birdy and I could have one weak drink each. I made two more Tom Collins. I put them on our cork-covered serving tray. The doorbell rang.

"Who on earth?" Margaret looked stricken. "Dinner hour on a Sunday? Could you get it, Roland? I don't have energy to be hospitable to more than one person."

I went to the door. I saw a brush cut and a tanned forehead. Terry.

"Is it a bad time? I just was in the area and thought I'd say hello."

"We have company." He had the unbearably hangdog look from the night before, and I felt terribly for him. "But come on in."

"Yeah? You sure? I don't have to stay long."

I took his hand coquettishly and led him into the living room.

"Hey, um, Barbara. This is Birdy's brother, Terry. He was in the area, so he thought he'd drop by."

"Hey, everyone. Hey, Birdy."

Birdy nodded. I could see him appraising his newly sexy brother. We were both fools for beauty, and Terry's taut body and hollow-cheeked, tanned face likely overrode any anger Birdy harboured toward him.

"Why are you here?"

"Y'know, I was in the area, thought I'd say hello. I ran into Roland the other day and—"

"You didn't say you'd run into Terry, Roland." My mother was ready to upbraid me for going out at night again.

"Yeah, the other afternoon," Terry said helpfully. He caught my eye—he was sexy *and* more socially astute than he used to be. "I drove past him. I think he was on the way to the library."

Margaret looked unconvinced but let it drop.

Barbara stood and shook Terry's hand. "Barbara Samuels."

"Oh yeah, okay, I'm Terry Perner. Birdy's brother. I know we're far apart in age. Birdy was a surprise baby. Our mum nearly died. She used to say that the blood whooshed out like a garden hose."

"How awful. Women's health is still just an afterthought—in Canada, and globally."

"No kidding, eh? Well, that's no good. I seen some of that in Nam. There was a guy there who made his wife walk ahead of him, so if there were land mines she'd be the one to get blown up. Sad, kinda. But I guess in some ways we're no better here in Canada. We've been terrible to the Native Indians."

Barbara shifted on the couch. "You were in Vietnam? Are you American?"

"No. No, no. Canadian. I volunteered."

"You volunteered? Why?"

"Oh, you know, no reason. Something to do. Tryin' to stay busy."

"Trying to stay busy. So you became an agent of genocide, for something to do."

My mom and I both issued the same singsong sigh to defuse things.

"Birdy and Terry come from a rather storm-tossed family environment," Margaret said, her hand on Barbara's thigh. "They've both tried really hard to chart their own course."

Barbara downed the rest of her drink and handed the glass to my mother. My mother looked around the room worriedly, then leapt up and went to the kitchen.

"So, Terry," Barbara resumed. "I really am fascinated by your story. You went to Vietnam and—what? Just sort of dove right into the—what to call it? The slaughter? Forgive my prying. I'm a writer."

There was a wobbly little chair by the front door beside a little table with a phone book and a phone on top of it. At first Terry had his knee on the chair, his backpack slung over his shoulder, but at Barbara's onslaught, he gingerly sat. He put down his bag and leaned forward with his elbows on his knees, and his head bopped wistfully as he stared at the floor.

"Hey, look, I didn't go looking for bloodshed, or however you put it. I was—somebody gave me this pamphlet and yeah, I was a bit lonely, didn't have anybody, shit job, I was alone in our house, the old house, nothing nice about the memories there, eh Birdy?"

"No." Birdy seldom said only one word, which made this one word cut through the tussle over Vietnam.

"And I want to say I'm sorry for adding to all that," Terry said. "I'm not gonna be a pest, Birdy. But I know I mostly just sat there like a lump, even when awful things were happening. That was not, that was not correct at all. I'm your brother. I've seen a bit of the world now, and I know what's what, at least a little bit."

Birdy was clearly moved, but he started scratching his face by way of camouflage. Barbara let out a scornful chuckle. Mom returned with a fresh drink for her.

"I find it fascinating," said Barbara, "that you gained such wisdom from, well, shooting people."

"What's fascinating about it?" said Terry, finally riled a little. "Like I said, it was a rough time. It's only once I got there that I saw how messed up the whole situation was."

"Sounds like a horrible ordeal," my mother said. "We're just glad you're back in one piece."

"Thanks, Miss Keener."

"Oh, Terry, call me Margaret, for heaven's sake."

Barbara drank her drink. "So do you live with great guilt? What are you doing to make reparations?"

"What's reparations?"

"Never mind. I am sorry. There's probably no point to this conversation."

That was when Birdy smacked his Tom Collins off the end table. The glass hit a bookcase, and gin splashed the spines of Margaret's reference textbooks. I shut my eyes.

"Why are you so mean? That's my brother. Nobody fucking cares that you're some shitty poet person. You're a guest here, you can't just drag people over the coals because they were in a bad situation."

"You're very young, Birdy. Eventually you'll learn the importance of speaking truth to power or, barring that, speaking truth to the foot soldiers of power."

"Shut up. *Fisting Desdemona*—do you know how disgusting that sounds?"

"Please stop, everyone," my mother said. "Barbara, I'm sure you'll find you have more in common with Terry than you realize."

"That's probably unlikely. But, really, Terry, Birdy, Margie, Roland—I apologize if I've delved too deeply. I'm terrible at cocktail banter."

"It's a process," my mother said.

Birdy kept looking at Barbara, taking her full measure. "And you're probably a hypocrite, *Barbara*. I bet your father was in the war."

Barbara did this long, long gasp, and her eyes went big and unseeing.

"Barbara, you're safe," my mother said, touching Barbara's brush cut. "You're in the present moment. It's August 10th."

"It's all right, Margie. I'm not disassociating. To answer your question, I no longer have a relationship with my father."

"That's not what I asked. I asked if your dad was in World War II."

"He was, as it happens. And he's a disgrace to me for that and many other reasons."

Birdy shook his head in disdain. I had no idea he was so patriotic. "If it weren't for people like your dad, we would all be in OVENS. Well, maybe not Terry, but for sure the rest of us."

"That is correct for sure," said Terry, visibly gaining vim.

"I would love to change the subject," my mother said.

"Yes, I'd like a reset, also," said Barbara. "Especially now that I'm being advanced upon by angry brothers."

"Nobody's advancing on you," Birdy spat. "I'm pretty sure my lyrics are better than your poetry."

Barbara smiled and put her arm around my mother. Her head was at a jaunty angle, like she was trying to replicate the author photo my mother showed me earlier that day, not the one on the back of *When Sappho Sat On Me* but the one on the back of the book before that. I can't remember the name of it. No, wait! *I Cried Out for Her Salad Tongs*—that was the name of it. Against all odds, I think I have a copy of it somewhere in the hall closet.

"Art is not a contest, dear Birdy."

"Yes it is. It's a major contest. They don't give out Grammys for being a nice person."

"Point taken. One to grow on."

My mouth fell open. My mother was falling in love with probably the least pleasant person I'd ever met. In less than an hour she'd alienated Birdy and his brother forever. And I would've been finished with her too, were she not my mother's girlfriend.

"Don't act so snooty with my brother," Terry said. "You should try to get along with people better."

Barbara tilted her head to touch my mother's in an unsightly attempt to turn a fractious situation into a reason for cuddles. My mother went stiff.

Barbara cleared her throat. "If I may, I'd like to recite a piece by Anne Sexton that has been a salve to me in recent years."

"Please don't," said Birdy. "Hey, Terry, do you want to go hang out at the house? I can't deal with this."

"Yeah? Sure. I got Swiss steaks in the fridge. We can play Yahtzee. That would be nice."

Terry put his backpack back on his back. Birdy put his shoes on.

"Roland. You wanna come with us? This is so dumb. It's only going to get stupider."

"I feel very strongly," my mother said, "that you be here for dinner, Roland. I seldom make demands, but this time I need you here. It's important."

I just sat there. I wanted to go with Birdy and his brother, but Margaret's insistence pinned me to my seat. She went to Birdy with wiggly, conciliatory hands. He didn't look at her.

"Please, you two, please don't leave. You're part of the family. I want you all to know each other, and I'm still convinced that we can all find common ground. It's so challenging to drop our defences and truly hear each other."

"Yes," said Barbara. "I know I'm unwieldy. It's been a lifelong obstacle. But, for what it's worth, I *am* interested in other perspectives. Birdy, I'd like to say that you're a very attractive young gay person. I'm excited for your future."

"Wow. Thanks."

BIRDY AND TERRY LEFT, and Margaret and I spent the rest of the evening listening to Barbara describe her perspective on men: she wasn't a man-hater; her response to patriarchy was really quite nuanced. She had, throughout her life, had vital friendships with men; it was possible to have affection for specific men while acknowledging that all men, given the chance, would annihilate all self-possessed women. She apologized again for being combative with Birdy and Terry.

"When I'm nervous," she said, "I become somewhat regal, which isn't always a good thing. I'm unstable. I really did want to make a good impression with your family, Margie."

"I know," my mother said. "There'll be time to mend fences. And you did make a good impression on Roland, so that's one down. Isn't that right, Roland? Tell Barbara that you like her."

My mother didn't, as a rule, issue such silly edicts. I paused. I didn't like Barbara at all.

"Yeah, she's nice," I said to Margaret.

"Say it to Barbara. Say, 'Barbara, I like you.'"

"Why? I'm not a parrot, Mom."

"It's really okay," said Barbara. "I do want to say that I like you, Roland."

"Thanks. I like you."

"'Barbara,'" my mother insisted. "Say, 'I like you, Barbara.'"

"Ugh. I like you, Barbara. Happy?"

NOW THAT I'M OLD, I can say with confidence that I'm pretty good at remembering the inflection points of my life. This surprises me; when the inflection points were occurring, at seven and ten and sixteen, love and death and other sudden endings, I was so overwrought that I felt as though my brain had shut off and couldn't possibly record the event at hand. But it was recording, faithfully if hazily, like a corner store surveillance camera. It even recorded absence.

Birdy never again slept at our house. He came by the day after the Barbara debacle to apologize for his behaviour and to pack a bag. We followed him through the house, incredulous and pleading.

"There's no need for you to leave," said Margaret in the bathroom, snatching Birdy's toothbrush from his grasp. "Barbara feels terribly about how the evening ended. She wants to get to know you."

"No, she doesn't. It's okay. I'm over it. I just want to hang out with Terry a bit. He's really changed a lot. We talked all night, and he really listened to what I was saying, even if he didn't have anything to say back. When I was little he used to spit on the floor and act all tough to impress my dad, but now he just sort of sits there, kind of peaceful. When I got up this morning he'd made porridge. He didn't call me a faggot once."

"He could still snap," I said desperately. "Yesterday he had a funny look on his face, like he was holding back from killing someone." It was such a flimsy lie.

"Ha ha. Come on. I still love you guys. I just want to spend some time with my brother. I don't have any other family. You guys have each other."

"And you have us," my mother said. "I don't know why I feel so upended by this. We love you, and everything is coming together for me, emotionally. You're very much a part of my vision of the future. Please don't leave."

"It's a ten-minute drive to our house, Margaret. You guys can come over whenever you want. We don't have to get all dramatic about it."

We followed him to his bedroom.

"Is he going to pay for your demo?" I asked. "He is, isn't he?"

"That is so ... cynical. No. Okay, yes, but that's not the major thing."

"I'll pay for your demo," Margaret said. "I'll happily pay for your demo."

"Thank you, Margaret. But like I said, it's not the major thing. I hated my brother, but now I like him. It's almost kind of a miracle."

I folded my arms and moved about the room, pretending to possess all knowledge, past, present and future.

"He's not going to be your forbidden gay love. Just so you know that."

"Oh, Roland, no." My mother lightly slapped her own face.

"Have I ever said I wanted something like that? Yuck. Yuh-uck. Some of us aren't perverts like you, okay?"

"I'm sorry. I am. I just don't want you to go."

"You can come over whenever you want, and I'll still come around. Anyway, I'm ditching school next year and moving to Toronto, so things are going to change one way or another. I was going to quit as soon as I turned sixteen, but Terry convinced me to at least finish grade ten."

"Yeah. I'd like to finish grade ten too, before we go, so ..."

Birdy didn't speak or look up from his suitcase. It was then that I officially started to worry that he would leave and not take me with him.

"That is a good plan," my mother said, now rubbing her fingers against her palms. "Give it a year, for sure. So much can happen in a year. You're technically still children."

We followed Birdy back down the stairs to the front door. My mother, the ultimate stoic, started to cry.

"Please don't cry, Margaret," Birdy said as she hugged him. "Why are you guys freaking out? I can't deal with it."

"I don't know why I'm crying. I can always account for my emotions, but suddenly I can't. I feel cold and frozen, like, like a utility chicken. That's a horrible analogy, but—"

Birdy laughed and kissed Margaret's forehead. "You're too much. You're both too much. Okay. I'm sure I'll talk to you tomorrow."

And then Birdy, so tall all of a sudden, so sure of his body, jumped on his brother's old ten-speed and was gone. That night my mother and I ate beans on toast silently, passing a bottle of Pepsi back and forth in the near dark, like boxcar hobos.

"A lot can happen in a year," she said again, as we dug spoons in a big carton of strawberry swirl ice cream.

"It's true," I said. A year can be hectic with eventfulness. A year can also be empty as a dirt valley. We'd known both sorts, my mother and I. There was no way of divining, not really.

A Year

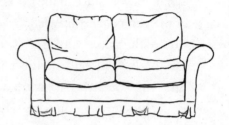

"**REALLY LIFT, ROLAND!** Really *hoist*! I can't do this without you." Barbara and I were struggling with her couch on the front steps. Barbara's couch was slightly longer than ours and covered in a rough brown fabric unpleasant to the touch. I much preferred our existing couch, but Barbara had a deep, unsettling connection to her own couch. "Gwendolyn MacEwan sat on this couch," she said, nearly tearful, when we went through her apartment, dithering over what to leave and what to take. She and Margaret had been a couple just over a month. In the end we left almost nothing behind, so our house now resembled a thrift shop. Stubbed toes were frequent as we moved about in the night in those early days of Margaret and Barbara and me.

At last it was done, Barbara's ugly couch stood where ours had been, and our couch was by the curb, to be surveyed by passing scavengers but always forsaken, rained on, and marked by the piss of multiple dogs.

Margaret fell upon the new couch as soon as it was set down. She'd started out so gung-ho about the physical work of moving Barbara in, beaming as she carried in tall bamboo lamps that looked like trophies for winning something vague. Then she started to drop things. At the end of a day her right foot dragged slightly. We insisted she let us do the rest of the work. Sitting on the new couch, she sighed happily, but when she started to speak, her voice sounded slightly off, filled with sloppy *S*'s and abandoned *R*'s.

"Wow. Never did I think I'd be moving in with someone this late in the game," she drawled.

"You're thirty-one, my love. The game is only starting."

"Oh, Barb, you really do lift me up."

"Like the couch!" Barbara laughed. (Sorry, I know she preferred Barb—elegant nomenclature was no longer a priority for my mother, just as Barbara's cloying lyricism had fallen away in a matter of weeks. They were well and truly Barb and Margie now, just your average benign lesbian couple with a hideous couch.) My mother laughed. I tried to laugh.

My house felt more like a non-profit drop-in centre now, with Barbara milling about; it was as though any stranger could walk in at any time and be met with coffee and a biscuit. Before Barbara moved in, my mother had sat me down and asked me squarely whether I'd be comfortable with the prospect, and I'd wanted to say no, but not as much as I wanted Margaret to be happy, so I said yes. And Barbara was truly trying, asking me for first impressions of grade ten, initiating protracted hugs in which her enormous and weirdly hard braless breasts pressed against my stomach. But the worst, by far, was when she'd sit next to me on the couch after I'd come from visiting Birdy and ask me how things were going with that.

The worst of those chats with Barb was the first one. Birdy'd been gone three days. I'd taken the bus to his parents' old house and listened to him plink away on the dilapidated upright piano Terry had bought for him. Every now and then he'd say something, still plinking on the piano.

"I've decided to cut my new demo at Arctic Sound. It's the best in the city. Terry and I drank beer last night. He told me about his nightmares. He dreams about kissing a Vietnamese woman and then her head explodes and then his head explodes. So horrible. I should tell you that I'm going to Burton Secondary for grade ten. Please don't be mad. It's just way closer now."

"How did it feel when Birdy told you he's going to another school?" asked Barbara, with her arm across the back of the couch.

"It was—I don't know. Surprising, but not really. It's fine." I thought of my old skid friends. To a person, they'd all dropped out of school to work in questionable auto body shops, or to sell weed, or to be pregnant and chew Bubblicious on somebody's porch. I was going to be alone again at school. Whatever. School solitude would prove to be a respite, away from a house filled with the chatter of new love: *Is it okay if I use tarragon? When I touch you there, do you feel endangered? I need to tell you something—I am not without anger. Hold me!*

"Young love is so ... bumpy. My first collection, *Medusa and the Embattled Pubis*, featured a whole lot of purple prose about my high school girlfriend. I know Birdy is less demonstrative than you'd like him to be, but you're both in constant flux at your age. Next thing you know, he could be the demonstrative one."

"We're not ... I don't know what my mom has told you about Birdy and me, but—"

Barbara patted me on the back. "Maggie hasn't said anything. I'm a writer—I'm constantly observing, processing, restocking the subconscious."

I looked away to roll my eyes. "Well. We're more than friends, but we're for sure not, like, dating. Birdy's—we love each other. Since we were little."

"What you have is special. Even I saw that right away. Some people live their whole lives without that kind of love. I'd made peace with the likelihood that I'd never know that kind of love. And then I met your mother. She has blown me open. I'm a blown-open woman. I'm truly shocked at my capacity for love. There had been so much austerity before ... My last lover—this is mortifying to share—our only intimacy was conducted through walkie-talkies, if you can believe it. The concessions we make in the name of love. Do you—do you want to call me Auntie Barb?"

"No, not really. That's okay."

She looked hurt but didn't persist. I knew that the only way I'd survive the year was if I avoided all controversy, kept my head down, focused on school, if only for the sake of distraction. I would stop going to Prior Park. I had to maintain an immaculate personal record to be worthy of a place in Birdy's big escape.

Barbara, for all her writerly bravado, was turning out to be a real sap, always clamouring for the smallest puff of affection, any tinny term of endearment. I found this previously concealed sappiness to be proof of pathology. I couldn't pinpoint the pathology— in between these saccharine episodes were long stretches of her usual severity—but in these early days of the new arrangement, I was on high alert for any proof of Barbara's capacity for betrayal. She worked three days a week at a bookstore; my mother was the breadwinner by far. I believed their love, but at fifteen I'd already learned from Birdy the soft treachery of the creative artist.

PEOPLE MOSTLY LEFT me alone at school. I'd reached my full height—a shade under six feet—and thinned out, so that I was no longer as boxy as I'd been only months before. I'd come into whatever manly allure I was ever going to have—a fuck buddy once described me as resembling a friendly werewolf—and maybe it was that sudden swarthiness that kept jocks from beating me up. My teachers were, to a person, the most uninspiring I'd yet had, four men and two women who all spoke in a monotone and announced new topics as though they were reporting tsunami fatalities. I returned to the obedient doggedness that had been my default prior to knowing Birdy, and it was good enough to garner steady Bs and the odd A-minus in English and history. My mother, run ragged by her practice and by Barbara's need for hugs and reassurance, seemed pleased with my effort.

And there was the boy with the limp. Stephen. He was pale, and his short blond hair caught the fluorescent light, and he always appeared startled by everything, so that fifty years later, I remember him as a kitten blinking newly opened eyes. He looked like a nerd but was an average student, even sub-average. When called upon in class his tiny kitten eyes would blink rapidly behind his wire-rimmed glasses, and he'd ask the teacher to repeat the question. Sometimes he'd ask the teacher to repeat the question more than once.

He was no great love of mine. We got paired in English to interview each other and then write biographical essays. He went first. I learned about his parents, Ukrainian immigrants, both doctors and busy getting their Canadian certification to practice. He had two younger sisters, I forget their names—one of them went on to dance with the Royal Winnipeg Ballet. Stephen didn't know what he wanted to be. He said this with eyes downcast, and later he'd tell me that his parents were gravely disappointed with his intellectual mediocrity, especially his father, who would go days without speaking to him and would cringe at the dinner table when Stephen said something stultifying about his day at school: his shoe coming untied, a paper cut.

We were marking time, Stephen and I. With Birdy gone I devolved into this provisional lump of a thing; my thinking slowed to the point where I could track an individual thought as it staggered across my mind like a poisoned mouse. Stephen was similarly afflicted, or at least he presented that way. Minutes could pass before he'd follow up on something I'd said or complete a statement that made no sense otherwise. I met his parents only once, walking single file on Portage with the children trailing, looking like a duck family. Stephen introduced me as a school friend. The father, his eyes even smaller than Stephen's, nodded at me, and they kept walking. Stephen's home life was probably silently hellish, but we were just marking time together. His hell wasn't my problem.

He came by the house a few times, and Barbara would pepper him with well-meaning but frightening questions: *Your future does sound rather opaque—does that make you nervous? I don't know if your parents ever share work stories with you, but there are so many prurient things I'd love to know, like maybe what were the most shocking things they've extracted from adult orifices? What do you think of our couch? Be honest.*

He stopped coming by the house. We kissed but once, behind the tool shed: our lips touched almost imperceptibly, and he drew back as if wounded, holding his mouth.

"Oh no. Oh no, no," he said through his fingers. "I don't want to do that ever again."

"Okay. It's not that big a deal."

He grabbed my hands and held them painfully tight.

"We can be friends for our whole lives." His tiny eyes seemed to retract into empty pits. "We can go camping. We can have families and then go camping, just the two of us. And we can—we can hug each other, for a long time."

I laughed. I already had an alliance like that lined up. Stephen took several steps back, deeply hurt; he'd just offered up a fantasy that had probably been germinating, torturously, for many years. We didn't hang out much after that.

BIRDY MADE HIS new demo that spring. He played it for me on the reel-to-reel machine his brother had bought him. It was dazzling in its own way, all those soaring, irrefutable melodies and masterful piano runs, and his beautiful, rangy tenor doing all sorts of gymnastic things as he sang his ungainly lyrics. For someone who'd seen so much, he seemed to have nothing to say. If I hadn't known him intimately but only known his work, I'd have pictured Birdy

O'Day as someone pining for a love so vague and inanimate that he could've been wooing an ice cube. Naturally I enthused endlessly. Birdy asked if I thought Margaret and Barbara would like to hear the new demo. I shrugged. I'd thought Birdy detested Barbara.

"I have to start getting along with people I don't like," he said, ever intuitive. "That's fundamental, if I want to be successful."

So, the next evening, Terry drove Birdy and his reel-to-reel to our house. Terry carried the machine inside the house as Birdy approached us, smiling and waving.

"Now, don't be grandiose, please," my mother whispered to Barbara.

"We are *so* excited to hear your new demo," Barbara beamed.

"And I am so excited to play it for you, Barbara! You're wonderful."

It was a barfy, hayseed, showbizzy moment. There would be many such moments to come, I knew, and I tried to wipe my face of all emotion.

Terry said he'd be back in an hour and sped off. We gathered in the living room, and Birdy stood by the tape machine on the living room table and waited for us to settle. He looked at once humble and regal as he took us in one by one.

"It means the world to me that you're all willing to listen to my new demo, Margaret, Barbara, and of course, Roland. It's been a really long journey arriving at this place, so much work and love has gone into the process. And I'm so grateful that it's already paying off. I'm so proud to announce that I'm going to be performing 'Won't You Please Come Back to Me?' on *Jumping Hildie*. I'm taping it this week."

"That is astonishing!" Barbara clapped her hands.

"I'm sorry, remind me," my mother said. "*Jumping Hildie* is a television show? Sorry to be so dim, Birdy. I so seldom watch TV."

"That's okay, Margaret. Yes, *Jumping Hildie* is a local variety show. It comes on after *Reach for the Top*."

"Oh, wow," my mother said. "It's all coming together for you, Birdy. I'm so, so pleased."

Birdy didn't say anything but bowed his head solemnly and pressed play on his player. The gorgeous music began, alongside the shitty lyrics. Barbara whooped and pumped her fists like she was cheering on a baseball team.

"Ooh, it's so good! It's so haunting! Your voice is magical!" It looked like she was lapsing into needy effusiveness again. "And the lyrics—it's clear that you really ... wrote them."

"That is so sweet, thank you. This is the one I'm doing on *Jumping Hildie*," Birdy said as "Won't You Please Come Back to Me?" started.

"It's so catchy, I can't get over it! You're going to be a pop star!"

"Thank you, Barbara."

"I've never known a pop star. Literary acclaim is one thing, but pop stardom ... it's so exotic!"

He nodded her way. "Won't You Please Come Back to Me?" faded out the way AM radio songs fade out. I considered saying that I preferred it when a song simply stopped instead of fading out, but there was no point. Birdy was lost in his mini masterpiece.

When the tape was finished, both Barbara and my mother were equally enthusiastic, although my mother's praise was more informed, given that she'd heard Birdy's songs many times.

"Probably the thing I'm most impressed with is how much your voice has evolved in just a few months, Birdy. It's stronger, more textured. You are a truly great singer." Margaret daubed at her eye. Birdy swept to her on the couch and threw his arms around her.

"Thank you so much, Margaret." I could hear some sincerity behind his patented kissy-poo patter. "I honestly couldn't have done it without you. You gave me a safe place to be creative. I'd be dead if it weren't for you."

"Stop, stop," my mother said, bawling now.

"It's true."

"You would've made it one way or another. Your tenacity is awesome."

"I think you're both astonishing," Barbara said. "I can't decide which one of you is the most awesome." Her palms went up and down like the plates of an old balance scale.

My mother shot her a brief withering look. This was new. I perked up: maybe the gossamer tedium of their young love was changing into something less annoying?

"Don't forget about us is all I ask, my dear Birdy. When you're a superstar, promise me you'll send the odd postcard, give us the odd phone call. Call us collect. I guess you probably wouldn't need to call us collect if you're a superstar, but the offer stands."

Birdy tried to do something brazen with his face but then started to sob. I saw my Birdy for the first time in eons. Were Barbara not such a sprawling amazon, I would've squeezed between her and Birdy.

"My mother knew I'd be safe with you. I love you. I'll call you every day."

"Well, perhaps not *every* day," said my mother, as she tickled the baby hairs on the back of Birdy's neck.

"And I'll be with Birdy too," I said, "so I'll make sure we call all the time." There was silence after that, and my mother hid her eyes in Birdy's hair. I wanted to die. They'd been talking behind my back about the futility of me being Birdy's assistant, I was sure of it. I felt my optimism drain away. "Unless I'm doing something totally unrelated," I said, to save face with my conspiring family.

There were more hugs and tender entreaties. Margaret said she'd set a timer in her office so she wouldn't miss *Jumping Hildie*, even if she had to jettison a patient. As Barbara and Margaret receded to the kitchen, Birdy took me in his arms.

"I love you, Roland. Please be patient with me. I won't let you down. Maybe nothing will come from *Jumping Hildie*, and things will go back to normal for a while. But things may also get crazy. But I'll be thinking of you, a lot. Do you still love me?"

I'm not sure how I was nourished by Birdy's egomania, but I was. Or at least I was warmed by the constant heat of him.

"Yes. I still love you. There's not much you could do that would make me not love you."

He looked toward the kitchen to see if we were being looked at, but Barbara and my mother were deep in an exchange filled with frantic hand gestures that resembled sign language.

He kissed me hard. I took the kiss but didn't press; these sweet entreaties were Birdy's domain, and I knew if I kissed him back he'd probably recoil or beg off some other way, citing a sore tooth or the like.

When Terry came to pick up Birdy, Barbara flew at him, all fluttery with contrition.

"Terry, I really want to apologize for how horrid I was to you the last time you were here. I get so worked up over the ethics of a situation. It's like I feel I could die somehow if I don't start an argument, it's like I could drown in my own saliva. I'm so sorry. I'm thirty-eight years old, but I've learned nothing. Nothing at all."

"No problem," said Terry brightly. "I'd actually kind of forgotten about it. Don't beat yourself up there."

"Oh! If only! If only I could do exactly that, Terry. Please excuse me, I need to—I'll be right back."

Terry took the tape deck. Birdy hugged my mother again.

"I have this stupid feeling," Margaret said, then stopped. "This feeling that I'm never going to see you again. Intellectually I know that's silly, but ..."

"That is so silly. You're going to see me next week, on TV."

"Right, of course." My mother looked disappointed by this response.

"We should probably get going, Roland. I got a stew on the stove and Yorkshire pudding ready to go in the oven." Terry seemed to be turning into a housewife. I looked down and saw baking flour handprints on the pockets of his jeans.

Barbara returned almost exactly when Birdy and Terry left, like she'd had her ear pressed to the bathroom door.

"I'm really glad I got the chance to clear the air with Terry," she said, sitting. "I'm not an ogre, I'm really not. I wasn't properly socialized as a child."

"It was big of you to reach out," my mother said.

"What does *that* mean?" Suddenly Barbara was all squirrelly again.

"It means that it was big of you to reach out, Barbara." Margaret looked tired.

"I'm sorry! I'm so sorry. Margie, Roland. I don't know why I'm so insecure these days. Living in such a loving, stable environment … it's all strange and new to me. Please don't abandon me."

My mother also sat. "You're not going to be abandoned. Why would you think that? I'm suddenly so tired. I feel like I've played three hours of tennis. Could we have a nice, quiet night?"

"Of course we can have a quiet night, Margie. I could make candy apples."

My mother's eyelids descended with a shudder, like metal office blinds.

"That's okay, sweetheart. Truthfully I don't really like candy apples."

"Fine. Love offerings are not welcome. I'll make a note."

I couldn't bear another round of their charged circular exchanges. I went up to my mother's room and watched a cooking show on the little black-and-white TV.

THE DAY OF Birdy's TV debut, Barbara went to the store for munchies and pop. My mother blocked off the hour. I'd heard her on the phone, rescheduling a patient. It was a protracted conversation that my mother ended abruptly, citing a death in the family and curtly encouraging the patient to seek hospital care if they were truly feeling suicidal. I was kind of shocked at my mother's tone; she sounded more like a harried taxi dispatcher than the painfully considerate therapist she'd always been.

Barbara and Margaret sat together on the couch. Barbara had poured Cheezies and corn chips into the cheap faux bamboo salad bowls she'd brought when she moved in and stacked with pride of place in the middle of the main cupboard. I sort of threw myself like a tablecloth on the floor in front of the recliner.

"Why am I so nervous?" My mother dug her fingertips into Barbara's knee. "He would've told us if the taping went badly. He's just so young. I should've—he's so young."

"You can't stop a star," said Barbara. "Normally I find it hard to be supportive of other creative people, but your young man will not be denied."

Jumping Hildie started, and I shushed Barbara. Birdy had told us that his segment was set for the last quarter-hour, but we whooped when Hildie, short and hyperkinetic, with a bobbing beehive, announced her lineup: "And, making his television debut, a very fine singer and instrumentalist, just sixteen years old, Mr. Birdy O'Day!"

My mother and I shared a quizzical look.

"O'Day? Since when was his last name O'Day? Is that his mother's maiden name, Roland?"

"How do I know? I guess he thought O'Day would be catchier than Perner."

"That's a red flag," said Barbara. "Next he'll be getting a nose job."

"It's not a red flag, Barb. Birdy O'Day does flow better than Birdy Perner. Don't you think, Roland?"

"I don't know yet. Yeah, maybe."

We waded through the first forty minutes. There was a woman who sued her landlord for evicting her because he thought she was practising witchcraft in her kitchen. There was the mayor, I forget which one, but he was breathlessly promoting the new wading pool on Florence Road, "where anyone can cool off on a hot day, regardless of race or religion."

"So unctuous," my mother said.

"Such a puppet," Barbara said.

Then there was an oddly stiff and expressionless mime. We all laughed when he mimed walking against the wind but failed to evoke wind, so he looked like he was walking and pushing a sheet of drywall on a dolly.

Then it was Birdy.

"I feel sick," my mother said.

"It's not that big a deal," I said, even as my own body shook with anticipation.

Birdy walked out in a sparkly red shirt and matching bell-bottoms. I puzzled over where he might have gotten such a getup, finally concluding that newly domestic Terry had taken up sewing.

"Hi, everybody!" he said into his hand mic, expertly held not too close and not too far from his mouth. He sat down at a white grand piano and stuck the mic in its holder on top of it. "This song is called 'Butterfinger,' and it'll be released really, really soon! I'm so happy to be here!"

He launched into his catchiest song. He gyrated on the piano bench. He made wild-eyed faces. We were witnessing the birth of his signature stage persona, and it was ridiculous and utterly new. Fifty years on I can describe early Birdy as a combination of Peter Allen and Bowie, vampy and strange.

"He's so good!" my mother said. "I know I had nothing to do with it, but I'm so proud!"

"A star is born," said Barbara. "Without question, a star is born."

"It's weird," I said. "He looks more relaxed on TV than he ever does in real life. He looks so happy."

"A star is born."

"Please stop saying a star is born. My mom and I already know that Birdy is a star."

"I'm sorry. I'm just trying to participate."

Birdy was finishing. At the end of "Butterfinger" he did a little keyboard flourish and threw his hands up like he had before he started. The studio audience, almost certainly composed entirely of seniors and housewives, let loose with croaky shrieks.

Hildie whatever-her-last-name-was beckoned Birdy over to the seat beside her desk. Birdy raced over and hurled himself onto the padded chair and then crossed his legs, one leg high-kicking and then wrapping around the other leg. So bold! This was 1971!

"Well!" Hildie purred. "All I can say is, where on earth did you come from?"

Birdy laughed the laugh he'd devised years ago, a fizzy giggle that telegraphed only fun, only good times and, mildly, erotic possibility.

"Winnipeg, born and raised, proudly so!"

"Mark my words, Birdy, someday soon we'll all be able to say 'I was there when ...' We have a few minutes left—will you honour us with another song?"

Birdy did the bashful, self-effacing face he'd perfected years ago, then bopped back to the piano. He did "Won't You Please Come Back to Me?" It was note-perfect. More broken squeals from the elderly audience.

What more is there to say? As Barbara said incessantly that afternoon, a star was born. Birdy called the house that evening.

"Did you see me? Was I okay?"

"You were amazing. You know you were."

"Oh, thank you. Oh, Roland, I should've have brought you to the taping. Terry went to the taping and he cried. Like a lot. Hildie wants me to come back next month, and she knows someone at MCA Canada, and she's going to talk to them and make sure they hear my demo! Can you believe it? It's like I've gone from zero to—a high speed or miles per whatever."

"That's so great. I'm so happy for you." It was hard to match his elation; I was tired, and Mom's foot had done its weird dragging while we were making dinner. I was starting to worry that she had some killer illness, a brain tumour or cancer all over her body.

"I'm still all worked up about it all, and Terry's out with this mousy girl he met at a pet shop. Do you want to go to the Stopper?"

"The gay bar? But we're underage."

"I'm friends with the owner."

"You're friends with Shit?"

"Yeah. She lets me in as long as I play piano."

"Interesting." I started to pant. Birdy had cachet over me everywhere, even at the Stopper. But I couldn't resist the chance to go to my first gay-ish bar.

WE MET OUT FRONT. Birdy was bopping in place and humming an improvised melody. I'd never been so excited about anything, except for Birdy's proximity in bed or on the big rock we used to sit on at recess.

As I remember it, the whole bar erupted in applause when Birdy walked in; they'd seen him on TV and wanted to rub up against a soon-to-be VIP. I also recall Shit screaming her appreciation and pouring him a big drink, but I may be wrong. I went on to be one of Shit's closest friends—when she died in '96 I was a pallbearer— and she was only ever remote and slightly bitter about everything, from the weather to gas prices to the impossibility of finding a Winnipeg dyke proficient in bondage. I've never laid claim to being an accurate reporter of the past.

She did come around the bar to slap Birdy on the back and to warily ask him who I was.

"This is Roland. He's—he's my boyfriend." It was pure posturing, just another instance of Birdy trying to be worldly, but this was the first time he'd called me his boyfriend, and my legs started to shake so badly I had to lock my knees.

"Oh, great," she said. "More jailbait. Well, if you sit quiet and act respectful, I'll let you stay this once."

Men approached us, smiling and purring cautious entreaties. Some of them were brawny and hardscrabble, others were coiffed and mincing, the old stereotype made flesh. There was more than one ascot. Every time someone came close, Shit bellowed, "Back the fuck off!"

We sat on the piano bench. There was a stack of sheet music on a little table beside the piano; Birdy leafed through the songs until he found one he liked and spread it across the music rest.

"I didn't know you could read music," I said.

"Yeah. I picked it up playing here. It's weird, I'm dumb when it comes to almost everything, but somehow I can learn musical stuff no problem."

He started in with "Gypsies, Tramps & Thieves." The whole bar sang along. Shit gave me a pint of dark, flat beer.

At the end of Tom Jones's "She's a Lady," one of the ascot gays approached us. He looked drunk. He studied me, then Birdy.

"Are you two sweethearts?"

Birdy smiled and nodded. I was too petrified to move.

"That's so nice. It's hard to find someone to love. I walked away from my one true love, and I can't remember why. You two hold each other tight."

"Oh, we will," said Birdy.

"You'd better, or I'm going to kick your ass. You promise to hold each other tight?"

"We promise."

"That's so nice." The man leaned against the side of the piano. "Don't bother with the faggots here. They'll stitch you up, steal your valuables. Do you know how old I am?"

Birdy and I looked at each other. The man looked sixty, easily.

"Fifty?" Birdy suggested generously.

"I am twenty-one years old. Let that sink in. I been used and discarded like fucking toilet paper. Passed around by the men in this dump like I was a dorm room bong, no lie. You two run as far as you can from this town. Hey—what should I do with my life? I'm asking, seriously. You tell me what to do and I'll do it."

"Marty! Sit your fuckin' ass back down on the bar stool!" Shit shook a beer stein with real vehemence. The man toddled off obediently.

Birdy played until his hands trembled with fatigue. Around eleven Shit said he could relax, and we found a tiny corner table. People pumped the jukebox with dimes. Birdy had finally burnt through the day's adrenalin, and we sat quietly, listening to music we hadn't heard before, mostly live recordings of jazzy women with ruined voices. I flashed on my mother, furious in the dark kitchen, waiting to give me hell.

On slow songs there was dancing. Men with men, women with women. A hooting woman in a fringed blouse, demanding that her fey male partner bend her backwards as far as she could bend. This was all new to me, and I frequently had to look away for fear I'd let rip with some outsized reaction to such a gorgeous spectacle. The last thing I wanted was to cry my first time at the Stopper.

But Birdy had seen it all before, and he swayed and sipped the pink drink that Shit had just delivered. Now and then he'd rest his hand on mine. Suddenly all this love and intrigue, after months and months of nothing special! This was how the rest of our lives would be: commotion, and music, and dance floors swirling with wholesome gay love!

The next song was "Unchained Melody." Birdy stood and bowed and extended his hand, like a southern gentleman.

"Really?" I couldn't believe he wanted to dance with me in public. "It's okay if you don't want to."

"Come on. Today was a great day. Dance with me."

Our table was a bit tippy, so I moved past it cautiously. I took his hand, and he yanked me artfully to an empty space on the dance floor. I was stiff armed, ready to dance as one might with a great aunt on New Year's Eve, but Birdy pulled me to him, and we were dancing close and slow. Red and purple lights turned our skin an attractive shade of dark pink. "Unchained Melody" sounded like a hymn to me, something we might've rehearsed when we were choir kids with Dr. Stock. This was twenty years before *Ghost* turned the song into pure cliché.

"Is this okay?" he asked.

"Yes. It's really nice."

I relaxed enough to put my head on his shoulder.

"Today was such a good day. I love you. I love everybody right now."

I wilted a little when he said his love was universal, but I let it go.

"Are you really going to take me with you?"

"Yeah. Course. I know I'm kind of—I don't know. But I don't go back on my word. Do you still want to come with me?"

"Yeah. That's all I want."

"Good. Get ready, then. I could be gone really soon. Things can go really fast in the music business."

"Okay. I'm ready."

The song ended, and one of the jazzy ladies started in with something slightly uptempo. I wanted to keep dancing, but I knew that Birdy liked to circumscribe romantic scenes, as though he were directing a movie.

"We can stop dancing if you want."

"Did I say I wanted to stop? I could do this all night."

I let my head fall back on his shoulder. It had always been my hope that with age, Birdy would settle into the ease of our love and stop perceiving it as inertia. Maybe that was what was happening now. If he could dance with me all night, he could, in time, just as easily buy a nice bungalow with me. We could adopt a rescue dog. We could, ten years from now, be sitting at our kitchen table, reading different newspapers, and I might pass him a particularly interesting article, and he'd read it intently, nodding now and then, and when he'd finished it he'd pour us more coffee, and we'd quietly gear up for the day's packed schedule.

We closed the place down.

"That's all she wrote, kids," said Shit, tossing glassware into a rubber tub. Birdy and I were both a bit sweaty from dancing. We got his backpack from the coat check. Shit unlocked the front door and held it open for us.

"You're nice kids," she said, tipsy but sincere. "You've got the world at your feet, you two. Don't fuck it up."

We walked up Smith toward our bus stops. The street lights on Smith were erratic, so we held hands in the darkness between them.

"Tonight was the best night I've ever had," I said. I couldn't bother to be circumspect anymore.

"It was really fun. I really like Shit. She's seen a lot. I relate to her. Ugh. Suddenly I'm all stressed out."

"Why are you stressed out? Everything's going so good."

He was quiet for half a block. "I'm already kind of tired. It's only going to get more intense. Maybe I can't cut it. What if I can't cut it?"

"If anyone can cut it, it's you." I wasn't sure what he meant by "cutting it," but it was time for me to start acting like his faithful assistant.

"I guess so. But if I start acting like I'm going to—I don't know—go all druggy like Jim Morrison, you'll tell me. Please say you'll tell me."

"Yeah, for sure. That's my job—isn't that going to be my job?"

"I don't know. Well, yeah. I haven't figured out all that stuff yet. But yes."

"Jim Morrison was so cute."

"I know. And Jimi Hendrix."

HE STAYED STRESSED OUT as we embraced and then awkwardly retreated to our respective bus shelters, occasionally waving across the street at each other until Birdy's bus came. Mine took ages to arrive, and when I got on, a woman was screaming at the back of the bus. "Why did I have fuckin' kids if I don't get to see my fuckin' kids?"

The house was dark. I braced for a blowout with my mother, but when I let myself in there was nobody downstairs. I sat down on the couch to reflect on the evening.

"No, I'm telling you I can't feel it!" I could hear the panic in my mother's voice, upstairs. "It's numb and then it's tingly!"

I went partway up the stairs.

"Maybe you slept on it the wrong way," Barbara said.

"No! I haven't been asleep. I can't sleep when Roland isn't home."

"Let me keep massaging it. I've been told that I'm a healer."

"Oh, shut up Barb! I don't care. There's something wrong. I think we should go to the hospital."

"You know the hospitals here. We won't be seen for hours. Can we go in the morning?"

"No, we cannot go in the morning! I'm telling you there's some-thing wrong. Don't you love me?"

"Okay, I'm sorry. We'll go."

I went to their room. Barbara was helping my mother put pants on.

"Roland! Where have you been? I've been so worried. There's something wrong with me. My right leg is numb, and I can't see colours. Everything's washed out."

"I'll drive you, Mom."

"Oh, could you?" Barbara asked pleadingly. "My bowels are in révolt. And it's probably better that someone be home in case— there's a phone call."

"A *phone call*?" my mother spat. I helped her to her feet. "Who's going to call in the middle of the night? Wow. That's rich, Barb. Huh. You really learn someone's character when they're faced with a crisis."

"That is so hurtful, Margie. I'm going to chalk it up to the situation."

"Gee, thanks. Don't upset yourself. You just settle in and wait for your precious phone call."

We hobbled to the car. Margaret told me to take her to St. Mike's Hospital; St. Boniface was embroiled in a big scandal after it had come to light that one of the janitors had been posing as a surgeon and removing gallbladders for no reason.

I drove too fast until my mother told me to slow down. "I'm not going into labour, Roland. There's no need to speed."

I was scared. She'd been having strange, fleeting symptoms for months, but this was the first time they couldn't be explained away. Maybe we'd waited too long and whatever she had, this tingling, mostly covert ailment, had eaten away at her nervous system or turned her skeleton to spun sugar, breakable by a single cough.

"Where were you all night? Were you at the park?"

"No."

"Then where were you? Now is not the time for you to be coy, Roland."

"Birdy took me to the gay bar. We were celebrating the TV show and everything."

"They let two underage kids into a bar?"

"Birdy's friends with the owner."

"Is he now? What next. Do you know the name of the owner? I would like to talk to him."

"It's a woman." I ran a red light. She didn't notice. "I don't know her real name, but everybody calls her Shit."

She laughed in disbelief at my low-rent night with Birdy. She smacked the dashboard.

"Don't do that! You could break something."

"Oh—oh. Things are clearly already broken. You're unrecognizable to me right now. And Barb—I am pretty much convinced after tonight that she is flotsam. *Flotsam.* After dinner I told her that one of my eyes was all blurry and she asked me if I wanted her to hold me! Like she could somehow kiss away a brain hemorrhage. People can be so atrocious. Turn right here. Here!"

We screeched onto Wayburn and parked by the emergency entrance. I saw some wheelchairs on the sidewalk.

"Maybe we should put you in a wheelchair?"

"Absolutely not. I'm going to walk into that hospital. It could be the last time I walk."

I scoffed, but it rang hollow. My mother was not a hypochondriac, so her bleak forecast carried weight. She was only just thirty-two. It had never occurred to me that she could die young.

"I'm sorry," she said, sensing that she'd just frightened her kid. "Whatever I have is probably chronic. If it were deadly, I'd be dead by now."

I put my hands around her waist like we were figure skaters and I was about to hurl her into an axel, and we walked into emerg. It was empty aside from a dishevelled, grey-haired man slumped in a chair. Whatever was wrong with him, it wasn't dire. They may just have been letting him sleep there.

We went up to the woman at the registration counter. She was knitting something grey. Eventually she noticed us.

"Hey, hon. Can I help you?"

"My mother—"

"I'm having some symptoms. Serious—they're serious."

"All righty. I just need for you to fill out—now where the hell did I put the clipboard? Oh, there it is."

MY MOTHER FILLED out the form. We sat. An hour passed. She expressed her dismay at the state of the health care system. Finally a bedraggled nurse called her name with some annoyance. We went into a room. The nurse checked her vitals.

"I'm fairly sure it's not something acute," Margaret said. "I think it's probably something neurological. Possibly MS? Pray god it's not ALS. But it's in that vicinity."

The nurse whipped her head like it was a typewriter cartridge and looked at the clock.

"You'll need to give that information to the doctor. Shouldn't be too long now."

We thanked her. She left. We waited. It was three in the morning, and then it was four.

"MAYBE WE SHOULD call Barbara," I said.

"What's the point? She's probably fast asleep, dreaming of Amelia Earhart or someone else in her fucking lesbian pantheon. Did you have sex with anyone at the gay bar? I mean, apart from Birdy."

I shook my head like it was an Etch A Sketch I was trying to erase.

"No. No! Not even with Birdy. He just played piano for everyone, and then we sat around and watched people dance." I was still rapturous about our slow dances and the thrilling things Birdy had whispered in my ear, and I wanted to tell someone. Margaret was a scold when necessary, but even during a tirade she could also appreciate the happy gravity of all my milestones.

"And then we danced, you know, together. And it was really great."

"Well—can you two not dance together in the safety of our living room? Why do you always run toward danger?" She kept opening and closing her bad eye as she said this.

THE DOCTOR CAME. He had a handsome face and a rubbery body that moved like a wind-tossed palm tree as he tested my mother's reflexes. When he tapped my mother's right knee, her leg only dangled.

"I'm pretty sure it's MS," my mother said, unable to hold back her own diagnosis. The doctor said nothing. "Do you think it's MS? Or do you think it's something worse?"

"We're a long way away from any sort of diagnosis." He sounded irritated. "I'd like to do a scan right now, but my best guess is that you're in for a week's worth of tests. I don't think you're in any immediate danger." He glanced at me. "Is this your husband?"

"This is my son, doctor. I would not marry my own child. So where do I go for the scan?"

"Third floor. Stay here for now. An attendant will come and get you."

The rubbery doctor went away. We waited another hour. I didn't want to add to Margaret's upset, but I got so bored that I started asking her about MS.

"MS stands for multiple sclerosis. My mother's sister has it— well, *had* it. I'm sure she's dead by now. When I was a little girl she walked with two canes. And then she was in a wheelchair. It's a slow killer, MS. I could have it for decades. Little by little, I'll deteriorate, until ... who can say? I don't know anything about end stage MS."

I couldn't think of anything to say for a long time. And then I was hit with the possible usefulness of an up-to-date family history.

"We should find your parents, Mom."

"What? Don't be ridiculous. Why?"

"So we can find out about what happened with your aunt."

"What's there to find out? She's either dead or she's a vegetable somewhere."

"But there could be more information your mom and dad might have."

"Please stop talking about my parents, Roland. We'll deal with whatever happens, you and me—and my flotsam girlfriend, I suppose."

SHE HAD THE SCAN, and the doctor let her go with an appointment for the next day. We drove home.

Barbara was very contrite, in her faded, pilly pyjamas.

"I'm so, so, so sorry," she said, trying to cry. "It's just—when there's something wrong with the love of your life, one goes a bit— if I lost you—oh. I'm so sorry."

"I accept your apology, Barb. There's no need for histrionics."

WE ALL THREE went to the appointments. Interminable days of sitting and standing and eating stale cafeteria pastries wrapped so tightly in saran wrap that we had to pass them to Margaret, the only one of us with discernible fingernails, to pick open.

Barbara was on her best behaviour, holding Margaret's hand, obsessively checking in on her in the plural.

"How are we? Are we okay?"

"I'm fine, Barb."

"How are we now? What's happening? Are we okay?"

"*We* are the same as we were five minutes ago."

WITHIN THE WEEK, my mother was diagnosed with MS. I remember us all nodding, sad and stunned despite her prediction at the outset. There was nothing to be done about MS in '71. We could only try to accommodate her infirmity as best we could. We put a handrail in the shower. We halved the front steps to make way for a gently sloping ramp.

Others have had it much worse, for sure. I know that. But throughout my life, it seems like contentment has been quickly interrupted by calamity—which is the case for most of us, certainly. But if I'm tired or drunk, I can sometimes lapse into a hammering self-pity and forget all about other people and their comparable troubles. I hate this about myself. I'm not a whiner. I avoid whiners whenever possible. I change tables at Club 200 if Rory Harper comes in and starts talking about his colitis.

But here it was: I danced with my one great love, and then my mother was given a death sentence. I know that there's no neat line between the two. It's just how I feel, sometimes, when I'm drunk.

THE DOCTOR SAID my mother could be fine for years and years. He said multiple sclerosis was an "eccentric, unpredictable, maddening malady," and Margaret and I both turned to watch Barbara bask in his pretentious turn of phrase.

"Until I forget how to walk or go blind, it's business as usual," my mother said firmly, at some point between hospital and house. "Okay? *Okay?*"

Okay, we said.

When I told Birdy, he was putting on eyeliner and mascara in his bedroom mirror. He looked particularly intimidating with eyeliner.

"When you say she's sick, what do you—is it like pneumonia?"

"It's MS."

"What's that?"

"It's a brain condition. Or a nervous system condition. I forget exactly what the doctor said. She could be fine for a long time, or she could go downhill in a wheelchair. I mean—she wouldn't literally go downhill in a wheelchair. You know what I mean."

"Oh no. Oh." Birdy wept. His tears were real, even as he reflexively turned to check his eye makeup. "Are there pills for that, or anything?"

"Not really."

"Oh no." He sat and put an arm around me. I'd already dealt with the crying stage privately, into my pillow, but his solidarity felt as real as our clinch on the Club 200 dance floor.

Terry walked past Birdy's room.

"Terry! Margaret has a brain disease! And she could be fine, or she could die."

"Oh, jeez. Wow. I'm sorry." Terry sat on the other side of me. He'd gained weight since I last saw him, and his pillowy thighs spread across the rest of the bedspread. His hair was longer, and he smelled like pasta sauce. It was like sexy, war-torn Terry was rapidly becoming Aunt Terry, life giving and quietly loving. It was weird. Not horrible, by any means. Terry clearly contained multitudes, and I admired each iteration of him.

"What can we do?" Terry asked.

"Yeah, what can we do? Seriously, anything."

"She's fine right now. There's nothing to do. I mean, she still has the draggy foot, and one of her eyes comes and goes, but she's still working a full schedule. We're all fine."

THAT EVENING TERRY and Birdy came by with two stacks of Tupperware.

"This here's a week of suppers for you all," said Terry. "If there's something you don't like, just throw it out."

"You two," Margaret murmured. Barbara put out her arms to indicate that she would like to hug them, if that was okay with them. Terry smiled, and Barbara wrapped her long, long arms around them. After that poor show the night of the emergency visit, Barbara was really giving her all. The past few weeks had softened me too; suddenly I was prone to offering up hokum sentiments during casual conversation. "We're all just people, at the end of the day," I'd say, watching Third World mudslides on the news with Barbara and Margaret. "You never can tell what life has in store," I sighed, when we got the news that the pretty young gymnast who lived next door with her handsome husband had slipped in the middle of a backflip and snapped her neck.

I guess I was at peace. I'm at peace now too, with Tony at home and my big-tipping faithfuls at the salon, but my peace at almost seventeen was airy, even facile, whereas my peace at sixty-nine is contentious and erratic. My present peace is something I'll only admit to after two beers, and always with the addendum that it could be so much worse.

I WAS HANGING OUT at Birdy's when he got the call from the guy at MCA Canada. MCA Canada loved the demo and the tape of the talk show, and they wanted to fly him down to Toronto for an interview and impromptu performance. Birdy kept having to cover the mouthpiece so the record guy wouldn't hear him hyperventilate.

"They like me!" he screamed, upon hanging up. "They want me!"

He grabbed me, and we jumped up and down. I was so happy for him, and so happy that, to put it crassly, I'd hitched my wagon to a star.

"So what's the next step?" I was breathless from jumping up and down.

"They said as soon as possible. They said next week would work for them."

"Next week! They must really, really love you. I'm really happy for you, Birdy."

"Yeah?" He kissed me roughly. His excitement turned sexy, and this time I was more than game to do things. We pulled off our shirts, our cut-offs, our dirty white socks. We grabbed at each other's cocks. We ground our pelvises together. Mouths and fingers. I'd never been so aroused. We were lovers, making love as lovers did. I flashed on the rest of our lives being laced with this sort of sweetness. I came too quickly under him, but he just stayed there, smiling, breathing, sliding mindlessly in our sweat. We didn't speak. A few minutes passed, and we started again.

There was only one hint that he might not have been as awed by the moment as I was: I took his head in my hands to kiss him softly and saw that he was looking up and to the right, wide-eyed, as though he were ogling a car crash. I assumed he was musing on the chaos of the coming weeks. As he drew closer to his goals, he frequently grew fretful, and it was my job as his agent of reassurance to offer ballast at all times.

"There's a lot to do in the next little while, but you're going to sail through it."

"What? Oh, you mean—yes, it'll be good. I'm ready."

"I can't wait to tell Margaret. She'll flip. Barbara's still kind of wobbly, so I'll have to make sure Mom has everything she needs before we leave."

He slipped off me.

"I was thinking, just for this first trip, it would be better if Terry came with me. Just for this first trip. I'm going to be so nervous, it'll be good to have a family member with me. You know what I mean?"

"No, not really. I thought I was a family member."

"You are! Oh, you really are. I want you with me for the whole rest of the journey. But just this first bit—Terry's gotten so patient and almost kind of maternal. It'll be good for me. Are you mad?"

"I—no. I understand." I turned my head away. My dick recoiled.

We dressed. Birdy asked me perfunctory questions about Margaret's condition. What did he know or care about her health? It was very hard, sometimes, to love Birdy. I am a sluggish organism; I need at least ten hours of sleep to function. His love—now chivalrous, now torrid, now nowhere to be found—was depleting me.

At the front door I stepped into the uncomfortable wooden clogs I'd recently bought at the Sally Ann.

"I really love those clogs," said Birdy.

"Oh. Thanks." In mere minutes we'd been reduced to shoe talk. Terry was mowing the lawn with an old-fashioned push mower. I nodded once by way of goodbye to Birdy and clomped down the driveway. Terry smiled and waved.

OUR HOUSE WAS filled with an old folk ballad sung by tenors on a record full of crackles and skips. On the couch Barbara was massaging my mother's greasy feet. Barbara appeared to be enjoying it more than my mother, and I recalled Barbara's first book, *Oiling Up Gretel*. Obviously this was a fetish of hers, but when she saw me, she wasn't furtive or apologetic, so I guessed her fetish was purely tactile and not sexual.

She said something, but the music was too loud. I went to the stereo and turned it down. Now I heard the slick smack of her hands on Margaret's feet.

"Just giving this lovely human some attention," said Barbara.

I sat. "You look like you're in pain, Mom."

"It's a good pain. At least I can feel something down there. No numbness at all today."

"That's good. MCA wants to sign Birdy to a record contract."

"What? Oh, Roland, isn't that something! His mother would be so proud. Poor Judy."

"Yeah."

"You sound—what's wrong?"

A little bubble of anger rolled up from my stomach to my forehead. "Barb, could I talk to my mother alone for a minute?"

"Sure thing. Give me maybe fifteen minutes and I'll be done."

"Barb," my mother said. "Please leave us for a bit."

Barbara flashed her long yellow teeth in response to this mild reprimand. "Sure thing," she said, and rubbed the excess mink oil into her palms. She turned the stereo off before she went away.

I waited a moment. "Birdy's bringing Terry to Toronto for all the meetings and everything. He said he wants a family member with him. It's so all of a sudden. School starts up in less than a month."

"Ah. And you feel rejected."

"Not really. Well yeah, kind of. He's my boyfriend. He said he was my boyfriend. We've been planning this for so long. And now he wants Terry to go with him. A few years ago he couldn't stand Terry. And now he wants him as a chaperone."

"This is all such uncharted territory, Roland. Birdy's nervous. And you're not even seventeen. It's understandable he'd want an adult he can trust with him. I really wouldn't take it personally."

"But I'm supposed to be part of this. What if he doesn't let me be a part of this?"

My mother pulled herself upright. She grabbed a roll of paper towel from the coffee table, tore off some sheets, and wiped her feet.

"Indeed. What if he doesn't? You know how I feel about that arrangement. You cannot fashion your whole life around someone else's career. That's the kind of thing that leads housewives into alcoholism. You have to have a Plan B."

"I have a Plan B."

"You do? What is it?"

"It's—I'm going to—I'm going to be a therapist. Like you."

She cocked her head, all canny doubt. "Come on. No, you're not. You're not going to be a therapist, Roland. I may have suggested that at one point, but that was just my own vanity. Some days I'm not even sure that I'm supposed to be a therapist. Have you given any thought to vocational training after you graduate? You could be an electrician, something fail-safe like that."

"Oh my god. Mom. I'm not a skid. Do you really think that little of me?"

"Roland, I have MS. I work sixty hours a week. My girlfriend makes me listen to sea shanties while she tortures me with awful massage. I'm pure pragmatist at this point—any remaining snobbery has been drained from me. And Barb has enough of that for the both of us. So, yes—why not learn a trade? As happy as I am for Birdy, it has sometimes gotten tiresome, all his talk of 'going for his dreams' and 'making it happen.' I'm here to tell you that there's nothing wrong with not having a particular dream. It's perfectly okay to enjoy the peace of mind of a union job with a steady paycheque."

I had no response. I had lived almost my whole life in the wake of Birdy's ambition, his tantrums and stunning keyboard runs; it hadn't occurred to me that I could be unremarkable without paying some sort of toll for that mediocrity. I didn't have to be anyone's handmaiden. I was grateful for the feedback, but I discarded it without a second thought. I thanked my mother, patted her on the shoulder, and went upstairs to starfish on my bed and picture Birdy and Terry on a flight to Toronto, sharing a tiny packet of cashews, and think of ways both tender and mercenary to force Birdy to take me with him on the next trip, the one-way to Toronto when we'd set up house, when I'd be subsumed forever, mindless, smiling, running through boring chores, all but forgetting my own name. I did have special talents, after all: I was my boyfriend's very best handmaiden, his doting catamite, the only helper he'd ever need. If my mother couldn't see that plainly, that was her problem.

THEY LEFT, WITH no set return date, and I spent the days whipping my head around like a flea-bitten chihuahua, desperate to bite at a body part just out of reach. He didn't call the first or second day. He called the third day, but I wasn't home, and Barbara answered. She said he sounded like he was having the time of his life, and there was lots of laughter in the background. She said it sounded like he was at a party. I decided that Barbara had made that part up just to be mean spirited. My mother didn't place much stock in celebrity, but Barbara did, and I could tell that she wished I was someone more delightful, someone with a record contract.

"Did you get his phone number in Toronto?" I asked.

"No. I didn't want to pester him with small stuff. He's so busy."

"But I want to talk to him. He's my boyfriend."

"Transcend, Roland. A serious artist is already overwhelmed with thoughts and feelings. You need to tread lightly."

I wanted to run to my mother and tell her that Barbara was being mean. But I couldn't be bratty. I had to put away childish things if I was to be a good personal assistant.

First day of grade eleven. Birdy and Terry had been gone a week. I felt brazen in Birdy's absence. Some new kid sat in the seat I wanted in homeroom, and I leaned over him menacingly and told him to hit the road. He moved without protest.

The math teacher was a short, haughty man straight out of teacher's college. At the start of class he talked breathlessly for at least ten minutes about his lifelong passion for numbers and how we'd be embarking on a "kind of pilgrimage that would be at once mystical and useful." None of us knew what the hell he was talking about.

At lunchtime I paced the parking lot of the church across the street, chain-smoking and shaking my head. If this was to be the start of my new life without Birdy, I wanted no part of it. I considered running off and embarking on my own big city odyssey, selling my blood and my body for sustenance as I traipsed from province to province. But that plan was only terrifying to me, and my mother would be gutted. Her illness might worsen.

By the end of the day I was catatonic. Margaret and Barbara asked me lots of thoughtful questions about my first day back at school, but I just pushed my nut cutlet around on the plate until both women also fell into a stupor.

The phone rang. I ran for it.

"Roland? It's Birdy!"

"I know. Don't you think I know your voice by now?"

"Things are going so great. I met Terry and Susan Jacks!"

"You haven't called." I couldn't hold back. I wanted to scream at him.

"I did call. Didn't Barb tell you?"

"I mean you didn't call back to get a hold of me."

"I'm sorry. I've been so busy. I've officially signed! They want me to go into the studio mid-November."

I turned into the hall, stretching the phone cord until its curls turned to kinks. "When are you coming home?"

"Saturday. Terry met a girl here. She goes to one of the universities. She says she can feel the prairie wind whenever Terry talks. Barf."

"I miss you. I feel like I'm losing my mind."

"Oh. Well, no. Don't go losing your mind!"

"You're being really glib. I think about you all the time. I know you're having fun or whatever, but I'm not. I hate everything. Am I still coming with you when you go back again?"

"Yeah. Definitely. I need all the help I can get."

I breathed hard, like a prank call masher, but it was only to keep from crying. "Can't you—can't you say something nice and—loving?"

He sighed. "You know I love you to bits. We're going to have so much fun. I have a manager who's really nice. She uses a walker. She reminds me of Margaret."

"My mother does *not* use a walker. She's doing really well, actually. Thanks for asking."

"Gwen is motioning me over. Gwen's my manager. She reminds me so much of Margaret. I have to go. Okay. Love you. Love you to bits."

"Thanks."

He hung up. I let out this caveman howl that made Margaret go "Oh!" I slammed the phone onto its cradle.

"What happened?" my mother asked.

"He's an asshole. It's fine. He's forgotten all about us."

"Oh, Roland. Sweetheart." This was Barbara, who touched my wrist and looked at me with a soft concern that made me fall into her arms. She held me too tight, but it was okay. I cried and cried.

"Let it out, bunny. Love is the shits. I know that's prosaic, but there's no other way to say it. My second-to-last girlfriend—I barely survived. She was monstrous, a total gaslighter. This one time there was a pine cone—"

"Barb, just let Roland be. You can tell the pine cone story another time."

WAITING FOR BIRDY, I vacillated between anger and a damp anxiety that felt sort of like the beginning of a head cold. Wednesday, Thursday, Friday, I was nasty to students and teachers alike. I told the uppity math teacher that math could never be mystical or even interesting. I knocked Elke Friesen's milkshake clear across the cafeteria for no reason. There was a waterbed store on the way home from school that had a floor model waterbed outside on the sidewalk. There was a plastic cocktail sword on the ground. I picked it up, looked around, and pierced the undulating mattress with it. I'd never done such a thing; as I walked away I felt like a jailhouse fugitive. For a few minutes I forgot about Birdy and pondered a life of small-time crime. But I was much too timid for that sort of thing. I still feel guilty about that waterbed.

Early Saturday morning, I filled my backpack with a can of Pepsi, a salmon sandwich, sliced dill pickles in tinfoil, and three digestive cookies, and set out for Birdy's house. It was already hot out, and by the time I'd made it to Birdy's, my T-shirt was stuck to me.

I rang the doorbell. Nothing. They weren't home yet. They'd probably booked a midday flight. I swept the grit off the stoop and sat.

Two hours passed. I ate a cookie. An elderly couple pulled up next door. I smiled and waved so they wouldn't think I was loitering.

At exactly noon I ate half the sandwich and a bit of pickle. I sipped my tepid Pepsi. The elderly couple came back out, in different outfits.

"Still waiting!" I said, much too cheerily.

"You could be waiting a long time," the man said. "We haven't seen 'em for a couple weeks. She wanted to call the police, but I said they're probably just on vacation."

"Yeah, they've been in Toronto."

"Toronto!" the woman said with a little sneer. "Oosh, no thank you!"

THREE P.M. I ATE the other half of my sandwich and finished off the pickles, but I was still dizzy and shaky from hunger.

Around four-thirty I started crying intermittently. I felt paralyzed; I couldn't leave my post, but all I wanted was to be home, in front of the air conditioner in the living room window.

Just after five, Barbara drove up with my mother. I was on the brink of passing out and briefly wondered if they were a mirage.

"Roland! Why haven't you called?" My mother had flung herself out of the passenger seat.

"You came. I called out to you and you came."

They each took an arm.

"You are absolutely soaked. You can't sit out in the hot sun all day like that. They haven't gotten back yet?"

"No. I called out to them too, but they didn't answer."

"Let's get you in the car," said Barbara, all but carrying me. "Your legs are shaking horribly."

We drove home. The wind in my face revived me a little.

"Their flight was probably delayed," my mother said. "I'm sure they'll be here tomorrow."

"What if they aren't here tomorrow?" My voice was high and tremulous like a little girl's.

"They will be. They have to come home sometime."

HA HA. HA HA HA. We arrive at the part of the story that I've shared countless times with people in every gay bar in town. I went back Sunday, and every day after school that whole week. They never came home. They didn't call or write. We took to watching the news for reports of a plane crash or double murder.

I went mute, except for when my mother sat on my bed at night, and then I'd cry and search my mother's face as I asked her again and again how something like this could come to pass. How could people just disappear? How could my most special friend abandon me without a word? What about their house? Were they just going to let their house stand empty forever?

"People are unknowable, in the end. Well, except for—a mother knows her own child inside out, if she's paying any attention. I'll always know you inside out, as long as you don't get hooked on hard drugs. But there too—I know you'd never get hooked on drugs. Birdy and his brother are behaving horribly, but you will get over it. May take years, but you'll get over this. Even if you don't want to get over it, you'll get over it."

"No. I hate him. How could he do this to me? How could someone be so—I don't even know. Cold?"

She looked up at the ceiling. The last owner had pasted moon and star stickers all over it, and we'd never bothered to remove them.

"You'd be surprised, Roland. Maybe it's better that you learn this now. All that you have is your own heart and mind. And Birdy—that degree of obsession with fame is mental illness. I see that now. He's not just a great young musician. He's ... sick for fame. That's all he cares about. You don't want that kind of company."

"Yes, I do! I do! I don't care! I do!"

I STILL CHECKED their house once or twice a week. Their lawn grew slipshod with angry weeds.

I WENT BY on a Wednesday in October. Wednesday, October 6, 1971. There was a "For Sale" sign stuck in the front yard. I looked in all the windows. The furniture was still there, but the place had been tidied up, and there were bulging boxes on the living room floor, taped up and labelled in artless black-marker scrawl. They'd come and gone, but when? Middle of the night?

I knocked on the neighbour's door. The woman answered. I asked her if she'd seen them come and go. The other day, she said. They came at dusk and left after she'd gone to bed. "The realtor stuck the sign out front yesterday. I don't see how they'll get a fair price without a fresh paint job inside and out," she said.

AND THAT WAS THAT. I went to school, zoned out all day, came home. Sometimes I'd sit on the toilet and imagine stabbing Birdy in both eyes, cackling like a Disney witch as he screamed. It was not cathartic.

My mother's head started to shake gently, like Hepburn's in *On Golden Pond*.

Mid-December, we put up our tiny fake Christmas tree, decorating it with all the chipped, poignant ornaments we'd all accumulated through the years. Barbara provided the star, old tin spray-painted silver. When we were done we sat on the couch and sipped the boozy eggnog Barbara had bought at the liquor store. We listened to the radio. Barbara and Margaret talked idly, and I watched them converse and was grateful for the music of them.

"This next one has really been lighting up our switchboard, and I do not tell a lie," the deejay said. "It's Winnipeg's own Birdy O'Day, with 'Butterfinger'!"

They both looked at me with concerned, crinkly eyes. I tried to bop along to the intro that I'd all but memorized, the choppy percussion and Birdy's wordless trill. Birdy was on the radio. He'd done it.

"He sounds really good," I said.

"He does," my mother said.

"Things move so fast in show business," Barbara said.

I Drink

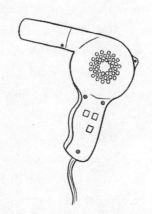

FEBRUARY 19, 1972

Dear Birdy,

They probably have some lackey at the record company reading and answering this, but I had to write anyway.

I'm very, very, very angry with you. You've been gone six months and I haven't heard a word from you. Do you think it's normal and human to just vanish and leave the people who love you to guess if you meant anything you said all these years? You said I was your boyfriend. That was obviously a lie. I'm not some fuckwit you can use and abandon. No, I guess I am, because that's what you've done.

That's some gratitude you've shown my mother, who took you in when you could've ended up in foster care—if your father didn't beat you to death first. Way to go. You've accelerated her MS. She can barely walk now. Nice one.

We've heard "Butterfinger" and the second single, I forget what it's called, but I do know that you didn't even write it. Mr. Genius Songwriter selling out already. Soon you'll be doing car commercials. Fuck you.

Please call me. Please! I love you. I will love only you for the rest of my life. I'm such a fucking idiot.

Roland

I showed my mother the letter.

"Oh, Roland. Please don't send this. It's too raw. Even if he does read it, it'll only worsen the impasse."

"I have to send it. I have to let him know how shitty I feel."

"I know, but—maybe put it aside for a week or two, and then send it?"

"Okay, yeah."

I sent it the next day, slamming the lid of the mailbox as hard as I could, as though Birdy might hear it in Toronto or Berlin or wherever his next big gig was. Ten days later I got a photocopy of an autographed 8 × 10: Birdy laughing wildly, showing his molars, with sparkles in his windswept hair. An ersatz glam rocker. I ripped up the picture and flushed the pieces down the toilet.

I TOLD MY mother I was dropping out of school. She asked me why. I said I wasn't learning anything, and I wanted to start my life.

"And what life is that?" she asked, arms folded. "I'd love to know."

"I'm not totally clear on it yet, but I'm going to get a job while I figure it out. I'll contribute to, like, the running of the house. You could probably even cut back on your hours."

"I don't want to cut back on my hours. I love my work. You know I will always encourage you as long as you are living your life with dignity and purpose. But you can't just hole up here for the rest of your life, pining away for Birdy. That ship has sailed."

"I think I know that! I know that ship has sailed. I think you're being kind of hard on me. Barbara only works one day a week at the bookstore, and she hasn't written anything for two years, and you're not sniping at her to get busy and have dignity."

"The particulars of my relationship with Barb are something else altogether. You are my child. I have to hold myself to a different standard with you." She stopped. "Why? Do you think

I'm slipping up in my relationship with Barb? No, don't answer that. It's none of your business. Just know that I worry about you constantly, and it would be a living death to see you waste your potential, your very real potential. Are you hearing me?"

I promised my mother I was hearing her. I quit school two days later. That night I went to the Stopper and told Shit I'd quit school. She bought me a shot of tequila.

"I fuckin' hated school, man," she said, as we clinked shot glasses. "Grade nine, the principal came home and caught me going down on his wife. He hit the roof. I said fuck this shit and never went back to school. I missed the pussy, but that was about it. I seen Birdy on TV last night, doing his new song. The song was no hell, but he was really good. How's he's doing?"

"I don't know. He left without a word. We haven't heard from him once."

"Yeah? Shit. Well, I guess he's real busy."

Plain-looking men bought me drinks. I danced a drunken, lazy dance alone on the dance floor. I drifted back to Shit.

"Hey, Shit. Maybe I could work here? I could help out with things, with anything. Is that possible?"

She wiped the counter down with a musty-smelling rag. "Fuck, buddy. I don't—well, I guess you could maybe—are you even eighteen?"

"Yes." I wouldn't turn seventeen for two months.

"Ah, fuck. Well. Is your mum okay with you working in a queer bar? She's full-on dyke now, right? She goes around with that fat butch who acts like her shit don't stink?"

"Barbara. Yeah."

"Well, you check in with your mum and make sure it's cool."

"I GOT A JOB."

"Already? I'm impressed. Where?"

"At the Stopper, busing tables."

"A bar. Naturally. I'm sorry, no. You're not old enough to work in a bar."

"It's fine. I'll be fine. Shit says she pays off the cops so they never give her trouble."

"Oh, well then. That makes all the difference. No."

Barbara poked her head in. "Shit, from the Stopper? She's pretty rough hewn, but ultimately a good person, Marg."

"See, Mom? What are you worried about?"

"The long answer? That could take all day. And please don't insert yourself into this, Barb. No, Roland. You could be beaten, raped ... do you think you're going to walk home every night? That right there is a bad end waiting to happen."

"I'll ride my bike."

"Only to get smucked by a drunk driver."

"Please. Just let me try it. I need to meet people. People in my— in *our* community. So I won't feel so alone, like I've been feeling."

She walked her stiff-legged walk through the kitchen, across the living room, and back.

"You can try it for a week. And during that week I don't want to hear you moan about Birdy's absence. And I don't want you writing any more poison-pen letters either."

APRIL 14, 1972

Dear Birdy,

I just want you to know that I'm getting on with my life despite your betrayal. I have a job in finance. It's really exciting. It's all coming together for me.

Your third single is AWFUL. I fear that you're heading into a downward spiral. How sad it is that your career is over before it even began. I know that the AWFUL single is charting in the States, but that means nothing.

I feel sorry for you, if I'm being honest. You know what my mother said about you? She said that your obsession with fame is mental illness. How sad. You sad fuckface. You probably have gone crazy. You're probably locked up, screaming. Good. Good!

I bet you're sucking lots of disgusting cocks in the nuthouse. What an achievement. You're going to win a Grammy for Best Case of Asshole Gonorrhea. Way to go.

I guess I'll sign off. I'm so busy. I have a date tonight with someone really sexy and rich.

Fuck off,

Roland

I worked a weekend at the Stopper. It was rocky at the start; I'd always thought a busboy should move slowly and discreetly through a bar so as not to disturb the ambience, but Shit kept snapping at me to move faster, and faster still, until I was literally running throughout my shift, pausing in dark corners to catch my breath. By Sunday I'd gotten the hang of it though. That night I drank with her and the other bartender, Brent, after we'd closed up.

"My back is so fucked," Shit said, trying to stretch even slightly, then seizing.

"Shit has a bad back," said Brent, a short redhead with dumb eyes that cast no light. He'd been staring at me all night; he was precisely the kind of bumbling gay who would make a faithful if somewhat dreary life partner, and if I hadn't been so mired in my hideous love for Birdy, we might've been a thing.

"Is it from an injury?" I asked, trying to be ingratiating.

"It's from standing and serving in bars for twenty years. And if you can believe, when I first started, I was high femme and wore heels. High heels to sling beer. But it was the fifties, so."

"We owe your generation so much," I said.

She rolled her eyes. "You don't need to butter me up with that crap, kiddo. We were assholes back then too. Only difference is I don't have to pretend I like cock now. And make no mistake—we step out that door, there's still a whole bunch of people who'd sooner slit our throats than look at us. "

Brent went "Oh ho ho ho ho!" like a hopped-up Santa. It wasn't laughter, but a kind of reflex, like he'd been poked somewhere ticklish.

"I know Birdy respects you a lot. He said you really helped him get his chops down, letting him play piano here. He said you're one of his favourite people. One time, we were going to see *Rosemary's Baby*, and he said he thinks you'll probably get some sort of life-time achievement award, from the community, like, when all is said and done. Oh. and he said—"

"Jesus Christ, kid, enough! I mean, thanks, but you need to wrap it up with the Birdy shit. He's gone for good. Fuck knows I wouldn't look back if I had the chance to get the hell out of here."

"I know he's not coming back. But we are in—or, we were in a relationship, so we have unfinished business. We need to address that."

"He's not going to address nothing, sweetheart. He's got his life, and you've got yours. It's time for you to bank some coin and start having your own kind of fun."

I nodded but stopped listening. I knew Shit possessed gritty wisdom, but she'd never been ensconced in anything as operatic as my Birdy situation.

Brent perked up belatedly. "Is your Birdy the same Birdy's that's famous?"

"I wouldn't say he's *famous*. He's making some headway, but it could all evaporate."

"I like him. He has such a nice singing voice. And he's really good looking. Oh, and I seen him on a show, and he seemed so nice."

Shit silently poured me another pint of Blue.

"He may seem nice," I hiss, "but he's not."

We drank until four in the morning. I biked on the sidewalk all the way home; the streets were busy with speeding meatheads. When I got home, my mother yelled, "FINALLY! WE HAVE TO TALK IN THE MORNING!"

ONE OF BIRDY'S peons sent the exact same photocopied photograph as before. This time I took it to my bedroom desk and drew jowls, laugh lines, and jagged teeth on his perfect if blurry face.

SHIT TOOK TO ME, and I started working six nights a week at the Stopper. Most nights I drank with Brent and Shit until near dawn, came home, and slept until three or four in the afternoon. This routine worked for me: I made money, shared boozy secrets with my co-workers, who quickly became like family (this bond would vanish when I left the bar, but at the time I felt like I'd found my clan), then biked home, where I'd fall into delicious, drunken sleep for twelve hours and then lope around the house in my bathrobe, sipping sugary coffee. I was seventeen years old. I thought I was acquitting myself rather well for a dropout with no ambition. This was all temporary! Despite my standoff with Birdy, I knew there was more to come between us, more combat, more … well, more.

BIRDY'S ALBUM, ENTITLED *More!* in a wacky synchronicity, finally came out after one top-ten single and two top twenties. I bought it as soon as Barry's Sound Centre opened on Tuesday morning, July 18, 1972. I wanted a covert transaction, but Barry wouldn't shut up about it when I placed the album with Birdy's face, done up like a sexed harlequin, on the counter.

"Ah, our local hero! I think he's probably a queer, but as long as he doesn't rub it in our faces, eh? You'll want a paper bag for this."

"Yeah."

I race-walked home and ran up to my room and my shitty little record player. I scratched off the cellophane. I pulled the record out of its fancy sleeve, which featured another shot of Birdy as a harlequin, but this time it was a full-body photo, with him sitting back on a rocking horse and kicking up his bare legs. When I look at that picture now, he looks like a skinny, pretentious drag queen, but at seventeen I saw a glorious, soft-focus ode to true beauty.

I flipped the sleeve over to the liner notes. And there it was: A paragraph of thank yous that included Birdy's mother, brother, and even his asshole father; my mother; and our long-ago choir leader, Dr. Caesar Stock.

At the bottom, in Birdy's florid cursive, it said, "This record is dedicated to RK, with love."

I pressed it to my chest. RK could only be me; surely he hadn't fallen in with another formative RK in the months since he'd been gone. I wailed like a Beatlemaniac, circa '63. "He still cares!" I cried. "He still loves me!"

My mother tapped her cane against my door.

"What is going on in there? You rattled my patient, Roland!"

"Sorry. Sorry. I'm fine."

"You cannot scream while I'm in session. If you have to scream, go out into the shed."

I PLAYED THE RECORD. Seven of the songs I knew. Two were written by someone else. And there was one new self-penned song, the closer, "Don't Mind My Madness," that I was sure was about me. The lyrics were inept but passionate, like all his lyrics.

The first verse went:

Sometimes I don't even know who I am
Sometimes it's wham, bam, thank you, ma'am
Sometimes I want to call you on the phone
And tell you that I want to come home

His voice was raw and whispery, like he'd been up all night. It was just him and his guitar. I cried again but was careful not to scream. How could I have been so petulant in my letters to him? How could I forget that he was broken from birth, that he could only give what he knew how to give: his music, his gorgeous music, so filled with inchoate regret and every heartfelt thing I longed for him to say flat out, in person? I'd been a shrew. I wanted to punch myself in the face.

"The whole record is like, I really feel, a letter to me." We were eating some bland, gritty, grey concoction that Barbara had made for dinner. I couldn't discern a single ingredient with any certainty. We ate the goop and listened to Birdy's album.

"It's very eclectic," said Barbara. "I love this sort of mariachi one. I've often thought about writing in Spanish."

"Do you know Spanish?" my mother asked.

"No. I'm so inept at other languages."

I saw my mother's upper lip curl a little. She and Barbara weren't growing apart, necessarily. It was more that they we were growing into each other, rapaciously, like duelling tumours.

I brought Birdy's record to work, but it was already leaning against the bar-top beer fridge.

Shit played it all night. People couldn't stop talking about it, about him.

"There's never been anyone famous from Winnipeg!"

"Yes—the Guess Who, 'member?"

"Oh, right. Well, but there's never been a famous gay from Winnipeg."

"His voice is so relaxing on the slow songs, and so energizing on the fast ones."

"Apparently his mother drank herself to death, and then his father too."

"You don't know that for a fact."

"Ooh, I like this one! It sounds like it's from Mexico."

"You mean it sounds like it's Mexican."

"Right, yes."

"Ooh, turn it over when it's done, Shit!"

All night I slipped around the room with adorable downcast eyes, like Lady Di when she still had hope for her marriage. I too felt like a famous wife—Birdy's girl, smiling shyly while everyone talked.

After work we drank, as we always did. At first I was tight lipped about the record, but as we tossed back the beer and the whisky shots, I found myself unable to stop talking.

"I know I've been maybe somewhat bitter these past few months, but I see everything with fresh eyes now. He dedicated the record to me, but it was more than that, if you know him like I know him. It was as close as he could come to a marriage proposal. I'm so happy. I haven't been this happy for so long."

"You know I think the world of ya," Shit said. "But you don't want to get too carried away. He's ignored you for a year and change."

"You couldn't be expected to understand. Anyway, I think the best thing for me to do is go to Toronto and track him down. That's what he's trying to communicate to me. He wants me to take the initiative."

Shit shook her head. Brent clacked his oddly long fingernails against his pint glass.

"What? Does that sound delusional? I don't think it is. Life is all about—it's all about—"

"Go ahead, baby," Shit said. "What is life all about?"

I looked at the silvery scar that ran down Shit's left temple and seized up. The nerve of me, talking life lessons with a woman who'd seen it all.

"I don't know. Do you think that's a bad idea? Going to visit?"

"Do you know where he lives?"

"No."

"Can I maybe say something?" Brent asked. "I was in love this one time? And he was a farmer in Saskatchewan, but he came to Winnipeg every few months for, you know, fun in the city. And so then I went to visit him at his farm, and turns out he had a wife and kids, and he ran me off the property with a rifle. He came to the city one last time. He peed on me, and I was suddenly filled with hope … I never saw him again."

I waved him off. "I'm sorry that happened to you, Brent, but your situation is totally different from mine. Birdy and I have been very, very close for a very long time. Since we were little kids. We're … inevitable."

"I think you should at least send him another letter," said Shit. "Even if they just send you another 8 × 10. At least they'll pass the info up the chain, and he'll have advance warning."

"Advance warning of what? I'm not a mudslide, Shit. I'm not a tornado." I was still in a bit of a snit after Brent's stupid cautionary story about the closeted farmer. But the next day I decided to heed Shit's advice.

> My lovely person who I love more than anyone ever,
> Your record is so good. Everyone in town is talking about it. I'm so proud of you. I love you so much, but still in a sexy way. I want to suck your cock and do sex things to your balls.
>
> Margaret was so touched that you thanked her in the liner notes. And naturally I was beside myself when I saw that you dedicated the record to me. Thank you for letting

me know in your private, special way that you still care about me. I know I was a little bit upset that you left so abruptly and that I haven't heard from you. For a while there I felt like I had fallen from the story, if you get my meaning. I was part of your very important story and then all of a sudden I wasn't, I was just some loser living with his mother and her lesbian lover. But that's behind us now. I feel like I'm part of your special story again.

So! Guess what? I'm coming to visit you! Of course, I don't have your address or phone number, but I'm sure when I tell the receptionist or whoever at your record company who I am, they'll point me in the right direction. Isn't that exciting? I really hope you think that's exciting.

I love you. I just want to be your baby. Nothing else matters. My heart is racing as I write this. I can't wait to see you. You're so great and nice. I love you. Okay, I should stop now!

XOXOXOXOX

Your baby,

RK

I bought myself some flashy clothes at Beyond, the funky clothing store that was run by two pretty sisters with extra-choppy Ziggy Stardust mullets. Their parents had bought the store for them, so they just lolled around the shop, smoking, utterly unconcerned that they had no customers.

I bought a jean jacket with starburst appliqués all over it.

"Oh my god, I cannot even deal with how good that looks on you!" said one of the sisters.

I bought a pair of bright-green spandex bell-bottoms. My inner thighs bulged in them, and my genitals looked like someone's first attempt at baking a tiny bran muffin.

"Caliente!" said the other sister.

I bought some shiny red platform boots. They were too small, but I loved being six inches taller and wobbled the length of the store, making up my mind.

"You're a total god in those! Those boots are made for buying!"

"**WELL, YOU DEFINITELY** look contemporary," my mother said, once I'd stuffed myself into the whole ensemble. "But you don't look comfortable."

"Oh, Margie," said Barbara. "Pay her no mind, Roland."

"Barb. Do not."

"Do not what?"

"You guys, it's okay. I know it's not my usual style. Please don't fight."

"We're not fighting, Roland. I'm only trying to parse the wreckage of my life."

"Your mom is punishing me because I dared to doubt aloud my ability to care for her, long range."

"You came up to me, and you fondled my cane fearfully as though it were some Satanic talisman. And then you said, 'Oh, sweet soul, what will we do when we're faced with the roiling bedpan?'"

I had to clench my anus to keep from laughing.

"It's okay, Roland, the correct response is laughter. She couldn't simply express her worry for the future and maybe take my hand. Oh no. And she had to speak in the *plural*, like we were both destined to shit the bed. Or maybe you were using the royal we—were you using the royal we, Barb?"

Eventually they forgot my presence as they fell to calling each other terrorists. I stuttered away in my platforms.

THREE DAYS LATER Birdy's letter arrived via express post. No 8 × 10 this time, no tacky postcard thanking me for writing. This was a letter from Birdy, on personalized stationery: "From the desk of Birdy O'Day," bracketed by tiny yellow roses.

Roland

I got your letter. DO NOT COME TO TORONTO. DO NOT COME HERE. I love you but I'm totally different person now, and I'm very, very busy. IF YOU COME HERE YOU WILL BE ARRESTED OR SOMETHING SERIOUS LIKE THAT, okay?

Yes, I dedicated the album to you, and I meant it. Why isn't that enough for you? When I was in Winnipeg, I honestly did think it would be nice and practical if you were my assistant, but now that I'm in the thick of my career, it's clear that was a bad idea. Terry got married to that brainy girl, and they're moving back to Winnipeg. That was disappointing, but I can't hold him hostage, can I? I see now that it's better not to have a personal relationship with my employees. I've signed with Capitol in the States and I'm starting a really long tour down there in a couple weeks. They're releasing the album next year, but they're making me change the title. They want to call it *Stop and Go*, which is fucking dumb but I don't care. As long as it's a hit.

I have to go, but I love you and DO NOT COME TO TORONTO, EVER. Okay? I'm sorry if this letter was harsh but I need to have boundaries. Morty—my manager—says I'm too soft hearted and it could be my undoing.

Please try to have some confidence in yourself. You have a soft touch—maybe you could get into massage or even hairstyling. Remember our corny science project? ha ha

With thanks

Birdy O'Day

For a good half-hour I was oddly calm. I straightened my room, tying back the curtains with their ties of the same fabric, I plumped my pillow, and I folded Birdy's letter in half and placed it in my desk drawer. I looked around the room with domestic satisfaction.

Then I went downstairs to the living room and collapsed at my mother's cold, numb feet.

I WENT TO WORK, drank, and bitched about Birdy with Shit and Brent, then came home and had a few more beer and went to bed.

Birdy broke through in the States with the singles he broke through with in Canada. I wanted to die. The album went to number fourteen. I wanted us both to die. He was on *Johnny Carson* in 1973, where he mostly only giggled with huge, new teeth—caps, probably.

In 1974, on a talk show hosted by Rona Barrett, she asked him if he wanted to confirm or deny the rumours of his "alternative" lifestyle.

"I can finally confirm the rumours, Rona," he said mischievously, his jumpsuit blazing with glitter. "I am proud to announce that I like ... *cock*-atoos!"

Rona laughed. So began Birdy's fifty-year stint of nauseating evasion when pressed to come out.

"Weak," I said. "He's such a fag."

"He'll come out when he's ready," my mother said, turning down the sound.

I STARTED MISSING shifts due to hangovers. Shit was indulgent at first, then took to hectoring me.

Brent developed a hole in his bowel and died of sepsis at twenty-eight. I'm ashamed to this day that I missed his funeral because it was too early in the day, but we threw a wake at the bar that night. At the end Shit was weeping with her head on the bar, until she reared up and screamed, "WHAT THE FUCK IS GOING ON IN THIS ASSHOLE WORLD!" It felt exactly like the season finale climax of a soap opera, and as I massaged her shoulders, I couldn't help but pretend that I was Mia Farrow in *Peyton Place* and Shit was Gena Rowlands in a guest spot.

With Brent gone I expected to be bumped up to relief bartender, but she hired this whiz kid young dyke dynamo to bartend instead. I tore into Shit's office before we opened.

"I have given my all to this bar for three years!"

"No. No, you haven't, Roland. You've been fucking up a lot. You miss at least one shift a week. You're lucky I haven't given you the boot. Sandy comes highly recommended. She knows how to make all those bullshit fancy drinks. The fags will love her."

"I'm so upset."

"With who? Me? Or you? Cuz you should be disappointed in yourself. It's not cute to miss work because you're hungover. Christ, you think I haven't gone to work with my head pounding like a fuckin' drum? You suck it up and you go to work. You're what now, twenty-five?"

"Twenty."

"Well, there you go. You've only got a couple chicken years left. Some queers would already pass you over for being too old. It's time to take stock."

"I thought we were friends." I hated the cliché as it left my mouth.

"Yeah? What's your point? How many fuckin' times have I told you work is work and play is play? Brent was my friend too, almost like a little brother, and he's in the goddamn boneyard, not even thirty. Only time he ever missed work was when he dropped dead."

I waited to speak, out of respect for Brent. "Well, I may have to explore other options."

She sighed. "Okay. Yeah, you do that, buddy."

I shrugged, turned precisely on my heel, and went out to work my shift. Sandy arrived. She was really cute with her thick black shag haircut and cowboy shirt, and she was genuinely nice, not obsequious at all. I watched her pour pints perfectly and shake her cocktail shaker with a friendly flourish.

I worked a few weeks more, then stopped going.

Shit phoned after I missed two shifts straight.

"That's all she wrote, you little bugger. You're out. Finis. All right?"

"Can I still come to the bar to, you know, drink?"

"I'll take your money, sure. I'll always take your money."

I WAS HAPPY to hear that. I grabbed two cans of beer from the fridge and took them up to my bedroom.

I guess I was depressed—beyond the dismal veil of daily alcohol withdrawal, that is. But once in a while, in the evenings, when I was tipsy but not yet hammered, I'd dance around my room, filled with an odd gumption and convinced that my path to fulfillment involved beer, somnolence, and masturbation. Those episodes were fleeting.

TWO YEARS PASSED. Birdy's second record came out, worldwide this time. The first single, "Sexy Ladies," went to number one in Canada, number three in the States, number seven in the UK, number seven in Ireland, and number ten in Norway. He went on a world tour. He played every Canadian city except for Winnipeg, and local deejays called him "ungrateful" and "off putting." My mother offered to take us to Saskatoon to see him. I said I'd rather eat barf. A weird vertical wrinkle developed on my forehead, like a crease but more pronounced.

My inertia infected the household; Barbara took to carping at the furniture. "Fucking recliner, what the fuck are you doing in the middle of the room … fucking coffee table!" She was as unhappy as I've ever seen a person, terminally baffled by the squalid predicament she'd fallen into, so far removed from when Gwendolyn MacEwan had sat on the couch that Barbara now cursed whenever she walked past it.

My mother wasn't happy about my indolence, but she was so focused on self-preservation, as her muscles shrivelled and exhaustion left her in a state of giddy uselessness by day's end, that she hadn't the energy to criticize me. She gradually ceded to her partner on all matters, big and small. But I'd sometimes catch her eye, opaque and watery, and know that she was trying to transmit disappointment.

I went to the Stopper and to the new bar, a slightly tonier place called Peekaboo. Peekaboo was fun if I felt like mingling with boys not yet beaten down by life's grief. Sometimes I'd see someone from high school, like Peggy Isner, with her pigtails and basic pluckiness, or Mike Brignall, who was fat and quiet in school but was now thin and gregarious, clearly basking in his freedom with a glee I was never quite able to muster. One night, fucked up on tequila and half a Quaalude, I nudged him into the bathroom and kissed his dry, thin lips. This went on for a few minutes, and the whole time I was thinking, like a fucking fool, *This is not Birdy this is not Birdy …*

I got a job at a shoe store. It was vast, almost like a warehouse: row upon row of cheap, dusty shoes. I quit at the end of the day.

I told my mother I got fired. She was eating a graham cracker very, very slowly.

"Oh, Roland. I know we all have our growing pains at different times, but you … I do get worried. If something happens to me and it's you and Barb locking horns every day … What a horrid existence."

"It's just like you said, it's growing pains. Everything will be fine. I'm actually really optimistic about the future. I am."

I'd said that so listlessly that I was sure she'd bust me, but she just went back to her graham cracker, like a hungry parrot. "Well, that's good to hear. That's a load off my mind, for sure."

TWO YEARS PASSED. Birdy won a Grammy for Best Male Pop Vocal Performance, and in his thank yous he thanked someone named Garth, wiping a tear from his cheek.

Garth. Clearly his new love interest. What more was there to say? He was running with upscale gays, beautiful, stupid, but somehow close to completing their doctorates in Chinese opera or the history of interesting furniture. Or whatever. I wanted to die.

I wasn't always drunk. I could go for days without a drink, and those days would be filled with remorseful housekeeping and a ticking panic I couldn't name that forced me to shut myself in the downstairs bathroom and sit on the edge of the bathtub, head between my knees. I was twenty-four years old. Even I had to acknowledge that it was probably time to get on with things.

My tiny life started to come apart the summer of '79. Birdy was riding high with "Time to Fly," a disco duet with Candi Staton. I was scavenging for cans and bottles to cash in for beer money. My mother had been enjoying a remission and started going for short walks in the neighbourhood. Barbara tried to walk with her, but my mother shut that down.

"It's a meditative time for me."

"But what if you fall?"

"If I fall, I guess I'll just lie there until I feel like getting back up."

"I'm losing her," Barbara said to me one day, after Margaret left for her walk. There's a … withholding. It's like she's drained the best of me, and now when she looks at me, it's like I'm a peach pit."

"A peach pit?"

"You know, like she's eaten the peach and now all that's left is the pit. But, you know, she can't throw the pit away because I live with her, or it lives with her—the peach pit, I should say—so it sits there, rotting, and when she sees it, she wants to throw up."

"Huh." It was often hard to remember that Barbara was once a poet of note.

ANOTHER GAY BAR OPENED. The Victory was all disco, all day and night. I'd start my night at the Stopper, where I'd drink at the bar and watch Shit and Sandy steal kisses between drink orders. They'd been a couple for years. Their love had softened Shit, and she would frequently buy shots for the whole bar. That was nice.

Then I'd go to Peekaboo and drink until I felt loose enough to sway alone on the dance floor and stare down any man who wasn't a blatant mutant. Occasionally these men would invite me back to their place, and I'd smile and sigh and slip away when they went to the bathroom, because I still had to go to the Victory and drink some more.

I was a fool for disco. Donna Summer, the Ritchie Family, Sister Sledge, Chic. I even loved shitty disco, all those phoned-in records by desperate has-beens like Ethel Merman and Frankie Avalon. Birdy's three disco albums were rather good. *Explosion* (1978) and *Catch Me* (1979) were both hits. *Dance with Me Forever*, released in '81, after disco's crash, was his lowest charting record on *Billboard*, peaking at 36. Personally, I thought it was one of his best, probably because he didn't write any of the songs.

I still wanted to die when I heard his music or saw him on TV, but when they played his songs at the Victory, something thawed in me, and I was able to savour his voice again. I threw my hands in the air. My fingers clutched and flexed. This was my only way of talking to Birdy, this awful, hopeless, sweaty prayer under the twirling disco ball and its speeding darts of coloured light.

After disco died the Victory owners tried to reinvent it as a new wave place, but Winnipeg queers couldn't be bothered with new wave, and straights stayed away from what used to be a gay bar. The Victory closed in '83.

I FINALLY NOTICED the chill between Barbara and my mother in 1980. Barbara would ask my mother if she wanted another cup of coffee, and my mother would close her bad eye and stare hard at Barbara with her good one. After an eternity, she'd go, "I don't care," like a bratty teenager.

I asked her if things were okay with Barbara.

"I don't know, Roland. I have so little energy these days after a full day of clients, I can't cope with her intensity. We've been together long enough that we should've arrived at a certain comfort level. But every day she comes at me with that needy, scary face, like some mask you'd hang by the front door to ward off evil spirits. I'm probably not even making sense."

"No, you are. It should be cozier, this far in."

"Yes, that's exactly the word."

"Have you talked about it with her?"

She laughed. "We've been talking for ten years. I mean, I've gotten better at communicating, but sometimes, especially when you're not feeling well, you just want to shut the hell up and watch *Jaws*."

I understood completely. I was a twenty-five-year-old alcoholic pill-popper who did nothing but sleep and stand around bars looking trashy but remote, but I understood the mechanics of a long, loving relationship. All I'd ever wanted was coziness with Birdy.

BARBARA STARTED SMILING coyly whenever we were all together. Like she was sitting on a big birthday surprise. Several times a day my mother would peevishly ask her why the hell she was smiling all the time, and Barbara would smile some more. It was like living with an enormous stone-butch kewpie doll.

One afternoon I was wrenched from sleep by a scream. I ran downstairs. There was an older couple, pale and plain, sitting on the couch. My mother stood in the middle of the room, braced by her lacquered canes. Barbara stood behind the couch, her long arms outstretched, forming a sort of awning over the couple.

"Look who it is, Roland!" Barbara said.

"I—who is it?"

"This is Hazel, and this is Bill—your grandparents! All the way from Saskatoon!"

This was such a non sequitur that it sounded like another language. Hazel and Bill looked up at me with their eyes but did not move their heads. Their snowy little faces conveyed only confusion.

"Well. Hi," I said. My mother bared her canines.

"Do NOT acknowledge them, Roland. I had nothing to do with this. It's the worst surprise ever. It really is the worst surprise, Barb. Please know that."

"I was only trying to make you happy, Margie. You've spoken so wistfully about your family situation, I thought maybe a reunion would be kind of curative, you know. Especially given your health situation."

Hazel took her boxy purse off the floor and put it in her lap.

"We would not have come if we'd known we weren't welcome," said Bill. "Your mother's been crying for twenty-five years, Margaret."

"Really? Wow. She must be very dehydrated."

My grandmother pulled a wad of wrinkled toilet paper from her bra and daubed at her eyes. "See, Bill! She's still so mean spirited and unforgiving, after all this time. Margaret, your father has phlebitis just awful but still, he made the trip."

"I'm sorry, but I don't care at all. Last time we spoke you called me a whore sent straight from hell—the logistics of which I still puzzle over—and you said that both I and my unborn child would be ripped limb from limb when we returned to hell, and then put back together, and ripped apart again, in a loop, forever. How loving. How comforting."

Margaret's mother put her palm out, like she was asking for change, then put her palm down again. The room was quiet a while.

"Maybe we should start with easy topics," Barbara offered. "Mrs. Keener, how were the crops this year?"

Hazel's mouth fell open. "We are *not* farmers. We live in Saskatoon proper. My husband managed a bank for thirty years, and I am very active in the community. I don't even keep a vegetable garden, although our land is lush. Do we look like farmers?"

"No. I'm sorry. I didn't know there was a stigma attached to agriculture."

No response from our guests.

"We were very sorry to hear about your multiple sclerosis," said Bill. "We've been estranged, but not a day goes by that we don't think of you."

My mother's legs were shaking.

"Mom, why don't you sit."

"I can stand. I'm capable of standing." But she sat.

I had no real stake in the standoff; I was very curious to know more about the people who created the strange, strong woman who'd raised me.

"Mom's having a remission right now." She gave me a murderous look. "She's doing really well. She goes for walks."

"Ooh, she goes for walks, how remarkable. I am not a poodle, Roland. Please don't make me sound like a poodle. I happen to be a highly respected psychotherapist."

"I know, Mom. I was just giving them an update."

"What's the outlook?" Hazel asked her daughter. "Your Aunt Flora went downhill from the get-go. Poor Flora ended up in a hospital bed in the middle of their living room, yelping and—oosh, I still get a chill—flopping around like a—well, what would you say, Bill?"

"Like a trout. A trout out of water. Flopping and yelping and gasping. Awful."

"Why are you here?" my mother hissed. "Did you come here just to taunt me with scary stories about Flora?"

"We came here, Margaret Yvonne, because your caregiver here said you were in a bad way and that you really wanted to see us."

Mom laughed, and I also laughed a little at the thought of my gruff mother tearfully calling out for her parents.

"Is that what Barb told you? That's a scream. Barb is not my caregiver, Hazel. She's my girlfriend. And all day, all we do is eat each other out. How about that?"

Barbara started laughing nervously, laughing and stroking the back of the couch. "I—oh you! I don't even know—you're too much!"

"Fuck off, Barb. The big-time dyke poet is suddenly shy to speak the truth. You should read them one of your poems. Recite something from *Fisting Desdemona*."

I assumed my mother was being sarcastic, but Barbara immediately closed her eyes and made the pulling-on-a-really-long-beard gesture she always did before reciting a poem.

She spackled the angry pubis with ointment.
"Stop!" I cried,
"Bend at the waist and spread for me, my darling,
my life raft!"

Barbara started to make gargling sounds. Margaret cackled, pleased to see the brazenly libidinous side of her girlfriend.

"I've always loved that one, Barb."

"Oosh, horrible!" Hazel gasped. "I'm going to throw up! This is Canada! Can't someone—call the police, Bill!"

"I'm sorry I jostled you," said Barbara. "I'm on the front lines of the avant-garde. The red shoes are dancing me to death. I'm possessed by art. Emily Dickinson didn't leave her bedroom for thirty years."

Bill patted his wife's somewhat bulbous knee.

"We shouldn't have come," he said. "We've been led into a vipers' den. When Mother Mary was led into the vipers' den and she cried out for fire, the vipers were set ablaze and turned into myrrh."

"Oh, shut up, Bill. That's not even a real Bible quote. I'm pretty sure that's something the mother in *Carrie* said to Carrie."

"Can't we try to be our best selves?" Barbara came around the couch and sat on the coffee table, leaning on her knees like a football coach exhorting his squad before the big game. "Can't we try to say neutral, loving things?"

"Barb. No. No, we can't. Not every relationship can be repaired by squishy conversations. Did you know that? Surely you must know that by now. Hazel, Bill. I'm sorry you came all this way for nothing. Now, if you don't mind, I'd like you to get out of my house."

"Oh, Margie. At least let me pour the coffee. You may never see your parents again."

My mother took several deep, rasping breaths. Her mother was leaning stiffly against her father, like a domino frozen in free fall.

"Fine. I need a cup of coffee."

Barbara went into the kitchen. We listened to coffee filling five cups. She returned with a tray. She put out a pitcher of cream and a pot of sugar. We all fixed our coffees the way we liked them. We drank our coffee and listened to the refrigerator's purr. Then they stood, my pious, wounded grandparents, and let Barbara lead them out.

"They're so old now," I said.

"Evil doesn't have an expiry date, Roland. Today was pure aggravation, nothing else. I've been with Barbara all these years and still she thought I'd somehow be enriched by this. What can be done with a mate who constantly mistakes you for someone you are not? Nothing. Nothing can be done."

"Well, that could've gone worse," said Barbara, when she returned. "They could've been a lot more ... crusty."

My mother looked at the carpet. She put two fingers to her lips. Barbara sighed contentedly in the silence.

"You cannot be trusted, Barb," my mother said softly. "There's nothing you won't do in your quest for corny scenes like the one I just had to suffer through. You can't be trusted. I don't know who you are."

As Barbara started in with some astrological excuse, I excused myself and went back to bed.

WHEN I AWOKE it was dusk. I heard my mother's canes thump against the floor in the hallway.

"I fell asleep, sorry. Is everything okay?"

"Barb is no longer with us." I pictured my mother beating Barbara to death with her canes. It was a possibility. "She's gone to a motel."

I was so relieved to learn my mother hadn't killed Barbara that I said "Oh!" way too brightly, so it sounded like I was happy that Barbara had been banished.

"I know. I'm sorry I subjected you to her for so long."

"You must be really upset."

"Oddly, no. I'm not. I have clarity. Weirdly, it's been a good day. It's rare that so much happens all at once."

"It's a lot to take in."

"Not really, Roland. I have a sense of myself for the first time in a long time."

"Because you saw your mom and dad?"

"Yes, because I saw that they'd grown older. I remember them as these monoliths, but now they're old and have phlebitis. They're still dumb, and hard. I can sort of fold them away now, once and for all. I'm cleaning house."

"That's so good. Way to go."

"Don't get too excited. You'll have to make some changes too."

"I'm open to change," I lied.

"Ever since Birdy left you've been living with hate in your heart. Hate has its place—today was a good example. But it's been going on eight years, Roland. Surely you don't want to live out your life like you have been."

My gut rolled at the thought of positive change—cathartic Spirograph art projects, some shitty janitorial job, jogging.

"You don't have to let go of Birdy, you really don't. If you can reimagine yourself as a fan of his, you can have the best of him, which, let's face it, is his music. He's pretty much a flop as a human being. Do you think you manage that change of perspective?"

"I think so." Could I be the sort of meek, benevolent creature who somehow massaged hate into fandom? It seemed so unlikely, such hard work.

"Oh, good. Good! How do you see yourself doing that?" she asked in her therapist voice. I'd only been awake for ten minutes; I couldn't possibly form a game plan right then and there.

"Should I send him another letter? No, that would be bad. I could … make a scrapbook? Of his achievements?"

"Yes! That's a fantastic idea, Roland. You can cut and paste little articles and things. And every time you scissor some little snippet from the newspaper, you'll be rewiring your brain a little.

I know it sounds corny, but several of my patients have had real success with that sort of thing."

AND SO, TO KEEP Margaret off my back, I started the scrapbook that I maintain to this day. The first thing I pasted into the scrapbook was an interview Birdy did with *Us* magazine, with several photos of him in a kimono at home: sprawled out in front of the fireplace; and in the kitchen, looking so surprised at the bowl of popcorn in his hands that you'd think he'd never seen popcorn before; and on an overstuffed floral-print sofa with a heavy-lidded, narcotic stare straight into the camera. In the interview, he was asked for the umpteenth time about his sexual orientation.

"I can appreciate the curiosity, I really, really can," he answered. "But fame is so exhausting that I find I need to keep my private life private."

Snip, snip, snip went my little scissors stolen from grade school. Cutting out that first article felt like martyrdom, and I groaned as I ran the glue stick across the back of it.

But my mother was right. As I pasted a picture of Birdy holding his People's Choice Award for favourite male singer, a small, bright spider of absurdity crawled across my brain, and for the first time since I was seventeen, I didn't want to howl at the thought of him.

I decided on beauty school, as Birdy had once suggested. My mother was very pleased. "The gay hairdresser is a cliché for a reason," she said. "I've only had my hair cut the once—you remember, it was after the healing retreat—but the gay man who did it had this beatific smile on his face the whole time. I'd never seen someone so fulfilled. He may also have been on drugs, but even so. I have the strongest feeling that hairdressing will serve you well."

I enrolled at Quantum Beauty School off Pembina Highway. I quickly mastered the basics. I had a talent—not nearly as significant as Birdy's, but still.

Now that I'd pacified Margaret, I went to the bars every night. I was there for the booze, mostly, but I did actively work on my flirting skills too. I'd made peace, more or less, with the fact that Birdy would never be my boyfriend in this lifetime, and I'd resigned myself to never finding anyone as memorable, so I felt free to go out and stare at men with daredevil persistence and say lewd or stupid things when they approached me. I went home with a few of them, after calling my mother so she could go to bed and not freak out that I'd been hit by a car. Always, with these men in their studio apartments, empty save for a bed, a TV, an ancient cat or dog, and strangely, more often than not a vase filled with dusty peacock feathers, I'd listen to them talk bitterly about their most recent boyfriend and how much they hated this or that bar regular, this or that coat check person. At some point they'd happen upon some paltry topic I could lock into, such as how pretty Olivia Newton-John was in *Xanadu*, or how perverse and snooty they'd heard Birdy O'Day was in real life. Then, like the drunken Birdy casualty I was, I'd quietly and solemnly announce my past with Winnipeg's wunderkind. Some of the guys didn't believe me, and some were so turned on by my proximity to celebrity that they'd brush aside their long bangs and lower their faces into my crotch as I studied the peacock feathers' faded iridescence.

I got pretty good at sex. I learned what men like, the stupid patter, the wide eyes agog at the always novel thrill of various acts and positions, the jocky, jovial punch to the pec as if to say *here we are, comrade, isn't this hot?* Some of the sex was fun. Some of it was intimate enough that vague plans would be made for a repeat. Most of it was boring and laboured, the two (or three, or four) of us desperately tugging our cocks to arrive at a chafed, dribbling finish. I learned gay sex. I felt a part of the community, a part of the dirty fraternity; I grew a beard and threw out everything that wasn't denim or plaid from my wardrobe.

A YEAR PASSED. I got a job as junior stylist at Fern's, a down-market salon by the airport where customers spoke gaily of their gangrene, wincing when I inadvertently grazed an infected ear piercing. They liked me, for some reason; they'd rattle on about their woes, and when I said "oh no" or "I'm sorry to hear that," they'd laugh incredulously, like no one had ever expressed sympathy for them before.

My mother's symptoms returned. She moved into the spare room off the living room, where she also saw patients. She lost a few ... inveterate basket cases who couldn't bear to watch my mother worsen or to see her heartbreaking bed in the corner.

We had a great time together. Now that she was immobile and I was no longer actively stewing about Birdy, we were able to sit late into the evening, gabbing about current events and the vagaries of life at the salon and the gay bar. She'd talk about her illness with philosophical remove—the ongoing surprise of it, the numb bits, the fatigue, how the whole predicament was something she'd never anticipated but wasn't altogether bad. She spoke of her sickness with the hushed nuance of a documentary voice-over, and I was fascinated by what she had to say.

"You know, you should probably clean up your act at some point soon," she said one summer evening, as we winced at each other through the tenacious sun.

"How so?"

"The drinking. And the sex. I mean, that's all totally fine, you're still young. But I'd love to see you with a nice boyfriend."

"I don't think I need a boyfriend. I'm like you—we don't need people in that way."

She laughed and knocked lightly on the arm of her wheelchair. "I'm not saying that you *need* someone. But you'd do great with a partner. Love would bring out new colours in you."

"I don't think so. I go to the bars every night and haven't met anyone interesting."

"You're not going to find a true suitor in a gay bar. You could take out a lonely hearts ad in the paper."

"Mother. I'm not that desperate."

"You are. What's wrong with a lonely hearts ad? I've thought about doing it myself."

"Nobody calls it a lonely hearts ad anymore. It's a personals ad."

"All right. All I know is, yours is not a solo journey. I know that for certain, speaking as the person who grew you. Reach out. Reach out, before you end up all fucked up in a wheelchair."

I'd not considered that I might also be felled by MS, but I held off on the personals ad. I went to the bars. Most nights were fun, or at least relaxing, after a full day of perming gangrenous customers.

BIRDY'S CAREER STARTED to sputter. We were nearly thirty, and he was struggling to stay pertinent in the era of angular synth pop. He put out an album called *Boing Boing* (1984) that was execrable, except for the cover, which featured Birdy so airbrushed that he had no nose and wearing a Claude Montana suit jacket with padded shoulders endless as airport runways. It grazed the very bottom of the charts in Canada and the US. I clipped and pasted an interview from *Graffiti* magazine.

> *Q:* Tell us about *Boing Boing*.
> *A:* What is that?
> *Q:* It's the name of your new album.
> *A:* It is? Oh! Right. Well, this record changed my life artistically, it really, really did. I've never cared more about a record, and that is the truth.
> *Q:* And how did you arrive at *Boing Boing* as the name of the album?
> *A:* I ... I was ... I saw a thing about ... I was—oh, right, yes, I was walking around, feeling really, you know ... I

don't know. And I suddenly thought, *You know what? Sometimes everything is just so, like, boing boing!* Do you know what I mean?

Q: I'm not sure.

A: You know what? Neither do I. And that, in a nutshell, is the nature of creative ... things. It's all very confusing. I love you!

I read that one to my mother.

"Oh, goodness. He doesn't sound lucid," she said. "He's floundering. I worried this would happen. That he'd get distracted by the trappings of celebrity and forget how to write."

I sent him a postcard—I couldn't help myself.

I love the new record! It's so unfair that it's such a flop. Margaret is worried that you're floundering and can't write anymore. I told her that was crazy talk. I mean, you were one of the six writers credited with "Time for Slammin' (We Be Jammin'!)," weren't you?

I'm well. Work is going great, and I'm very much in love with someone rich.

Love, Roland

I STARTED TO accrue a roster of faithful clients by 1985. I flirted shamelessly with Emilio, the salon owner, a cheery guy in his late thirties who favoured chunky gold jewellery and left his shirts partly undone, exposing thick black chest hair. I swooned when he swept in every morning in a cloud of Kouros, the ubiquitous cologne of the era that smelled like a urinal cake. I wanted him. My love for him wasn't lyrical like my love for Birdy; I wanted to keep house for Emilio, and rub his furry shoulders at the end of the day, and take him inside me, gasping and screaming.

I procured him the day his father died. His father lived in Palm Springs with Emilio's stepmother. She called Emilio at work, and he let out the most devastating wail at the front desk. Emilio had worshipped his father, and they were inseparable in the years after Emilio's mother died. Then his dad had met Verna, the stepmother, a woman who'd seen Liberace in concert fourteen times and loved to lie in the Florida sun every day until she burned. She called it "the sizzle." "Your dad and I are just heading out to get a good sizzle," she'd say. Emilio hated her.

We closed early and drank red wine from Styrofoam cups. We all listened to Emilio reflect on his father's life, and everyone grew weepy and talked about their own losses. I'd only lost Birdy at that point, which seemed like a frivolous loss next to Emilio's, so I stayed quiet. The other stylists—all women—gradually fell away to pick up their kids or return to worried husbands, until it was just Emilio and me.

I was drunk, so I forget the particulars of our conversation except for the moment Emilio threw his empty cup across the room and said, "I mean, what the holy hell?" And then our knees were touching, and we had more wine, and we kissed, and he drew the blinds and I sat back in my stylist's chair and hoisted my legs apart and he fucked me, murmuring thrilling things like "Who are you?" and "Who do I have before me?"

He came over for dinner, and when he left, my mother said she'd never met anyone as tied to the earth as he was. I asked her what she meant.

"I want to say that he's earthy, but it's beyond that. When he was talking he gave off this elemental shimmer, like he was formed by the tundra, the topsoil. He's good, Roland. I like him."

I moved in with him. He was minutes from my mom, so there was no wrenching departure; I was back and forth constantly, and Margaret grew so fond of Emilio that she'd yodel his name whenever he came through the door.

We had a good year, wonderfully humdrum and filled with great, cheerful sex. He fucked me with the placid diligence of a farmer. When it was time to have sex, it was time to have sex, simple as that. I was occasionally bored by his reliability and thought back to the havoc of Birdy. But I was happy. I was thirty-one. We still went out to the Stopper once or twice a week (Peekaboo closed in '85, after years of barren dance floors), but mainly to dance with each other or to play inept, giggly games of pool. I was an average person with a good job and a nice boyfriend. My mother was happy for me. Emilio taught me how to crochet.

My boyfriend was the first person I knew to get sick. He'd been lethargic for months; I chalked it up to ongoing grief over his father. I was cutting his hair at home one evening when I found a lesion on his scalp. I'd read pamphlets, I knew what to look for. I gasped when I saw it but didn't say anything until we were in bed.

"I found a spot—a purple thing, right above your hairline."

"Yeah," he said. "I saw it a few weeks ago. I didn't want you to get all worked up."

"Oh my god. Oh god. Okay. Well, if you have it, I have it."

"We don't know that. We don't even know if I have it."

We got tested. We spent the two weeks' wait doing busywork. My brain was like a kid's pencil drawing of a tornado, a blazing black scribble. We both tested positive.

We should've used rubbers. I know that. I know that. We were idiots to think we were safe way up north like we were, so deep in love like we were. I look back as, miraculously, an old man, and I think I would've been much more cautious. I don't care if it would've doused our intimacy; I'd have surrendered Emilio to the fog if it meant that I wouldn't have the lipodystrophy that has hollowed my face and placed an ugly pad of fat at the top of my back, or that I wouldn't have to take eight pills a day for thirty-eight years, or that my put-upon liver wouldn't periodically issue scary numbers that make my doctor hector me about never drinking again. If it meant that Tony and I didn't have to have such fearful sex in the years before PrEP, I likely would've left my sweet Emilio to tussle with his own fate, alone.

I took care of both Emilio and my mother, running back and forth between houses until I forgot who had which sickness. Emilio went downhill pretty quickly, while my mother simmered, stuck in her chair but sharper than ever, so untethered to worldly concerns that she sounded like an oracle, even when she was asking me to change her bedsheets.

"AIDS is not a plague sent by an angry God," she said once, when I was cutting her toenails. "Because there is no God, obviously. This disease is a chance for us to show our humanity. There was a wonderful woman on TV who said that AIDS will show how strong and resourceful gays and lesbians are when they're pushed to the limit."

I clipped her baby toenail—the shard darted across the room.

"This is the selfish mother in me, but I am so, so relieved that you don't have it."

"Me too." I hadn't told Margaret that I was positive, and I would not tell her for another eight years. I was well, I reasoned, so why inflict more worry on my put-upon mother?

Emilio was a big, bulky man, but AIDS turned him into a panting skeleton in the span of six months. I was running the salon and tending to him and my mother. The effort left me tired and wired at night, afraid of sleep, as though my wakefulness was the only thing keeping them alive, and I'd sit in the kitchen, drink coffee, and chain-smoke until dawn.

He put himself into hospice. I wept and insisted I could handle the workload.

"I know you think I don't fully understand you," he said, as we sat on our neatly made bed, waiting for the taxi to come. "But I've been watching you like you were my favourite movie since we met. I know when you're really up against it. I know when you need a rest. What kind of boyfriend would I be if I didn't know such things about my guy? You need a rest. You need a good rest, and you need to glue those little articles into your Birdy O'Day scrapbook to relax. I'll be fine."

Emilio died in August of 1987, after ten days in hospice. We had a little gathering at the Stopper after the funeral.

"He loved you hard," Shit said at some point that night. "If you think Birdy fucking O'Day could have loved you like that, you can hit the road. I don't want to hear no more bitching about how unlucky you've been with guys."

Shit was right. I'd been well loved. I was lucky. Emilio left me some money, so I cut back at the salon to three days a week. This gave me time to sit on Barbara's old couch in my mother's house and shake with fear over some indistinct threat, not just my HIV but something unnameable, shaping itself to the lilac bush out front until it was hidden, then drifting through the hall and dragging its horrible, horny toes, a constant, breezy threat. There was no safe place now.

So I started drinking full on again. I'd push all my appointments to the afternoon and close the bar every night. I was thirty-two now, and my drunkenness was no longer cute. I fell in with the old-timers at the Stopper, and we'd line the back wall, not talking, watching the young and unencumbered laughing in packs over nothing, their heads whipping back like Pez dispensers.

MEANWHILE, BIRDY SPENT three years in Vegas and made slightly alarming appearances on *Good Morning America* and Joan Rivers's short-lived nighttime talk show. ("Joan, do you know how pretty you are deep down inside? I had a dream about you, and there were buttercups everywhere, and I had such a feeling of … looking out the window.") He was quiet for all of 1988, then put out an album called *This Is Birdy O'Day*, intended as a fresh start, a bid for legitimacy after the soulless folly of *Boing Boing*. On the album cover he was shown emerging from a lake, no makeup, with big, penitent panda eyes. Song titles included "Please Forgive Me," "Pure and Simple," "I Come in Peace," and "You," a love ode that is as close as Birdy's ever come to coming out.

> *You're big and tall*
> *To you I give it all*
> *When I look into your eyes*
> *I know I'm in for a surprise*

It was another flop. Birdy went back to Vegas and took humble TV gigs, cooking shows and a regular spot on a very short-lived game show called *What's That Smell?* I did not delight in his decline; my anger had gone, and as I dutifully updated my scrapbook, I remembered Birdy as I'd loved him, with his soaring tenor and fascination with homely ornate things, like doilies and the Royal Doulton notions that gave his mother such pleasure.

With the money Emilio left me and my own savings, I opened Keener and Company in May of 1990. It was sleek and minimalist, all black, white, and grey, with conical steel lights swaying from the ceiling. We were an instant success; even our junior stylists had waiting lists. I couldn't believe it. Keener and Company remains my greatest achievement.

But throughout there was the virus, smouldering in me as it killed all my friends. Massive doses of AZT gave me diarrhea so intense that I lived on the toilet, whimpering when I had to wipe my chapped anus. I drank and did coke, furtively snorting in my basement office. Short of needle drugs, I did everything possible to douse the panic that sang in me always. There were so many terrifying ways to go: Dwayne was fine one day and comatose the next, Jeremy woke up thinking he was twelve and thrashed about with a fever so high that his body's heat made us slough off our coats in his hospital room, and Colin held on for four years, losing hair, teeth, and weight until he was an ancient, wisecracking newborn holding court in one of the soft chairs that Shit brought in for all the besieged, bony asses of our friends.

I dated a few guys, all positive, all very nice, but always our outings would devolve from phoned-in flirtation to shared fear. There were those of us who dove into sex with other positive men, scathing orgies soaked in every possible body fluid, and I might've joined in were it not for the fact that I've never had that kind of abandon, that capacious libido that could override reason and hygiene.

I was thirty-five years old and living with my mother again, but we both liked the arrangement. We were both going to die fairly soon, so we savoured our days together. I'd often catch her staring at me with a look of affection frozen on her face.

My mother's constant fatigue made her scale back her practice. I could tell whenever she was telling a client about her partial retirement; there would be bleating and pleading coming from her office. Her patients adored her.

I started having vague symptoms. Brief fevers, harmless but persistent skin infections, and my own case of unshakable fatigue. We'd sometimes nap together, Margaret and I, curled into balls on either end of the couch.

"You have to quit drinking," she told me one day, while we were dozing. "That's going to kill you, not HIV. You need to start looking after yourself. You're nearly forty."

"I know. I will. As soon as I have a good nest egg. Then I can take a break, or even sell the business. Until then I can't make any big changes. I have to plow through."

"That may not be your decision to make, Roland. Your body is going to rebel."

I didn't want to hear it. Course correction in the midst of so much anxiety felt impossible to me. But she was right, more or less.

I started drinking at work, my work grew slipshod, I lost clients. Then there was the staff walkout, me screaming and shaking my fist as they filed out. Keener and Company went under.

BIRDY MADE TWO consecutive Christmas albums, cheap and tinny and sad, sold exclusively through TV commercials: *Oh, Wait, Is It Christmas?* (1992) and *Christmas Is Really Interesting* (1993). I only listened to them once. Apart from hating Christmas music, I found Birdy's voice had deepened and coarsened, like he'd been chain-smoking since infancy. I saw him sing his very first hit, "Butterfinger," on *The Dini Petty Show*. He'd lowered the key by an octave and still struggled to get through it. His face was strangely puffy, and when he did his trademark gestures, his hands shook.

Birdy went into rehab in 1994, the day before I got pneumonia. The pneumonia was bad enough that I finally told Margaret that I had AIDS, after she levelled her harsh, crowlike eyes at me and demanded I come clean. She sat with me every day in the hospital, rocking in her power chair, eyes shut, like she was deep in desperate prayer. I even asked her at one point if she was praying. She laughed and said she was thinking about Barbara's tits. I told her I'd die if she got back together with Barbara. She said that wasn't funny, paused, then admitted that it was kind of funny.

I got over the pneumonia, but I was weakened. I got winded after taking the two steps to our front door. I remember holding hands with my mother across the kitchen table, crying, asking how it was that things could be so horrible.

"Happiness is an aberration," she said. "Some of us get to glide through life. Some of us can only withstand a token bit of misfortune. Dead grandparents, dead pets. You know those kinds of people. I was born under a hideous set of stars. Barb did my chart once. She started crying and wouldn't tell me anything else. She said Anne Boleyn had a similar chart. Roland, I swear, if there had been some way of warning you in the womb what you were being born into, so you could choose to live or to just float away like a dandelion seed, back to the earth ... I'm sorry. I'm honestly very sorry."

"Birdy O'Day's Journey Back to Sanity" was the title of the *Maclean's* article about Birdy's stint in rehab. It was filled with quotes like "I was just sick and tired of being sick and tired" and "what other people think about me is none of my business." All the recovery jargon. The article was accompanied by a picture of him jumping jubilantly in the air, as though rehab had left him without a care in the world, all his bedrock problems resolved in two months.

He got out three weeks after I'd been discharged. There were no further statements from Birdy on the state of his recovery. But there were several tabloid reports of relapse and two more stints in rehab. I felt no schadenfreude in my weakened state; I only wanted him to live.

He did make several bizarre TV appearances in the ensuing years, but in those he was manic, not sedated. His enthusiasm would've gone without mention if it were a young Birdy crossing and uncrossing his legs as though trying to tamp out a tiny fire in his crotch and jerking his head around as though jostled by a sudden scream, but this was Birdy at forty. Nobody is naturally that jerky in their early forties. But I can only speculate.

I HOBBLED ALONG until the antiviral cocktail came along in '96. All of us at the Stopper, spectral and dull weeks before, regained our vim almost immediately, and we continued to gather, stunned but gleeful, wondering how long these new miracle pills would work. We'd all been betrayed that way before with the noxious AZT. But our health held. Shit, who'd been holding it together as our sweet matriarch for decades, finally imploded as her own body rebelled with chronic fatigue syndrome, and Sandy sent her to Cancún, where she died, dozing on a beach lounger.

I rented a chair at the salon I work at to this day. I cut back on my drinking, devising an intricate set of booze rules: never two days in a row; never before six p.m.; only one big binge once a week, on a Friday or a Saturday; no hard liquor, ever. This arrangement worked for me. Margaret noticed the difference. "Abstinence is classist, in my experience. You're doing great, I think. Your complexion is so much less blotchy, and you're up at a reasonable hour. I'm fifty-seven years old, I can't walk, and I sound like I'm drunk when I'm tired, but I'm content. My son is getting on with things, doing the best he can. We're not in the poorhouse, and we have our nice evenings together, watching the nature shows. 'Lower your expectations,' I'm always telling my patients. In fact, get rid of all your expectations. Nothing bad will happen. We all have this nasty little schoolmarm in our heads, demanding that we do better or—oosh—*go for it*, and we have to banish that bitch. Oh! I just had an idea—let's have breakfast for dinner!"

BIRDY GOT HIS own talk show on CBC in 1996. I found it enjoyable. He asked thoughtful questions of his guests, regardless of the topic. He wasn't as jumpy as he had been. He'd had an obvious facelift, and his hair was now a shade of beige not found in nature, but otherwise he looked good. I liked watching his show, kicking back in the recliner with a Diet Pepsi. I was a middle-aged man with a steady job. I was no longer dying.

Birdy had become what they call a legacy artist: no longer a hitmaker but still capable of filling a good-sized auditorium, occasionally tickling the Adult Contemporary chart with one of his mushy ballads. Some deejay in Brazil remixed "Butterfinger," and it went to number one on the dance charts. When interviewed by

Entertainment Tonight about that unlikely bit of success, Birdy shrugged humbly and tried to force his waxy face into a smile.

"Score one for the old-timers!" he said, leaning into the hard *r*'s of the clipped prairie accent he'd camouflaged for so many years.

MARGARET RETIRED IN 2002, at sixty-three. She was falling to pieces. Her face had fallen into a permanent rictus of discomfort, no matter how happy she was, and she had to hold her head up with a fist steadied by the arm of her wheelchair. She'd been sick for so long.

"Do not for one second think that you need to take care of me forever," she said to me. We were sitting in the backyard, in the feeble sun of late September.

"Why do you say that?"

"I can get the home care woman to move in, or something along those lines. You had to wipe my ass last month, and I will not let that happen again."

"It really wasn't a big deal."

"It was for me. You're still relatively young—there's every chance you'll meet someone else worthwhile. Don't you want that?"

I looked at the lawn. It was overdue for a final trim before winter.

"I don't know. I've been loved. That's over for me now."

A chuckle came out of her pained face. "You can't say that with authority. You're a handsome man who's out and about every day. Anything could happen."

I put my hand on my mother's hand, the one that wasn't holding her head up. She'd been so kind to me, almost always. She could have so easily turned into an ogre—she was physically beautiful and had reason for bitterness, the way so many beautiful people tend to spend their beauty. But she'd refused. And I'd acquitted myself well enough to be her companion. My friends through the years have shared horror stories of intolerant parents who beat them, put them into conversion therapy or reform school, or simply threw them out of the house, as my own mother's parents did, never to see them again. I'd been lucky. I've been lucky.

I MET TONY that same year, when I was forty-seven. He was on the construction crew putting up a modest office tower next to the salon. He'd say hello to me whenever I went out for a cigarette. He was so beautiful, like a young Sal Mineo, with a lock of sweaty black hair always falling out of his hard hat and down the middle of his forehead. I assumed he was being excessively polite because he was new to the crew and wanted to prove to his co-workers that he was civilized and not likely to punch out passersby. Because he looked like the type.

The workers wrapped for the day. Tony came up to me, hard hat in hand, and asked me for a cigarette. Despite his copious courtesy, I was still afraid of him; he had an angry vein running down his forehead next to the lock of sweaty hair. I gave him a smoke and lit it.

"How's the hair business?" he asked me. I noticed how guileless his eyes were, even with his permanent squint from a life in the sun.

"It's good. Business is good."

"Good stuff, bud."

"How's the construction business?"

"Shitty. Wouldn't trade it though. Well. Guess I'll see you tomorrow."

And that was the end of our first meeting. I finished up at work and took the bus home, thinking of the handsome, guileless construction guy, happy to know that there were nice straight men even in the butchest of professions.

We had an identical exchange the next day, and the next. Then he asked me if I liked to play pool. I thought of Emilio and me, laughing as one of us attempted a fancy shot. I said yes, I did love pool.

"We should go play pool at Toddy's sometime."

Toddy's was the diviest of dive bars, a place old women would run past no matter how hobbled they were. I was sure I'd meet my demise if I ever dared enter.

"Yeah, that sounds good."

"Cool. Well, how about tonight? Friday night, after all."

It still didn't occur to me that he might have designs. I thought he might be a nice guy who, for whatever reason, didn't have any friends.

We went to Toddy's. I was treated decently; Tony seemed to inspire goodwill from the patrons, which extended to me. I decided to make it my beer binge night, and Tony matched me through to last call.

On the street I put out my hand to shake goodnight, but he pulled me to him and kissed me expertly, an obvious veteran of men's mouths.

"Is this okay?" he asked.

I choked on my tongue. "It's—yes. I'm just surprised. I thought—"

"You thought I was a straight dude with no friends."

My mouth fell open. His assumption was almost telepathic. Telepathy is the sexiest. Birdy had read me with accuracy, but that was because we'd shared the same child-sized frame of reference. No one can pluck insight out of the air like Tony does.

That's pretty much it, the story of Tony and me. It started as an impossible thing, the stuff of listless gay porn: the construction stud and the adoring queen. Then we fell into each other. It was so easy, easier than Birdy, easier than Emilio, who could sometimes, even before he got sick, give way to a dusty Old Testament fatalism inherited from his superstitious, deeply Catholic mother. There was none of that with Tony. We were gently fused from the outset. He slept over at my mother's house; I slept over at his tiny apartment on Broadway, which featured a couch, a TV, an aquarium soupy with fish effluent that three exhausted goldfish tried to wiggle through, and a mattress on the floor in the bedroom. It looked like a crime scene, but it was oddly tranquil, redolent with Tony's innate sanity. We got a place together in 2005.

My dear mother passed at sixty-seven from pneumonia, surrounded by former patients who'd become friends since her retirement, and Barbara, with whom she'd reconciled, and Barbara's partner, Enid, who smelled of mothballs but was otherwise very sweet and wispy. And there was Tony and me, obviously.

Eighteen years passed. While Tony and I canoodled, washed and dried the dishes, lolled on the couch and watched must-see TV, Birdy's career continued to crumble to the point that I'd have nothing new to clip and paste into the scrapbook for months at a time. I do know that he sold his California mansion for "something more manageable and rustic" in Connecticut (*Canadian Living*, "Catching Up with an Icon," August 2011). I visited his website once or twice a week. At first it was updated on the regular, but as his gigs became more and more mortifying—the 2016 Happy Baby Festival in Minot, North Dakota, opening for Juice Newton (free admission with fair pass); a short set in 2017 at a Taco Bell ribbon cutting in Sioux Lookout, Ontario—the updates petered out. Late in 2019, I typed in "birdyoday.com" and got a page that said, "This domain is for sale."

TONY HAS TURNED OFF the television, and I can hear him shuffling through the broadloom in the hallway. He knocks on the bedroom door before he opens it.

"Christ," he says, "I thought you'd died in here. What the hell have you been doing?"

"Nothing," I say. "I fell asleep. But I'm awake now."

"I was gonna turn in."

I make room on the bed. He slowly undresses. He's been mostly inert for ten years but retained his athletic, rangy body and six-pack abs. He grimaces as he places himself on the bed. His pain is always worst at the end of the day.

He turns off the light. He pats my chest.

"Did you put the clipping in the Birdy book?"

"Yes."

"Good. You're such a weirdo."

"Fuck off. You're a weirdo too."

"Guess we'll have to stay together."

"Okay."

He drifts off quickly as his bedtime meds kick in. When he's asleep I pull the Birdy book from under my pillow and gently place it on the floor.

An Evening with Birdy O'Day

TONY CALLS ME at work.

"Are you sitting down?"

"I'm working. Why would I be sitting down?"

"This woman called and said she's Birdy's assistant. She wants to give us tickets to Birdy's show, and she said Birdy wants to see you after the concert."

"Really. Huh." I refuse to get excited about an *audience* with Birdy, the boy who used to sleep next to me, curled into himself like a sad cat.

"That's good, isn't it?"

"I'm not sure. I don't know."

"Come on, Rolly. You guys can talk and have a cathartic-type thing."

I pull the plastic wrap from my client's head to see if the bleach is lifting evenly.

"I can't really talk right now. I'll come straight home today. We can talk about it then."

"Don't go all apeshit about this. I know you're going to go apeshit and get hammered at the club."

"No, I'm not. Like I said, I'm coming straight home today."

My client looks up at me with mild concern. I tell Tony I have to go.

"Is everything okay?" my client asks.

"Yes!" I chime. "Absolutely. Ooh, you're lifting nicely. I definitely think ash blond is within reach."

AFTER WORK I go to the club and get hammered. I sit with some
guy from Fargo. I tell him the whole saga. I can tell he's bored, but
I can't stop talking. I am absolutely the kind of tedious drunk I run
from, but I can't stop talking, gesturing wildly, grabbing the guy's
wrist for emphasis.

"This mother*fucker*, who hasn't put out a decent record since
nineteen-fucking-seventy-two, thinks he can swoop in and play
the hometown hero at the fucking Centennial Concert Hall, doing
his shite songs with his wrecked voice, but you know what? You
know what? People see him for the bullshit artist he is. We see
right through him. He knows he's washed up, and it's either do
a big, splashy homecoming concert or sing 'Butterfinger' for the
millionth time at the opening of someone's new garage door. You
know what I'm saying, Marvin?"

"Mark."

"You're great, Mark. Not like some people. You know what?
I was very serene before all this bullshit about the concert and the
visit. I was turning into a nice little old man. Like, little kids with
their folks on the sidewalk smile at me and wave, because they can
sense that I'm nice and don't want to fuck them. You know? My
husband is still hot, and we still like each other. Now comes all
this bullshit from fifty years ago, and it's like I haven't made any
progress at all. If I see Birdy, who's to say I won't smash his face
in? What do you think I should do?"

"Well. If you think you might smash his face in, I'd say you
probably shouldn't go."

"Yes! That is really insightful. But then again, life's all about the
big moments, eh? Don't you think? I mean, yeah, I might smash
his face in, but if I don't go see him I'll be—my mother used to talk

about how so many of her patients were half lives half-lived, and she wouldn't stop working with them until their half lives were whole. I don't want to be a half life half-lived. Do you know what I'm saying?'

"Oh, gee," Mark says. "It's almost eight o'clock. I should skedaddle."

"Okay. I love you like a brother. Hey, you know what, you know what, Marvin? You're my brother."

IT TAKES ME so long to get my key into the front door lock that Tony has time to shuffle across the living room to open it.

When I see his face I smile my drunken, apologetic smile—eyes sewn shut by hammy guilt, mouth grotesquely turned down, all of it meant to be cute and conciliatory—and Tony only sighs and goes back to the couch.

"I'm sorry, I am. I didn't think I would get hammered. But I am. I am hammered."

Tony drags on his spliff. "Dude, I know you. That's always how you deal with surprise news. You get hammered. It's fine, just don't pretend you're a Sober Sally, cuz we both know you like your beer when you're fucked up."

It's so nice being known, even in Tony's gruff, prosaic terms, and I fall upon him on the couch as softly as I possibly can.

"I love you so much, Tony."

"I love you too, but please get off me. My hips are throbbing. Feel like I've done the fucking Ironman, and I've been on the couch all day."

"I wish I could take away your pain."

"You're just loaded and you want to suck my dick, but thank you."

"You're so sweet," I say, and mean it. I'm drunk and full of kissy reverence, so even his dismissals sound like poetry. I doze briefly, my cheek pressed to his outer thigh, devoted and slobbering like a very old dog.

I'VE NO MEMORY of going to the bedroom, stripping, and tucking myself neatly under the duvet. I awaken with a painful pulse in my temples and jaw and tongue. Tony is already up and about. Despite his pain and the morphine that pushes it into the background just enough that he doesn't jump off our filthy balcony, he still keeps construction hours. I love his pride and valour.

He's halfway through his first pot of coffee.

"I don't remember going to bed. Did you put me to bed?"

"I nudged you along, yeah. Do you remember being at the club?"

"I—yes. Definitely. Yes. I talked to some guy from Fargo. About Birdy. I talked for hours at him. Poor guy."

Tony pours me my coffee: lots of sugar, lots of whole milk. "I got a call from Dr. Eadie just before you got up. Dr. Eadie himself, not just his receptionist. There's some brain thing, a study thing, where they put, like, electrodes in the brain, and it blocks the fibro pain."

"Wow, that's major. And he thinks you'd be a candidate?"

"Guess so. I don't know if I'll do it. It's early days, the whole study. But some woman in Sweden had it done, and she's been pain free for three years."

"Tony. That's incredible."

He shrugs. We've been down this road so many times—so many drugs, so many arcane therapies. He doesn't want to get his hopes up. I don't want to get my hopes up either, partly out of concern for him, partly—and ruthlessly—because I'm scared that if he does get healthy again, he won't love me anymore.

My first client isn't until one o'clock. I drink three cups of coffee. I try to go back to bed, but I'm too wired—from the caffeine but also from a sickening sense of my whole body whipping around in a centrifuge until it spits out toes and fingers. I know I'm freaking out over nothing. Birdy's coming to town, and we'll hang out for a few minutes, issue each other air kisses, and that'll be it. But my galloping heart is all drama: Birdy's visit augers chaos! I'll lose my boyfriend and my apartment and my job, and I'll trundle nude and sooty through the streets of Winnipeg until I throw myself in the river, just like my mother's boyfriend sixty years ago!

Tony comes into the bedroom for socks.

"I'm freaking out, Tony."

"About what? The brain study thing? That's a long way off, and I'm not even sure I'll go through with it. I don't want some asshole sawing away at my skull."

"I'm freaking out because ... what if Birdy's visit is an omen, and everything's just going to fall apart and—yeah."

"Do you want one of my Ativans?"

"That's not a very thoughtful response."

"It's ten o'clock in the morning, and my whole body's on fire."

"I'm sorry. Yeah, maybe could I have an Ativan? Will it make me drowsy?"

"Ha ha. Bitch, you're the one who used to pop Quaaludes like they were fuckin M&M's. You'll be fine."

Tony opens one of the little plastic doors in his plastic pill calendar and shakes out an Ativan. I put it under my tongue. Within a minute I feel synthetic contentment coursing through my chest and extremities. Drugs are so nice. Birdy's crazed, fanged face recedes from my mind. I sigh like someone in a commercial who has finally found the right mattress. I fall into a light sleep.

Tony shakes me awake at noon.

He waves an envelope in front of my face. "Look what just came express post. Front-row tickets, and VIP passes, and a little note from Birdy that I haven't read yet."

"Huh? Oh, could you read it for me? I don't have my glasses."

He clears his throat and unfolds a piece of pink stationery.

"'Dearest Roland, I can't believe I'm going to see you in a few days! I'm so sorry that I haven't been in touch for a while—'"

"A while! It's been fifty-three years!"

"Shush. 'Sorry I haven't been in touch for a while, but it feels so good to be resuming contact. I hope that you're flourishing, and Margaret too, as well as your love interest—my assistant Chrissie did tell me his name, but it escapes me at the moment. This tour has been so exhausting, all I can do between shows is lie in the dark. This will definitely be my last major tour—I'm too old for all this travel. Can you believe we're nearly seventy? It's obscene! Seventy! Tina Turner did her last big tour at seventy, and she said it nearly killed her. Tina's a doll. I had dinner with her and her husband in Zurich a couple years ago.

"'There's so much to say, isn't there? And yet there's nothing to say, is there? Because we'll just pick up where we left off. Our bond is magical that way. I'm at a real crossroads personally and professionally right now, and I find myself pining for my familiars, my special ones from childhood, that depth of understanding.

"'Hugs and kisses, your Birdy.'"

"Ugh. He thinks his old bullshit is still going to wash with me. He wants something. He probably has a colonoscopy coming up, and he feels old and wants to feel young again."

"You don't know that. Try not to have any expectations. Do you want another chill pill?"

I wave him off and wrench myself out of bed to shower for work.

MY CO-WORKERS ARE divided about Birdy's virtue when I tell them about his impending visit.

"You can finally have some nice closure," says Sonya, whom I've known for thirty years.

"Once a taker, always a taker," says Millie, twenty-six, who's been divorced for three years but still calls her ex in the middle of the night to make angry cat noises before slamming down the phone. "My ex fucked my mum and still hit me up to buy him a Camaro. Once a taker …"

"You should just go and check it out," says Jason, thirty and gay, but preternaturally positive (his parents were hippies). "Try not to have any expectations."

"That's exactly what Tony said. The fucked-up thing is that I didn't have expectations. I was so over it all, wasn't I, Sonya? Haven't I been like a totally different person these past few years?"

"Well, kind of, probably."

I glared at her.

"Yes, I should say. Definitely. You've been real peaceful."

"Right? And now I'm all fucked up. I wish he'd never been in touch. I wish he'd cancelled the concert."

THE DAY OF the show Tony doubles his doses so he won't be in agony for a long night out, and he takes me to dinner at the Keg. I order steak and lobster, but it all tastes like boot leather. Tony is stoned out of his mind and eats both his plate and mine.

"This is nice, eh? I think they changed the carpet in here."

"Restaurants should never be carpeted. It's so unhygienic."

"Oh, Christ, Roland, get the bug out of your ass. I haven't been out for so long. I want to have a nice time."

"I'm sorry. I'm just anxious. I'm really trying, Tony."

"Maybe when we get home I can pop some Cialis and fuck you. Would you like that?"

"It's okay. I know you hate fucking me now. My ass has gotten so—so flabby."

"Have I ever said that? Have I ever said your ass is flabby and I hate fucking it? No. Not once. I know it's a nervous time for you, but don't make problems where there are none. We're all good, you and me. Okay?"

I want to cry or release my tension in a showy way, but the Keg is not the place.

TONY WANTS TO smoke a few joints before the concert, and we make it to our seats just as the lights are dimming. The opening act is a young Indigenous woman named Beverly Robichon with a velvety voice, serious guitar chops, and a collection of songs that startle us with their lyrical precision and odd chord choices. I remember that she played a short set at last year's Pride. She should be headlining, not opening for some has-been.

"She's so good, it's blowing my mind," Tony whispers. "We have to get her CD at the merchandise thing in the lobby."

I nod vigorously. Beverly ends her set, smiles and waves, praises Birdy O'Day as a great ambassador for the Manitoba arts community, and snakes into the stage-left curtains.

Birdy's band assembles in the dark. They all have long grey hair, and for a second I wonder if Birdy has reunited the Rubies for his Winnipeg return. But then the houselights brighten by half, and I see that they are just old session men.

"Please welcome Winnipeg's own," lead-guitar old guy announces, "the legendary Birdy O'Day!"

There is courteous applause—more applause than when we saw Luba at the casino ten years ago, but less applause than when we saw Diana Ross at the casino five years ago—and Birdy strides out in a shockingly modest black three-piece suit. He is still lithe, if somewhat hunched, and he appears to favour his right leg. I attribute the slight limp to wear and tear, because there hasn't been mention in the press of a hip replacement or significant injury.

He paces the stage, applauding our applause, smiling, blowing kisses via heavily ringed fingers. He stops directly in front of me and narrows his eyes, wondering if the wan, wrinkled person I've become is his old friend. He does finally recognize me and waves wildly. I put up my hand in greeting.

He pulls his mic from its stand, and the band starts in with some slow, soupy preamble.

> *I've been so lost, so locked away*
> *No one to talk to, no one to say "hey"*
> *I've roamed the world in diamonds and fur*
> *I had a little kitty who liked to purr*
> *But then it died*
> *I felt so fried—*

"Jesus Christ," Tony mutters to me. "A dead baby could write better lyrics."

"I guess he tried to write a song for the occasion. Poor thing." I squeeze Tony's knee.

> *I was pushed to the limit*
> *I was a flibbertigibbet—*

"The fuck is a flibbertigibbet?"

"It's from *The Sound of Music*. Shush!"

> *Then it occurred to me that if I wanted to be happy*
> *I should go home*
> *Like a dog with a little something known as a "bone"*
> *Ha-wanna-hey-a-ka-ka-pow*
> *I'm here, Winnipeg, and I am wah-ah-ha-aha-aha-ah-wow!*
> *I'm here, Winnipeg, and I am wah-ah-ha-aha-aha-ah-ha-a*
> *WOW!*

"Thank you!"

"Fuck, dude. That fuckin' sucked," Tony whispers.

Birdy throws up his arms to bask in applause that does not occur. I'm shocked: at least half the audience is made up of middle-aged gay men, and even if they aren't big Birdy fans, they should at least acknowledge an earnest, if atrocious, intro tune. Yes, his voice is shot, with a wide, wobbly vibrato that one might hear at a nursing home singalong, but still. Have people gathered to gently chide a prodigal son? It can't be. Tickets weren't cheap. I brace for disaster. I don't want him to fail. I've pictured tonight as an unqualified love-in, chockablock with spontaneous avowals of fandom, shouted requests, sweet asides, a healing evening for all concerned. I watch him wilt a little and feel as protective as I did whenever he was cruelly lampooned on the playground.

"It's an indescribable feeling, being back home after—gosh— fifty years! Could it be?"

"Fifty-three!" someone yells.

Birdy points and smiles. "I stand corrected! Fifty-three years. Wowee. That's—yes. A long time. I have no explanation for why I haven't visited, I really don't. I love you. I—love you, and it's always hardest to tell the ones you love the most that—woo! Do not cry, Birdy O'Day! I am a gay Manitoban, and I can finally say that I'm proud of that fact. At sixty-nine!"

The dark ions in the room evaporate. Finally, there is hearty applause, and half of a standing ovation. I well up. I look at Tony; Tony's welling up. Birdy covers his face with his hands, like he did in times of distress when his social mask slipped and he had only his bare self to show. His lead guitar guy sidles up to him and tries to put an arm around his shoulders. Birdy bends, impish but decisive, to avoid his touch. Lead guitar goes back to his post.

The rest of the evening is as all that I'd hoped and more. Birdy runs through his hits, along with several unexpected covers: "Love and Affection" by Joan Armatrading, "Just Breathe" by Pearl Jam, "Harvest Moon" by Neil Young. This is a Birdy I've never seen before. Joan Armatrading? I get a sense of Birdy's private mileage all these years without me. All the frothy interviews I've clipped and pasted, the silly talk show shenanigans—all that time he's been collecting these sweet songs that speak to his greedy, sad, weird heart. We have a really good time, Tony and I, and after his initial nerves and the audience impasse, Birdy does too. He is crying freely throughout the last encore, a slowed-down, elegiac version of "Butterfinger," an old ditty that is suddenly a prayer.

Birdy's assistant, a tiny woman with a lot of damaged blond hair, runs to us as Birdy is leaving the stage for the last time.

"Mr. Keener and—Tony, I'm so sorry, I don't know your last name."

"DiCresce. Don't worry about it."

"I'm so sorry. Hi, I'm Chrissie, Mr. O'Day's assistant. We're so, so excited to have you with us. And—is your mother not attending, Mr. Keener?"

"Oh no, she passed away many years ago."

Chrissie bends forward in grotesque contrition, a pose familiar to anyone who's ever worked a job they desperately need. "I'm so, so sorry. I had no idea."

"It's fine, Chrissie, really. Birdy would have no way of knowing."

"I see, okay. Okay. Well, I'd really—I'd love to take you backstage to see Mr. O'Day, if you're okay with that?"

"Lead the way, Chrissie," Tony says, standing with the aid of the silver lion's head cane I bought him last year to replace the hideous foam-handled drugstore cane he'd been using for fifteen years. We struggled to keep pace with busy Chrissie, who was practically jogging through the shadowy bowels of the backstage.

We arrive at Birdy's dressing room. Chrissie knocks.

"Mr. O'Day? I have your friends here. Is it okay—"

Birdy throws open the door. When he sees me, he gasps and wraps his spindly arms around me.

"I can't believe it. I cannot! Roland. Oh wow, Roland! You look so good. I know I look like death warmed over. I'm in litigation with the guy who did my brow lift. My temples are completely numb." He turns to Tony. "You must be Tony! Oh, hi!" Birdy hugs Tony gently. "Wow, Roland, he is really foxy. He looks just like— you look just like Sal Mineo, Tony! Sal Mineo but more chiselled. Sal Mineo crossed with George Maharis from *Route 66*. Woof."

"I don't know who those guys are, but thank you."

"Come in come in come in." Birdy grabs a cigarette from a bowl of cigarettes on his makeup table. "Lighter ... lighter? LIGHTER!"

Chrissie bolts over to him with a lit lighter. Birdy takes several puffs, his eyes falling shut. He looks exhausted. Impossibly exhausted, as though the only remedy would be several months in a medically induced coma. I last saw him in peak teen health, and here he is now, looking so depleted but for nervous hands and rapid speech. I assume he's powered by some powdery stimulant, but fuck knows we all need a reason to get out of bed at this age, be it chemical or delusional. I still think I can be a world-famous hair guru, even though I have to pound on our shitty dishwasher like it's a war drum to make it start. If Birdy has to huff something to make it through the day, more power.

He urges us to sit on the sunken couch opposite his makeup mirror. I sit; Tony hesitates.

"I should let you guys have some time alone together."

"No, stay," I say.

"Yes, for sure, stay," says Birdy. "You're Roland's life partner. How long have you guys been together?"

"We're—what is it, twenty-three years?" Tony asks me, sitting on a couch arm, grimacing, then sitting down next to me.

"Yeah," I say in a small voice. I don't want to brandish our marriage. Birdy might be single. He may never have known long-term love.

"Isn't that wonderful?" Birdy says, puffing, drinking from a black glass, patting down his beige hair. Oh! I was with my guy for thirty-one. Ralph. My hubby's name was Ralph, isn't that insane?

He died last year. Lung cancer. I'm coping. It's a choice. I'm moving toward the light." He starts to sob and smack the makeup table. Brushes and palettes bounce and rattle. I want to go over and console him, but I can't move. It's been fifty-three years. Birdy said in his letter that we would pick up right where we left off, but that is not the case. I am different. He's different—wistful, worried, slightly out of breath. We are strange with each other, as he daubs at his tears with a kimono cuff and throws his head back in a silent laugh, exposing six decades of silver fillings.

"Did Margaret—was Margaret not up to coming?"

"Mom died in 2006."

"No! Oh, I can't stand it! Was she—did she suffer?"

"No, not really. I mean, she had the MS for many years, but she was so sanguine about it all, you remember. No, in the end it was pneumonia. We were all gathered around her. It was a good death, as they say."

Birdy starts crying again. "I'm sorry. I should've been there. I'm awful, I know I am. That whole year I was on this *unspeakable* oldies tour with Leo Sayer and Tiffany and this horrid Bananarama tribute act called Bananaramarama, playing tiny casinos that smelled like piss."

"Rolly and me like to go to the casino whenever we can," says Tony.

Birdy and I both nod thoughtfully. We play the slots at a tiny casino exactly like the ones Birdy describes. Our casino also smells like piss; the diehards void into diapers so they don't have to leave their favourite machines. As we sit in Birdy's frigid dressing room, sighing through the fumes of old cologne, I can't say that I'd want to swap our lives. I'd much rather play the slots at the casino than perform there. The stage at our casino is the size of a shoebox— how could all three girls in Bananaramarama possibly fit? Tony's knee, probably throbbing this late in the day, shakes against mine. It feels nice.

"Was the show okay? You can be honest. I know my voice is shot. My vibrato sounds like a dying car engine. One day I went into my little studio at home to do a guide vocal, and my whole top end was just *gone*. I'd go to hit a note, and there'd be nothing there. I know how to fake it, but it's not the same."

"I thought you sounded damn good," Tony says. "Better than ever, I thought. You've got a raspy thing going on now, kinda like Kenny Rogers."

"You're so sweet, thank you so much. Roland, you can tell me the truth, really."

"You were really good, Birdy. Your phrasing is so—you reminded me of Édith Piaf, that depth of feeling. I mean, yeah, you've maybe lost some range, but all singers go through that, don't they?"

He shrugs. "I know. You just don't think it's going to happen to you. When I turned forty I was on top of the world. I looked great, felt great, sounded great. I thought time would stop, you know? But—ha ha—it didn't, did it? Fifty wasn't bad, but sixty! Wasn't sixty awful?"

I think back to my sixtieth birthday. Tony took me to *Holiday on Ice*. Nancy Kerrigan was the headliner; she looked bored out of her mind and didn't do any jumps or spins. When we got home *The Deer Hunter* was on TV; Tony fell asleep but I watched the whole thing. I cried and cried when Christopher Walken shot himself in the head. It was a pretty okay birthday.

"Sixty wasn't too bad. Sixty-five was pretty brutal though. Not that I can ever retire."

"Oh yes, right—you're a hairstylist, no? That's great. Remember our science project? I was so queeny, even then."

"Rolly is the best hairdresser in the city, I think," Tony says. "He's won a lot of awards. Some of the old barkers he's made pretty, you wouldn't believe."

"That's great. Just great." Birdy stands, looking distressed. "Where did Chrissie go? I need Chrissie. Oh god, did something happen to Chrissie? CHRISSIE!"

Chrissie comes in.

"Oh, Chrissie, I got so worried. Are you okay?"

"I'm fine, Mr. O'Day. I was standing right outside."

"Oh. Okay, good. You can go back to calling me Birdy, by the way. That's just for show. Roland and Tony are old friends. Could you get me a blue one and half a pink one?"

Chrissie pulls a clear plastic bottle from the waiter apron she's wearing. We watch Birdy's knees bounce as she taps out the pills.

"So how are things?" I ask him, in the most soothing voice I can muster. "You seem a little bit on edge."

"I know, I'm sorry. My nerves—my nerves are bad. She's just giving me a beta blocker and half a Klonopin. I'm pretty much sober otherwise."

"No judgment here, Birdy. I still like my beer, and we both like pot. Tony has a prescription for it."

"Oh no. Are you not well, Tony? You look marvellous."

"Yeah? I feel like hell. I used to work construction, but yeah, I've had fibromyalgia for years. This will be my big night out for the month. Tomorrow I'll be wrecked."

"Oh. Oh no." Birdy puts his hands out stiffly: one of his patented air hugs. I find him inscrutable, at once forthcoming and cagey. "I know all about chronic pain. I've had both knees and both hips done. Spinal fusion. I have to wear a back brace. I shouldn't have been so kicky in my shows through the years. I could've just sat at the piano, like Elton. Oh well. What about you, Roland? How is your health?"

I hesitate. I want to be a titan for him. "I'm all right. I've been positive for thirty-eight years."

He growls with empathy. "HIV? No. Oh, please, no. I've lost hundreds of friends. The plague years—let's not even talk about it. And it's a miracle I'm not positive myself. I've had many lovers. Many, many lovers. I got lucky. Were you very sick before the—the inhibitor pills?"

"I was. I was touch and go many times. But I'm still here. I'm glad ... you're still here too."

Softened by the pills, he gets up and kisses me on the forehead. "That means so much, Roland. Really. I'm so glad you're not angry with me anymore."

"You kidding?" Tony blurts. "He's kept scrapbooks of all your press clippings."

"Didn't I tell you not to mention the fucking scrapbooks? They're therapeutic more than anything, Birdy. I was angry for the longest time. So the scrapbooks—well. Not that I'm not still ... somewhat hurt, and somewhat confused, by your actions since you left Winnipeg."

"Oh, I know, and I could just howl like a dog whenever I think about it. I have no excuse. It's—once I started getting famous, it became ... weirdly important that I felt like—it sounds dumb—this creature with no past. I even banished my brother and his wife. I bought them a house in Santa Fe—she's very into, you know, seashell earrings and looking at her vagina with a hand mirror, that sort of thing—and I told them not contact me with any less than six months' notice. I've no excuse. Terry passed from COVID in 2020, but she's still hanging on. Like a vampire bat."

"I'm sorry to hear about Terry. I liked him. I always wondered what happened to him."

Tony turns his torso this way and that, his face creased with pain. He'll have to go home soon.

Birdy claps his hands. "You know what I'd LOVE? My driver's parked outside, ready to go. It would be so great if we could drive around town, looking at all the old haunts. I think that would be really inspiring for me. I used to tell Ralph all sorts of stories about Winnipeg, and you and me, and Dr. Stock, all of it. I will always regret that I never brought him here to show him the sights and ... I was weak. I didn't have the fucking guts to show the world the man I loved. I was so weak. Yuck. Yucky."

"Sometimes I'd read in one of the tabloids about guys you were dating."

"That was all bullshit. It was always only Ralph. Well, apart from the hustlers and groupies. And now Ralph is gone. He was a lot like you, Tony. He did landscaping, but more high end. That's how I met him. He did my place in California. He put in all these shrubs that were supposed to protect me from evil energy. I still went crazy and had to be institutionalized, but it was worth it. I found my person—that's what Chrissie calls her girlfriend, her 'person'—and for that, I'm so, so grateful. So! Shall we do a little tour of the town? It'll be so fun."

I turn to Tony. His eyes have an odd cast to them; he needs to go to bed. But he'd never call an end to such a momentous evening, not even in agony.

I survey Birdy's face, its surgical sheen and pastiness, and the remnants of his beauty, the symphonic bone structure, his huge eyes and their throbbing blueness, undimmed after fifty-three years. I hear a tiny bell chime, so clear that I look around the room for it. But there is no bell. I've no explanation for why I heard a bell ring. Maybe an angel got their wings, like in *Miracle on 34th Street*.

"I don't want to be crass," Tony says, in his late-night radio baritone, "but I need to take the crap of my life. Where's the WC?"

"If you can believe it, my dressing room doesn't have a bathroom. I was incensed when I realized. I threw a shoe. It's two doors down, on the left."

"Thanks. I'll be back." Tony mentally prepares to stand, then slowly stands and heads out to find the bathroom.

Birdy dashes to where Tony was. Grabs my arm, hard. He looks slightly crazed.

"I'm so lonely, Roland. I'm so alone. I can't be alone. I haven't slept since Ralph died. You have to help me. Please, help me. Please. Please?"

"Sure, yeah, of course. But how can I help? I can start writing to you again, if you like. I only stopped because you asked me not to contact you."

His whole face flickers, like a TV on the fritz. "No, no. I want— I've been thinking about it—it's all I've been thinking about, and I—you and Tony are probably—well, not *struggling*, but you're probably kind of hand-to-mouth. So I thought, I thought just now, what if—hear me out, I know this is a real leap, but what if the two of you came and lived with me in Connecticut? It's just me and the dogs. You could have a whole wing to yourselves. We wouldn't have to see each other at all, except for maybe dinner every other evening, and special occasions. What do you think?"

"Wow. Well, that's really generous, Birdy. But I don't—our lives are here in Winnipeg. We've both lived here our whole lives. And Tony's doctors are here."

Birdy takes this in. He looks like he's adding sums in his head. "Okay. That's fair. What if—what if ..."

He cups my face with his hands. His hands are very cold. "What if I said that—that I'm still in love with you? What about that? Because I am. Well, I could be. I absolutely could be. We could get Tony nice and settled in a nice—a care home or something like that, independent living but with nurses, that type of thing, and then you can come and live with me and—I—yes—I could be your baby again. Wouldn't that be great?"

His frantic leaps of logic make me laugh and play with the hem of his silky sleeve. I think of my apartment three streets over, its dusty surfaces and thin walls; I think of my job, the one I'll work until I collapse; I think of the best of my friendship with Birdy, how young we were, how ephemeral our bond was, how we very likely wouldn't have gotten along if we hadn't been pressed together by circumstance; how Birdy's desperation in this freezing room might eclipse the worst of mine from any given point in time these past sixty-nine years; how long Tony is taking to shit.

"Birdy. What I would've given to hear something along those lines like fifty years ago. This is so fucked up and ... on the nose in such a fucked-up way. We're so old now." He seems impervious. "Do you not feel like we're too old for this sort of shakeup?"

"Possibly. I mean, yes, time has passed. But I'm so lonely. I can't be alone. What do I do?"

If someone at Club 200 told me they were lonely, I know what I would say. I'd tell them to meet me for lunch sometime, and to keep coming back to the club, where everyone is either a friend or a friend we haven't met yet.

"You have endless resources, sweetie. Why not hire a companion?" I've lapsed into my hairdresser voice. "You could hire some nice boy who'll pamper you."

He sways in a circle, annoyed by my crap advice.

"Do you not think I've done that already? I have a whole staff. They'd fuck me over for a pair of sunglasses. I'm still the same person I was when we were friends. I'm still that boy."

"I know. But. I don't know what to say, Birdy. I'm not the boy I was. I thought I was—I thought I was stuck in amber like a fly, forever ten, you know. Writing you letters and doing my stupid scrapbook. But, against my will, I changed. I changed a lot. You can't tell me you haven't. You've been all over the world. You won an American Music Award and, like, twenty-five Junos. You'd have to be a robot not to have changed."

Birdy plants his feet a foot apart, like Shirley Bassey about to belt, like drunk but plucky Garland. "I don't want to talk about things that changed us. I mean, I do, but not right now. I read your letters, Roland, even though the fan mail people answered. I read all about your love for me, and your anger. I know how you feel, okay? And I'm saying hey, hey there, I want to be your baby again. Don't you want to be my baby?'"

"I already have a baby, I can't be your baby—oh, god, why are we calling each other babies? We're nearly seventy."

Birdy offers a dejected nod. "It's game over for me. All the love and the ... good fortune is all in the past now. I feel that very strongly. Why bother? I'm so—I'm so angry. At Ralph. For leaving me alone. I'm sad. I'm sad all the time."

I hug him tight. I've always loved him the most in that taut moment when his bravado dissolves and he's left defenceless.

Tony's here now, still tucking in his dress shirt.

"How we doing? We okay?"

"Birdy's not doing very well. He's grieving."

"Aw, bud. We've all been there. My one and only before Rolly, he died of AIDS in '94." Tony joins our hug, and for a second we are a very small lacrosse team before the big game. Tony starts to hum softly; he does this when he comforts me, and I love it. Makes me feel like a babe in arms. "Sometimes, Birdy, when it's really bad, all you can do is tuck yourself into bed until the worst of it passes."

"That's good advice," says Birdy. "Do you guys want to have a three-way?"

I laugh. Tony sighs. "Dude, that's not what you need. That's the last thing you need."

"You're right. Force of habit. Whenever I want to die, I suck cock. I'm sorry."

We come apart—not abruptly, but only because the group clinch has served its purpose.

We all sit again. I don't know what else to say. When Tony deigns to enter a conversation, his tender common sense tends to stifle further conjecture, like a cleric citing scripture.

Birdy clears his throat. "So, after tonight it's Saskatoon, Regina, Calgary, Edmonton, Vancouver, then all down the US west coast. I don't know how I'm going to get through it. I want to cancel the whole tour. But I'm building a new house in Miami. I need the money. I don't know."

I look at Birdy's small, supple feet in terry cloth slippers. Fifty-three years of pained speculation, pointless woolgathering, fifteen photo albums filled with yellowing reviews and interviews, and we sit here like codgers in a barbershop, filling time. It kills me to see him in a state of such hard, unsolvable pain, but I am not his lover. He is someone I used to know.

There is grotesque silence.

"Hey," says Tony. "You want to come over to our place? We can smoke some weed and make grilled cheese and listen to tunes."

"Oh, Tony, I'm sure Birdy's much too busy for something like that. And we haven't vacuumed in a month."

"Just an idea," Tony says.

"I'd love to," says Birdy, finally showing the earnest face I couldn't help kissing when we were twelve. "I mean, if that's okay? My flight's not 'til the afternoon, so, yeah. And would it—I don't want to leave the limo driver waiting on the street all night—would it be okay if he came up with us?"

"The more the merrier," says Tony. "What's his name?"

"I have no idea. He seems nice. Well, we haven't actually spoken, but yeah."

"And did you want to bring your helper lady along?" Tony's eyes dance at the thought of actual company in our apartment.

"Chrissie? Oh no. She gets so hyper in social situations. She's an Aries. If we could just drop her at the hotel on the way, that would be great. Okay, you two go relax in the little green room at the end of the hall. I'll be ten minutes. Oh, this will be fun!"

We go to the green room, where there is a table with a platter of wan little sandwiches and a coffee machine.

"Jeez," says Tony. "This is no hell, eh? This is the best Winnipeg has to offer? Shit. Surely they had a nicer spread for Sheena Easton when she played here last year."

He leans lightly against the long table. Our heads touch, forming a tiny steeple between us. Neither of us is used to being out past ten o'clock, and we coo drowsily.

"I really didn't think he'd want to come over," I say.

"He's not a bad guy. He's for sure not a monster. But everyone gets mellower with age. Crankier, yeah, but mellower too. You know what I mean."

"Yeah. But I've never seen him so sad. Not even after his mom died. She had the same sadness sometimes. I wish there was more we could do."

"He'll sort himself out. Grief is no fun. Well, we'll get him nice n' baked, have a nice chat. It would be cool if he'd let us play his records, and he could tell us everything that was happening when he was making them."

"Yeah. That would be fun." I don't tell him that I already know almost all of the behind-the-scenes stories, from my scrapbook clippings and the fan club quarterly. Temple to temple, we keep our sweet steeple and wait for Birdy O'Day, who is stepping out of his Birdy O'Day costume and into something more comfortable. Probably something puce, possibly tangerine, definitely velour. We wait for him, humming songs from the concert to stay awake.

I have taken a little artistic licence with the air dates of television shows; though Roland mentions watching them in 1966, *The Carol Burnett Show* didn't start airing until 1967, and *Laugh-In* didn't air until 1968. Also, though they are depicted in the novel as performing on the same episode of *The Ed Sullivan Show* in the summer of 1966, Diana Ross & the Supremes performed "Love Child" on September 29, 1968, and Mary Hopkin performed "Those Were the Days" on October 27, 1968.

ACKNOWLEDGMENTS

Love and thanks to: early readers Morgan James, Jessica Westhead, Sky Gilbert, and Zoe Whittall, sweeties all. My Winnipeg family, who were unstinting in their support and invaluable in helping me fill the gaps in my memory of Winnipeg queer lore: Kyle Smoley, Sara Brasseur, Tara Fraser, Dan Doucette, Anita Stallion, Danny Dumas, and the dearly departed John Cardinal, a.k.a. Joan Costalotsa. Thanks to my friends Gloria McIsaac, Andrea Gerardi-Peterman, Patricia Matte and Jack Constable, Patricia Wilson, Frank Mancino, Chris Mitchell, Olivia Roblin, Kate Tunney, Matthew Hays, Flavio Belli, Julie Di Cresce, and Philip Evans for their kindness and encouragement during the awful years. Thanks to my warrior niece Danica Hayes and my father. Oh! And thanks to Lisa Foad and Suzette Mayr for their gorgeous blurbs.

The deeply talented team at Arsenal Pulp made this the most satisfying publishing experience I've ever had. Publisher Brian Lam, designer Jazmin Welch, editor Catharine Chen (who was so incredibly deft, and so indulgent of my AIDS brain fog as we worked to update the text and nail down its chronological particulars), publicity director Cynara Geissler: your enthusiasm has been so restorative. Many thanks also to Robert Ballantyne (associate publisher), Erin Chan (marketing & publicity assistant), and JC Cham (assistant editor).

Samantha Haywood, you've been an incredibly patient agent, advocate, and friend. Thanks also to Transatlantic Agency allies Eva Oakes for her bracing feedback, and Megan Philipp for her administrative acumen.

Thanks to George Pratt and his staff at the Cock Bar—Morgan, Alberto, Rob, Joey, Steph, Lenny, Rick.

And to my late husband Robert Matte, my Birdy and Tony in one: how lucky I was to know and love you.